ADVANCE PRAISE FOR *LAND OF SILENCE* AND OTHER NOVELS BY TESSA AFSHAR

Land of Silence

"No one brings the Bible to life like Tessa Afshar. *Land of Silence* grabs hold of the woman who stole healing by touching Christ's hem in a way that brings us all to a place where we can recognize that we, too, are daughters of the King."

DEBBIE MACOMBER, #1 *NEW YORK TIMES* BESTSELLING AUTHOR

"Tessa Afshar's *Land of Silence* is a biblical novel in a category all its own. Moving, believable . . . this inspiring, uplifting story encouraged me at a heart level. A wonderful story—not to be missed!"

JILL EILEEN SMITH, BESTSELLING AUTHOR OF *THE CRIMSON CORD* AND THE WIVES OF KING DAVID SERIES

"Tessa Afshar's captivating and emotive story is about one first-century woman's pain and struggle. But the hope she describes is real and for you and me today."

CHRIS FABRY, BESTSELLING AUTHOR OF *WAR ROOM* AND *DOGWOOD*

"Tessa Afshar's novels draw you in so that you're both captivated and changed by the power of story. *Land of Silence* is no exception. You're in for a treat with this one—enjoy!"

SUSIE LARSON, NATIONAL SPEAKER, RADIO HOST, AND AUTHOR OF *YOUR BEAUTIFUL PURPOSE*

In the Field of Grace

"Afshar writes unforgettable biblical fiction."

ROMANTIC TIMES

"This is one of my favorite books of the year. Beguiling, exciting, romantic, and a much-needed reminder of the Creator's steadfast faithfulness, even to those the world deems undeserving."

NOVEL CROSSING

"Once again, Tessa's seemingly effortless talent breathes new life into this beautiful love story and makes it come alive."

RELZ REVIEWZ

"Tessa Afshar breathes new life into the old, stale story we think we know and cracks the door wide open for a beautiful story of a tragic life turned upside down by forbidden love and immeasurable grace."

JOSH OLDS, LIFEISSTORY.COM

Harvest of Gold

"Afshar has created a treasure of a book. Brilliant characterization, adventure, intrigue, and humor coupled with deep emotional impact garner a solid five stars."

CBA RETAILERS + RESOURCES

"Engaging. Inspiring. Heart-stopping and heart-rending. A fabulous biblical novel that sent me straight back to God's Word!"

MESU ANDREWS, AWARD-WINNING AUTHOR

Harvest of Rubies

"There is so much depth to *Harvest of Rubies* that readers will happily drown in its message of God's unfailing love and mercy while diving headfirst into the captivating plot and precarious romance. . . . This is a great read!"

BOOKREPORTER.COM

"Afshar brings readers biblical fiction with mysterious twists and turns . . . that fascinate and claim the reader's full attention. The story will have you laughing and crying."

ROMANTIC TIMES, TOP PICK REVIEW

Pearl in the Sand

"This superb debut should appeal to readers who enjoyed Davis Bunn and Janette Oke's *The Centurion's Wife* or Anita Diamant's *The Red Tent*."

LIBRARY JOURNAL, STARRED REVIEW

"A riveting and compelling book. . . . Fantastic research and stellar writing make this one you don't want to miss!"

ROMANTIC TIMES, TOP PICK REVIEW

"*Pearl in the Sand* is a lovely story, vividly written, and is sure to please devotees of biblical fiction."

TITLETRAKK.COM

Land of Silence

TESSA AFSHAR

Land of
Silence

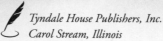

Tyndale House Publishers, Inc.
Carol Stream, Illinois

Visit Tyndale online at www.tyndale.com.

Visit Tessa Afshar at www.tessaafshar.com.

TYNDALE and Tyndale's quill logo are registered trademarks of Tyndale House Publishers, Inc.

Land of Silence

Designed by Ron Kaufmann

Edited by Kathryn S. Olson

Published in association with the literary agency of Books & Such Literary Agency, 52 Mission Circle, Suite 122, PMB 170, Santa Rosa, CA 95409

Land of Silence is a work of fiction. Where real people, events, establishments, organizations, or locales appear, they are used fictitiously. All other elements of the novel are drawn from the author's imagination.

Library of Congress Cataloging-in-Publication Data
Names: Afshar, Tessa, author.
Title: Land of silence / Tessa Afshar.
Description: Carol Stream, Illinois : Tyndale House Publishers, Inc., [2016]
Identifiers: LCCN 2015040791| ISBN 9781496414007 (hc) | ISBN 9781496406460 (sc)
Subjects: | GSAFD: Christian fiction.
Classification: LCC PS3601.F47 L36 2016 | DDC 813/.6—dc23 LC record available at http://lccn.loc.gov/2015040791

Printed in the United States of America

22	21	20	19	18	17	16
7	6	5	4	3	2	1

To John

"I found the one my heart loves."

SONG OF SOLOMON 3:4, NIV

If the LORD had not been my help,

my soul would soon have lived in the land of silence.

When I thought, "My foot slips,"

your steadfast love, O LORD, held me up.

When the cares of my heart are many,

your consolations cheer my soul.

PSALM 94:17-19

ONE

I have been forgotten like one who is dead;
I have become like a broken vessel.

PSALM 31:12

WHEN I THINK OF THE RUIN my life has become, the slow wrecking of my dreams, the destruction of every love, I always return to the bee. That one tiny sting, which robbed my place of favor in my father's heart and changed the course of my destiny.

Sorrow came to me on a beautiful afternoon, with the sun shining and just enough heat in the day to warm the skin without scorching it. Wildflowers were abundant that year, and the hillside where Joseph and I had come to pass the hours was covered in a blanket of yellow and pink. I remember the scent of them tickling my nose and filling my lungs, making me laugh for the sheer beauty of the world.

Joseph ran amongst the soft stalks, piercing the leaves

1

with his make-believe sword, playing Roman soldier. He knew better than to play the game with our parents around. They were staunch Jews whose lineage in Jerusalem went as far back as the days of Ezra. Romans may have been generous patrons of my father's wares, but they were still dangerous enemies. My parents certainly did not consider them a matter for fun and games. But Joseph was four, and he loved the Roman horses, their uniforms, their rectangular painted shields. He wanted to be one of them. And I let him, seeing no harm in a little boy running wild and pretending to be something he could never become.

"Elianna, come and play," Joseph called over his shoulder and thrust his invisible sword in my direction.

"Hold a moment," I said. "I will come soon."

I was distracted, sitting on the coarse felt blanket I had brought, twirling a pink flower, trying to fathom a way to leach out its color and use it for dye on linen. A large shipment of flax had just been delivered to our workshop and we would have plenty of fibers for weaving. My father traded in luxurious fabrics. He even had a small but brisk business in purple, the lavish dye that was derived painstakingly from sea snails and remained more expensive to produce than any other color. It was a measure of his success that he could afford this particular trade.

Joseph had been left in my care that afternoon because everyone in the household was busy working on the flax. Even my mother, who rarely participated in my father's business, had been drafted to help.

My father bought his flax already steeped and dried, with

the seeds separated from the stems and discarded, and the stalks beaten to pull out the fibers. His workers were left with the task of combing out the fibers, making them ready for spinning. The stalks of this particular harvest were thick, which produced coarse linen, and would be used for weaving towels. With Romans and the new Jewish aristocracy so fond of their baths, towels were in high demand throughout the main cities of Judea.

I was twelve years older than Joseph and more than capable of caring for him. My mother, suspicious of my passion for my father's trade, and looking for ways to distract me from my fascination, had given me charge over Joseph for the afternoon. Her plan worked to double advantage: it got my exuberant brother out from under the busy feet of the adults while at the same time withdrawing me from direct contact with my father's work, lest it feed my obsession with the secrets of his trade.

"Leave that to the men," she always told me, thrusting some feminine task into my lap before I grew too enraptured with the mysteries of creating a better grade of dyed fabric.

"Elianna!" Joseph's voice bellowed from farther down the hill. "Come. Now! You promised when you brought me here that you'd play with me."

I grinned. My little brother could be imperious. No one had expected the birth of another child to my parents at their advanced age. When Joseph was born, we were all a little dazzled with his mere presence in the world and became instant slaves to his charm. Add to that the reality that he was a boy—the son of my father's dreams—and, well . . . even a burning seraph could be excused for being a little spoilt under the circumstances. If he seemed bossy, the fault belonged to us. By nature, Joseph was so sweet that the overindulgence of a hundred adults could not render him tyrannical.

"You better hope I don't catch you," I said as I rose to my feet. "My sword is a lot sharper than yours."

"No, it's not. I'll defeat you." He let loose a fearsome bellow and began to run up the hill, his short legs pumping under his hitched-up tunic at a speed that made me flinch. I needed my whole strength to keep up with that boy.

"Hold fast," I cried, catching up with him at the top of the hill, thrusting my pink flower forward as if it were a deadly weapon. Joseph doubled over, giggling.

"That's not a sword! That can't even cut thread. You're such a girl, Elianna."

"You dare insult me, Roman dog? I shall have your head for that."

Joseph rushed toward me, his imaginary sword pointed at my abdomen. "No, you won't. My horse will eat you for breakfast." He did a fair imitation of a parry and then followed with a quick thrust, his little fist hitting my ribs. I grabbed my side as if in pain.

"You will pay for that, young man." With a quick motion, I reached forward to untuck his tunic from his belt. Distracted, he looked down, and I shoved my flower in his face, leaving a powdery yellow stain on his nose and forehead.

I laughed. "You still need some practice, Roman." Just behind him, I noticed a lone sheep chomping on a bush. I looked around, trying to locate the shepherd or herd to which it belonged. It seemed to be alone. I walked over to examine it for any hurts. A shepherd somewhere must be missing the fat fellow.

"Elianna!" Joseph called. "Come back. I am not finished. . . ." And then, inexplicably, he swung his arm in a wide arc. "Go away. Go away!" His voice emerged high-pitched and shaken. He made a half circle around himself, his hands flapping about him in frantic motion.

The sheep had my attention, though, and I ignored Joseph's cry. Up close, I could see that it was well cared for, its wool healthy and clean. I knelt down and ran my hand over its back. "Where did you come from, little fellow?"

From the corner of my eye I could still see Joseph flapping around. Then he cried out, "Make it go away, Elianna!"

I thought it was a fly at first until I saw the flash of yellow, heard the angry buzz. "Don't fret so. Stay calm, and it will go away of its own accord." I didn't want to leave the lost sheep, in case it wandered away and became even more lost. Joseph was old enough to deal with a buzzing bee. Really, we had overindulged him. I tried to make my voice soothing. "Calm yourself, brother."

My words had no effect on Joseph. The creature was buzzing with fierce intention around his head, and he panicked. He flapped his arms harder and started to run. "No! No!"

I threw my hands up in the air and came to my feet reluctantly. "Joseph, it's just a bee."

I understood the source of his unreasoning fear. The year before, he had been stung on the ankle. He had broken out in hives and his entire leg had swollen to the size of a young tree trunk, and he had been in terrible pain. He had never forgotten the experience. But in my mind, that had been an anomaly. We all had to contend with bees. It was part of life. I watched in frustration as he ran himself ragged for a few moments.

Finally, I caught up to him and reached out my hands to flick at the bee, although I could no longer see it. Without warning, Joseph let out a piercing wail that made my belly lurch. He rubbed at the side of his head, and then I spotted the insect caught in the hair near his temple. I grabbed the bee in my palm and squeezed. Half-drunk from having released its venom, it was easy prey in my violent, clenching fist. I dropped it to the ground and knelt before Joseph.

Fat tears squeezed out of his eyes. He was crying so hard that he began to wheeze. I cuddled him in my arms. "I am so sorry, Joseph. It will be well. I've gotten rid of the little monster. You can stomp on him, if you wish."

"Hurts." He took a breath that shook his chest.

"Where, dear heart? Where do you hurt?"

He pointed to his temple, and I saw that it was already swelling. I gave it a light kiss. "Is that better?"

His gaze brimmed over with accusation. "No." He pushed me from him. I noted a red welt on the back of his still-chubby hand. "Did it sting you twice?" I frowned as I stared at the raised mark, spreading like spilled dye on his baby skin. Joseph shook his head. Hives, I realized with a wince. Just like last year.

He took another breath that shivered down his body. He

sounded as if every inhalation was an effort. I thought it was fear lingering in him, robbing him of breath, and tried to calm him. But with each moment, he seemed to grow worse. His wheezing became harsher and unremitting. Confusion caused me to delay. He had had no difficulty breathing the last time he was stung. Was this panic?

I should have helped him sooner, come to his aid at the start, when the bee first began to pursue him. And then it occurred to me that the bee might have been attracted to the scent and powder of the flower I had pressed on his face. Perhaps it would not have come near Joseph at all if not for my silly prank.

I saw that he was growing worse and picked him up in my arms. "I am so sorry, Joseph. I'll take you home. You can have a honey cake, and Mother will make you an herb potion to soothe your pain." Against me, I could feel his thin little chest battling for every breath. I began to run. Somewhere down the hill, my sandal came off, caught on a stone protruding from the ground. I stumbled, then righted myself and kept on running without tarrying to retrieve the lost shoe.

"Sick," Joseph said, his voice weak. Before I could turn him, he threw up, soaking my shoulder and my chest. Normally I would have groaned with disgust. But terror had seized me. I sensed that against all reason the bee had caused my brother's tiny body inexplicable damage. It was as though the poison in that accursed bee somehow robbed him of the very air. I was desperate to arrive home, to give him into the care of my parents, who would know what to do.

I barely stopped to wipe his befouled mouth, only shifting him to my other shoulder so I could start my race again. He was heavy, too heavy for me to carry all that way. My heart pounded in my chest like a metalsmith's anvil. The strain of holding on to his sagging body made my arms tremble. "Joseph! Joseph, speak to me!"

He moaned. I staggered to a stop, unable to continue my haphazard run, and fell to my knees with him still in my arms. My head swam with a wave of dizziness when I saw his face. His eyes had swollen shut, and his lips had become an unearthly blue. His whole mouth had turned into a tender, purplish bruise. I bit down on a scream and hefted him up again, forcing my legs to run, faster than before.

Pray, I thought, my soul frantic with the horror of what I had just seen. *Pray something.* But all I could think of was *Eli, Eli,* the first part of my own name. *My God! My God!*

When I saw the large wooden door to our house, I loosed the scream I had swallowed for the past hour. My voice emerged as a broken croak and no one heard me. "Help me! Father, please help me." Joseph had gone limp in my arms. I knew he had fainted some time before, fainted from lack of air.

I kicked at the door with the last of my strength and fell against it. One of the servants pulled the door open and I slumped backward, Joseph still held tight in my grasp. The woman cried out, and before long we were pulled inside together. I was still clutching him, his face pressed to my shoulder. My parents came running.

I saw my father's face as he pulled his son out of my arms.

He turned white. My mother started to scream. I didn't think I could feel more fear. But her cries—shrill, unnatural sounds that pierced the courtyard—filled me with a chilling dread that robbed me of speech. Why wasn't she helping my brother? Why did she stand there, screeching, pulling at her veil, pulling at her hair?

My father collapsed, Joseph held against him. His head drooped over the unmoving child. "My son," he moaned, rocking to and fro. "My boy."

I turned in shock and saw my younger sister, Joanna, sitting against the wall, sobbing quietly into her hands. The servants wept. My father, shaking and silent, convulsed around the inert body of my brother while Mother's screams continued to fill every corner of the courtyard, piercing me like jagged shards of broken glass.

That's when I knew. My brother was dead. The bee had killed him.

I reached out to cling to my father, in disbelief, in horror, in desperation, hoping for a miracle, seeking comfort. He looked up and the blank despair in his eyes lifted for a moment, only to be replaced by a coldness I had never seen there before. "What happened? What has done *this* to my child?"

I stepped away from him. "A bee . . . It stung Joseph. On his temple." Perspiration dripped down my sides and with a trembling hand I wiped my brow. "It was my fault. We were playing . . . And I . . . I shoved a flower in his face; I think the bee was drawn to its scent. I should have come to his aid sooner, but I was distracted by a lost sheep." I remembered that I had merely thrown words at Joseph, as if my instructions were enough. I owed Joseph the truth no matter what punishment I faced. He deserved that much, at least.

My father swept the hair away from Joseph's swollen flesh with tender fingers. I flinched when I saw his beautiful face, distorted by the obscene hand of death, and swayed where I stood.

"But you knew how sick he became last year, after he was stung. You knew how scared he was. Why didn't you just swat it away? He was a little boy. He was helpless." My father moaned. "My little boy!"

"I should . . . I should have . . ."

His words grew iron-hard and sharp. "You were supposed to look after him. What did you do? Just stand there and watch it happen?"

"No! It wasn't like that, Father! I did help. But I was too late. I was too late!"

"This wouldn't have happened if you had watched him better."

I was struck dumb with guilt. He had grasped the heart of my failure. I had not tried to get rid of the bee from the start. "Father, please . . ."

"Be silent!"

I closed my mouth. Swallowed my excuses. He was right. I had failed Joseph. I should have taken better care of him. I should have wiped the pollen from his face, swatted the bee sooner, come home faster. I should have saved him.

"Get out of my sight." My father's voice emerged scratchy soft and bitter as gall.

I gasped. With broken movements, I forced myself to stand, to walk. I went inside the house, leaving a faint trail of blood with every step where I had cut my foot on the jagged stones during my flight home. Huddling in the corner of the room where I slept with my sister and Joseph, I finally gave vent to the tears that I had quenched earlier. Joseph's blanket was neatly folded in a corner. I grabbed it and, pushing my face into its folds, breathed in the scent of him and knew that I would never hold my precious brother again.

And it was my fault.

My father made up my name when I was born, putting together two Hebrew names: *Eli*, which means *my God*, and *Anna*, which in our tongue signifies *favor*. When he first set eyes on me, my father said, *"My God has favored me,"* and that became my name, for my birth was a sign of God's favor and grace to my parents.

For eight years after they were married, he and my mother had remained childless. I came when they had given up on physicians and their useless potions. I came, but I was a girl. Still, my parents were too happy to have a child at last to complain about my gender. Three years after I was born, my sister arrived, long-limbed even at birth, with wide eyes that seemed to cover half her face. Then when no one thought it even possible, Joseph burst into our lives with his lusty cry and his irresistible smile.

It wasn't as if my father loved me less when his son was born. It was only that he loved Joseph so much more. More than my mother or my sister or me or his business. More than life. Joseph was the light of his heart.

Until now. Until I caused his death. I felt as though I had destroyed the greatest treasure the earth had to offer.

Hours passed as I sat unmoving in a fog of disbelief. Death had swallowed me up along with Joseph. In taking him, it took me, too. Though I breathed and my heart beat with strong regularity, my wound was incurable. The thought of what my parents must be feeling made me wish it had been I who had died instead of Joseph.

The sound of the wailing of mourners penetrated my distracted thoughts. I became aware that a great crowd had gathered downstairs. They must already be preparing Joseph's body for his burial. I could not bear the thought.

The exuberant boy I had adored for four years, the child who had made me laugh and hope and rejoice, was gone and we would never have him back. I pressed my hands against my ears, trying to drown out the sounds of wailing. I felt lashed by their sorrow, guilt eating at me with voracious hunger.

"Elianna." Gentle hands took hold of my wrists and pulled them away from my ears. "Elianna," he said again.

Ethan.

My betrothed. The man I had loved since before I became a woman.

TWO

Therefore, I will mourn and lament . . .
I will howl like a jackal and moan like an owl.
For my people's wound is too deep to heal.

MICAH 1:8-9, NLT

I FLINCHED. I did not want Ethan to see me like this, my shame plain as smeared ink on my face. Then a spark of hope made me sit up.

"Did my father send you?"

His fingers cradled my jaw. With his thumb he wiped my cheek, and I realized that my face was wet with tears. "Come down," he said. "You should be there."

I did not miss his prevarication. Ethan had noticed my absence in the crowd and come in search of me himself, not at my father's bidding. I shook my head and moved my face away from his touch.

"You won't come?"

I shook my head again. He stared at me, his gaze unwavering. Ethan had unusual eyes—I always thought of

13

them as angel eyes. I had never shared this odd conclusion with anyone, least of all him. But I felt convinced that there was something of heaven in them. He had curious irises, like a mosaic, made up of flecks of gold and green and brown, shifting hues, depending on his mood or the light. Today, they were more autumn than summer, full of golds and browns as they looked at me.

I felt compelled to explain my resistance. "My parents won't want to see me. They . . . Joseph was with me. When it happened."

I shoved a fisted hand over my lips, biting the soft flesh at the base of my thumb to try and stuff back the sob that my own words had pulled out of my depths. It wouldn't be quenched. Sob after sob rolled out of me. Roughly, Ethan pulled me into his arms. "Elianna," he said, his voice gruff. "Be still now." It was the first time he had ever held me close. If not for the extraordinary circumstances, he would not draw this near now, though we were betrothed. Jerusalem had become a conservative place since being conquered by foreign powers.

Ethan's chest was massive and warm. It felt like leaning against a padded shield. He pulled my hand into his own and examined the mark my teeth had left. I had not realized that I had bitten through the skin. He wiped the blood with the corner of his sleeve. "You did nothing wrong," he said as his thumb caressed the palm of my hand.

"My fault. It was my fault," I groaned and wrenched myself away from him, huddling against the wall.

Ethan raked unsteady fingers through his hair and

rubbed the back of his neck. "How could you have prevented Joseph's death?" He had been kneeling by my side. Now he shifted so he could lean back. "Elianna, will you not speak to me of what happened? It may bring you a measure of comfort."

I had given only short snatches of the afternoon's events to my father. No one had yet heard the full account. I thought about sharing the story of Joseph's suffering and death, of speaking the words out loud and reliving those moments. Bile rose in my throat, bitter and sour. Comfort? It would crush me. "I don't want to speak of it."

Ethan reached out and took hold of my hand again. I struggled against him, but he held fast to me. "Hush," he said. "You need not talk of it if you don't wish." He held on to my fingers in silence for a few moments. "Come down with me. Sit with your mother awhile."

I trembled at the thought of facing everyone, and pulled my hand free from his warm hold. "My father hates me."

He looked away and said nothing. It dawned on me that he had given me no assurance to the contrary. That was unlike Ethan. He always saw the good. The hope. His silence was the same as a formal agreement. What had my father told him? I did not want to know. "I'm not coming down," I said.

"You will let them bury your brother without you?"

"They'll wait till the morning. I'll come then."

Ethan shook his head. "I don't want you to be here alone."

"It's the only relief I can offer my father. He will hurt more if I am there."

He closed his eyes and rubbed the bridge of his nose.

"It's the shock of losing Joseph. In his heart, Benjamin hasn't turned against you. He will come around. Give him time."

"Does everyone know that he blames me?"

"No. He spoke only to me and my father. And your mother, of course."

I took a deep breath. It occurred to me with vivid clarity that before long Ethan would also reject me. He hadn't wanted me very much to begin with. His father was a merchant who imported madder and indigo, as well as more exotic dyes, into Judea. He had known my father since boyhood and often worked with him. They had arranged our marriage between them when I was fifteen and Ethan twenty-one. I had been ecstatic at the prospect. Ethan, lukewarm.

"I won't marry you until you turn seventeen," he warned the day my father told me of his plan. "Not one day sooner. I won't get myself bound to a child."

"A child! I have a half-dozen friends my age already married."

"I am well aware of that fact. As I said, I will wait until you are at least seventeen."

I flushed under his hard stare. Along with a good portion of Jerusalem's population, I was aware that one of those friends I had mentioned had married Ethan's brother before reaching her fifteenth birthday. Seven months after their wedding, the girl had returned to her father's home, filled with tears and complaints. Ethan's brother had waited patiently until his wife came back to him three months later. But it was well known that she spent more time under her mother's roof than under her husband's. I suppose Ethan wished to avoid such a disaster in his own domestic life.

I was offended by his cold resistance. Could he not see that I was different from Avigail, his brother's wife? More responsible? Mature? Faithful?

I had loved Ethan for as long as I remembered. I longed to be his wife. Ethan obviously did not feel the same. And now, he would see that I was not the woman he would want for his wife—or for the mother of his children—no matter what my age. If I couldn't be trusted to look after my own brother, how could he entrust his sons and daughters to me? It was a matter of time before he would seek an excuse to break our betrothal.

"You better leave before they find us here, unattended," I whispered. In truth, I cared nothing about how they found us. My objection was a thin excuse to send him away; I did not want to see the cold look my father had given me reflected in Ethan's eyes.

Ethan lingered, ignoring me. "You shouldn't be left alone. You aren't well."

"Please, Ethan." My throat was thick with tears I refused to shed. "Go before you cause me more trouble. It isn't right that you should be with me here, in my chamber."

He hesitated, his lips tightening into a flat line. Then he rose. "I'm not going far. Just below stairs. Call for me if you need anything. Promise me, Elianna."

I nodded. Somewhere during my haphazard dash home, I had lost my veil and my hair had come undone. He ran his fingers through the tangled curls once, twice. Then he rose and walked out. I curled into myself, a little circle of misery on my pallet. I smelled of vomit and sweat. I smelled of death. And it would never wipe off.

⁊*

Hours later, Keziah, a quiet maidservant who often rushed to help anyone in need without waiting to be asked, brought me a plate of warm raisin cakes. The smell of cooked raisins and slightly charred wheat turned my stomach. I don't know why the sight of those cakes made me choke with despair. Perhaps it was the ordinariness of them. They sat on the plate mocking me with innocent irony, because I knew nothing could ever be ordinary again. To this day I cannot smell hot, cooked raisins without feeling queasy and a little hopeless.

I dozed for a few moments in the night and awoke with a start, my memory confused with exhaustion and shock. For an instant I forgot Joseph was dead. Something loomed in the back of my mind, like a dark monster waiting in the shadows. My skin prickled and I shivered. And then memory swooped down again, irrevocable and final. Joseph was gone.

Gone.

I did not sleep after that, but sat frozen in the dark. Long before sunrise I rose to wash and sent Keziah to bring me a garment of sackcloth, appropriate for the burial of my only brother. In the courtyard mourners had gathered in sleepy groups, making ready for the procession to the new tomb, which my father had purchased the year before. For his own

18

burial, he had said. He would lay the body of his precious boy inside that dark cave instead.

I stood on the edge of the crowd, avoiding everyone's gaze, fearful of what I might find there. Ethan noticed me and came over. I blinked when I saw him. He had cut his beard in a show of mourning, and in spite of the dark circles under his eyes, his face looked younger and more ruggedly beautiful than I remembered.

"God be gracious to you," he said, his tone grave. A formal greeting for a dark day. God be gracious to me? Too late for that, I thought.

"Did you sleep?" Ethan asked.

"Not much. You?"

"I tarried with your father. My parents are here also. Come. They will want to see you."

I followed him to the corner where his parents, Jerusha and Ezer, along with his younger brother, Daniel, had gathered in the gray light. Jerusha folded me into her arms as soon as she saw me. My mother had never been physically affectionate with any of us. It was not part of her nature to touch and embrace with ease. Jerusha's warm embraces had been a welcome comfort to me since my childhood. She was one of those rare people who knew how to fill you with approval and acceptance with a quiet word.

"My poor girl. What you have been through. I am so sorry," she said as she held me against her soft bosom. For once, her sincere comfort backfired. I wriggled out of her arms and stepped away. I feared that if I gave in to it, I would break down and never stop.

"Elianna hasn't slept all night. She is exhausted," Ethan said, trying to explain my rude silence, I suppose.

"Of course she is." Jerusha gave me another hug and stepped away.

My parents approached us. Turning rigid as one of the marble statues the Romans were so fond of carving, I bit into dry lips. To my surprise, my mother grabbed my hand and squeezed it. That was all. One small, warm touch before she let go. I thought I would melt with relief. She loved me still, that touch said. She forgave me.

My father would not look at me, but he bestowed a stiff nod in my direction. It was a great concession, under the circumstances. I could see how hard he was trying.

Jerusha drew my mother to her side. "Here, Elizabeth, lean on me." My mother began to weep as if unable to bear even this small kindness. She had lost her voice after screaming so long yesterday, and her tears now came plump and mute.

The professional mourners gathered, carrying the bier that held my brother's tiny body. He was wrapped in strips of the whitest linen cloth, his face covered by a spotless napkin. That linen had been woven for some great lady's veil. For feasts and joy and celebration. Instead it covered the suppuration of death. The scent of the aromatic oils and spices with which they had washed and anointed Joseph's body filled the air. So much spice that the stench of death could not compete.

I thought I might be sick.

Then the wailing picked up again, loud and unrelenting.

What had the prophet Micah called it? Howling like the jackals, and moaning like owls. We were led by a menagerie of grief, the noise fearsome in its hopeless sorrow.

꙳

After we laid Joseph's body in the tomb, we returned to the house. The servants had prepared refreshments for our guests, and I spent the afternoon carrying trays of food, filling up platters and jugs of wine as they emptied.

I felt like I had dropped into a world of nightmares. It seemed implausible that I should be engaged in something as innocuous as offering food to polite guests while my little brother lay dead in a grave.

Father leaned slumped against a wall, his shaking hands fisted in his lap. Seated next to him was his friend Gamaliel, a popular religious teacher and member of the Sanhedrin. On his other side lounged Rabbi Zakkai, a Pharisee I did not know well.

Gamaliel leaned over to my father. "You will see your Joseph again at the resurrection. You will have him by your side, Benjamin."

Rabbi Zakkai picked up a stuffed date and twirled it in his fingers. "True enough. Unlike this fellow Johanan and the rest of his Sadducee brothers—" he pointed his bushy chin at a man sitting to Gamaliel's left side—"we Pharisees believe in the resurrection of the dead."

Johanan, a thin man with very dark hair, gave a cold smile and said nothing. What could he say at the funeral of a little boy? Have no hope? You have lost him forever? He took a deep swallow of his wine.

Rabbi Zakkai seemed disappointed by the stretching silence. "Of course," he continued, "that may not be such an advantage where there is great sin."

Gamaliel frowned. "What sin can a four-year-old boy have committed?"

The Pharisee waved his hand. "The boy, nothing. The sister, now. She is another matter. She is at fault for her own brother's death. How is God to forgive such a sin? It would be better for her if she had not been born. The resurrection of the dead is not good news for such a one, I tell you."

My father looked up, his eyes burning. I choked. The tray slid out of my hands and fell to the ground, splattering melons over the clean tiles. My father rose unsteadily and walked away.

"Benjamin!" Gamaliel cried, but my father would not stop. Furious, Gamaliel spun to face Zakkai. "What infernal rubbish are you spouting now? The death of that child was nothing but a sad accident. How could the sister have prevented it?"

The Pharisee raised a hand, palm flat, and brought it down against the low table before him with a hard slap. Lifting his hand, he held out a dead fly between two pinching fingers. "Like that?" He pitched the fly on the ground and wiped his hands on the linen napkin next to him with fastidious care. "How hard is it to swipe away a bee? Or kill it? Her negligence in caring for that poor child is clear. Believe me, my friend, when I tell you her punishment is coming."

Gamaliel's cheeks turned puce. "Nonsense! You are turning the Law into an executioner's ax instead of a signpost that leads the way to salvation."

Johanan the Sadducee leaned over. "Still think the resurrection of the dead is a comfort to the grieving? We Sadducees may give no false peace to the people, but at least we don't tear their hearts out with our good intentions, either."

THREE

Do not despise these small beginnings,
for the LORD rejoices to see the work begin.

ZECHARIAH 4:10, NLT

OUR PATRIARCH JACOB had been mourned for seventy days, the Scriptures said. So for seventy days, my family remained in formal mourning. The goat-hair sackcloth I wore every day had started to chafe my skin in the heat of the day, leaving red, itchy patches. In a perverse way, I clung to that small discomfort. I deserved to suffer for what I had done.

Ethan and his parents kept telling me I was not at fault. They meant well, but they could not understand. Joseph wouldn't even have been on that hill if I hadn't taken him there. I had chosen that spot because of the flowers. He had wanted to play in the lane just outside the house. I had dragged him to the hilltop with promises of merry games and entertainment.

My family stopped work on the flax. We ceased all labor and mourned. The looms sat quiet, gathering dust. The vats of dye remained empty except for the spiders that liked to spin their webs across the cool stone.

One morning as I was entering the courtyard, I ran into my father. He nodded. "Peace," he said without looking me in the eye. He never looked me in the eye anymore, though he had at least resumed talking to me. Desultory words that rarely seemed to make a full sentence. Greetings and passing requests. He never called me daughter or cuddled me or pulled my braid in the old teasing way we had.

I don't know which hurt more: when he started talking to me like I was a stranger, or when he refused to acknowledge me at all.

"Ezer is coming to see me today," he said. "I will receive him in my workroom. See that we are not disturbed." He turned and took a step away. Then with a distracted air he said over his shoulder, "Food and drink. Don't forget, Anna." Father had taken to calling me Anna, as if he couldn't bring himself to speak the name of God and mine in one breath.

At noon, I fetched the food myself on a heavy tray to my father's workroom, which he kept in the house in order to deal with his accounts and meet with visiting patrons. I heard the sound of raised voices as I approached. The door remained shut, but even through the wood and the mud-brick wall and layers of plaster I could make out the words.

"A whole year will be too long, Benjamin. The seventy days of formal mourning come to an end tomorrow. Everyone will understand if you return to work. You know as well as I that most folks return to their lives after thirty days." I recognized Master Ezer's gravelly voice, sounding urgent. "Your customers will find other merchants if you delay longer. You're not the only man to sell fine fabrics in the city, you know."

"I care not," my father shouted.

"You ought to care. You still have a wife and two daughters who depend on you. Servants. Workers. What will become of them if you give up your business?"

"Isn't my son worth a year of tears?"

"And more, Benjamin." Silence reigned for a few moments, and then I could hear the sound of sobs—wrenching, male sobs that came from a deep well of suffering.

My legs gave way and I slid down against the wall. With the last of my strength, I set the tray roughly on the stone floor and buried my mouth inside the bend of my elbow to muffle the sound of my own convulsive weeping. I had never heard my father sob, not even when they laid Joseph's body in a freshly hewn cave.

"Benjamin, no one expects you to stop grieving for your child. Everyone knows how much you loved him. But for the sake of others, you must return to the world of the living."

"I cannot." I almost did not recognize that broken voice.

"You can and you will. Ethan and I will help where we can. And you have Elianna. She is clever and quick to learn. If she has asked me one question about my trade, she has asked a hundred. This business is in her blood. Let her help you."

I held my breath. If my father made an answer, it was too

low for me to hear. Then I heard movement and, afraid of discovery, ran back into the courtyard.

I did not have much hope that my father would take Ezer's advice and ask for my help. In recent decades, Jerusalem had become a strict community in spite of the fact that its elite had grown fond of Roman ways. Most of our women played a very minor part in the world of commerce. Master Ezer traveled widely throughout the empire for his business, and his views had stretched accordingly to accommodate a more flexible outlook. Ethan was the same. But my father had too much of the old ways in him to shift and change. And my mother would do everything in her power to sway him even if he did consider Ezer's advice in a serious light.

The next morning my father sent for me. "Tell the servants to resume work on the flax," he said.

"Yes, Father." I had never been entrusted with such a charge. Although my father's workshop was situated behind our private residence, separated by a large garden that helped to protect us from some of the unpleasant odors associated with the business of dyeing fabrics, I rarely visited there for long and did not know his servants well. I worried that the workers might not take me seriously, being young as well as female. I need not have worried. In their anxiety for their own future employment, they were quick to leap to their task, no matter who brought them the orders.

Hours later, I was still in the workshop, observing how the workers processed the flax fibers, using iron hooks and combs to get them ready for spinning. I had spent the whole day avoiding my mother, trying to learn the details of flax preparation. It seemed wise to learn everything I could if my father needed my help.

One of the women held up her rough flax comb. "I should try using this on my husband's grizzly head," she said.

"It might do some good," another replied. "He has more tangles in his hair than you'd find in a Canaanite goat's fleece."

"You would be wasting a good iron hook. The iron is sure to bend against that rough mess growing out of his head," the foreman said, motioning for them to continue their work.

Their hands grew busy again. Laughter coloring her voice, the first woman said, "I could always wait until he falls asleep, then cut off his hair and sell it to the master as sheep wool." She shot me a playful look from under thick eyebrows.

I sensed her comment was a small test. She wanted to know how I would manage—whether I would take offense or enter the congenial spirit of banter amongst the workers without losing my place of respect with them. The room became very quiet.

"Watch out; that particular wool might become very popular with our Roman customers." I threw a tangled ball of discarded fiber into the air and caught it again with a quick motion of my hand. "They might demand more. And then where shall we be? We will have to contend with the men of Jerusalem walking about with bald heads. Their wives might have a few objections." Everyone laughed, the tension draining from the atmosphere.

The workshop had grown stuffy by early afternoon. Sweat stained my drooping tunic, and my light veil, damp and shapeless, began to itch. I cared not. My eyes followed the quick movements of the laborers as I committed to memory every detail of the process. No aspect of the work seemed tedious to me.

Towels were not dyed, so we would not have to worry about that step. We only needed to weave the fabric on the vertical looms in my father's workshop. Because my father only bought steeped flax, even this coarser grade of plant would yield softer towels. Nothing scratchy for our discriminating customers, many of whom were Romans and accustomed to the finer things of the empire.

"Elianna!" My mother's voice made me jump; I hit my head against the frame of a loom resting near me and winced. My mother threw her hands up in the air. "What are you doing, loitering here? I've looked for you everywhere. Come away from this place at once."

"Father sent me." Of course he hadn't told me to linger once I had organized the start of the work. But she did not need to know that.

She narrowed her eyes and stared. "Benjamin?"

I shrugged. "I think Master Ezer was concerned for the welfare of the trade should it remain dormant much longer. He might have suggested that Father use my help for now. While he . . . while he grieves." I felt my cheeks heat.

"I see." And that, to my disbelief, was that.

Except that after we finished eating the evening meal I overheard her complaining to my father about the madness

30

of allowing an unmarried young woman to get mixed in trade. "What next?" she said. "Will you have your daughter running around Jerusalem, reeking of mordant and selling towels?"

"Of course not, Elizabeth. But I need help; can't you see that? I cannot cope with the workshop at the moment. She is eager enough for it. If it weren't for her, none of this would have been necessary. It's only right that she make a little sacrifice now, for all our sakes."

My mother said nothing after that.

At my mother's command, the servants had removed Joseph's bedding and chests from our room. Joanna had pulled her pallet closer to mine, and more nights than not, she would slip into my bed and hold me in her slim, cold arms. I returned her embrace with all my might. I held her with the strength of two affections, knowing I could never hold my brother like this again. I missed him every moment. I even missed what used to annoy me: his habit of waking up early and insisting that Joanna and I join him; his demands for attention when I wanted to concentrate on something else; his insistence on traipsing after me wherever I went. How I longed to have him back. His absence turned into a hole that never filled.

It was a relief to return to my father's workshop and find a distraction from the pain that had become my shadow. In addition to the towel-grade flax, we also had to process a new delivery of linen fibers, this one fine enough for ladies' tunics and veils. We would deal with this delivery later in the year. We stored the processed fibers in a cool, dry shed, where a large order of wool also awaited our attentions.

One afternoon, before the weavers began their work, the foreman approached me.

"Mistress Elianna, do you want us to weave the towels plain, or have a stripe woven into them? In the past we have either woven a plain blue stripe on each edge and in the center, or we have added a Roman key design. What would you like this time around?"

More and more, the servants turned to me seeking direction, for although in the evenings, just before the workers finished for the day, my father would come for a perfunctory inspection, we could tell his heart was not in it.

"I will let you know in the morning." An idea had been asserting itself in my mind all day, but I could not authorize a new plan without my father's approval.

Even women of rank were allowed to embroider, and I had a special talent for it. Before dinnertime, I drew a design of leaves and flowers. After choosing three hues of yarn for the embroidery, I took my design to my father.

"I thought we might try something new on the towels. What about a simple embroidery instead of the usual weave?" I placed my design before him on the table.

He rolled his eyes without examining my drawing. "Just do what we always do."

"Yes, Father. Only . . . we are over two months late, you see."

He gave me a swift look before turning his back. "So?"

"The Roman key weave is common enough, as is the stripe pattern. Every fine merchant in Jerusalem will have been offering stacks of similar towels, and they are months ahead of us this season. But if we have a unique offering, the delay won't matter so much. Customers will buy from us what they can't find elsewhere."

My father tapped his fingers on the wooden table. I noticed his nails had grown too long and were dirty. He picked up my drawing and looked at it for a moment. "Do as you wish," he said, dropping it back on the table.

I had hoped the design would elicit a response from him. A hint of approval. Instead, he seemed uncaring one way or another. He had barely looked at my drawing and ignored the colors I had chosen. I crossed my arms at the elbows, my fingers digging into my flesh. Without his guidance, I felt lost. Grave doubt about my scheme assailed me. Who was I to decide that a new pattern was what we needed? What if I proved wrong? What if no one had any interest in towels with a floral motif? What if I caused an enormous financial loss?

I wrapped my design and the sample yarns in a piece of linen and took Keziah with me to visit Ethan's family. Jerusha welcomed me with her customary kiss and asked after my family as she set out a gold-edged platter of fresh figs and grapes.

"I came to ask your opinion." I opened the linen cloth and showed her my diagram. "Would you buy towels with these flowers embroidered on them?"

She bent over and studied the drawing with shrewd eyes.

"It's beautiful, Elianna. I would love to own towels so elegant. But you need Ethan and Ezer. They know what sells. They will be back soon. Can you stay for supper?"

I nodded, relieved, and sent Keziah to my mother to let her know that I would not come home for the evening meal.

Ethan and Master Ezer arrived an hour later. My words got tangled at the sight of Ethan. After so many years of knowing him, he still had the power to make my breath catch with his mere presence. He was not overly tall, but he was wide and powerfully built, more like a charioteer than a merchant. Heads turned his way when he entered a room; he was hard to miss.

His mother explained my need, and after dinner Ethan looked at my flower motif.

"This is lovely, Elianna."

"Do you think so?" I brightened at his compliment.

"But it will take longer to complete than a simple weave. Longer hours mean more pay. Less profit, if you sell at the old price. And if you raise the price, you run the risk of not selling at all."

My heart sank. "So you think I shouldn't do it? Stick to the old patterns instead?"

He shrugged a broad shoulder. "I didn't say that. Your concerns are valid. Your father's business is behind by two months. Many have already made their purchases. A narrower margin of profit is better than none. How much longer will it take you to embroider the towels rather than weave a design into them?"

I thought about it and realized that by making a few

34

adjustments to the shape of the leaves, I could make the embroidering go faster without affecting the overall design too much. I estimated the time it would require to finish one towel and compared it to our normal woven patterns. "There will be a difference of five, perhaps six hours for each towel."

It took Ethan less than a moment to figure the sums in his head. It would have taken me an hour, and I probably still would not have had it right. Perhaps because he had thought he would never have a son, my father had provided me with more education than common amongst women. That privilege had not enabled me to master the art of figures, however. I feared no amount of study ever would.

Ethan told me how much money we would lose. "Your profit will be smaller. But," he said, "I think it would be worth it. You might find new customers, establish a whole new trend. If you receive a greater number of orders than usual, you will make up the loss."

"Do you believe that is possible? Having increased custom, I mean."

"With the right seller, I believe it probable."

My shoulders drooped. Father would have no interest in establishing new customers. He had no patience for people these days. He certainly would have no motivation to reach a different clientele. "I don't think my father will be able to do it."

Ethan smiled, his eyes lighting up. "We don't need to bother him with this. In all Jerusalem, you shall not find a better dealer than your servant." He bowed, Roman style.

"Leave it to me. Flower-adorned towels will be the new rage in Judea this season."

Ezer and Jerusha laughed, and I found to my surprise that I was laughing with them. I had not even smiled since Joseph died.

Ezer slapped Ethan on the back. "I would tell him off for being boastful, except that I believe he tells the truth. My son could sell sackcloth to a Roman lady on her way to dine with the new emperor, Tiberius. If anyone can make a success of your scheme, it is he."

If was not a word I dared to contemplate.

FOUR

Good people pass away;
the godly often die before their time.

ISAIAH 57:1, NLT

THAT NIGHT MY SISTER, Joanna, came into my bed and
wrapped her long gazelle limbs around me. "It was my birthday today and no one remembered," she whispered. "I'm
fourteen years old."

I groaned and turned to embrace her. "I am so sorry,
beloved. I can't believe I forgot."

She sniffed. In the faint light of the lamp that we always
left lit through the night I saw her rub her eyes. Jews did not
celebrate birthdays with gifts and lavish feasts the way our
Roman conquerors did. But those who could afford it at
least acknowledged such a day and commemorated it with
a special meal and a gathering of family and close friends.

I shoveled one more sin on the growing pile that weighed down my soul. Joanna had been forgotten in the shuffle of our grief. A grief I had brought upon our heads.

Like a thousand times before, I looked back on that dark afternoon and imagined ways I could have prevented Joseph's death. If I had not taken him to the hill. If I had delayed by one hour. If I had wiped his face. If I had come to his aid sooner, killed the bee faster. If I had brought him home before it grew too late. It was a useless game I played in my head every day, trying to change the outcome of that dreadful incident.

The problem with death is its very irrevocability. Still, I could not help engaging in this painful exercise, thinking of ways to prevent Joseph from dying. I wondered if my parents did something similar. Were they held captive by their secret regrets as I was? If so, they kept their torment as hidden as I did mine. We all suffered. But we did not share the weight of our anguish with each other.

The next morning I rose before Joanna to tell my mother about the birthday we had forgotten. Promptly, she burst into tears. Her weeping no longer tied my stomach into a knot. It had become too common a sight and I had grown accustomed to it, the way one grows used to the searing heat of the sun in the summer.

"Shall I arrange a special meal for this evening?" I asked gently.

Mother wiped at her eyes and nodded. "My head is in agony. You organize everything. And see if Ezer and his family can come. Joanna would enjoy that."

After arranging the details of the supper, I returned to the workshop and told the servants to begin the work of weaving plain towels. I found it a relief to hear the hum of their swift shuttles filling the chamber. Before long, we would have lengths of linen fit for towels and napkins in Herod's own palace.

I spent an hour with the foreman, coordinating the upcoming embroidery work, since my plan presented as much a new venture for him as it did for me. My mother, Joanna, and I would join in this effort; even my strict mother had no objections to the work of embroidering. We could bring the towels inside the house and work on them in the privacy of our chamber, which offered a respectable alternative to visiting the workshop.

Over dinner that night I noticed Ethan staring at me with peculiar intensity. "What?" I whispered under my breath so only he could hear. Master Ezer was recounting the story of his last journey to Caesarea and everyone was listening to him with rapt attention, affording Ethan and me a veneer of privacy even though we were in public.

"Your birthday is two months after Joanna's, isn't it?"

I shrugged my shoulder, not comprehending the significance.

"You will turn seventeen, I believe."

I could feel the color leach out of my skin. Seventeen. The age I had been impatient to reach for over a year. The age when my betrothal would come to an end. The age of marriage. I pretended the roasted lamb in front of me held an indelible fascination and reached out to pick up a piece of bread. My fingers shook so hard that I dropped the bread. I lowered my hand to my lap with a quick motion.

"Elianna?" I could feel the question in Ethan's voice.

"Yes?"

"Will you look at me, please?"

I forced myself to look up. A band of pain had started to pound on one side of my forehead and I squinted. Sweat broke out over my upper lip.

"You don't want to be married to me?" Ethan's voice was steady and soothing.

"Do you want to be married to *me*?"

"Of course I do. Why do you think I have waited all this time? The question is you."

"Me?"

"You don't seem too eager."

"My brother . . ."

He took a deep breath. "I know. We can wait a year if you wish. That's what I wanted to say. That I am willing to wait."

I could not understand the relief his words brought me. Once I had found the waiting onerous. Offensive. Now it assuaged the panic that threatened to rise up and tear into me with its sharp teeth. Ethan had given me time, which meant I did not need to examine these strange responses for now.

I did not know myself anymore. It was as if Joseph's death had somehow entombed a part of me, and what remained was a stranger. I could only live from one day to the next. No dreams. No hopes. Then I realized that was not quite true, either. I had my father's work. That remained the one place I allowed my dreams to live on and to grow.

We finished the embroidery faster than I had estimated and Ethan turned his attention to finding new customers while we approached Father's old patrons. My father visited with a handful of his customers himself and made good progress, but his interest waned rapidly. He had lost his enthusiasm for work, for people—for life itself, I sometimes thought.

"Send Joel," he said. "He will manage." Joel was a young man in his employ who had on occasion dealt with customers in my father's absence.

I packed Joel off with sample towels and a rolled-up list of potential patrons. His palms were sweaty and his thin beard twitched as he pulled at it. He was unaccustomed to this much responsibility. But we had no alternative. If I had been a son, I could have gone myself. As a woman, I had to stay home and twist my hands and hope that Joel would find a way to overcome his inherent shyness and inexperience and sell my towels.

To my surprise, Joel returned home to tell me that the towels were selling themselves.

Within weeks, Ethan found us as many new buyers as we already had for the towels, doubling our custom with his efforts. We had to get busy embroidering the linen remaining in the workshop. The clamor for our new design wiped us out of every scrap of coarse linen in our possession. I tried to pay Ethan a portion of our profits, but he would have none of it.

"This is business, Ethan. I may need your help for months

yet. You cannot afford to give me your time without charging for it. If you refuse, I will stop asking for your help. And then where shall we be?"

The breath hissed out of Ethan's nostrils. "You wish me to charge my own betrothed for a kindness? What manner of man do you think I am, Elianna?"

"Not kindness. Commerce. I will not abuse our relationship. Look, thanks to you, we have more than sufficient profit. I can afford to pay what is fair. My father will agree with me, I have no doubt."

"Your father will agree that his daughter's future husband should be paid for helping in her time of need?" Offense leaked out of him like a churning river.

I knew him to be wrong in this matter. I could accept help once, but no more. If I allowed myself to become a charity in his eyes, he would soon lose respect for my family and me. I would turn into the burden he had to carry. "Take my offer or not, Ethan. I will not waver on this."

Without a word, Ethan turned around and left. I had never seen him this angry. I sank down on a chair. Had I offended him so badly that he would not return? My mouth went dry at the thought. I wanted to run after him and beg his forgiveness. I wanted to tell him that he could have whatever he wanted. Instead, I gritted my teeth and let him go.

Ethan was one of the most levelheaded men I knew. Even his anger was leashed under an iron band of control. But lately, I had come to see that there was a deeper well of emotion in him than I had realized. We had been dealing together as adults for some time now. I had ceased to perceive him through my childish haze of adoration. I saw him as a woman sees a man. He was not perfect. He was not beyond anger and resentment. Hardship and sorrow hurt him much more deeply than he allowed others to see.

And I had wounded his pride.

Better his pride than my place in his heart, I thought. He would get over his pride, no matter how much it smarted now. I was not so sure I could find my way back into his affections once he turned from me.

Master Ezer came that same night and closeted himself with my father in private. I sat stiff and unmoving in my chamber, chewing my nails. Were they discussing how to break the betrothal agreement? Had Ethan sent his father to free himself from me, once and for all?

I ran downstairs as soon as I spied Master Ezer leaving our house. My father was just emerging from the dining room. He seemed gray and smaller than I remembered.

"Did he break off the betrothal?" I asked, my voice trembling.

"What? No."

I leaned against the wall for a moment. Then, wishing my father peace, I hastened back up the stairs to cry with relief.

Whatever passed between Master Ezer and my father, I never knew. But after that, Ethan gave us his help for a share of the profit. The lower the profit, the lower his pay. He never came himself to collect his coin. He sent a servant or his younger brother.

I was careful not to refer to the money when we were together. I suspected that his father had forced his hand, and that Ethan had not acquiesced willingly. Pulsing beneath the surface of his calm exterior, Ethan had a deep vein of resentment about the whole situation.

⁂

Lambs were born, plentiful and healthy that year, and everywhere herd owners celebrated their good fortune with such enthusiasm that the sound of their merrymaking kept us awake late into the night for weeks. I had been born the same month as the new lambs and my birthday came and went with considerably less remark than the advent of the new flocks.

Under different circumstances, we would have been planning my wedding feast. My mother brought up the matter with me once. I explained that I could not face marriage while she and Father needed me so much. She did not try to argue. We both knew that Father still relied on my help. He had not recovered from Joseph's death as we had hoped and seemed to live under a veil of malaise that never lifted. His interest in the world of the living remained marginal at best.

We could not expect Ethan to let me continue to work for my family once I married. As his wife, my time and talent belonged to him. I should be helping *his* business flourish, building a legacy fit for any sons and daughters God chose to give us.

"Is Ethan willing to wait?" my mother asked.

"Yes. He is probably relieved, if you think about it. He seems so set on having an older bride."

My mother gave a wan smile. "He is a good man. He loves you, Elianna."

"He *is* a good man," I said, keeping my opinion to myself about whether he loved me or not. Ethan felt protective of me. He cared for me. But he had never given me reason to believe that he loved me with any serious attachment.

The months had tumbled one into another in a blur of grief-washed activity. It was winter. We had already spun the fine-grade flax delivered to the workshop in late summer, which I had had to store at the time. I now turned my focus to dyeing the fine linen yarn, producing beautiful shades of blue, red, and a pleasing green hue, which I, along with the help of our dye master, had developed.

Ethan and Master Ezer had been an invaluable resource to me, answering my many questions with inexhaustible patience. They visited with my father regularly and always lingered with me afterward to ensure I did not feel overwhelmed with the many new tasks before me. Between them, they knew as much about fabrics and the process of dyeing them as my own father, who had three generations of knowledge running through his veins.

If Ethan felt any discomfort about finding his betrothed more involved in a textile workshop than in the affairs of the household, he never betrayed it. From his manner you would have thought all the women of Judea spent their time developing new shades of dye.

I felt safe sharing my ideas with him. He would listen with his habitual silent intensity, as if nothing in the world could be so important as one of my new schemes. I lived for those rare moments when his light eyes would sparkle with approval. "This . . . this design is worthy of a princess. Well done, Elianna." I clung to his approval the way a blind man clings to a guiding hand.

Once, he told me that I had more talent than any man he had ever met. I worked all the harder to win those rare words of approbation from him, knowing I would never have them from my father.

Colors dominated my world. While the quality of our fabrics remained a key focus, their unique color palettes would ultimately win us our select clientele. So I learned everything I could about dyes.

The roots of the madder plant produced numerous shades of red, but in order to make madder colorfast, the fabric needed to be treated with a mordant. Each dye master had his own secret recipe for assorted mordants. Because our house was so close to my father's workshop, he forbade the use of truly putrid materials, such as old urine, which was both cheap and popular. Instead, he preferred substances like iron salts. These produced softer, more demure shades of red, which our workshop specialized in creating.

To make our green dye, we first used a special indigo solution. This produced a celestial blue color; then we immersed the blue yarn into a second bath, this one made of a yellow dye extracted from weld. The resulting green, a misty, dark, leafy hue, had a luscious sheen that drew the eye and captured the attention. I knew it would become popular as soon as I saw the yarn drying in the sun.

In spite of the cramped, often malodorous process of

coloring fabrics, I loved visiting the dye room in my father's workshop. Although many weavers dyed their fabrics before the process of spinning and weaving began, in my father's workshop we did most of our dyeing after we completed spinning the yarn. This produced a more uniform color, which translated into better fabrics. One of the reasons my father's customers sought his wares year after year had to do with the intangible quality of everything that came out of his stores. Whether linen or wool, we produced some of the finest textiles in all of Judea.

Our workers washed the large deliveries of fresh wool in the famous spring of Fuller's Field so that the oil could be leached out of the fleece properly. But the majority of the remaining process took place in the workshop itself, which was surprisingly humble in size. There were nine cement-lined vats against two walls and a narrow stone bench against another where I often sat to oversee the process. A large stone cistern for rinsing completed the furniture in the simple chamber.

For me, this became the magical room. Nothing was as it appeared. Dyes went into the vats looking one color, and yarns emerged to dry into a different hue. Only experience and careful planning could give you the result you wanted. Using dyes required an internal knowing, almost a kind of faith. You created them not by the evidence of your eyes, but blindly, by the knowledge of your materials, and by the feeling in your gut.

I spent day upon day learning and creating, living in a world of my imaginings. I dreamt of colors and textures.

Of beauty. And when dreams of death came, as they invariably did, I taught myself in the wakeful, shivering hours following their onslaught, to think instead of formulas and solutions, of vats of indigo and madder, of new shades and heart-stopping colors. I hid in a cave made of glorious creations. And I forced myself to forget what I had lost.

FIVE

The LORD will keep you from all evil;
he will keep your life.
The LORD will keep your going out and your coming in
from this time on and forevermore.

PSALM 121:7-8, NRSV

ETHAN HAD LEFT on an important purchasing trip just before my birthday, taking no one but a trusted servant, and I had not seen him for two months. His father, having grown tired of seasickness and the inconveniences of travel, trusted Ethan to do most of their purchasing now.

I knew him to be brilliant at this work. He managed continually to discover better sources of unique dyes and had an infallible sense of what would become popular. His father's business thrived as a result of his acumen. But I could not help worrying for him when he was gone. Travel, even in the civilized Roman Empire, was a dangerous undertaking. Unpredictable storms, ruthless bandits, violent sickness—anything could happen when you were far from home on a vulnerable ship or a deserted road.

He walked into the workshop unannounced early one afternoon. The workers were in the garden, eating their noonday meal, and I alone remained indoors, distracted by a new crack in one of the vats. My delight in seeing him after so long an absence made me forget everything and I ran to him, forcing myself to stop a mere breath away. I could not suppress my smile, which must have flashed with the stunned joy of a drunk poet discovering a jar full of free aged wine.

"Ethan!" I cried, shoving my hands up my sleeves to keep from enfolding him in an inappropriate embrace. That would have shocked him.

His answering smile made me gulp. There was a new assurance about the way he held himself, as if he had won a battle and liked coming away the victor. His eyes turned warm in acknowledgment of my obvious welcome. He always liked it too well when I could not hide my affection for him.

"I brought you something." He extended a small, flat package, carefully wrapped in clean cloth.

Nonplussed, I made no move to take the package from him. He had never brought me a gift before. "Well?" His chuckle brought me to myself. "Don't you want it?"

"Of course." I unwrapped the cloth with care to find a magnificent tapestry the size of a small window, worked with delicate wool in captivating shades of blue and scarlet and green. Everything about its construction—the ornate borders, the sharp-edged flowers and leaves, the luster of the precious gold twinkling in clumps, even the slight hint of fading in certain parts of the tapestry—indicated its old age.

I turned it over. The back had been cleverly woven so that

there was scarcely any difference from the front panel. No knots. No tangles. This was the work of a master weaver, the kind that surfaced only once every generation. Upon closer examination, I found that the tiny holes that were invariably created from looping the different colors back and forth on the loom in order to create each pattern had been painstakingly sewn shut.

"Babylonian!" I breathed. "Is this genuine Babylonian work? From the time before Persian rule?"

"Trust you to know the origin with one look."

"How did you find it? It's breathtaking, Ethan. You couldn't have given me a better gift." Babylonian tapestries were legendary. Endless generations had revered the work of the weavers of Babylon who shared their secrets with no one. Antique productions like the one Ethan had brought me were difficult to find and exceedingly valuable. Usually, they were huge in size, covering the length of a whole wall. I guessed this piece was a fragment of a border to a much larger work.

He seemed pleased with my enthusiasm. "I hoped you would like it. I thought of you when I saw it."

I made a pretense of giving all my attention to rewrapping the tapestry with care, trying to hide the inexplicable flash of tears his words had aroused. He had thought of me. He had not forgotten about me while traipsing about the empire, having adventures. I swallowed hard and remembered that I should ask about his journey.

Lifting my head, I noticed the man standing just behind him. It showed the measure of my distraction that I had not seen him until that moment, for he was a giant, towering over Ethan by almost a head. Broad, with muscles and a thick neck that could have held the weight of a bronze table, this man would have looked at home in the arena. And though I was no expert, I was sure that not many gladiators could have matched him in size. A thick scar ran from under his right eye and disappeared into his beard.

I stared at him, forgetting to close my mouth.

"This is Viriato," Ethan said, his lips twitching. He had switched from Aramaic, the language we spoke in our daily lives, to Koine Greek. The Roman Empire had united a vast portion of the world with its might. In a way, the diverse dialects and languages of these different nations posed as great a challenge to Rome as their weapons and armies, for how were they all to communicate in a world that grew smaller every day? The language that brought so many races and peoples together was a common form of Greek rather than the Roman tongue, or even the classical Greek that their poets and playwrights liked to use. Most of us spoke at least a smattering of Greek. Like many men and women of my class, Ethan and I were fluent.

"Viriato is my new friend from Lusitania," Ethan continued.

Viriato smiled. Instead of softening his face, it had the strange effect of making him look like a grimacing bear about to attack. "He means I am his servant, which is enough for me. I would still be a slave if not for his generosity."

He spoke Koine Greek with the facility of an educated man. "A slave?" I raised my eyebrows and looked from one to the other.

Ethan scowled. "Don't encourage him. He will bore you to tears with his endless prattling. I should know. For weeks, I was stuck on a ship with him as we traveled home."

Viriato laughed, his voice booming around the workshop, making the weavers stare with curiosity. "He doesn't want me to tell you how we met; that's his trouble. Too modest, your betrothed."

Ethan ran his hand through his hair, making it stand up in tufts. "You are the hero of the story, as you well know. I did little enough."

Being the daughter of a merchant had certain advantages. I had more freedom than other women my age, most of whom would not be allowed to talk to strange men. My father's business, however, had brought me into contact with strangers since before I could walk. Managing the workshop had stretched my freedom even more. We lived in an age of upheaval and change. I was not the only female who pushed at the boundaries of propriety with my work. Some of our synagogues were led by women. At the same time, it was still considered scandalous for women to hold conversation with men in a public place.

I shrugged. "I sense a good tale. Come into the house, and I will offer you sweet wine while you tell me about your adventures with Ethan."

After all, Ethan had brought the man to me himself, and I did not wish to miss what promised to be a fascinating story.

Ethan groaned. Viriato rubbed his hands. I hid a smile and walked ahead.

✻

Back in the house, I brought the men into the outer chamber, where we sometimes entertained my father's Gentile clients. Here we offered them wine and, if they merited extra attention, pastry and fruit, though we never partook of food with them ourselves as the Law forbade Jews from eating with heathens. Since Viriato was obviously a Gentile, I decided that we could gather here, around a rectangular low bronze table carved with lotus flowers and overlaid with silver. It was our best table, on show to impress potential customers.

I sent for my parents. My mother had gone to bed, battling another headache, the servant told me. Father came in, his tunic askew, his hair uncombed. I noticed his eyes were red and glassy. He had been drinking. Again. But he was gracious to our guests and said the right things.

"So, tell us your story, Viriato," I said.

"I was a slave in a cinnabar mine in Hispania," he began.

I could not silence a gasp. Cinnabar was a highly valuable mineral, more for its mercury content than the vermilion that it also produced. But anyone working in a cinnabar mine, no matter how young or strong, would eventually succumb to the poison that seemed to linger in the air. Which is why only criminals and undesirables were put to work there.

"Indeed?" I said, my voice unsteady. What was Ethan thinking? Why would he invite a criminal back to Judea with him? Call him friend? Bring him around to the house of his betrothed for conversation and sweet wine?

"I had gone to examine the cinnabar there," Ethan explained. "A colleague told me that a new, rich vein had been found, producing vermilion of exceptional color."

The Romans adored vermilion red, and the wealthy used it to paint their villas, their doors, even their faces. The fashion had spread into Palestine amongst the very rich, and Ethan's father, who had an instinct for such things, had become one of the premier merchants offering the dye in Judea.

"The manager offered to show me around the place." Ethan shrugged. "I had always been curious to see the inner workings of a mine. We had just begun when, on the rock face directly above us, one of the slaves who was pushing a cart full of mineral lost control."

"He suffered from tremors, that man. It's common amongst those who work the mine. Restricted vision too." Viriato rubbed the palm of his hand over his face, and I sensed that beneath his good-humored joviality lay a wealth of somber memories. "He probably lost his footing due to a bad tremor."

"All I know is I heard a creaking noise, and when I looked up, the cart was tilting right on top of me. I would have been dead if that much cinnabar had landed on my head. Before I could gasp, this hulking giant threw himself across the cart and prevented it from falling below, crushing me."

The thought of how close Ethan had come to dying made me turn white. I could taste bile in my throat.

"I did say he was the hero of the story. The cart was at such a precarious angle by then that he might have plunged down with it. He hung on for several moments, his feet dangling in the air, pushing down as the cart teetered over the edge. Finally, he managed to stabilize it. He earned himself a few bruised ribs for his efforts."

"Why?" I asked, too stunned to think of tact. "Why would a slave risk his own life for a complete stranger?"

"I became a slave. I did not stop being a man. I could no more prevent myself from helping a fellow human in the midst of danger than I could will myself to simply stop breathing."

I could see what Ethan saw in Viriato. Not merely the physical strength, the impressive size. It was the man himself. A certain nobility that scars and slavery had not managed to ruin.

"I thank you, with all my heart," I said. "I could not have borne to lose Ethan. Tell me, Viriato, how did you end up in a cinnabar mine?"

The giant scratched his beard and looked at his shoes. "I hit the wrong man. Broke his jaw. And his nose. Perhaps a few ribs. Seemed like the right thing to do at the time, but he didn't agree with me. Since he was a centurion, his opinion mattered more than mine."

"Why did you hit him?"

"Not to be indelicate, but it involved a lady."

"He made overtures to your . . . ?"

"*My* nothing. She was a respectable maiden from an impoverished Lusitanian family. He seemed to think that being a Roman citizen and a centurion gave him the right to—" He puffed out a breath through inflated cheeks and looked to Ethan for help.

"The right to force himself upon a young woman."

"You defended her? From *that*? And they put you in a cinnabar mine?"

He shrugged. "You can't go around assaulting Roman citizens, no matter what the provocation."

"So what happened? After you saved Ethan's life, I mean?"

"Ah. The impossible." Viriato clapped once, and intertwined his fingers. "I had been thrown into that mine to rot. The life span of slaves in cinnabar mines is notoriously brief. I thought I would end my days there. Your betrothed changed that. I don't know by what trick or charm he convinced the manager to sell me outright. Must have cost him bushels. He won't tell me how much. But you can't buy a slave with a criminal past unless you are unusually generous. I figured being his slave beat working at the mine any day. So I was happy to leave with him.

"Imagine my surprise when our first stop was a visit with the magistrate. He made me sit outside the door as he conducted his business. I spent the time wondering if I had already offended him in some way, and whether he meant to lodge a complaint against me. I figured I had enjoyed the shortest respite from the mines in all of Rome's history. I considered making a run for my freedom."

"Did you flee?"

"No. I sat where he left me and mourned my imminent arrest."

"But Ethan did not have you arrested."

"No. I was mistaken on that account. Ethan had another plan. He emerged from his visit with the magistrate and handed me a roll of papyrus. 'Here is your certificate of manumission. You are a free man today,' he said to me."

SIX

Do not be afraid; do not be discouraged.
Be strong and courageous.
JOSHUA 10:25, NIV

MY FATHER LEANED FORWARD. "What did he ask in return?"

"Nothing. After informing me I was free, he turned his back and began to amble down the road, whistling. It took me a few moments to comprehend his words. I thought he was playing with me. But when I glanced at the papyrus, what do you think I found?"

"Your certificate of manumission," I said, smiling so wide my cheeks hurt.

"I was dumbstruck. In my whole life, I had never known such an act of generosity."

"Don't exaggerate," Ethan said, his voice gruff. "I told you. I walked away alive from that cinnabar mine because of you. It was only right that you, in turn, should walk away from it because of me."

I stared at Ethan as if I were seeing him for the first time. "What did you do then? How did you end up traveling with Ethan?"

Viriato shrugged a massive shoulder. "I told him that the very least he could do was allow me to buy him a meal. As thanks for giving me my life back."

Ethan's lip curled. "He also asked to borrow money to pay for the food, the big lout."

"Don't laugh, mistress," Viriato said. "You ought to pity me. First, he refused to eat at a proper inn, because the food might be unclean. Such delicious smells were wafting out of that place. My stomach grumbled louder than a dancing girl's ankle bells as we walked right by, ignoring the inviting aroma of roasted fowl. Instead he took me to the house of a Jewish merchant and purchased cold bread and watery cheese. Then he made me sit apart, in case my Gentile skin might contaminate him."

"You were still close enough to talk through the whole meal. Gave me severe indigestion. I had to sleep in the middle of the day for a whole hour to recover."

Viriato smirked. "I needed to talk fast if I was to prove what a nice, trustworthy fellow I am. How else were you going to hire me to be your faithful servant?" Viriato spread his arms wide. "So here I am."

My father, who had stopped drinking from his cup some time before, shook his head. "What an extraordinary tale. Why did you come to Judea? Why not return home to Lusitania?"

Viriato dropped his head. "There is no place for me back

home. The centurion I hit is still stationed there. My return will only bring my family more trouble than I already have caused. It is better for them if I stay away."

We were silent for a beat. "What shall you do for Ethan?" my father asked.

"He has already made himself useful, actually," Ethan said. "Viriato's father raises sheep. Very fine sheep. He knows more than I do about different grades of wool, as well as what kind of dye works best on each variety."

"Sheep, eh? What's so hard to figure out?" the big man said, his cheeks turning an endearing shade of red at Ethan's compliment.

Ethan leaned forward. "He would be a good help to you, Benjamin."

My father furrowed his brow in confusion. "Me? He is your servant."

"Well, yes. Then again, not entirely."

It wasn't like Ethan to be so obscure. I gave him a sharp look.

"The truth is, I purchased his freedom partly with your money, Elianna."

"*My* money?"

"Your father's, I mean."

"*My* money?" my father said.

Ethan tapped perfectly trimmed nails on the table before him. "The money you have insisted I receive for helping with your trade. I had been saving it to give to Elianna on our wedding day as a present." He shrugged. "I needed it to free Viriato from that death trap. I would not have had enough funds without it. How could I leave him there? I felt I owed him for saving my life."

I nodded. "It was your money to use as you wished. For what it's worth, I am happy you used it in such a worthy manner."

"As I said, I had set it aside as a gift for you. So really, it was your gold I spent. Which makes it only right that you should use Viriato from time to time."

Before I could make a vociferous objection to this circular and ridiculous argument, my father nodded. "Thank you, Ethan. We will be happy to have Viriato's assistance upon occasion."

My eyes grew round. I could not very well go against my father. I tried to think of an argument that would cut through the web Ethan had managed to weave. "Father, Viriato is a freedman. Surely he deserves to choose for himself where he is to work?"

Viriato gave his bear smile, the scar puckering high on his right cheek. "I would be privileged to help where I can, mistress. Ethan and his father only deal with dyes, you see. I miss working with wool. It will be a pleasure to get my hands on some superior fleece again."

What could I say? I nodded and smiled, though it made my cheeks hurt.

On the way out, Ethan sent Viriato to await him at the door and turned to me. "Don't look so sour, Elianna. You can't always have your way."

"With you around, that won't be a great problem. I'm not likely to have my way. Ever," I added.

"'It is better to live in a corner of the housetop than in a house shared with a quarrelsome wife,'" Ethan quoted. "Solomon must have been an expert on the subject, what with all those wives."

Without taking time for a breath, I quipped, "'An excellent wife who can find?' If King Solomon couldn't find one, think of *your* chances. Poor Ethan. Destined for a lifetime on a corner of the roof."

He laughed. His eyes had turned dark and liquid. "King Lemuel said that, and he probably did not have the breadth of Solomon's experience. In any case, I have some pleasant news to share. May I tell you, or are you still too angry to listen?"

Curiosity got the better of me. "By all means, share your good news. I will forbear to be happy for you."

"My brother's wife is with child. I am going to be an uncle."

I promptly forgot my ire and bounced on my toes with excitement. "What a great blessing! I am so happy for you all, Ethan. Jerusha must be overjoyed at the prospect of having a grandchild."

Ethan pulled on one of my curls peeping below my scarf. "Her feet have not touched the ground from the moment she heard. Best of all is seeing Daniel smile from one poky ear to the other. It has been a long time since I have seen my brother so happy."

After Ethan and Viriato left, I sat in the courtyard, lazily tending the herbs growing in large clay pots. In the stillness of the sunset hours it occurred to me that Ethan had never overcome his distaste for accepting money from me. He had merely come up with a different way of getting his own way. He was far more complex than I had understood, more patient and persistent. I hardly knew whether to laugh or be vexed. He refused to take my money, yet he did not hesitate to give every spare coin he had—what he considered mine as well as his—to save a man's life from slavery and death. It dawned on me that I was betrothed to an extraordinary man whose sense of honor, generosity, and mercy surpassed that of anyone I had ever known.

I choked on that thought. Ethan deserved a much better woman than me for his wife.

We turned our attention to the last large bundle of wool that had been delivered to our workshop late the previous summer. It was now spring, and this would be our final major undertaking before orders of fresh wool and flax started to come in. The sales from our store of wool would have to carry us into midsummer, when the new wool and flax could be processed for sale. We were running behind, never having managed to catch up after losing over two months in our busiest season.

Viriato was with me the day we went to examine the wool in the storehouse. According to our records, this was fine wool from Syrian sheep whose soft fleece and broad tails were held in high esteem by Jews, Romans, and Greeks alike. I touched a fleece lying on top of a large bundle and frowned. It was coarser than I expected, the color not quite white, lacking the brightness and delicacy such grade of wool should have. I pulled out another fleece from under the pile and found it the same. Then another and another.

I thought perhaps I was mistaken. "What do you think?" I asked Viriato.

"Middle range, at best."

"It's meant to be the highest quality, equal to Tarentine sheep." The sheep of Tarentum were famed for their shiny, soft fleeces. Legend had it they were hand-fed, kept clean, and coddled, even brought into the house like babies every night.

Viriato pulled his fingers through his beard. "Not this pile, in any case." With swift movements, he went through fleece after fleece, pulling them randomly and examining them in the light. He shook his head. "I'm sorry, mistress. These are good for blankets. Carpets, maybe, if you were in that business. No fine tunics in this bunch. Your aristocratic ladies are going to run the other way at the first touch."

I sank on a high pile of fleeces, my head starting to pound. The difference between what we could make from blankets and the income from fine artisan wool fit for elegant clothing was too enormous to contemplate. I needed to find out how much my father had paid for this shipment. Perhaps he had come by it more cheaply than I assumed.

I found him in his room with the door closed. In spite of the half-empty cup of wine resting on the table, he managed to locate the parchments related to the purchase with alacrity. We bent over the scroll, scanning the details. The fleeces had come from a new source, the name of the merchant unfamiliar to me. My father understood the numbers sooner than I and pushed the scroll away with trembling fingers. I jumped as he smashed his hand on the wooden table.

"I should have examined the fleeces before I made payment."

The delivery would have arrived mere weeks after Joseph's death, while we remained deep in mourning. I thought of my father then, a ghost of himself, unable to focus, barely able to think. "It's not your fault," I said as gently as I could. "We'll work something out."

He drank the wine in his cup to the dregs. "You don't understand. Sums don't come easily to you. The loss here. It is incalculable."

"Can we return the fleeces?"

He gave a bleak laugh. "No chance. These people are new to me. They were cheaper than the merchants I regularly work with, so I decided to give them a try. When I placed the order, I had nothing to lose. I figured once the fleeces were delivered, if their quality did not match the price, I would return them and refuse to pay. But I was in such a fog last summer that I simply paid them without examining the quality of the stock."

The silence stretched. No obvious solutions presented themselves to my mind. "So . . . blankets, then?"

He leaned heavily against the back of his chair. "Or we can spin and dye the wool and sell it to carpet merchants as yarn."

"Which brings more coin?"

He threw his hands up in the air. "Who can tell? Blankets,

if you could sell them. But people can make their own blankets at home. What can we create that would tempt them to purchase from us at a decent price? At least with the yarn, we make something."

I stayed awake late into the night, thinking about what my father had said. If we wanted our customers to buy blankets from us, we had to offer them a unique product, one they could not create at home. I crawled out of bed as quietly as I could so as not to disturb Joanna.

She stirred. "Elianna?"

"Go back to sleep, beloved."

She sat up. Like me, she was a light sleeper and, once awake, had a difficult time falling asleep again. "What's wrong?"

"The wool is only good for blankets." I found my design materials, lit another lamp, and sat cross-legged on the carpet, trying to think of something that would tempt the rich and elegant in Judea.

It was like staring into a lightless cave. There wasn't even the ghost of an idea.

"Why don't you embroider them as you did the towels?"

"Blankets are too thick for that. It won't work."

The emptiness of my mind felt like a tomb. I could not think of a single clever idea. Not one.

Lord, I began, then stopped. I had not been able to pray since Joseph's death. I waded through the prayers of my parents with respectful silence and visited the Temple, going in as far as the second court, where women were allowed. I participated in the Jewish feasts regularly. I stood when I was supposed to stand, spoke when I was supposed to speak, fell on my knees when I was supposed to fall on my knees. I ate the right foods and avoided the wrong ones. I tithed the herbs and vegetables I grew in the garden.

But I did not pray.

The Pharisees taught that righteousness depended upon our perfect pursuit of the Law. If we performed our duty, God would bless us. If we failed, he would remove his hand of care and protection from us. Our faith revolved around a simple legal transaction. We could not be right with God if we did not fulfill our end of that transaction.

And I had lost all right to God's favor when I destroyed my brother and shattered my father's and mother's hearts by doing so.

Every time I tried to pray, the distant echo of Zakkai the Pharisee's words would tumble back into my mind. How could the Lord forgive my sin? Why would he care what I wanted? How could he look past my shame to bless me with an answer to my prayers? The stain of my guilt would not wash off.

I fidgeted with the parchment and beat the end of the stylus against my forehead. Spreading my fingers on the floor, I stabbed the carpet peeking through between each finger with the sharp end of the stylus as fast as I could without piercing my flesh. I held my breath and managed to count to sixty-one before I had to release it. I must have wasted a good hour on useless activity to keep myself awake. Nothing.

Lord, I began again. *I need your help. Not for me. But for my family. Please, Lord. Don't turn your face from me. My family is innocent of my wrongs. For their sake, show me a way.*

I looked up. And there was Ethan's tapestry twinkling faintly in the weak light of my lamp. I frowned and fetched it down from the wall. With delicate care, I examined it first one way, then another.

"You want to make blankets with that pattern?" Joanna asked, her voice sleepy.

"Not possible. It's too complex. You couldn't create something this intricate with midgrade wool. Besides, it would have taken the weaver months to complete a work of this quality. Even if we had the artisans, we couldn't sell them. They would be too expensive."

"What then?"

"I was thinking we could use a simple pattern—just a border, say, at the top. And dye the wool in beautiful colors. It would be much cheaper than an embroidered bedcover. Yet still attractive and warm." I drew a few designs until I was satisfied. Crawling into my bed a few hours later, I fell asleep before I had a chance to exhale.

Showing my designs to Ethan and Viriato the next day, I stood at tense attention, waiting for their opinion. Viriato shrugged. "Not my area of expertise. I know nothing about stars and flowers."

But Ethan nodded. "I can sell these. They are attractive and uncommon. The warmth of a blanket with the loveliness of a woven bedcover. How much will each one cost to produce, wages included?"

I told him my calculation. He gave me a wry glance. "Have you checked that with your father?"

"I was waiting for your opinion."

Ethan nodded. "Ask. This is worth pursuing."

To my surprise, Father showed more interest in this project than he had in anything since Joseph died. I think the recognition of his mistake came as a hard knock—the realization that he could lose everything if he continued his careless approach.

Viriato gave me a few helpful suggestions about processing the wool so that it would produce as fine a yarn as possible given its grade. To my relief, the resulting yarn was soft to the touch, yielding a cozy, warm fabric.

I chose three initial designs for the weavers. In the first, we dyed the yarn a delicate sky blue, using indigo and plant ash. Then we wove a pattern of white waves into the top of the blankets. Wool absorbs color better than linen, and the blue of the blankets, highlighted as it was with white waves, though simple, was surprisingly appealing.

For our second design we used madder on the blankets. Madder is hard to work with and requires several immersions in the dye vats in order to get exactly the right hue. My father had a talent for working with different shades of red and managed to coax a glorious deep red out of the madder, no easy accomplishment. Since Romans were especially fond of the deeper shades of red, I knew this design would do well with our Gentile clientele. For the border of the red blankets, I had designed a flame pattern, blue at the center, cleverly flowing into orange and fading into yellow at the tips.

My favorite design was a midnight-blue blanket with a border of five-pointed stars woven in bleached white wool. We splurged and embroidered tiny stars, made of real gold thread, at the centers—a star within each star. In lamplight, the stars stood out and twinkled as though we had captured a fistful of celestial matter and sprinkled it on fabric.

As we turned our attention to selling the new merchandise, we discovered unexpected depths of talent in Viriato. In addition to being an impressive source of useful information about processing wool, he showed prodigious aptitude for sales. I had expected that his height and girth and scarred visage might turn customers away. But Viriato could display an overwhelming charm when he chose.

I once caught him talking about chariot racing with a Roman official. You would have thought he had spent a lifetime racing chariots in the Panhellenic Games. For all I knew, perhaps he had. Viriato did not speak of his life at home very often.

The depth of his knowledge about horses and racing impressed not only me, but also the Roman. As he conversed, Viriato absentmindedly caressed the man's horse, spoke a few words of praise about its gloss and condition, diagnosed a minor problem with its shoe, and won the horse and master over in the course of a few moments. By the time they were finished, the Roman official had placed a large order for blankets for his wife and daughters—and for his horses.

He had also placed a sizable bet over an upcoming chariot race. Viriato won.

With women, he became gentle and funny. After a particularly heavy rain, a portion of the road outside our house turned into a huge muddy puddle. I saw Viriato take off his crisp woolen cloak and lay it on the mud for an elegant lady to step on so that she would not get any dirt on her dainty shoes. She purchased more fabric than she could use in two years.

My father and Viriato sold our whole stock of ready blankets within one week, and we spent the next month spinning and weaving and dyeing the last bit of fleece we had left over. The demand for the blankets proved so enthusiastic that I barely managed to keep one sample of each design for our own home.

Because of the exorbitant cost of the fleeces, the profit margin for each blanket was small, but we had sold so many that we managed to pay all our expenses, taxes included, and still have enough left to order supplies for the following season. My father returned to his original supplier of wool, but he added ten talents of medium-grade fleece to our usual order of fine wool. This time, he paid a fair price for them, which would more than double our profits for next season's sale of blankets.

"Work on some new designs," he told me as he handed over a copy of the order. It was the closest he had come to showing me his approval since last summer. My heart warmed with hope. I thought perhaps he had begun to forgive me.

How great an anguish is hope! For when it disappoints, it ruptures old wounds and gouges out new ones, so that you are left worse off than when you began.

SEVEN

ONE LATE MORNING Keziah came running into the work-shop. "Master Viriato asks you to please come, mistress," she huffed out, trying to catch her breath. How Viriato had managed to earn the title *master* within weeks of entrenching himself in our home, I have no idea. I found myself wanting to call him by that appellation myself more than once. It suited him far better than former slave to a cinnabar mine.

I arched an eyebrow. "What does Viriato want?"

"He has brought a beautiful Roman lady to meet you. I think she is someone important."

"I see. Thank you." I rushed back to the house, wonder-ing why Viriato had asked for me rather than my father, who dealt with customers. The servant girl had not exaggerated the lady's allure. She was no older than I, but much taller, with a figure to make a sculptor's heart sing. Her dark-golden hair looped around her shapely head in artful braids and tucks, winking with jeweled combs. Clad in an exquisite blue *stola* and a darker *palla*, she seemed to me the epitome of Roman elegance. Viriato stood to one side in silent respect as the woman examined a wall hanging, one of my father's treasures imported all the way from India.

"My lady, you are most welcome," I said to the back of her head. "I am Elianna, daughter of Benjamin. Do you wish me to fetch my father for you?"

The lady turned, her face wreathed in a wide smile. "Viriato tells me you are the one I should see."

Viriato bowed. "Lady Claudia, allow me to present to you Mistress Elianna. Lady Claudia is wife to Titus Flavius Lepidus of Rome, mistress."

I had never heard of Titus Flavius Lepidus. But it seemed clear, even to my untutored eyes, that Claudia was a lady of some consequence. I wondered what the likes of her was doing in Jerusalem, moldering in our unfavorable weather and troubled politics. I bowed my head, lost for words.

Claudia seemed to sense my confusion. "Did you design those charming blankets? And the towels with the delicate embroidery?"

"Yes, my lady." I found myself flustered by her compliments. Since I rarely dealt with customers, I did not have opportunity to see their response to my designs firsthand.

"I have purchased a dozen of each and sent a large bundle

home for my mother and sisters. You have a unique talent for making ordinary things beautiful. Tell me, Elianna, daughter of Benjamin, do you have other designs that might interest me?"

"I have a number of freshly dyed fabrics that might suit your needs, my lady. If you like, I can design embroidery for each piece."

The large hazel eyes sparkled. "That sounds lovely."

I spent the whole hour before noon showing fabrics and sketching designs for our new patron. For the first time, I felt that a client had come for the sole purpose of seeing my creations. Not my father's. Mine. This sophisticated woman who had no doubt traveled through some of the most splendid parts of the empire was interested in my ideas. I could hardly keep myself from grinning like a fool.

Once we started speaking of flowers and leaves and designs, Viriato slipped out. I noticed him wiping his brow with a handkerchief.

The lady Claudia caught my scrutiny and smiled. "He knows his wool, and has great charm, but for all his girth and strength, I think talk of fashion reduces him to a trembling lamb."

We looked at each other and burst out laughing. I sensed an odd affinity for her, this highborn Roman woman whose world and mine could never touch. I found myself wishing she could be my friend. A strange and untenable thought for a Jewish girl. I had no liking for Romans in general. They had conquered our land and were hard on us. Daily, they squeezed us with their unjustified taxes and the force of their cruel army. But that day I began to learn that you could dislike a whole nation and still grow fond of the individuals in it.

⁂

Time sprinted ahead. A year passed. For the first time I noticed gray sprinkled at my father's temples and wrinkles at the corners of my mother's eyes. Joanna celebrated her fifteenth birthday and I turned eighteen. And yet oddly, nothing changed. It was as if we were trapped in ice, slowly suffocating. I continued to work in the workshop. My father sank deeper into his drink, and Mother grew more retiring, suffering from headaches and tears that came with unreasoning regularity.

My family disintegrated before my eyes with a quiet, inexorable force. Helplessly I watched, unable to alter anything. I worried most for Joanna. I had my work, my father his wine, and my mother her household management. But at an age when she should have received the most attention, Joanna started to fade into a terrible obscurity. She disappeared into the background of our lives, forgotten. She grew trapped in our sorrow, like a delicate sparrow with a broken wing caught in a dark barn.

Joanna was not like me. She had no interest in fabrics or business. I could not involve her in my world. She avoided the workshop as one might avoid a venomous snake.

My sister's passions centered around the household. She loved attending the chores, seeing to our meals, guiding the servants. But these were my mother's responsibilities, and while she took pains to share them with her daughters, she could no more relinquish her position as mistress than she could stop the beat of her heart. This left Joanna with little to engage her mind and senses. She flitted about lost, lonely, and unmoored.

No one spoke of marriage arrangements for her, though I knew Joanna would make the best of wives. By now my parents should have spoken to her of the possibility. They should have sought the connections that might lead to such an eventuality. The hope alone would have brightened her heart. No one spoke of the future in our home, however. Too much grief bound our family in its poisoned tentacles. We were entrenched in the dark past; the future held no appeal for us. Neither of my parents showed interest in anything as joyful as a possible marriage for their younger daughter. My sister sank like a stone under the weight of our despair.

It had been some time since I had visited the market near the fortress of Antonia; I had little time for pleasurable pastimes anymore. I spent so many hours dealing with the needs of the workshop that my normal practice of visiting the market stalls—bakers, jewelers, cobblers, herb sellers, metalworkers, silversmiths, potters, and all manner of wonders—had gone by the wayside. In the old days, the markets would have provided me an enjoyable distraction even if I bought nothing.

Now, even though I needed to purchase a few necessities from the stalls, I would have preferred to send a servant. We had a large order of wool that needed my attention. But I had a good reason for wanting to go myself. It gave me an excuse to drag Joanna out, knowing how much she would enjoy meandering through the market. Joel and Keziah accompanied us, and we traveled through Jerusalem's narrow streets on foot rather than bothering with the cart. The fortress of Antonia was not far from our home.

A large wall extended from the fortress, arching over the northern part of Jerusalem, enclosing a number of markets. By the time we reached the stalls, I had managed to make Joanna smile three times. I intended to make her laugh before we returned home. I felt my heart lift at the sight of the sparkle in my sister's eyes, and I realized that I had allowed work to swallow up too much of my time. I vowed to make more room for Joanna; nothing, not even my father's business, could equal her happiness. She could not enter my world, but I could enter into hers, no matter the price.

The silversmith's wares drew Joanna's attention and we approached his table, examining delicately carved rings and hair ornaments. Joanna had just picked up an ebony and silver armband to show me when a man shouted, his sharp voice causing me to jump out of my skin. Joanna gave me a dismayed look, and we both turned to find the source of the unusual clamor.

"We don't have any!" The unpleasant screech belonged to the merchant in the next stall.

"Isn't that sweet incense on display behind you? You have a number of amphorae that seem to contain what I am

TESSA AFSHAR

looking for." I knew that soft, patrician voice. It belonged to Lady Claudia. I had seen her a number of times in the past year. She had become a faithful and enthusiastic patron.

"I've already sold those," the storekeeper said and turned aside to spit on the ground. "I told you; we don't have anything you want."

I gaped, aghast at the rudeness of the man. Lady Claudia stood, regal and unflinching. Her maid, red in the face next to her, pulled on her mistress's arm in an effort to move her away from the stall.

I narrowed my eyes and marched over, my sister, Joel, and Keziah at my heels. We must have made quite a cavalcade.

"What is going on here, Reuben?" I knew the young man minding the perfumer's stand. His father owned the business, and the son sometimes helped, though his sour disposition and foul temper made him a poor merchant. Ever since he'd taken up with a group of zealots intent on overthrowing our conquerors by violent means, he had grown more petulant than ever. He was a disaster waiting to happen. I had no fondness for our subjugators myself and would see them gone if I could. Yet I knew that the violence of the zealots against a fierce power like Rome would only win us blood and misery in the end.

Besides, I liked Claudia, never mind her people.

"This Roman wants to buy something I don't sell," Reuben said with a rude gesture.

"This *lady* wishes to honor you by purchasing something from your shop. Now show me what you have, Reuben, and make no delay about it."

I turned to face Claudia and gave her a smile. "My lady. Please forgive our rough manners."

"I've heard of the fire of resentment that burns in some of your people. Palestine has become legendary for the trouble it causes our army. I thought supporting the locals might render them less acrimonious."

"Most of the merchants are happy for your custom, my lady. Some—" I gave the perfume seller a warning glance—"are unsociable by nature."

Reuben slapped a marble amphora in front of us.

"Several more, if you please, Reuben. How about the one your father sold Lady Jerusha last month? I might wish to purchase a small jar myself; my mother admired it, as I recall." I turned to Claudia. "If you like a touch of cinnamon, you will love the scent of this particular mix."

Reuben slammed a few more miniature urns and amphorae in front of us before slithering away and leaving Claudia, Joanna, and me to survey his goods at our leisure.

"Who is this ravishing creature?" Claudia asked, gesturing toward Joanna.

"This is my younger sister, Joanna." Joanna bowed her head, her cheeks turning vermilion.

"Beauty runs in your family, I see. Venus herself must be jealous of two such stunning kinswomen."

I had heard of Venus, a Roman idol that heathens worshipped with a great deal of enthusiasm. She had her own temples around the world, and many avid followers engaged in unspeakable acts in her name. What these unspeakable acts might entail, I had no idea. I only knew they were exceedingly vile.

Once, while travelling with my father to Caesarea, I had seen a marble statue of her as it was being transported to some temple far from Judea. Naked except for a drape of fabric over her hip that tied low in the front, the marble goddess stood unashamed of her bare body. In spite of this callous exhibition, even I had to admit she was lovely. My father, catching me staring at her, had covered my eyes with the palm of his hand, though not before I noticed him staring at her himself.

I had no desire to make her or anyone else in the Roman pantheon take the least notice of me. But I did not know how to say so to Claudia without causing offense.

Thankfully, Reuben's father turned up, rendering a response unnecessary. After that, our time passed in a far more pleasant fashion, especially after the merchant dispatched his malcontented son to parts unknown. Claudia chose two expensive bottles of incense, enough to put a smile on the perfumer's face, and I bought the one I knew Jerusha admired.

"You have been very kind, Elianna. Thank you for coming to my rescue. Won't you and your family join Titus and me for dinner one night?"

I felt heat rise in my face. "That wouldn't be possible, my lady."

She tapped elegant, gold-adorned fingers against her forehead. "I forgot about your food laws. Forgive me. I am still new to your land." A shadow crossed her eyes. I had the sense that she had not landed in Jerusalem under happy circumstances. "And please, call me Claudia," she said after a moment of hesitation.

How lonely she must feel, I thought, away from her home and family, in a world and culture so foreign to her. We Jews felt superior to Romans because we considered them heathens. Far from God, with no hope of salvation. The Romans felt superior to Jews because in their estimation we were weak, lacking their military might and glory in battle. But both felt sorrow. Both felt the bitterness of isolation and rejection. Rich, powerful Roman or conquered, weak Judean. How different were we, really, despite our prejudices and objections to one another?

"How long have you been in Iudaea, Lady Claudia?" I was careful to use the Roman word for the province of Judea, which also encompassed Samaria and Idumea.

"Two years."

"It seems a strange place for a lady of your rank to settle in. I would have thought someone like you would grace the palaces of Rome."

Claudia looked away. "I have lived there all my life. This is a new venture. We came here shortly after Titus and I were married."

How hard it must have been for her to adjust to so much change after a sheltered life. "Your husband must be a great adventurer," I said with a smile.

Claudia's eyes warmed at the mention of her husband. "My Titus *is* adventurous, but we did not land in Jerusalem by choice. This was the fruit of his honesty, I fear. In Rome, if you don't learn to mind your tongue, you will find yourself in all sorts of strange places. If my father did not hold such a high rank, Titus would have ended up in an elaborately crafted sarcophagus, instead of the heat of Palestine."

We had been wandering slowly from stall to stall, examining trinkets as we spoke. I stopped dead when she made her last comment. "Jerusalem is a far lovelier place than the inside of a sarcophagus, my lady. Even if some of the shopkeepers are unfriendly."

Claudia laughed. "Don't let Sejanus, the new Praetorian prefect, hear you say that. He is under the impression that he has consigned us to a fate worse than death, which keeps him satisfied."

"Ah," I said. Jerusalem was, after all, no longer even the official capital of Judea. The Romans had bestowed that honor upon Caesarea. Of course, for the Jewish people, Jerusalem remained the heart of Israel and the seat of God and his holy Temple. To us, this was the center of the world, whereas to the rest of the empire, our city was a fading backwater. "So he is the one responsible for your present predicament?"

"The very man. Titus can charm most people, patrician and plebeian alike, but the prefect is another matter. My husband's brother worked for Sejanus. He was killed under very suspicious circumstances and Titus challenged the prefect openly. A grave mistake, since the emperor holds the man in high esteem. Of course, Sejanus had his revenge on us. Here we are, and here we stay until he says otherwise."

I made a sound of sympathy. Jerusalem was my beloved home. I could not bring myself to think of it as a punishment.

"I am convinced that Tiberius will one day regret trusting that man," Claudia said. "Eventually, he is bound to see what a crooked lout he has placed in charge of the world."

This talk approached treason. I could not afford to engage in open criticism of the emperor or his trusted henchmen. I tried to find a safer topic. "What does your husband do?"

"Poor Titus is in charge of requisitioning for the garrison at Antonia. Only two years ago, he served as quaestor, with hopes of standing as praetor one day soon. Instead, he has become a glorified procurer. Can you imagine?"

I shrugged. "Still far better than the inside of a sarcophagus. Besides, think of the good your husband can do for all those Romans. Most men in his position pocket some of the money allotted for the garrison and buy poorer fare for the men. As long as your husband is at his post, at least the soldiers shall eat and drink something decent."

Lady Claudia gave me a sparkling glance. "Fat, happy soldiers won't trouble your people nearly as much as hungry ones who are always in a foul mood."

"You see. Perhaps the Lord sent you and your husband to us for both our peoples' benefit."

We dissolved into laughter. I noticed to my joy that Joanna joined us. It had been a very long time since either of us had laughed aloud.

Claudia reached for my hand. "You have done me a world of good, Elianna. I wish I could repay you for your graciousness."

"No repayment is necessary," I said.

"It has been lovely to spend this hour with you, my lady," Joanna added shyly.

Claudia brightened. "I have it. Herod Antipas is coming from Galilee for a short visit. My husband knew him from his childhood days when Antipas resided in Rome. Titus was a young boy at the time, but Antipas knew the family and spent many afternoons with them at their villa.

"There is going to be a banquet in his honor when he arrives. I shall see to it that you and your parents are invited. Surely your father cannot refuse. Think of the potential benefit to his business. Besides, Antipas is as Jewish as you. No doubt they will observe all the necessary dietary laws for the occasion."

"Well," I said, "the tetrarch is of Jewish heritage, that much is true." The Herodians were famous for many things. But sticking to the religious laws was not one of them. Still, Claudia had a point. My father could not very well turn down an invitation from a Jewish ruler, the tetrarch of Galilee and Perea no less. "It would be an honor to our family to receive such an invitation, Lady Claudia," I said.

Next to me, Joanna flashed a smile so big and bright, it put the Judean sun to shame.

EIGHT

One who heard us was a woman named Lydia, from the city of Thyatira,
a seller of purple goods, who was a worshiper of God.

ACTS 16:14

ETHAN CAME TO VISIT US that evening with an invitation for my family. "My father asks that you join us for supper tomorrow evening, Master Benjamin. It has been too long since our families broke bread together."

My father nodded. "True enough, Ethan."

"After supper, we shall have other guests. A dye seller from Thyatira and his young daughter, Lydia, are joining us. They have a more affordable purple dye they wish to show us."

My father made a slashing gesture with his arm. "I know all about the cheap purple dye from Thyatira. Instead of sea snails, they use the madder root. I don't like the results. It produces a reddish purple that fades too quickly. People want the deep imperial purple that only sea snails can give you.

It grows even brighter and more beautiful with wear. Don't waste your time with this Thyatiran rubbish."

Ethan smiled, not taking offense at my father's lecture even though he knew a lot more about the subtleties of different dyes. "You are right, of course. In general, the economical purples are inferior to the more expensive variety. But this Eumenes claims to have improved on the process. His dye is colorfast. He sent me a sample. A rich, bright purple as good as anything you may find hiding inside a sea snail. And it costs about half of what you pay for royal purple. Of course, that is still not cheap. But think of the increase in your sales if the quality proves as good as Eumenes claims."

"Since I will already be there, I will listen to the man. Mind you, I have no great expectations. Clever men have tried for over a hundred years to improve on that formula to no avail. You and Ezer are wasting your time."

"I am sorry, Ethan," I said as my father walked away. "He isn't interested in anything these days."

Ethan clasped his hands behind his back and stared at his sandals. "You seem very tired. Are you working too hard?"

I shrugged. "Of course not."

"Then why are there dark shadows under your eyes? Why have you lost weight? Why do you smile so rarely?"

I felt pelted by little sharp stones as each accusation found its mark. He made me feel insufficient, somehow. As if I had failed him by being miserable and faded. "I . . . had a bad night. That's all."

"You dreamt of Joseph." It wasn't a question. I said

nothing. If he felt like making pronouncements, he didn't need my response.

"You are very quiet."

"'A silent wife is a gift of the Lord,'" I quoted from Sirach.

Ethan let out a long breath. "If I wanted a silent wife, I would not have looked to the daughter of Benjamin of Jerusalem." And then without a word of farewell, he swiveled around and traipsed off. My mouth almost came unhinged from my jaw, I was so surprised. What ailed him now?

⚜

Master Eumenes turned out to be a man of learning as well as a shrewd craftsman. The samples of cloth he had brought with him were impeccably dyed, as vibrant as the petals in a fresh posy of viola. Even my father appeared impressed.

"And you used no sea snails to make this?" my father asked, not bothering to hide his skepticism.

"Oh no, master," Lydia piped up. She was a child of ten or eleven, with hair like ripe wheat and eyes the color of Persian turquoise.

Children would not normally have been allowed at such a meeting—half social gathering, half business venture. We had ignored this strange oversight by Master Eumenes since, strictly speaking, no women should have been present at the discussion either, and there I was. Although my mother, along with Jerusha and Joanna, had slipped out after the family dinner to retire in a different chamber, I had remained with the men at Ethan's request. He must have mastered his earlier displeasure with me; if he still harbored any resentment, he hid it well.

At the sound of her voice, we all turned and stared at Lydia. It was one thing to have her present in the room, but quite another for her to take part in the discussion with such enthusiasm. Seeing all eyes trained on her, she continued, undeterred by our astonishment.

"My father does not use a drop of mollusk secretion." It was hard not to be impressed by her vocabulary as well as her boldness. She knew bigger words than I did.

"I see," Master Ezer said kindly.

Viriato scratched his beard. "I am sure I will agree as soon as I've figured out what you said."

Lydia smiled sweetly at Viriato. "It would be too expensive to use," she said without a hint of self-consciousness. I wondered if all the children in Thyatira were this confident. Somehow I doubted it. "My father is brilliant, though he is too modest to say so. No one has managed to produce such a color without sea snails. He has worked for years on this formula."

Eumenes smiled. "You must forgive my daughter. She has too high an opinion of me. I cannot find it in myself to correct her error."

"If this color is any indication, you deserve her high esteem." Ethan turned a piece of fabric over, his fingers caressing the edge. "May we keep these samples for a week? I would like to examine them under the brightness of the sun."

"Go ahead and wash it too," Lydia said. "Once, I washed a piece of dyed linen one hundred times. My father said

I tested my sums as well as his dye. The color faded only a tiny bit. You would hardly have noticed if you didn't compare it to the original."

"Are you always such a good saleswoman?" I asked.

"Oh no, mistress. Sometimes people don't seem to appreciate it when I speak. A Roman lord once offered to buy me from my father. Not because he liked me so much, he said, but because he felt sorry for my father."

I swallowed a smile. "I take it your father did not accept the man's offer?"

"He said he would think about it. Sometimes he threatens to write the Roman a letter of acceptance."

"You don't seem too worried," Viriato said.

"Of course not. My father would be lost without me."

At that, even the men could not keep silent. Everyone laughed. Lydia gave us a haughty glance. Clearly, she had not been jesting.

The dye, though expensive, cost less than half the price of the famed royal purple derived from sea snails. One jar of purple dye had the same value as pure silver. Master Eumenes' dye, by comparison, offered great value.

Because Ezer had invited us to this meeting, my father and I could have purchased the dye directly from Eumenes, saving ourselves the middleman's portion. Ethan's generosity never ceased to touch me. My father, however, was not easy to convince. No one knew Eumenes in Jerusalem, and though his letters of reference seemed impeccable, and he belonged to the famed trade union of Thyatira, an immediate purchase would have been risky.

It was a risk I would have taken. To my surprise, Master Ezer declined an outright purchase as well. Instead, he settled for a number of samples and a promise to contact Eumenes soon.

Before leaving, Lydia placed a short length of purple fabric into my hands. "I dyed it myself. It's not large. Enough for a summer mantle. You are so pretty, Elianna. I couldn't resist giving it to you."

"And you are precious," I said. I embraced her warmly, wishing I could sneak her home with me. "Thank you for my gift. I regret I have nothing to give you in return."

"It isn't necessary. Besides, I pinned our address to one corner. Once you wear that mantle, you will be convinced that nothing matches our new dye and will want to buy bushels of it."

"Maybe I will offer to buy you from your father as well. You can come and work for me. We shall double our sales with you on our side."

Lydia grabbed her father's hand and kissed it with tenderness. "I could never leave my father."

He ruffled her hair with absentminded affection. "Sweet girl. In truth, I can't bear to part with her myself. Her mother died two years ago. It's only us now. So I drag her around the world whenever I travel. I suppose it's selfish of me. I ought to leave her safely in Thyatira, minding our home. Instead, I give in to her pleas and let her join me. Where would be the joy in life without my daughter?"

I felt like someone had pierced my heart with a knife. The obvious affection between father and daughter was a painful contrast to my own circumstance. My father would happily leave me behind. I had little joy to offer him. My eyes filled with tears.

A warm hand enveloped mine. Startled, I looked up into Ethan's eyes. He said nothing. His hand, wrapped over mine, felt solid and reassuring, his gaze steady like a bracing touch. He hid our intertwined hands in the folds of my tunic. I felt the shaft of pain leave my heart, bit by bit, as if melting in Ethan's comforting grip.

"I miss him," I said, my voice soft and sad. Ethan alone heard. He alone understood.

"I know."

The barley ripened early that year, and the month of Nisan sprang upon us before we were ready. Herod Antipas came to Jerusalem in time for the barley harvest and Passover. He liked to give the impression that he was an observant Jew and had come to Jerusalem in time to make his sacrifice at the Temple. Not that anyone believed his fervent posturing. He praised God with one side of his mouth and declared his love for the Roman Caesar with the other. Still, popular or not, he was ruler over a quarter of Israel and a man of great wealth and influence.

Of course my family accepted Claudia's invitation to the banquet that was given in his honor the week before Passover. The feast was held at the Roman prefect's palace. Valerius Gratus was the governor of Judea at the time, and he had gone to some trouble on Herod's behalf. The banquet room blazed with hundreds of lamps and numberless servants and slaves mingled amongst guests, tending to their needs.

My father grumbled under his breath as we arrived. Attending such a feast, though a great honor, did not come free. According to the Pharisees' interpretation of the Law, we would have to ritually purify ourselves merely for entering the Roman governor's house or we would not be able to partake of the feast of Passover at the end of the week.

Claudia herself welcomed us before introducing us to her husband, Titus. I could see why she seemed so smitten with him. Good-looking, with fair hair and a clean-shaven square jaw, Titus demonstrated none of the usual Roman superiority common to men of his class. Instead, he welcomed us as though we were the most important people in the Roman Empire.

"Your daughter came to my wife's rescue in the market, as you no doubt have heard," he said to my father. "I owe her great thanks."

I had not bothered to tell my father the story. He had shown so little interest in my life these past two years that I had fallen out of the habit of sharing anything with him that did not relate to business. He gave me a sidelong glance, caught off guard by Titus's words. "Thank you for your invitation, my lord."

"I hope you shall meet many new customers this evening. Claudia has been singing the praises of your wares to every Roman she can find. She would speak to the Jews as well, if they would actually listen."

My father cleared his throat. "You are both most kind."

Claudia drew Joanna, my mother, and me to a quieter corner and settled us on a soft couch, knowing our discomfort amongst this mixed company of strangers. We were not poor people and ate well enough. But that night I observed such luxury as I had never seen before.

The smell of lamb, domestic fowl, and fried game mingled with expensive spices and rich sauces. Pastries sweetened with honey, fruit, almond and walnut paste sat on silver and gold trays in artistically arranged pyramids. At one point they brought in a whole peacock, fully cooked and then decorated with its own feathers and eggs. Such an abundance of food was on display that it took four whole hours to serve everything. We could have fed half the city of Jerusalem with what they put before us at Herod's banquet.

I almost lost my appetite when I saw a platter full of oysters pass right under my nose. We Jews were not allowed to eat shellfish and sea creatures without scales, and thank God for his favor, I thought! Why would anyone in possession of half a brain wish to put such things into his mouth?

Claudia pointed out a beautifully decorated dish to me. "Stuffed dormice with minced pork. A great Roman delicacy." She burst into peals of laughter at the looks on Joanna's and my faces. "I suppose I ought not point out the snails to you, then."

I had once seen a bust of Herod Antipas as a young man. He had seemed well-favored to me then, with a comely nose, chiseled mouth, and a strong jawline. But even the cold marble had revealed a subtle hint of cruelty and debasement in that face.

The man in the governor's palace was a far cry from the youthful face caught in stone. He had gone to fat; the thin lines of his mouth hinted at a spoilt, selfish nature. He spent most of the evening eating a lot and drinking more, saying barely a word to his companions. I tried to see what he put in his mouth and whether he avoided unclean foods. But he was too far, and in any case, I lost interest when I saw saliva dangling from his decorated beard.

In spite of the richness of the repast before us, I had a simple meal that night, too fearful to indulge in anything lest it prove a violation of God's commands. The vegetables seemed safest, and like the prophet Daniel, I stuck to them. I tried artichokes, asparagus, sweet parsnip, and a plain wheat roll. Joanna ate even less. At one point in the evening, I noticed her staring several times at a particular corner, reddening, and lowering her head, only to stare again. Curious, I turned to see what held her interest. I found nothing there but a tall young man with brown curly hair and the most besotted expression on his face. He was looking straight at my sister.

I turned to Claudia. "Who is that young man?"

Claudia squinted. "He came with Herod's household. Part of his staff, I believe. Now let me see. Oh yes. His name is Chuza; his father is Herod's steward."

"You don't know him well?"

"Never spoke to him in my life." She lowered her voice so only I could hear her. "He looks over here a great deal. The object of his interest seems to be your younger sister. He has good taste—this much we can say about him."

"She seems to be looking back," I whispered.

"Say no more. I shall discover all I can about him. Leave it to me."

I grinned. "Mind you don't breathe a word to her about what we are up to. I don't want to encourage her until I know what manner of man he is."

Claudia left on our clandestine mission to unearth what she could about Joanna's admirer. Chuza could not resist Joanna, it seemed. He kept inventing excuses to come near us until even my mother, who was busy speaking to an acquaintance, took notice. "What is that man up to? He stares at Joanna as if she were a piece of pastry. I will fetch your father if he keeps this up."

"Oh, please, no, Mother!" Joanna gasped. "I am sure he means no disrespect. Please don't embarrass him."

A few moments later, Claudia returned. "You will like what I have to say, I hope," she whispered.

"What is that?"

"He comes with glowing references. Good character, upstanding family, quite well-connected. And of course, he is a Jew."

"Too bad he lives in Galilee."

"Not for the next two weeks. He and his father remain in Jerusalem with Herod until after the feast of Passover. What we need is a plan. A means of bringing Chuza's father and yours together. Allow the families to meet and become friends. One fact is in our favor. Herod's wife, Phasaelis, is a genuine princess—the daughter of King Aretas, the Nabatean ruler."

I wiped my forehead with my hand. "I will regret asking this, no doubt, but what has the lineage of Antipas's wife to do with our domestic plans for Joanna?"

"As a princess, Phasaelis will have a love for beautiful fabrics. Doubt it not. She will wish to purchase piles of things from your workshop. And of course she will have to send Chuza's father as a go-between. In fact, give me a moment with Titus, and I can guarantee that she will."

"Another hour, and we shall arrange the future of the empire between us," I said, wagging my finger.

Claudia flashed a sparkling smile. "I am up to running the world."

"Well, I'm not. I can hardly run my own life."

Claudia slumped. "One's own life is always more difficult to manage than the whole world put together. The emperors and governors of this world have it easy. It's wives and daughters who have to struggle the hardest."

We burst out laughing. A young slave, clad in a minuscule tunic that showed off his hairless bare arms and legs, came over and offered us a tray of figs dipped in honey. I goggled in spite of my best intentions to appear as sophisticated as the other women in the banquet. I had never seen that much of any adult man's flesh on display. Joanna leaned over. "Don't you think he is very handsome?"

"Who? The slave?"

Joanna choked on her fig. "No, of course not. I mean the young man with the curly hair. The one over by that wall."

"Oh, you mean Chuza?"

"Chuza? You know his name? How did you find out?"

"I have my ways," I said with a smug shrug of my shoulder. Joanna shook my arm. "Don't tease, Elianna. Who is he?"

"He is the son of Herod's steward. He lives in Galilee and helps his father in Herod's household. According to Claudia, he has an impeccable reputation. Satisfied?"

Joanna's eyes sparkled like the lampstands in the Temple. "I knew he would be good. Did you say Galilee? Why does he have to live so far away? I shall never meet him." She groaned.

"The Lord has not forgotten about you, my lovely sister. And neither have Claudia and I. We have an inspired plan. But you must make me a promise, Joanna."

"Anything."

I did not wish to encourage Joanna too readily, before we found out more about Chuza and his family. Caution dampened my growing enthusiasm. I was happy to see Joanna come to life with hope. But I wanted to temper that hope in case it came to nothing.

"We don't as yet know enough about him. Chuza may not turn out to be what he appears. Remember the words of the wise king: 'Promise me, O women of Jerusalem, not to awaken love until the time is right.'"

"Who spoke of love?" Joanna mumbled. Her foot caught in the hem of her tunic as she turned; she stumbled and would have fallen if I hadn't steadied her.

NINE

Hear the word of the LORD, O children of Israel,
for the LORD has a controversy with the inhabitants of the land.
There is no faithfulness or steadfast love,
and no knowledge of God in the land;
there is swearing, lying, murder, stealing, and committing adultery;
they break all bounds, and bloodshed follows bloodshed.

HOSEA 4:1-2

TO MY UTTER ASTONISHMENT, Chuza and his father, Shual, accompanied by Claudia and her husband, showed up at our doorstep the very next morning. My father knew nothing about the whole affair, except for a passing remark of my mother's about a young man whose eyes chased after Joanna all night. He only knew that a company of important customers had descended upon him.

Claudia asked for both my father and me, and we arrived almost at the same time.

"Master Benjamin," Titus began, "allow me to introduce you to my friends. We have come this morning in search of a few special tokens. As steward to Herod's household, Master

Shual has many needs. My wife assures me that you are more than able to provide what we seek."

My father bowed. "You are welcome, my lords. My lady. I believe Lady Claudia has honored us with several purchases before."

Claudia spread the skirt of her green tunic. "As you see. Elianna embroidered these flowers with her own hand. Or was it your sister, Joanna? I forget."

"I designed them and Joanna embroidered most of them. I was working on the matching *paenula*."

"I remember now. It is too fine a day for a cape, sadly, or I would have worn it. Where is she, Master Benjamin?"

"Where is who, my lady?"

"Your younger daughter, Joanna. Let Herod's steward see the hands that create such fine work."

My father scratched his head. Claudia's request was unusual. But how could a merchant turn down a great lady's request? "If you wish."

Joanna arrived dressed in a simple ivory tunic, her hair covered demurely by a light veil. I saw her so often, it slipped my mind how ravishing she was. Claudia placed her finger under Joanna's chin and lifted her lowered face. "Simply charming," she said. "Do you not agree, Master Shual?"

"Beauty has been generous to your family, Master Benjamin," Shual said. "Two daughters as beautiful as jewels. Tell me, have you any sons?"

My heart stopped. I saw the blood drain from my father's face; he turned white as marble and just as still. I could not breathe. We lived in a small community. Everyone knew us.

Since Joseph's death, no one had had cause to ask such a question. The room grew heavy with awkward discomfort.

To my shock, it was my shy sister who came to our rescue. "My little brother died two years ago, Master Shual." Her voice was soft and wistful. "We miss him terribly."

"Of course you do. Forgive me. May the Lord bring you his comfort and bestow upon you the oil of gladness."

My father nodded, his eyes misty and out of focus. One of the servants came in with sweet wine just then, a mercy from the Lord, I thought, and the distress caused by the simple question started to dissipate.

Titus addressed my father and Shual, talking of the news from the West and the latest gossip from Rome and other nonsense I could not retain. Word by gentle word, he changed the atmosphere of the room until all of us started to grow calm. Titus Flavius had a gift with people. He took their measure and approached them with a subtle diplomacy that bordered on genius. I could not have been more grateful to him for his intervention that day if he had given me a royal palace.

I caught Chuza staring at my sister, his eyes glittering as if he had a fever. His whole face had turned the color of a ripe beet. Joanna seemed struck by the same malady. She flushed until her cheeks turned into radishes. Beets and radishes, I thought. They ought to make a nice salad together.

Whether Master Shual had been forewarned of the true purpose behind this visit or he was a particularly shrewd man, I cannot say. He looked from one to the other. A smile tugged at the corner of his mouth before he covered his chin with a be-ringed hand.

"Tell me, child, do you often work for your father?" he asked Joanna.

"No, master. My sister does most of the work. I only help with the embroideries if we grow very busy."

"We can provide any of our fabrics to you plain, so that your own servants can do the needlework, or if you prefer, we can design and do the work for you here." My father, utterly in the dark, held fast to the business at hand. Meanwhile, Chuza and Joanna stole glances and turned redder by the moment.

Shual drew my father apart and kept him busy for a good hour while the rest of us passed the time in conversation. In truth, Claudia and I spoke, while poor Titus Flavius tried to engage Chuza. He made no headway that I could see. The young man showed as little interest in Flavius's conversation as Joanna displayed in ours. They were in a world of their own, those two.

When the time for departure arrived, Master Shual said, "You have many fine fabrics here, I see, Benjamin. I must consult my lord before I make any purchases, however. Chuza and I can return the day after tomorrow. Would that suit?"

For the next two weeks, that suited everyone very well. Eventually it dawned on my father that Shual's many excuses for his return visits might have an ulterior motive. He made a few good sales in the process. But he also began to take the measure of Shual in a manner different from a mere business acquaintance.

To my joy, Joanna began to bloom. She laughed at Keziah's silliest jokes and hummed under her breath as she walked. A new lightness entered our home, one that had been lacking for two years. Cautiously, we were learning to hope again.

⁂

After Joseph's death my father's participation in the running of his business remained more limited than before, but he did not relinquish the administration of his accounts to anyone else. This gave me great relief. My education, though more thorough than many of my contemporaries', was still not the equal of a man's. I had a vague idea of what we were earning and what we had to pay out, but I knew few details. Father continued to take care of the workers' wages, as well as ordering and paying for supplies.

One of the most complicated aspects of managing a substantial trade, particularly one like my father's that imported goods from different regions, was the taxation. Romans took their share of everything. They taxed our land, our water, our roads, even our salt and meat. In Jerusalem, you had to pay a house tax in addition to your land tax.

Hardest of all, perhaps, was the fact that at every official checkpoint on the road your goods were levied heavily, so that by the time we received the merchandise, it sometimes cost us thirty or forty times the original price. And then we had to pay taxes again after we sold the final product. When you consider the dishonest publicans who added their own unreasonable sums to the imperial demands, it's a wonder we survived.

One morning, my father declared that the Roman tributes were due. He intended to go into the city, near the Roman governor's palace where the chief publican was stationed. At the mention of the governor's palace, I sat up straight. A small but exclusive market had recently been established near the palace, which I rarely had the opportunity to visit. It was too far from our home for convenience.

Impulsively, I said, "May I come?"

My father flushed. "There is nothing for you there, Anna. Merely a long line of merchants paying their taxes."

Once he would have welcomed my company for any excuse. The obvious brush-off hurt. Long months of being subjected to his rejection had done nothing to cool the sting of it. I do not know why, but the hurt turned into anger that day. Why could he not forgive me? He was my father. My *father*! Why could he not overcome the weight of my sin? Why could he not reconcile with me?

My jaw felt stiff as I answered. "I didn't intend to stay with you. I only wish to go as far as the market. You can collect me after you have completed your errand. It would be easier to travel with you in the cart than on foot."

Something in the coolness of my voice caught his attention and he looked at me for a moment. His eyes slid away. "Come, if you wish."

"I do. Just for the market." I raised my chin to make sure he received the message that I was not going for his company. I was finished begging for his affection.

My father disliked traveling through the busy thoroughfares of Jerusalem. He detested the stench of sweat and dung and unwashed bodies, the dirt of the road, the shepherds who clogged the streets with their cattle. He had an aversion

to having to wait for Roman soldiers as they led their arrogant cavalcades with little care for the inconvenience they
caused. So rather than travel through the center of Jerusalem,
which would have been the quickest path to our destination,
he decided to loop around the city and travel outside the
protection of Jerusalem's walls.

Viriato was helping Ethan and Master Ezer that day. So
my father brought with him one of the weavers, Dan, a large
man whose impressive girth ought to have warned away any
bandits. I brought Keziah because she never complained, not
even about riding in the back of a dusty, swaying open cart.
We sat together in the cart, sharing the cramped space with
the iron box containing my father's denarii. There were only
the four of us in our party, with my father on horseback and
Dan driving the cart.

Our house was located near the Sheep Pool, not far from
Fuller's Field. We left the shelter of Jerusalem's walls and
circled south, traveling past the Water Gate. We intended to
enter the city again on the west side of Jerusalem.

We were just about to emerge from the Hinnom Valley
when we found ourselves hedged in by a band of rough-
looking men, some on donkeys and several on foot. They
brandished daggers and short swords, and one clutched an
iron-tipped spear in thick fingers. In the twinkling of an eye,
we were surrounded from every angle. I counted six or seven
before I gave up, terror making rational thought impossible.

We were too close to Jerusalem for thieves. I could see
the walls of the city; a few steps and I would have been able
to touch them. We should have been safe. But desperation

drove men to unreasonable acts. This group of audacious bandits, once too afraid to come near the city, now dared come this close to its walls in broad daylight.

"You know what we want," said the one with the spear. "Give us your money and be quick about it." He had a country accent with a lilt that hinted at the distant hills of Judea.

One of the men on foot approached the cart and hopped in. His bloodshot eyes widened when he saw my face. To my shock, he bent down and shoved my veil back. "Look at this morsel!" he cried. "Have you ever seen anything so pretty?"

I snapped to my feet to put a bit of distance between us; he followed my movements, straightening then leaning, his face too close. I could smell the stench of rotten teeth and sour sweat. It turned my stomach. I slapped his hand away as it reached to touch my cheek. The man laughed and shoved his fingers into my veil instead, snatching it off my shoulders and tucking it inside his belt. With the fingers of his other hand, he grabbed a hank of my hair and yanked until it came loose from the combs that held it in place, spiral curls falling wildly about my face and shoulders.

"I want this one!" he cried as he pressed his torso into me. I could feel his dirty beard scratching my chin. I slithered backward until my back came against the wall of the cart.

"Stay away!" Fear clawed inside me, and I had to clench my jaw to keep from screaming. Keziah had no such compunction. She started to cry out with terror. I winced when the man's hand flashed out, giving her a heavy backhanded blow. Her screams turned into pathetic whimpers.

In the periphery of my vision, I could see Dan and my father struggling with the other men, trying to come to our aid. But it seemed a hopeless struggle to me. They were too outnumbered.

My legs shook, but I forced myself to sound stern. "Why don't you take the money and leave us alone?"

"I will. In a little while," he said and lunged toward me. His fingers clamped onto my arms as he pulled me toward him. Ignoring the bruising force of his hold, I fought him with every bit of strength I had. I kicked; I scratched; I bit like a feral animal. I even got in a few good punches until his nose began to spout blood all over both of us. But he would not let go. His hands seemed to be everywhere at once, grabbing parts of me that had known the touch of no one. I tried to fend him off, but I was growing tired. It began to sink into my horrified mind that he wasn't playing with me. He intended to violate me right there in front of my father and the others. My strength waned with each passing moment. No one interfered. No one held him back or tried to dissuade him. The cackle of coarse laughter and incomprehensible comments barely registered through the harsh sound of my own labored breaths as I continued to pelt my assailant with my weakening fists.

Then with a sudden twist, the man's weight lifted off me.

"Easy now, mistress. You might hurt the poor fellow." In the throes of panic, I could still pick out the thread of amusement running through that deep voice. I heard the accent—Roman—and then through the tangled net of my hair, which had fallen over my face, I saw the uniform.

Decurion? Centurion? I could not tell. I only knew that he had come to our aid just in time. His men were rounding up the other bandits and chasing those who had run off at their approach. The Roman horses proved fast and effective. The bandits stood no chance against their agility and hard-earned discipline.

Whatever had held me together under the threat of the bandit's molestation collapsed when I gained my freedom. My legs began to wobble and I sank to my knees. The sound of Keziah's soft keening penetrated the terrified haze of my mind. I bit my lips to keep them from trembling, shoving down the rising hysteria in my own chest so that I could comfort her.

"It's all right, Keziah. You're safe now." I tried to sound calm as I caressed her hair.

I watched the Roman officer who had rescued me from my attacker get the band of thieves under guard. He was clearly in charge of the other soldiers and comfortable in that role. Every once in a while he would bite out an order and someone would run to obey it. At his feet now lay my assailant, unconscious and bleeding from his head as well as his nose. I had seen the Roman bring him down with one well-placed blow to the side of the head when the man tried to fight his way free. I am ashamed to admit that I enjoyed witnessing that blow with fierce satisfaction. I only wished I had been strong enough to deliver it myself.

My father approached the Roman. "Thank you for saving us, my lord," he said. His face looked gray and clammy. "I am Benjamin, a seller of dyed cloth in Jerusalem. I hope you will come back to our house and allow me to express my thanks more appropriately."

The Roman nodded. "I am Decimus Calvus. You were lucky my men and I decided to circuit this way. Your Judean thieves grow bolder every day." He pointed at the thieves with his clean-shaven chin. "As soon as I have dealt with these miscreants, I will escort you back home to ensure your safe return."

"I am grateful," my father said. "We were on our way to pay the publican."

"Tomorrow, I will return to escort you and make certain you get there in safety. Today, you had best return home and recover from your adventure." His gaze strayed toward me.

Something made me lift my chin. No Roman would catch me looking weak and pathetic. Not even one who had saved me from a horror I could barely imagine. I felt perspiration dampen my forehead and tickle down my sides. The Roman continued to stare at me, brown eyes unflinching and bold. With a distracted movement I reached for my veil. Then I remembered that the bandit had taken it off me, and that I was sitting there before a dozen strange men, my hair a twisting mess hanging to my hip. I looked down and felt heat spread under my skin when I realized that my tunic had ripped at the neck in my struggle, exposing the slope of one breast, and one sleeve had torn at the shoulder, hanging against my arm.

With a gasp, I straightened the tunic, covering myself to the best of my ability. Shame overwhelmed me with a rush. It wasn't merely the state of my hair and clothes. These men had witnessed me being pawed at by that squalid bandit. They had observed my humiliation. Something in me cracked. With a sob, I threw myself from the cart, twisting my ankle as I jumped, and ran stumbling to my father. In the haze of my shame and fear and shock I forgot about Joseph. I forgot that my father had not held me in two years. I forgot that he could scarcely bear to remain in the same room with me. I knew only that I needed him to hold me, to make me feel safe and clean again.

For a moment he allowed me to cling to him. Then he set me aside, his movements stiff. "We'd best leave," he said and turned his back on me to grab his horse's bridle.

I felt cold and hot, at once sweaty and shivering like I had a fever. Something soft touched my hair, and I jumped. The Roman had retrieved my veil from the bandit's belt and brought it to drape over me. Up close I saw that he had short stubble on his cheeks; there were bags under his eyes, as if he had stayed up too late with wine for company. His uniform, I noted, marked him as a centurion.

"Thank you," I whispered and pulled the veil close around me, taking refuge under its cover before limping back to the cart.

TEN

Do not rejoice when your enemy falls,
and let not your heart be glad when he stumbles.

PROVERBS 24:17

ONCE THE CENTURION had discharged his soldiers to take their captives to the Roman garrison, we set off for our house. It took us half the length of an hour to return home. It felt like a whole day to me. I spent the time clamping shut my jaw and willing myself not to be sick.

Before the cart came to a full stop, I jumped off the back into our courtyard, intending to run above stairs so that I could hide in my chamber. The leap from the cart was too much for my bruised ankle. To my dismay, that shaft of unanticipated pain proved my undoing. I had borne the shock of the attack, my father's withdrawal, my horrifying public humiliation. But this one final insult against my flesh I could not bear. My head began to swim and I felt myself sway. I tried to reach out and anchor myself against the side of the cart, but it was too far.

A strong arm wrapped around my waist and pulled me up before I fell. They were Roman arms that held me, a Roman chest against which I leaned. Before I could protest, Decimus Calvus swung me high against him.

"I've been wanting to do that since the moment I saw you fight as fiercely as Hippolyta the queen of the Amazons," he said, his lips close to my ear. He had the audacity to smile at me. Something about that smile made me cringe. It was too calculating. Too intimate. I pushed at his chest with the flat of my palm.

"Put me down." I made my voice as cold as winter.

"Elianna!" My eyes shut in relief when I heard Ethan's voice.

"Thank the Lord," I whispered as I saw him running toward us, followed closely by Viriato. He came to a sudden stop several steps away. Even in my dizzy state, I noticed the color drain from his face as he took in the scene before him. Too late, I realized the impression he would receive—my clothes torn, my face tear-stained and pale, an enemy soldier cradling me in his arms as I struggled.

Ethan made a gasping sound. His hand jerked in an uncontrolled motion in front of him.

"What have you *done*?" He sounded hoarse, as if he wanted to swallow a scream and couldn't quite manage it. "Take your hands off her!" To my horror, I saw him pull out a silver dagger and point it at the centurion's heart. It happened so fast, I had no time to reason with him, to think, to act.

An image of the cinnabar mines flashed before my eyes. I saw Ethan as a slave, poisoned by the rotten atmosphere, dying one day at a time. It made me choke.

"No, Ethan! No!" Struggling wildly, I flung myself from the Roman's grasp, wondering if it was too late. If the very fact that Ethan had dared to flash a weapon against a Roman officer would earn him some unimaginable sentence.

"He saved me," I screamed, half incoherent in my fear, throwing myself against him and missing the drawn point of his dagger by a hairsbreadth.

"Have you gone mad?" he yelled. "I could have stabbed you!"

"Put that thing away." I pressed myself against him, grabbing his shoulders. "He *saved* me. He saved me from the bandits that attacked us."

The dagger slipped from Ethan's fingers unheeded, landing tip first in the earth. He stared at me. His eyes had turned pure green, darker than oak leaves in late spring. Heat stained my skin as he took in my torn clothes, my disheveled appearance, my slipping veil.

"You were attacked by bandits? They did this to you?"

I bit my lip. Softly, I said, "One man. He . . . he did this." I expected to see revulsion in his gaze. Disgust. Rejection. Instead, he wrapped his arms around me and pulled me closer, heedless of the many eyes that watched.

"Elianna." His lips brushed my hair. I could feel his fingers shaking against me as he caressed my back, my shoulders, any patch of me that he could get his hands on. "What did he do to you?"

I shook my head. Before I could speak, he cradled my face in his hands. "I do not care. I do not care what he did, do you hear me? You are still my bride. You are still mine." I had never heard him sound so vehement.

"*Mine,* Elianna." He touched my lips gently with his thumb like he was committing them to memory.

I shuddered at his touch. His words. It took me a few moments to find my voice.

"No! I mean, yes, I am still yours. But he did not . . . he did not do what you think. He tried. But Decimus Calvus and his men came just in time."

"He didn't . . . ?"

"No." My lips fell open as his words sank into my dazed mind. He had claimed me even when he thought I had been violated. Thinking that I was no longer pure, he still wanted me. Amongst our people, a woman's purity was held in highest esteem. Once lost, be it voluntary or otherwise, a woman's value was diminished. Some even claimed that according to the Law, a violated woman was unmarriageable. But Ethan wanted me besmirched or clean.

For the first time I wondered if Ethan truly loved me. He may never have spoken those words, but in every other way he had stood by me. My eyes filled with tears. I raised a shivering hand to caress his cheek. "Ethan, I—"

"Am I interrupting?" A half-amused, half-impatient voice inserted itself with annoying insistence into my happy thoughts. Decimus Calvus bent to retrieve Ethan's dagger from the ground, flipping it into the air, allowing it to twirl and capturing it, hilt first, with disconcerting speed.

"You are," Ethan said, pulling me closer, burying my face in the crook of his shoulder. "But I am too grateful to you to bear you any ill will."

"Whereas I resent having a dagger pulled on me."

The breath caught in my chest. I pulled myself out of Ethan's arms. "No, please! He meant nothing by it. It was the response of a moment. He would never have harmed you."

"Oh, I think, considering what he believed I was about to do to you, he would have harmed me with great pleasure. Or tried." Decimus Calvus surveyed Ethan through narrowed eyes, then laughed. With unexpected speed, he flipped Ethan's dagger up in the air again and sent it flying toward him. Ethan plucked it with ease midair, the hilt resting comfortably in his broad palm. The Roman raised a dark brow. "Well, well. How clever of you."

He turned to look at me. After a long moment he said, "Considering the circumstances, I suppose I can forget about your show of violence toward a representative of the empire."

Ethan bowed his head a fraction. "Thank you. For Elianna and her father."

My father approached us then. He had been speaking to my mother, no doubt recounting our adventure and reassuring her of our safety, and had missed the drama that had unfolded between the Roman officer and Ethan.

"My lord, come and partake of refreshments," he said to Calvus. "My servants shall wash your feet and see to your comfort. While you eat and drink, I will gather a few trinkets for you. A token of our appreciation for your kindness."

The Roman shrugged. "I did my duty. No more."

"You saved our lives, for which we thank you, my lord. Tell me, have you a wife back in Rome? A mother or sister? I have beautiful lengths of fabric fit for a queen."

Calvus's face grew shuttered. "I have a wife I have not seen in two years. She will appreciate a length of fabric to keep her warm, since I cannot."

I was surprised to hear he was married. Given the way he had held me and spoken to me earlier, I had assumed him to be a bachelor. I had forgotten that Romans could be lax about their marriages, especially the soldiers who lived far from home and family. It was no business of mine. Faithful husband or not, he had saved me from a horror I could not have borne with ease, and I owed him much.

"I will fetch you food," I said.

"You will not." Ethan's tone sounded unusually stern. "You are in no condition to play mistress of the house. Elizabeth will see to Decimus Calvus. You need to rest."

To my amazement, he swung me up in his arms and began to walk toward the stairs that led to my chamber. "Benjamin, I will take care of Elianna. Please add to the centurion's gifts a length of the green linen at my expense."

My mother, now aware that I felt unwell, ran to our side. "Are you hurt? What happened?" she cried. Her hands fluttered before her like confused little birds.

Hastily, I tucked my veil over my torn dress. "I am well. My ankle twisted when I jumped from the cart. It's a trifle. No need to worry."

"This is the centurion I told you about, Elizabeth." Father

patted her arm. "He and his men came to our rescue before those bandits could rob us."

"Bandits a stone's throw from the walls of Jerusalem." My mother pressed her temples. "What next? Will the Temple itself be pulled down about our ears?"

"Of course not. We are all well, as you see," I assured her.

Ethan shifted me in his arms. I could feel the muscles of his chest tighten against my cheek. "I know you must see to the centurion, Elizabeth. Perhaps you would send one of your servant girls to help Elianna? A wash, I think, and fresh clothes. And herbs to help her rest. I will remain with her until the servant arrives." He gave my mother a reassuring smile, his face a study of tranquility. No one would have guessed that minutes before he had pulled a knife on a Roman centurion.

My mother, soothed by the air of calm he exuded, sighed. "You are right. It won't do to ignore an officer of the empire."

Ethan strode to the stairs, taking them two at a time, as if I weighed nothing. In my chamber he came to a stop, still holding me in his arms.

"You can put me down now," I said.

"You are shivering."

Now that the danger to Ethan was past, my body was starting to fall apart. My teeth began to chatter and I felt assailed by dizziness again. "It's nothing," I managed to say. "I am fine."

Ethan ignored my words and looked about him in the empty chamber. He seemed to consider my bed for a moment, but instead of taking me there, he grabbed a blanket from a chest and sat against the wall near the door, with me still cradled in his arms. He wrapped the blanket around me, tucking the edges under until I felt its warmth start to seep into my icy limbs.

I traced the pattern of stars that adorned the corner under my chin. "Why are you sitting on the floor?"

He lowered his lashes. "If I take you to your bed, I'll have to let go of you. I can't seem to bring myself to do that yet." His eyes bored into me. "Can you tell me what happened out there? You don't have to, if it proves too hard. But I should like to know."

I slipped my hand back under the blanket, where I could clench it unnoticed. My stomach churned at the thought of telling him the details of the attack. Of the bandit's brutal hands on me. Of my fear. Of my father's rejection. But I sensed that knowing was important to Ethan. Healing, even. He would be able to live with the truth better than with the images his imagination might awaken.

With halting words, I told him what had happened.

He turned the color of ash when I described my helplessness as the thief grabbed me. I did not detail the man's offenses. But by Ethan's expression it was plain he knew that the thief had touched me in ways no one had. Not even Ethan. When I told him about making the man's nose bleed, Ethan threw his head back and laughed. To my own surprise, I started to laugh as well.

"You should have seen the Roman knock him on the head. He went down like a felled tree. I wished I had hit him that hard."

"I wish I had hit him much harder." His voice had turned icy and sharp.

"We are terrible. Remember what Solomon said?" I forced myself to sound obnoxiously prim. "'Do not rejoice when your enemy falls, and let not your heart be glad when he stumbles.'"

"What would Solomon know about it? He had seven hundred wives and three hundred concubines, our wise king. He could spare one or two. Whereas I—" he pulled me up against his chest—"only have you. I can't afford to be quite so generous with evil men."

I pulled my hand out from under the blanket, dislodging it. Ethan's eyes narrowed. "That son of a she-dog. Look at what he did to you."

I looked down and saw a large bruise near my collarbone, already turning purple. Shoving up the torn fabric of my dress, I lowered my head. My cheeks were burning.

Ethan put a finger under my chin and lifted it. "You have nothing to be ashamed of. Do you understand?"

"My father wouldn't agree with you."

"What can you mean?"

I shrugged, pretending an indifference I was far from feeling. "After it happened, I ran to him. For comfort, I suppose. For an embrace, a reassuring touch. Anything. He pushed me away. He didn't want me, Ethan."

"In this, you are wrong, Elianna. I don't believe he turned away from you because of your shame. Or even because of Joseph."

I winced. Sometimes Ethan's habit of forthright speaking

could be like sitting in a room filled with sharp knives. Eventually, you were bound to cut yourself. "Why then?" My voice sounded small and young in my own ears.

"Because of *his* shame. Elianna, do you know how horrifying it must be for a father to have to stand by and watch his daughter come under attack, and be utterly helpless to stop it?"

"What could he have done about it? He did his best to come to my aid. There were simply too many of them."

"The heart is not always conversant with the ways of wisdom. It has its own logic. Your father will feel that he let you down. If he won't look you in the eye, it is his own shame that drives a wall between you. Not yours."

"He has never forgiven me, you know. For Joseph. For what I did."

Ethan's eyes softened. I thought for a moment that he might kiss me and sat mesmerized, unable to move. A noise on the stairs distracted me, and then one of the servant girls burst through the doors, forgetting to knock. She skidded to a halt when she saw me in Ethan's arms.

Her face turned a curious shade of purple. She pulled her scarf lower over her forehead and cleared her throat. "Your mother sent me with this medicine, mistress."

If Ethan felt embarrassed, he did not show it. "Give it to me and I will make sure she drinks it. Now fetch some hot water for a wash as well as a tray of food. Broth, I think, to settle her stomach."

My eyes grew round. I had not told him of feeling nauseated. How he had deduced that, I could not fathom. He ignored my wide-eyed perusal. "I will remain with Elianna until you return," he told the servant girl.

"Yes, master." She handed the silver goblet to Ethan and ran out.

I rolled my eyes. "Now there will be trouble." I wriggled, trying to get up. His arms wrapped around me like bands of iron.

"Be still. I want you to drink this."

I nestled back into the comfort of his embrace and, grasping the goblet, took a small sip. It tasted bitter and smelled like a wet sheep. Wrinkling my nose, I pushed it back at him.

Ethan took the goblet and placed it on the ground without comment.

I sighed, relieved that he had not chosen to fight me over drinking the contents. I should have known better. My relief came to an abrupt end when he spoke into the silence.

"Elianna, I don't want to wait anymore. It's time we married."

ELEVEN

Wait for the Lord;
be strong, and let your heart take courage;
wait for the Lord!

PSALM 27:14

MY MOUTH FELL OPEN. "What . . . what brought this on?"

"Give me an answer."

"Soon."

"No. Not soon. *Soon* means *later* in your tongue. I want to marry now."

"You barely even wanted to marry me two years ago! Why this sudden haste?" I glared at Ethan, forgetting the tenderness he had shown me for the past hour.

He raised a dark eyebrow. "I see I offended you by asking you to wait after our betrothal. But it was for your sake as much as my own that I insisted on that condition. I didn't want you to be forced into the arms of a husband before you were ready."

I shrugged and looked away. "Who said I wasn't ready?"

"I did. And it was no easy task to wait, I assure you. For quite some time, I've had to battle my own desire for you, resist my longing to start our life together."

I gasped. "You never showed it."

At last, he was telling me the words I had been desperate to hear. Ethan wanted me. He wasn't marrying me out of duty or resignation. He wasn't marrying me to please his father and mother. He wanted *me*.

He shifted, bringing my face around with resolute fingers until our eyes met and clung. "Have I been so obtuse? Of course I wanted you, Elianna. Why do you think my father approached yours in the first place? I knew if I did not claim you soon, another man with no qualms about your age would grab you from under my nose. So I devised this long betrothal. But I have waited long enough. You turned eighteen five months ago. I don't wish to delay longer."

My stomach turned into a painful knot. I felt as if in one stroke he had delivered both life and death to my soul. I still could not face the thought of marriage. Grasping at the most obvious problem, I said, "I cannot marry you yet, Ethan. My parents need me."

"Then we will help them together. I will add my efforts to yours in order to make their lives easier."

"That's not right!"

"What's not right is how you make us wait for no good reason. I shouldn't have to sit against the corner of your room and flinch when a servant girl walks in. I shouldn't have to fight myself every time I want to hold you. Kiss you."

I took a sharp breath. "You said you would wait. For Joseph's sake."

He nodded. "I sensed how crushed you were when he died. Not merely because you lost a beloved brother, but with a weight of guilt I could not fully fathom. Although you tried to hide it, I sensed that you felt responsible for his death.

"I thought with time you would learn that you are not at fault. In truth, I would be willing to wait if I thought it would help you. Help heal this wound in your heart. But time is only making your sorrow worse. You try to hide this mountain of guilt beneath your work, and still it follows you. You aren't getting better. Joseph's death still haunts you. You have paid enough for whatever indiscretion you are convinced you committed, Elianna. It's time you put it behind you."

I flung myself out of his arms and stood trembling before him. He did not try to stop me, but remained leaning against the wall, his legs bent at the knees where I had rested not one moment ago. "You know nothing about it, Ethan. Ask my father, if you don't believe me. Ask him about my disgrace."

He waved a hand in the air, as if he could sweep my words away with one gesture. "I know how your father feels. And though I hold him in high esteem, he is wrong in this. No doubt he will relent eventually; one day he will regret his own treatment of the daughter he once treasured. But by then, your heart may shrivel. You could be destroyed under the weight of remorse. Living here is not good for you, Elianna. In this house, you are constantly reminded of Joseph's death and the fault you think you bear."

"The fault I *know* I bear!"

"Explain it to me, then. Explain how you are culpable for this tragedy."

I paled. "You already know—"

"As it happens, I do not. You have never spoken of it."

I owed this to him. This truth. This suppurating wound. This horror. But I could not say it. The words clung inside my throat and refused to leave. I shook my head.

He took a deep breath. "If we marry, you will have me by your side every day to care for you. And at least you will be out of this place of sorrow."

"Perhaps in a few months when—"

"No, Elianna. I'm done waiting."

I bit the side of my thumb. The thought of marrying Ethan, moving into a home of our own, going to sleep in his arms, and waking up in their gentle embrace made my bones melt.

Then he said, "If the Lord wills and we have children of our own, you will be too busy loving them to worry about your father. In them, you will find your healing."

I felt the blood drain from my face.

I did not trust myself with the life of a child. What if I managed to harm my own baby with my incompetence? I could not bear the thought.

I almost thanked God aloud when the door swung open and the servant returned, her arms heavy with a laden tray. Heaven had sent me a reprieve from having to give Ethan an answer.

"Here you are," I mumbled. "I need to change out of this tunic. It's sticky with sweat and that man's blood." I said this not only because it was true, but also because Ethan could not remain in my chamber once I started disrobing. He gave me a hard look that told me he knew exactly what I was doing.

At the door, he turned. "I will want an answer this week, Elianna. I won't stand for more delay."

The following morning, Ethan sent word that his brother's wife had borne her child, a plump boy with ruddy skin and dark eyes, according to my mother, who went immediately to visit. Both were healthy, thank the Lord. With the bustle of the new birth, Ethan grew busy for a few days and did not come to our house. Disappointment warred with relief in my chest. I missed him every hour. Then again, he couldn't press me about the matter of our marriage if he wasn't present.

Two days after our terrifying experience with the Judean thieves, Decimus Calvus came in person to fetch my father, as he had promised, and accompanied him to the tax collector's booth. To my surprise, my father seemed to hold the centurion in high esteem.

"That's a good man, even though he is a Roman," Father said. "He stepped in to ensure the publican's rates remained reasonable when I paid our taxes."

The next afternoon, Calvus sent my father an official letter that would render military road inspections easy and painless when we imported goods from other regions. My father had not asked for such a favor. Calvus offered it freely.

In exchange, my father invited him to our house on most

days and welcomed him with open arms. He was served the best wine and the choicest meat and never left our home empty-handed.

One morning I saw him leaving with a cart full of fabrics, blankets, towels, and an extremely expensive purple cloak we had been saving for one of our wealthiest customers. My eyes bulged. A year's worth of an honest general's salary wouldn't cover the price of everything piled up in that cart. I would be the first to admit that we owed the man a great debt, but surely my father had grown excessive in his generosity. We could not afford to give so much merchandise away.

Calvus noticed me goggling at him and the hard line of his mouth softened. He had eyes the color of flint, but when he smiled, they turned a warm gray color. "Lady Elianna." He gave me a formal nod.

"My lord."

"Call me Decimus. Surely we are friends after all we have been through together."

I frowned. The familiarity he offered by asking me to use his praenomen was unusual. Roman men saved their first names for family and close friends. Did saving my virtue, perhaps my life, give him the right to such an intimacy? Although I sensed that I might be violating the bonds of propriety, I did not wish to offend him over such a simple request. "Decimus."

He rewarded me with a smile. "What brings you out so early?"

I glanced at the shadow clock in the courtyard. It was still the first hour; the sun had just risen and the air had that crisp, fresh quality of when the day is young. "I was about to ask you the same question."

He laughed. "I came hoping for a glimpse of you. What else?"

I pursed my lips. "Now you've had it."

"And it isn't nearly enough."

"Then I hope you enjoy your consolation prize." I gestured at the brimming cart.

His eyes turned frosty. "They will keep me warmer than your tongue, for certain."

⚜

"I saw Calvus early this morning," I told my parents as we ate lunch. I tried to sound offhand. "He had a cart overflowing with merchandise."

"He has good taste," my father said. "Everything he chooses is quality. Talked me out of the purple cloak. We will have to make another, though I am out of purple dye."

"Don't you . . . don't you feel that you have given him enough gifts?"

My father coughed. "Gifts? He bought every item in that cart. You think I want to bankrupt myself? I wouldn't have given away so much for free, not even to the Messiah if he were ever to come."

Joanna choked on a piece of bread and burst out laughing. My mother made a disapproving noise. But I grinned with relief. "We can always use new customers."

The silver knife next to my plate glinted in the shaft of sunlight that poured through a lattice window. I picked it up and twirled it in my hand for a moment. "How can he afford so large a purchase? I wouldn't have thought a centurion would have the kind of income that allowed for such extravagance." Centurions were in charge of eighty men. They were not poor; neither were they known for their wealth.

Father shrugged. "I gather he is from an affluent family. It's a pity he is a Roman. I like his company."

"Has he already paid his bill?"

"Of course not. He can settle with me later."

This was not unusual. In the case of many of our established patrons, accounts were settled by the end of the month, not at the time of purchase. I shrugged, relieved that my father had struck up a new friendship.

Our unpleasant experience on the road had started to haunt me. Sometimes, without warning, I would be filled with an overwhelming sense of anxiety. At other times, with no reason or explanation, I seemed to smell the stench of my attacker's rotten teeth and sweat-stained body as palpably as if he were standing next to me. I knew this was a trick of my mind and still could not stop myself. I would go rigid with the horror of it, barely able to contain the dread that made me want to hide under the covers of my bed like a little child.

I realized that if I gave in to this fear, it would soon rule my life. I had no desire to leave the security of our home and found excuses to avoid going outside the house. Anxiety sat at my door, threatening to become a permanent state if I were not careful.

I sent a message to Claudia and asked permission to visit her. My mother frowned upon my friendship with a Roman. But she had grown lax in her discipline since Joseph's death, and I found myself making bolder decisions with the passing of time. I think my father saw the benefit of my relationship with a highborn Roman. Or perhaps he had ceased to care. In any case, he made no demur.

I traveled through Jerusalem's streets for the first time since we had been set upon by bandits. Of course, I kept within the confines of the walls. That lesson, I had learned. Joanna insisted on tagging along, and we brought two male servants with us. Still, by the time we arrived at Claudia's comfortable quarters near Castle Antonia, sweat covered my whole body and my hands trembled like butterfly wings in the wind.

"You look as pale as a naiad out of water," Claudia declared when she saw me.

"A what?"

"A naiad. You know? A water nymph. May Diana come to my rescue. How can you know so little about anything?"

"May the Lord come to your rescue. How can you know so much about things that matter so little?"

"What put her in such a grumpy mood?" she asked Joanna.

"It's the bandits. She hasn't been the same since they attacked her on the road."

"*What?*"

I threw myself on the couch and stretched my legs. "I almost lost my life, my purity, and my favorite veil to a bunch

of nefarious thieves. And they were smelly and ugly to boot."
I tried to sound lighthearted, but my voice shook. "It's the
first time I've left the house since it happened. I would have
run back home when we lost sight of our front door if Joanna
hadn't pressed me."

"Great heavens! What happened?"

I found that telling the story to a woman differed a great
deal from telling it to my future husband. Claudia made
me laugh by taking the sting out of my horror. Not that
Ethan had made me ashamed for even a moment. Ethan
had wanted to kill those men with his bare hands. Claudia
wanted to cook their private parts and feed them to dogs.
I cannot explain it, but there is a difference. I had needed
Ethan's protective response. It made me feel cherished. In a
different way, I also needed Claudia's hilarious one.

After that day, I stopped being haunted by my experience.
I overcame my fear with laughter.

TWELVE

There are those whose teeth are swords,
whose fangs are knives.

PROVERBS 30:14

LATER THAT WEEK, Ethan came to fetch me so that I could visit Daniel and Avigail's baby. He did not mention our marriage as we walked to his house. I had expected him to pelt me with dates and plans and felt a disproportionate relief when he avoided the subject.

Master Ezer's home was a Sabbath's-day journey from my father's, and Ethan spent the short time singing his nephew's praises. I could tell he was smitten with the little fellow. It made my heart contract. For the first time, I realized how deeply Ethan wanted to be a father. I listened to his descriptions in growing silence, my stomach in knots.

Daniel's wife, Avigail, was resting in her chamber with the

baby in her arms when we arrived. According to our tradition, a woman remained in the home for seven days after the birth of a boy and fourteen for a girl child. Avigail had been at home for six days when I came to visit her, and she seemed restless from the enforced confinement.

Ethan stopped just outside the door to Avigail's chamber. It was deemed improper for any male other than the child's father to go into the room. But he smiled at me with a brilliance that made me stumble as I entered.

Feeling shy, I first greeted Jerusha, who sat folding linens by the foot of the bed, and then Avigail's mother, who reclined by her daughter's bedside, cooing to the baby. Daniel grinned at me, looking very pleased with himself.

"May the blessings of the Lord be upon you, Avigail," I said. "You must be so proud."

The young woman shrugged. "He almost tore me up on the way out. Wait till you have to give birth, Elianna. It's horrible."

"The Lord's hand was with you." I peeked over the soft linen blanket wrapped around the baby's swaddling cloths. "He is beautiful."

"Is he not marvelous?" Daniel plucked the baby from Avigail's arms. "Look at the way he can grip my finger. I think he's going to be an athlete. I foresee he shall beat every Greek and Roman before he reaches twenty."

I bit my lip.

"You are laughing at me," Daniel said. "But you will see. Fifteen years from now this little man will be entering chariot races and winning the Panhellenic Games."

"If he is anything like Ethan, he will," I said.

"Ethan! Any fool can see he looks just like his father. But I won't hold it against you. You are betrothed to that brother of mine, and it behooves you to sing his praises. Would you like to hold the splendid fellow?" He held out his son toward me with gentle care.

I reached out to take him; the baby started to wail. Avigail screeched, "Don't give her my baby, Daniel! I don't want her to touch him."

Daniel's head jerked up. "What? Why not?"

"Have you forgotten what happened with her own brother? Joseph died under her care. For all I know she will drop my son on his head."

I felt like someone had slapped me. My fingers trembled as I laid them against my mouth, covering the gasp that had slipped from my depths.

Daniel's whole body went rigid next to me. "Don't be foolish, Avigail."

Jerusha shook her head. "Avigail, my daughter, how could you say such things? This is malicious gossip. Elianna does not deserve it."

Avigail had turned red. "I have said nothing that half of Jerusalem has not said behind her back. Saying it to her face is honest. I don't want her to touch my son."

Daniel's voice shook. "Well, she can hold my baby anytime she wishes." He held out his son to me again.

I shook my head, horrified. Not a single word came out of my mouth. What could I say? Remaining in that room became impossible, but Ethan still stood at the door, his wide shoulders filling the doorframe. His face was whiter than Avigail's sheets.

I went to push past him, but he restrained me with an iron grip. "Elianna, don't listen to Avigail's foolish talk. It means nothing."

All the pain and shame of the last few moments turned into an arrow of anger in my breast and I pointed it at Ethan. "The answer is *no*. I will not marry you. Soon or ever." I wrenched my arm out of his grasp and pushed against his chest. Caught off guard, he stumbled backward, and I slithered past him like a wounded animal in a hunt. I ran home, crying the tears I had not allowed to fall in Avigail's chamber. Poor Keziah could barely keep up with me, getting covered in dust as she stumbled in my wake.

Not only my father, but all of Jerusalem condemned me. And they had every right to do it.

Ethan gave me an hour's reprieve. Then he came to our house to find me. I had sought my solace in the workshop, trying to bury Avigail's words in the soothing murmur of the weavers' voices.

"Peace be with you," Ethan said to the workers as he walked into the workshop.

They knew him well. Most of them had worked for my father for years and had seen Ethan come in and out of the workshop with Master Ezer since before he had grown a beard. They wished him peace and asked after his brother's baby.

He lingered long enough to answer their questions. Not by one gesture did he betray his impatience to end the pleasantries. After he had answered everyone's inquiries, he turned to me. "Elianna. Come out for a moment, please."

I thought about ignoring his request. But the workers would have perceived it as shockingly disrespectful. I would lose their esteem; cantankerous, belligerent women are not popular amongst my people. Sighing, I rose and followed him outside. He stopped halfway between the house and the workshop, far enough from both that our conversation would not be overheard. His face was wiped clean of expression, but his eyes had turned a glittering gold. Shining, cold, and hard.

Neither of us spoke. My throat turned so dry that I could hardly swallow. I had never known him to look at me with such hostility.

"Is that what you propose to do every time the world throws hardship at you? Run?" he snarled with sudden fury.

I hugged my elbows. "No."

"Do you intend to take your woes out on me whenever someone speaks to you unkindly?"

"Of course not."

"Good. Because I expected better from you."

"Forgive me, Ethan. I did not mean to hurt you." I dropped my head. "Though I regret the way I spoke, I meant what I said. I cannot marry you. Do you not see how impossible it is? You deserve someone better."

"Look at me, Elianna." His voice had gone very soft. Against my will, I looked up.

"Come here."

I shook my head.

His mouth crooked up on one side. "You won't come to me? Then I must come to you." He took a long step forward, closing the distance between us until we stood so close that barely a breath separated us. Still he would not touch me. "You are my betrothed. By law. By custom. By the word of our fathers. By a signed contract. You are already mine. Is it such a light thing for you to break your promise?"

"Of course not. I am doing this for your good, Ethan."

"I decide what is for my good."

I threw my hands up in the air. "Not if you decide wrong."

"Elianna, I will not set you free. My answer would be different if you wished to part from me because you couldn't bear to live with me. I would agree to break this betrothal under those circumstances. Since I know that is not the case, I am not going to give in to this mad idea. If you press me, I will press back. Make this a public battle. Do you truly want the weight of such a scandal to break over your house and mine?"

I thought of Jerusha and my mother and how they would feel if instead of a quiet divorce, a public storm blew into their households because of me. Our fathers could no longer remain friends. There would be a gale of gossip that would destroy our quiet lives. Had I not done enough damage to my family? I hung my head. "I cannot be the kind of mother your children deserve. Everyone in Jerusalem knows it. Why can't you accept that I am wrong for you?"

"Do you think I had not heard that rubbish before today? Do you think Avigail's accusations came as a surprise to me?

But rubbish it is, Elianna, and you are a fool if you listen to this nonsense and allow it to sway you. How many times do I have to tell you that Joseph's death is not your doing? You will make a wonderful mother—loving and tender. Wise. I will not allow a bee to rob me of my dreams."

I shook my head. For Ethan's sake only one option remained to me. The truth. I must tell him what happened that day on the hill. Tell him so that he would let me go. And be free to live his life.

"Ethan . . ." I gulped, feeling nauseous and light-headed and full of hatred for myself. "Ethan, that day with Joseph. It *was* my fault. I took him to the hill. He didn't want to go. He wished to play with his ball in the back alley. I wanted to enjoy the wildflowers and pressed him into coming. When we arrived on the hill, we started playing and I shoved a flower in his face, marking him with its powder and scent, which must have attracted the bee. I should have wiped his face. Then when that wretched creature began to buzz around him, I refused to help. A sheep had gotten lost and I grew distracted by its plight.

"Joseph . . . O God in heaven, have mercy . . . Joseph cried out for help. He was so scared. So little and helpless. I just told him to stay still. It took me a long time to finally go to his aid. By the time I arrived, the bee had already stung him.

"He gave me such a look, Ethan. So hurt and accusing. I could see it in his eyes: he blamed me for leaving him." I bent over and dry-heaved wretched sobs as my stomach churned and my heart broke and my soul shattered again. "I killed him, Ethan. I as good as killed my own brother."

Strong arms wrapped around me. Ethan pulled me against him and held me. He said nothing for a long time. What could he say? Words that could comfort me had not been invented.

"Is that it? Is that all that happened?" he said finally, after my sobbing subsided.

"What do you mean *is that all*? What more do you want?"

He lifted my face to his gaze. "Elianna, beloved, I cannot take away this burden. I cannot wash away this guilt that you feel. I *can* tell you that I will stand by your side as you walk through it." He bent down and gave me a light kiss, sweet and tender and chaste.

I wrenched out of his arms. "You mean you still want to marry me?"

"More than ever."

I gaped at him. "You have lost your sanity."

His smile was half exasperated, half sad, and completely stubborn. "What shall it be? Will you marry me willingly or do you want a public fight on your hands?"

I wilted. "You win. Only by winning, you lose."

My father and Master Shual maintained a regular correspondence once the steward returned with Herod to Galilee. Not a month after they had left, my mother told Joanna and me that Master Shual's whole family was traveling back to Jerusalem to visit us and that Chuza and his parents would be coming to dinner.

"Wear your new blue dress with the gold fringe," my mother instructed Joanna.

I knew there could be only one reason for the whole family to traipse all the way to Jerusalem so soon after leaving it, and it wasn't dinner. They were coming to ask for my sister's hand in marriage. In the two weeks that Chuza had remained in Jerusalem following Herod's banquet, he had managed to visit with Joanna many times. The two of them were rapturously in love, any fool could see.

Affection, however, did not forge matrimony in our world. Infinitely more mundane interests such as family connections and wealth and social position weighed in the matter. We had mergers, not love affairs, no matter what King Solomon liked to write on the matter. Of course, fathers often took the desires of their children into account. Still, no one could deny that their primary concern rested with practical issues such as the amount of the dowry or the size of a wedding or the acceptability of a bride price.

Socially, we were of the same standing as Master Shual. But he had higher connections. He had a high position in the home of the tetrarch. I suppose he could be said to be above us. He could have sought higher for his only son.

Yet here he was, wife and son in tow, looking to bring our families together. As much as I dreaded the thought of my own upcoming marriage, the thought of Joanna's betrothal made my heart lift with joy. I knew she had never wanted anything so badly, and from what I had seen of Chuza, he seemed a good and kind young man. Of course, I was disposed to loving any man who adored my sister with such obvious fervency.

For days we slaved to prepare a feast worthy of the occasion. My mother wanted to prove that although we had no royal associations, we could provide as good a banquet as any found in the house of Herod himself. There would be only seven of us for dinner, but we had prepared for seventy. I was worn out by the time the evening came.

I knew that if my father and Master Shual did not manage to come to a financial understanding, the grandest food from the emperor's own palace in Rome would not bring about this betrothal. Between them, the men had the power to forge or disband. Even in a love match, money reigned. We were stable enough, financially. Stability was one thing, however. Extra coin quite another. There just wasn't that much spare cash. If Master Shual proved greedy, this wedding might remain a dream in Joanna's heart.

My mother forbade Joanna from doing any work that day. Instead, she sent her for a long bath, and Keziah spent hours curling and adorning her hair, although of course it would be covered by a veil as long as she was in the company of men. Chuza's mother, Merab, would have the privilege of seeing her while we ate our dinner apart from the men. Before dinner, sweet wine and dainty delicacies would be served in mixed company.

My parents welcomed Master Shual and his family warmly, and we all settled on the freshly cleaned couches. Joanna arrived last, veiled as expected for an unmarried maiden. Not even a veil could hide the radiance of her beauty, and Chuza gaped, forgetting to greet her. Everyone laughed.

"There is no hiding the fact that my son has set his heart

upon your daughter," Master Shual said, addressing my father. "We are here to ask for her hand, Benjamin. If she is willing, of course." He threw Joanna an expectant look. "What do you say, child? Are you willing to come to my son and be his wife?"

If I could manufacture the exact shade of red that stained Joanna's cheeks, I would be a rich woman, I thought. "Yes, master," she said and stared at the beads on her shoes.

"Good. Good." Shual rubbed his hands together. "Your father and I shall discuss the details over dinner. Such delicious smells are coming from your kitchen, Elizabeth. My stomach is grumbling like a roaring camel."

"I shall have them serve the meal at once," my mother said before leading the women to an inner room already prepared for our supper.

The two mothers spent most of the dinner hour bragging on the excellence of their children.

"How old is Chuza, if I may ask, Merab?" my mother asked.

"He is twenty-four."

"So old? I am surprised you have not found a wife for him before this. My Joanna is only fifteen."

"It is a woman's business to get married as soon as possible, and a man's to keep unmarried as long as he can. I think Chuza is too young, if you ask me."

My mother stiffened. "He does not seem to think so."

"My son is brilliant in almost every way. We expect a great future for him. But like all young men, his head is turned by a pretty face. What can a mother do? We have to bear with our children's lapses."

I bit my lip. My mother, I could see, was not pleased to have her favorite daughter described as a *lapse*. A chill settled over the room after that.

I could have bowed down and kissed the carpet with relief when the men rejoined us. By then the edge between the two older women had grown as sharp as an Egyptian dagger. Clearly neither one felt that anyone was good enough for her progeny.

I noticed my father's mouth was a tight pale line. Chuza, on the other hand, sported a big grin, so I guessed the betrothal had been agreed upon, though perhaps not according to terms that pleased my father.

"What news, Father?" I dared to ask.

He took a deep breath and placed a hand on Chuza's shoulder. "You shall be my son-in-law," he said, sealing the betrothal with the formal words once spoken by Saul to David. I sighed with relief. Everyone blessed God with various degrees of enthusiasm.

Chuza approached Joanna and reached for her hand. "A gift for you until the full bride price is delivered. Think of me when you wear it." He slipped a ruby the size of my earlobe onto her finger.

I grimaced, disinterested in the dazzling beauty of the jewel. That ring must have cost a fortune. They would expect us to match its grandeur with the dowry we provided for Joanna. How were we to secure such a vast sum? I could see why my father sat quiet and pale, not joining the excited chatter in the room.

At least we had a year to prepare. My own wedding was set to take place in one month. Two weddings in one year. I had helped my father set aside a portion for my own dowry. I knew that Ethan and Master Ezer would take me even with a small offering, but I had my pride. I refused to come to my husband empty-handed. As it was, I brought him a mountain of trouble and shame. I could at least get this one thing right.

THIRTEEN

In their hearts humans plan their course,
but the LORD establishes their steps.

PROVERBS 16:9, NIV

"I DON'T UNDERSTAND what the problem is," Ethan said, leaning against a gnarled olive tree. We were alone in the garden, within sight of the house, but too far away to be overheard. "You know I will help you after we are married. Why this urgency to provide for Joanna's dowry? You'll have months to work it out."

I shrugged.

"Elianna, I haven't seen you so much as an hour over the past ten days. The only reason we are speaking now is because I cornered you in the workshop. Have you even slept above three hours a night? You will make yourself sick at this pace."

"Ethan, leave it be. I know what I'm doing."

The golden eyes narrowed. He pushed himself away from

the tree trunk and bent toward me until our faces grew level. "Explain it to me so that I can understand, then."

I swallowed a groan. He would not give up until he had what he wanted. "It isn't merely her dowry."

"You are breaking your back for *your* dowry? You think I care?"

"I care. I am not coming to you with one denarius less than what our fathers agreed upon."

"Benjamin has already set that money aside, Elianna. He told my father last month."

I hung my head. "He had to spend some of it. He placed a larger order of wool than usual and we were short of cash when it was delivered. We need to have more merchandise this year if we are to have enough for Joanna's dowry. So our purchases have had to expand, and we weren't ready for the extra outlay of capital."

"Your father can pay your dowry later. I know he is an honest man."

I shook my head. "We will keep our promise to your family. I have worked it out. We are almost finished with the vermilion and dark-blue wool lengths. With Viriato's help, we can have enough to pay your family everything my father promised."

"How can you be so stubborn, woman? You are going to come to me a corpse on our wedding night. It's not exactly what a man dreams of at night when he thinks of his marriage bed." His eyes burned with a fire I had not noticed before.

My heart started to pound like a military drum. I was speechless. Ethan laughed at the look on my face. "You need more rest. If you refuse me, I will complain to your father and he will force you to stop working altogether. I will insist on it."

"You would not!"

"Without hesitation. If you wish to keep working, then you have to cut down your hours."

"I don't have time, Ethan."

"And," he continued as though I had not spoken, "you will join your parents and mine at the feast in Avram's house."

Avram Ben Hesed was a wealthy Jewish merchant from a noble family whose connections extended to Roman gentry, Jewish aristocracy, and every major merchant in Jerusalem. His annual banquets were legendary. My parents never missed them. No one who had the honor of being invited would consider missing the greatest feast in Palestine unless they stood at death's door. This year, I had declared that my work prevented me from coming.

"If your father can spare one free evening for a banquet, I don't see why you shouldn't," Ethan insisted.

"My father has given the running of the workshop into my hands. It is my responsibility now, not his."

He ignored me. "I shall come to fetch you myself. Don't be late." Whistling a tune under his breath, Ethan turned his back and walked toward the gate. To my utter vexation I realized he was whistling a bridal song.

❧

On my way back to the workshop, I ran into Calvus. He had another pile of fabrics in his arms, stacked so high he could barely walk straight.

I raised my eyebrows. "More purchases? You have bought enough fabric from my father to clothe a small army."

"That is precisely what I intend to do, O alluring daughter of Vesta."

"My mother's name is Elizabeth," I said, my voice sharp. "And what do you mean that is what you intend to do?"

"Our soldiers are wild for your father's creations. They pay good money to have them. Your father has no interest in expanding his business into the garrison. So I buy from him and sell at higher prices. We both profit."

I gaped. "You must be jesting."

"Why? Your father knows what I am about."

"He *knows*?"

"And gives his blessing. Ask him, if you don't believe my word."

Sweeping my skirts, I walked past him toward the house, my back rigid. His low laughter rang in my ears long after I could no longer hear it.

To my stupefaction, my father affirmed Calvus's claim. "What harm can it do? I am not going into the garrison to barter with Roman lowlifes."

"And he is paying you full price for everything?"

"He will." My father shrugged. "In the end, I will have increased our sales and lost nothing by it."

⚜

The eve of Avram's feast dawned too soon for my liking. By the time I left the workshop and ran home for a hasty wash and change of clothes, Ethan had already arrived. He kept his thoughts to himself as he saw me fly up the stairs to my chamber. I heard my mother make an apologetic comment before I slammed the door shut.

For a moment I looked in the mirror. Curls flew wildly about my face, my tunic was wrinkled, my shoes stained with blue dye, and my skin seemed sallow and dry. The disarray of my hair and clothes caught me off guard. Being the daughter of a fabric merchant meant that I was always expected to appear to best advantage. My attire made a statement about our business. When had I grown so haggard and slovenly?

My mother and Joanna came to help me. We dashed about my chamber, combing my hair and stripping me at the same time, grabbing fresh clothes and pieces of jewelry as we went. By the time we descended the stairs, I presented a more respectable sight. I worried that Ethan might be displeased by my lateness. Instead, I caught him laughing silently.

"What?" I asked, with a half-hearted attempt at sounding annoyed. He had scared me with his threat of putting an end to my work. I felt relieved that I had not angered him by being late.

"New fashion?"

I looked down where he was pointing. My feet were still encased in my dye-stained work shoes. Tucked in one corner of a shoe, unnoticed by me, sat the wrinkled handkerchief with which I had washed. With every step, I was dragging it on the ground behind me.

✤

Someone nudged me hard in the ribs, waking me up from a restless sleep. I blinked, bleary eyed and confused by the noise before I remembered Avram and his feast.

My mother shoved a goblet of new wine under my nose. "Don't shame us, Elianna. Try to stay awake."

"Yes, Mother." Dutifully, I took a sip before replacing the goblet on a low table. Avram's feasts were a mingling of Jewish and Roman custom. Men and women remained in the same grand hall, though the women were assigned to one side and the men to the other. Through an ornately designed colonnade, we could observe one another. I saw my father speaking animatedly to Calvus. Many other Romans were present in the room, and to my delight, Claudia joined my sister and me before long.

Fanning herself with a fan made of peacock feathers set in gold filigree, she reclined on the couch next to me. "By Apollo, it is hot in here."

Several women ambled to the other side of the hall carrying lutes and citharas. Their clothes were scanty by any measure and I wondered how much skin would be on display when they bent over. The thought of Ethan seeing all that bountiful female flesh made me cringe.

"Oh good. We are to have music," Claudia exclaimed before catching my expression. "Do you not like singing?"

I flushed, embarrassed to be caught in my moment of jealousy. "I do, of course. Only these musicians are not . . . well, they are not wearing much."

"And?"

"I find I don't like the idea of Ethan looking at them. Can you imagine what he will see when they bend over?"

Claudia dissolved into laughter. "In one week you will be married to him, and you can blindfold him when you bring him to a feast, if you like."

I gave serious consideration to the idea; it seemed doubtful that Ethan would allow it. No more feasts at Avram's house, I decided. The lamps were smoky, the hour annoyingly late, and the air stuffy. Ethan would never miss it.

The offending musicians began to play and sing, and I had to admit with disgust that they were excellent. Their voices blended in beautiful harmony and their instruments filled the hall with a haunting melody.

"In Rome, we had music every night," Claudia said, her tone wistful.

I gave her hand a squeeze. "Homesick?"

She leaned her head against my shoulder. "Not so much now you are here."

The food started to arrive on large silver and gold platters. Some of the dishes were new to Claudia, and I explained their contents to her. Avram might have Romans for guests and eat and drink with them, bringing the frowning displeasure of many Pharisees upon him, but he drew the line at eating what the Law forbade. To Claudia's disappointment, the food before us bore no resemblance to the meal provided at Herod's feast. There were too many things we Jews were forbidden to eat that appealed to a Roman's taste buds.

Weariness began to overcome me as warm food and sweet

wine filled my belly and the mellow music of harp and lutes quieted my stretched nerves. My eyelids kept falling shut of their own accord and I had to battle just to keep them open.

"Look at this poor girl," Claudia exclaimed. "You must be exhausted."

"She's been working day and night," Joanna said.

"Then we must bundle her home." She signaled one of the servants and sent him to fetch either my father or Ethan.

We rose and made our way to the courtyard. By the time we arrived, both my father and Ethan were waiting. To my surprise, Calvus tagged behind. A servant fetched the cart in which the women had driven over. My father and Ethan had ridden horses, an indulgence for which both men had a weakness regardless of the great expense. But when my father attempted to mount his horse, he found it had gone lame.

"It's no good," Calvus said, shaking his head as he examined the poor creature's hoof. "You cannot ride him tonight. Take my horse, Benjamin."

It went against the grain with me, being indebted to Calvus. Again. I could not fathom my aversion toward the man. He had shown us many kindnesses over the past months. Yet there always seemed to be an expectation attached to every generosity—an unnamed, unspoken calculation.

No one else seemed to experience this discomfort around him, and I kept it to myself, knowing my father's fondness for the man. Still, I tried to circumvent the offer of his horse. He made it casually, but to give one's personal ride to another entailed a significant act of trust and generosity. It was simply too intimate a gesture. "You can ride in the cart with us, Father." I patted the seat next to me.

Father frowned and shook his head. I sensed that his dismissal of my suggestion had more to do with his desire to avoid sitting next to me than his enthusiasm for accepting Calvus's offer. My heart contracted at his rejection. I never lost it—that odd, hollow feeling every time he distanced himself from me.

"How will you get home if I take your horse, Calvus? I will walk," he said.

"Don't be foolish. Your house is much farther than my quarters. Come. I will give you a hand. Prepare for the ride of your life." Calvus stretched a hand and beckoned to my father.

Father grinned at the thought of riding a Roman-trained horse. Once mounted, he looked down. "He is certainly tall."

Calvus shrugged. "He is not one of your pretty Arabs, I grant you. But Perseus is strong and reliable."

"My thanks."

We began our journey at a brisk pace that jarred my bones as I held on for dear life to the edge of the cart. Ethan guided his horse near where I sat. "You are fading before my eyes. Take note of what I say, Elianna. You are not to rise out of your bed before midmorning tomorrow."

I ignored him. I had never slept that late in my life and I was not about to start now.

"Elizabeth, I charge you to care for my wife. She is not allowed to do any work until after the noon hour. Can I trust you to keep her—" He stopped speaking abruptly and drew in a sharp breath. Without another word, he dug into the sides of his horse and, pulling on its bridle, left my side at a gallop.

I stared after him, stupefied. The sight that met my eyes made me freeze with dread. My father was weaving atop Perseus as the animal clipped forward at alarming speed. It was clear he had lost control of the mount. Without warning, the horse rose on his haunches and screeched as though in agony.

In slow motion, I saw my father lose his hold on the leather bridle. His hands waved wildly in the air. I gasped, my nails digging hard into the side of the cart as I saw him waver. Then he grabbed at the horse's mane and for a short moment managed to steady himself as the horse's hooves gained the ground again. But then the animal screamed, his cry an unearthly sound that made the hair on the back of my arms stand on end. With greater violence than before, Perseus rose on his haunches again.

This time, my father could not hold on. He toppled from the saddle, flying backward, somersaulting in the air like a Minoan acrobat. He landed on the ground with a bone-crushing thud. I stopped breathing. My mother screamed. Next to me, Joanna slumped forward in a faint. Our driver brought the cart to a tooth-shattering stop, trying to calm the donkey that had been spooked by the violence of Perseus's movements.

Relief washed over me when my father raised himself up on his elbows. With trembling fingers, he rubbed his ribs as though they ached. But he was all right. I could see by the way he moved that he was not too badly hurt. God had preserved him!

He will be sore and bruised tomorrow, I realized with relief. My father was a grumpy patient. We would have a difficult week tending to his needs. I grinned at the thought.

Then the unthinkable happened.

Once again, Calvus's horse rose up on his haunches. My father looked up. His eyes widened and he cried out, his voice rough with alarm. He had no time to roll over. To crawl out of the way. Perseus brought his hoof down with intentional violence. It caught my father in the head with a knock so hard we heard it all the way in the cart.

Ethan arrived by their side at that very moment. He leaned so far out of his saddle that only his toes held him fast to his mount. With an agility that defied ordinary human strength, he reached out and grabbed Perseus's bridle, which was now hanging uselessly by the horse's side. Ethan pulled on the leather with a vicious tug. For a moment I thought the horse would unseat him with the force of his resistance. But Ethan proved too powerful and Perseus grew tame under his guidance.

I jumped out of the cart and ran to my father.

"Have a care, Elianna!" Ethan shouted. "I don't have Perseus fully in hand."

I ignored him and knelt by my father's prone body. My stomach turned as I saw the side of his head. Blood caked his face and soaked the dirt beneath him. It even trickled out of his nose and ears. To my great relief, I saw that he still breathed. As gently as I could, I swept his hair aside; what

I saw made me retch. His skull had been fractured, and a small sliver of bone stuck out of the wound.

I could hear my mother wailing in the cart. A great commotion made me look up. "Elianna, move!" Ethan cried.

Perseus had pulled the leather bridle out of Ethan's hold. The horse's big brown eyes were rolling and wild, and he screamed as though in pain before flying toward me. Ethan threw himself in the savage creature's path, trying to impede Perseus's trampling speed as he headed straight for me. Perseus knocked Ethan down, but Ethan's heroic lunge had slowed the horse's imminent arrival. It gave me time to throw myself to one side and avoid the deadly hooves by a mere breath of space.

The horse galloped past me, back into the dark street from which we had come. I could only hope he would injure no one else in his mad scamper. "Ethan! Ethan!" I cried, choked by the tears that were running down my face. If he had been hurt trying to save me . . . I could not finish the thought.

FOURTEEN

You keep track of all my sorrows.
You have collected all my tears in your bottle.
You have recorded each one in your book.

PSALM 56:8, NLT

ETHAN COUGHED. "I'm all right, Elianna. He just knocked the wind out of me." To my relief, I saw him rise and limp toward me. "How is your father?"

"Oh, Ethan." Words failed me.

He dropped to his knees next to me and examined my father with care. "This wound is grave. But there is always hope while he lives."

"What should we do?" My mind had grown numb with shock. I could not think of the simplest practical measures in that moment. Thank the Lord Ethan had kept his presence of mind. He ran to the cart and helped my mother and Joanna down. My mother, holding on to Ethan's arm, made her way to my father's side. Quickly I covered his wound with my scarf, knowing the sight of his injury would be her undoing.

I put my arm around her shoulder. "He breathes. You see?" She slumped against me with a whimper.

Ethan and the servant brought the cart as close as they could. To my astonishment, Calvus ran into our midst. "What's happened? Perseus returned foaming and riderless. I feared an accident."

"Your horse threw Benjamin and kicked him for good measure," Ethan said, his voice clipped. "Now you are here, help me get him into the cart."

Calvus knelt next to me. He reached his hand to remove my scarf from around my father's head. I grabbed his arm to prevent him from exposing my father's awful state to my mother's eyes. Calvus looked at me for a moment. "Why don't you take your mother to where your sister is reclining? Ethan and I will care for your father."

"No."

"Elianna, he is right," Ethan said. "Come, Elizabeth. Give us room to move him." He grabbed my mother's hands and pulled her up.

"Thank you," I said, but refused to budge. I intended to stay with the men and help my father. Ethan sighed and hurried my mother to the other side of the street where Joanna sat, leaning against a wall.

"I am sorry my horse harmed your father," Calvus said. His voice was low and heavy.

"Why did you insist that he ride that infernal creature?" I hissed at him, fear and shock rolling into anger. "That horse has the very devil's temper."

"I am sorry," he repeated, his voice calm. "Perseus is rambunctious, but he is rarely vicious without reason."

"Not vicious? He is a war horse, trained to kill alongside his master! What were you thinking, pressing him on my father?"

"Elianna, this will not help," Ethan said as he rejoined us. "We need to get him to a physician quickly. You can hold on to your recriminations a while longer." He bent down and slid his hands under my father's torso. "Help me get him up, Calvus. Gently. Elianna, you keep his head as steady as you can."

I sat next to my father in the cart to hold his head immobile. Joanna and my mother squatted at his feet, clutching his hands, begging him not to die, weeping noisily. I wanted to scream at them to be quiet. Their words drilled into my heart like fiery darts.

"There was something wrong with that horse, Calvus," I heard Ethan say. He had thrown our servant on the back of his own horse and sent him to fetch a physician, while he drove the cart as fast as he dared.

Calvus, sitting next to him, shrugged. "Animals can be unpredictable."

"No. I tell you, he acted as though he was in pain. Check under his saddle. Perhaps he has developed a sore or a cut."

"I saddled him myself this afternoon. Nothing wrong. This was a tragic accident, no more. I am deeply sorry for it. Poor Benjamin. I fear he is done for."

I gasped. Ethan threw Calvus a filthy look. "One more word out of your mouth, and I promise to hit you so hard, you will swallow your teeth along with your words. I care not if you *are* a Roman soldier."

I could not observe Calvus's expression from where I sat. I only saw his hand tighten on the hilt of his sword for a moment before relaxing. "Calm yourself, Jew. I said nothing she hasn't already worked out for herself."

༝

The physician came and did what he could. Ethan slipped out at his arrival without telling me his destination. I remained with the physician as he examined my father, anxious to hear his prognosis.

"I am amazed he lives," the man said, mopping his brow. "I don't know if he will survive the night."

We stayed with him, keeping vigil, helpless to do anything for him. A few hours later, Ethan returned, oddly silent and distracted.

"Where did you go?" I asked. We had already sent a servant to inform Jerusha and Ezer of my father's accident, and they had come to be with us in our trial. To my surprise, they had told me Ethan had not returned home after leaving us.

He took a deep breath. "The fortress of Antonia. I wanted to examine Perseus for myself."

My eyes widened. "How did you get near that creature in a fort full of Roman soldiers?"

"A generous bribe can soften a hard heart, Roman or otherwise. The guard remained by my side to ensure I caused no mischief while I examined the horse, but he allowed me to do what I needed once I gave him a fat purse of silver."

"What did you find?"

"Something odd. On his back, where the saddle sat, there was a narrow but deep wound. It wasn't a sore or anything natural. It seemed like a puncture, as if someone had placed a sharp nail under the saddle. With the pressure of a body's weight, it would have been pressed into the poor horse, causing him pain and terror."

"You mean someone did this on purpose?"

"I am almost sure of it. There was nothing under the saddle, so whoever set the trap had removed the sharp object by the time I got to it."

"Why would anyone want to kill my father?"

"Not your father. Calvus, I think. No one could have guessed that the Roman would offer his horse to someone else at the last moment. Whoever set up this trap wanted to harm Calvus. Your father had the misfortune of riding that horse at the wrong time."

I gasped. "Did you tell Calvus?"

"I had to. If someone is trying to murder him, he has a right to know."

"Did he dispute your claim?"

"Not when he saw that deep puncture wound on Perseus's back. He didn't say anything. But for once that arrogant smile was wiped from his face."

✻

Rabbi Zakkai came to visit my father. We Jews believe more in the Lord's healing power than we do in a physician's arts. At first, I felt encouraged by the rabbi's presence and grateful that he had taken the time to come. Perhaps his prayers would succeed where the physician's herbs had failed. Then he opened his mouth.

"God is punishing him," he said. "Benjamin must have done a grave wrong in the sight of the Lord to be so stricken."

Ethan was in the chamber with us. He bolted upright. "Surely, Rabbi Zakkai, not every calamity is due to God's displeasure."

The rabbi snorted. "The Lord himself declares, *If your soul abhors my rules, so that you will not do all my commandments, but break my covenant, then I will do this to you: I will visit you with panic, with wasting disease and fever that consume the eyes and make the heart ache.* It is the words of the Law that accuse Benjamin, not I, young man."

"Have a care, Rabbi Zakkai, for you begin to sound like the friends of Job. I know this teaching has gained popularity amongst many of you Pharisees. I know you preach the conviction that our sufferings are always a result of our sins. But as I recall, when Job's friends accused Job in the same way, the Lord said to them, *My anger burns against you . . . for you have not spoken of me what is right.* Be mindful that in your zeal you do not malign our God, lest he say the same of you."

To my relief, the Pharisee never returned to our home. And yet his words left a bitter taste in my mouth that his absence would not cure. Were we cursed by God because we were evil? Was every stripe of our sorrow a punishment from his hand?

For seven days the physician came and went, bringing his herbs and potions. Nothing helped. My father never awoke. There were bruises behind one ear and under his eyes, turning his skin into a quilt of washed-out white, stained with purple and blue and yellow. Other than the change in the color of those bruises and the odd way his eyes sometimes flickered, nothing altered in his appearance or condition.

"I do not know what keeps him alive. I doubt it is my ministrations," the physician said on the eighth day.

"Will he get better?" I asked, out of my mother's earshot.

"I expect not. He needs a prophet armed with miracles now, not a physician with a bag of medicinal herbs. I will keep coming if you wish and do what I can for him. But I am an honorable man. I will not give you false hope or take false credit."

A day would come when I would learn to appreciate such honesty. For the moment, I only felt numb with the horror of our hopelessness. I returned to my father's side after seeing the physician out. Both Joanna and my mother had been sent to bed to sleep and I was left alone with my father.

I had managed to hold a tight rein on my emotions until then. I had stayed strong so Joanna and my mother could have the freedom to fall apart. The physician's words proved too much for me. My tenuous grasp on self-control slipped away. I fell on my father's chest and wept.

"Please, please wake up!" I wailed. "Please, Abba. I love you so much. I need you. Don't leave me. Don't leave me without forgiving me. I am sorry about Joseph. I am more sorry than you can know. Abba, Abba. How will I go on? How will I take care of Mother and Joanna without you?"

His eyes flickered. Nothing more. No signal to show me that he had heard. I beat softly against his chest. "Come back to us! I miss you. I need you. I need my father!"

A pair of strong arms wrapped around me from behind and physically lifted me off.

"Elianna, hush now." Ethan pulled me closer and held me in his arms as I sobbed like an inconsolable child.

"I'm sorry," I said when my tears were spent. I had no business clinging to Ethan this way. We weren't even married yet. I gasped as awareness sank in. This was to have been our wedding day. "Oh, Ethan, the wedding!"

He gave a lopsided smile. "Don't concern yourself. I cancelled that days ago, when the accident first occurred."

"Forgive me." I knew he must be disappointed. He had waited so long, and once again, I had frustrated his wishes.

He pulled me out of the room. "This is not your fault, Elianna. I am disappointed, of course. But the world does not always go as we plan."

"How can you be so accepting? How is it that you are not screaming with frustration?"

"I've been spending more time in prayer. I am learning that obedience to God means that you do not put your eyes on your longings, but instead, you simply place one foot ahead of the other into the space that the Lord opens. Tired, wounded, overwhelmed. It does not matter. You merely keep moving where God directs and stop focusing on what you wish you had. It's teaching me patience."

"I wish I were as close to the Lord as you are."

"You could be."

"Maybe one day," I said, without a grain of hope.

Ethan rubbed a finger against his temple. "God is mindful of your sufferings, Elianna. He knows every tear you shed. He has not abandoned you. You must try not to abandon him."

"I have not." I shook my head for emphasis. "I have not lost my faith. It's that . . . I cannot draw near to him." I crossed my arms over my chest until my hands were tucked under my armpits. "Ethan, we must discuss practical considerations."

He nodded. "The physician told me his prognosis just now, on his way out. We should make arrangements to take care of your family."

We had stopped by the olive tree in the garden. I sank to the ground and leaned my back against its narrow trunk. "I have no strength left, Ethan. How am I to run this household? How am I to provide for my sister's dowry and my father's business?" Tears sprang fresh from my eyes again. "I am overcome."

Ethan squatted in front of me. "Remember the prophet Isaiah's words? He promised that the Lord gives power to the faint. And to the one who has no might, he increases strength. You can trust him, Elianna. He will care for you and your family."

I sniffed as a tear rolled down my face. With an impatient

hand I dashed it away. What did God have to do with such a one as me? My own father had rejected me. How could the God of earth and heaven not do the same? Why would he help me?

"I want to suggest something," Ethan said as I remained mute. "Don't refuse me before you think it through. I want us to be married, simply and quietly, in respect to Benjamin's illness. I will move here and take care of your family's business."

"There is nothing to think through. It would be out of the question, Ethan. Master Ezer told me just this past month that he has stepped away from running his business and leaves most of it in your hands. I know Daniel takes care of the accounts, but he has no interest in the rest of your work. He rarely travels or deals with your customers. It's all on your shoulders now, Ethan. Your father cannot do without you."

"I will not abandon him. Our trade will continue to receive my attention. And I will look after your family's interests as well."

"You know that is impossible. You cannot manage both the businesses. I won't ask it of you."

Ethan's eyes narrowed. "Why can't you trust me, Elianna? I know it will be hard, especially at the start. But I can manage."

"I am not saying you aren't capable. But the cost of such a sacrifice is too high. I will not ask it of you."

"We could do it together, you and I."

I shook my head.

"Sell your father's business, then, and bring your family to live with us."

I hid my face in my hands. "I cannot! It would be the end of my mother to lose her home as well as her husband. And Chuza's father will not take an impoverished girl as bride. He is not like you and your father, Ethan. He thinks very highly of his dignity and position in society. No matter how Chuza feels about Joanna, his parents will not consent to their wedding if I cannot meet their full demands for a large dowry."

Ethan rose to his feet and rubbed the back of his neck. He looked exhausted, and for good reason. He worked long hours during the day and then came to spend every spare moment at our home, helping with the workshop and offering support to three needy women.

My heart brimmed over with love for him. I felt no man on earth could compare to his goodness. For a moment, I weakened. The thought of moving into his home, of placing myself in his care and allowing him to take responsibility for the tangle of our family's affairs tugged at my soul with such a force that I had to shove my hand over my mouth to keep from speaking out. What kind of love would that be? How could I selfishly take so much and give so little in return? How could I burden him with my mountain of problems?

"I wish I could run the workshop without my father's help. But there is no chance of that. No one in Jerusalem will want to buy the merchandise of a business run by a woman."

Ethan remained quiet for a moment. His face had gone white and still. He opened his mouth once and closed it, as if he could not bring himself to say the words that were on his mind.

"What is it?" I asked.

He swallowed hard. "There is a way, I believe, to make that happen. No one knows the extent of your father's injuries. We will keep it a secret. Let it be known that he is sick and unable to leave his bed. But we'll allow people to assume that he is able to run the business behind the scenes. Viriato can come to you permanently. He can take over what your father was accustomed to do.

"As long as your father is believed to maintain control and direction of the workshop, even if it is behind the scenes, your customers will continue their patronage."

I sat up, brightening for the first time in a week. "Do you think so?"

"Without a doubt. They have heard of your work in the trade already. No one has turned their backs because of your increased involvement, save a small handful of staunch conservatives. This will make no difference, so long as we are able to keep your father's secret."

"Ethan." I bit the corner of my nail. "You want me to run my father's business?"

His mouth tipped up to one side. "*You* want to run your father's business. I am merely telling you that it is possible."

FIFTEEN

A friend loves at all times,
and a brother is born for adversity.

PROVERBS 17:17

TO MY BEWILDERMENT, Calvus began to visit us every moment he was free, especially during the first weeks. Perhaps he felt guilty for my father's accident, thinking this should have been his own fate.

He never told us who had attempted to harm him. I tried to ask him on several occasions and found that neither charm nor pestering worked on him. He would either evade the subject or turn mute. Either he did not know or he did not wish me to discover the name of the culprit. I had to be satisfied with my ignorance. One thing I began to grasp about Decimus Calvus during his many visits: he was unshakable. You couldn't persuade him into a compromise. If he did not intend to reveal the name of the guilty party, no inducement or nagging on my part would change his mind.

He could also be thoughtful. Some days he would arrive with an armful of exotic fruits, accessible only to Roman officials. At times, he would unclip his scarlet cloak and help the servants move a heavy chest or carry an oversize loom. And he never rode Perseus into our home lest the sight of him upset my mother.

Many an evening found Calvus sitting by my father's side silently, watching him with an unreadable expression. My anger melted in the face of his obvious care.

"Why don't you sell Benjamin's business?" he burst out a few days after the accident. "You cannot hope to continue in this vein. You will kill yourself trying to run this trade. It's no work for a woman."

I arched a brow. "Perhaps Roman women are not equal to it. But we Jews are made of sterner stuff."

He threw his hand up in a wild gesture of disgust. He had an expressive way of speaking with his whole body rather than just his tongue. "You are the most stubborn creature the gods ever put on this earth. If you were my wife, I would beat you."

I sorely wanted to retort that if he treated his wife that way, then no wonder he found himself alone, halfway across the world. I managed to keep my words to myself. He already thought me a shrew. "Then I thank the Lord that he saw fit to betroth me to Ethan. I should also mention that the gods did not put me on this earth. The Lord did. In fact, the same holds true for you."

"At least let me help you."

"I don't need help."

"Of course you do. Your taxes are due soon. I will arrange for you to make the payment privately so that you don't have to contend with long lines or a surly publican. How much do you owe? Can you afford the full amount?"

"I don't know."

"Give me your books and I will sort out the taxes for you. I am not just a comely soldier with great battle skills, you know; I am also very gifted with accounts."

I had to bite my lip to keep from laughing. "Ethan will help me," I said, walking away. At the door I turned back. "Thank you, Calvus."

※

The day before the anniversary of Joseph's death, I found myself alone by his grave. It still looked new, the cave freshly hewn. I sat dry-eyed and thought of the little boy we had lost, and it came to me that this fate awaited all of us. No one escaped death. It would have you in the end, slow step by slow step, bits of strength worn down, flesh worn thin, heart worn out. Beauty and strength and brilliance couldn't save anyone from its ravages. In the end, death would swallow all of us whole and we would join Joseph in the ground and turn into bone and dust.

What fools we are! I thought. *We have no answer for death, so we turn our hope to this world. As if this life could assuage our longings and truly make us happy.*

I couldn't deny that life had good things to offer. Good things that could dazzle you and take your breath away. But even those good things couldn't last. In their own way, they joined Joseph's bones and turned to dust. Dreams died, as surely and irrevocably as the flesh.

Then I had a strange thought. God could bring meaning into all this. Bring light and hope and life into what no one could undo. He alone could breathe life into that dust and breathe meaning into the things that pass. He alone could alleviate our hunger and conquer our great enemy, death.

But God had no interest in me. His grace had passed me by. If the Pharisee Zakkai proved right, his judgment awaited me, harsh and forbidding. Not so different from the condemnation my father felt for me. After an hour, I returned to the workshop, and the growing pile of my responsibilities drove these deeper considerations from my mind.

Viriato became the support that held our trade together. He dealt with the customers while I ran the workshop, produced new merchandise, designed fresh colors and textures, and with Ethan's help, slowly revolutionized our productions. Month after month, my father remained unchanged. Mother and Joanna tended to him with fastidious care. I think he remained alive by the sheer force of their love and the excellence of their ministrations.

Perhaps God spared him to us so that I could continue to provide for my family. Slowly, new merchandise began to accumulate, and our sales increased. A small mound of savings was growing in a box marked for Joanna's dowry. By late fall, we had produced substantial quantities of wool and linen fabric. Much had been sold, but a large assortment of fabrics still remained.

"How much income will there be from this lot, do you think?" I asked Viriato, wondering if I could cover Joanna's dowry in full after selling the pile growing in the corner of the workshop. She had celebrated her sixteenth birthday two weeks before, and Chuza had sent her a heavy gold necklace to mark the day. To Joanna, his token was a source of joy; to me, merely another reminder of the need for us to increase our earnings.

Viriato shrugged a wide shoulder. "I won't know until I go through each piece and estimate the price."

"Let's do that today." I had the men move everything into my father's office, while Viriato and I tried to appraise the potential profit in each piece. Viriato priced the pieces with his sharp, experienced eye, while I tracked through my father's accounts to tally the bills we would have to pay in the coming months.

"Why don't you hire a scribe?"

"Scribes cost money."

"Not having them costs more. What if you commit an error?"

"Don't give me a sore belly, Viriato. My stomach is in knots as it is."

He flashed a wide grin through his dark beard. "Fear not. Ethan will take care of you. You keep doing what you are so gifted at. Make these fabrics, and I will sell them, and the denarii will come rolling in." He flipped a green piece of wool over. "Ah, this is a masterpiece. Using the saffron instead of weld definitely paid off. And that thread of silver woven through afterward makes it irresistible. I will fetch you a good price on this one."

I smiled. "You fetch me a good price on every piece. I don't know what I would do without you, Viriato."

He folded the green wool with care and picked up a piece of red linen. "I enjoy it more than you know. Every day of my freedom is like a dream to me."

He had told me more about his experiences in the cinnabar mines, the years of backbreaking labor and remorseless cruelty. The sickness that surrounded him and his own health that had begun to deteriorate with alarming rapidity. I could not imagine how he had survived. His reminiscences had been so vivid and moving that they had planted a deep well of dread in my heart. I would do anything to protect those I loved from such a fate.

"You are stronger than most men, Viriato. And I am not speaking of your prodigious muscles."

"Don't be fooled, mistress. I still have nightmares about the mines. Many a night I wake up, soaking in sweat and fear, shivering like a little boy. Then I remember that I am free. I tell you, it's almost enough to make me believe in your God."

I laughed. "I see Ethan has been talking to you."

"He took me to your Temple once. To the outer court where foreigners are allowed. I listened to some of the teachers of the Law. They are not so boring as they first appear."

I tried to hide my surprise. I knew of other Gentiles who gravitated toward our God. Some gave their whole heart to him. Grown men would submit to the excruciating pain of circumcision in order to join his household of faith. Many more remained God fearers, honoring God, praying to him, but stopping short of the formal process of conversion and circumcision. I wondered if Viriato had begun to lean into that path. If it were up to Ethan, he would certainly convert. Ethan's affection for Viriato had grown into a fierce loyalty that could not bear the thought of the Lusitanian perishing in his unbelief.

"Viriato, are you thinking of converting to our faith?"

"What? And give up roast suckling pig forever?" He shuddered. "The God of Israel has much to offer a man's soul. But he is hard on a man's stomach." He bent and examined the corner of a yellow length of fabric with more care. "This one has faded on the edge. We will have to cut the price."

I sighed and recorded the number he quoted in the book. When we finished with the whole pile, I added the numbers. Even after paying the accounts that would come due soon, we would have enough left over to cover Joanna's dowry in full as well as pay for the fresh orders of wool and linen that we needed for our new line. I could have danced with relief.

Viriato left to meet with a patron, taking a few samples with him. I went to visit my father for a little while. I had taken to speaking to him every day, although I knew he could not hear or understand me. In a strange way, I felt closer to him now than I had since Joseph had died. I was free to demonstrate my heart to him. He could not object or withdraw, not even when I touched him. I tried to ignore the ache of knowing that he could never return my affectionate caresses or hold me in a fatherly embrace again. Before his accident, I had always had a sliver of hope that his heart would melt toward me. Now I had no hope. But at least I did not dread his constant rejection, either.

"Abba, I have such good news. We have made enough money to pay for Joanna's dowry!" I leaned over and kissed his brow. "And we have done it a few months early. She will be able to marry her Chuza now."

I smoothed his hair back from his forehead. The bruises had long since faded. He had lost a great deal of weight and lay in his bed unmoving and skeletal thin. I could see his chest rising and falling and pulled the blanket up to his chin. It was one of the first ones we had made—the design with the twinkling gold stars. I smiled at the memory of our scampering efforts to avoid disaster. I had come a long way since then and learned a great deal about our trade.

His fingers in mine were cold and stiff. I squeezed them gently. "I must return to work. I miss you, Abba. I wish you were awake to tell me what to do."

Joanna waylaid me in the office. She shoved a bowl of stew into my hands. "You eat that. No skipping another meal. I made it for you myself. Go on. I want to know if you like it."

She had taken to cooking for me personally instead of allowing the servants to do it. I could never refuse any food she offered me, knowing how hard she had worked for every morsel. She sat on the edge of the desk and watched me eat.

"I hope to send your dowry to Master Shual within the month. If you want to include a token for Chuza with the package, start working on it. The striped linen would make a fine tunic for a man of his height." I had never allowed Joanna to find out how much pressure her wedding had placed upon us. She should enjoy every day of her betrothal, free from worry or guilt.

"I miss him," she said, her expression dreamy. My answering smile was sympathetic. I knew how I felt when Ethan was gone on one of his business trips. I had come to depend on him so much that his absence felt like a hole in my inmost being. Nothing felt right with the world until he returned.

Joanna reached out to caress my cheek and I turned to kiss her palm. "This stew is delicious, little sister. Thank you for making it for me. Now I really must concentrate on these accounts."

She ruffled my hair before rising.

"Wait!" Indicating the mountain of fabrics folded in one corner, I said, "Choose a few pieces for yourself before you go. You will need new clothes as a married woman. And a present for Chuza."

Joanna squealed and dove into the pile like an osprey chasing after fish. She picked out three pieces. I added three more and sent her off to my mother, hoping the thought of working on her wedding clothes might cheer both. The sparkling smile she gave me as she left the room was reward enough for all the hard hours of work over the past few months.

I was going over my calculations to make certain I had made no mistakes when Decimus Calvus walked in, uninvited.

He frowned when he saw me poring over the accounts. "Have you not given up on those yet?"

"Of course not. You can't run a workshop without tending to the figures. I have good news. We are doing well this season. As soon as I have sold this lot," I said, pointing at the pile of fabrics sitting neatly in the corner, "I can finally give attention to these books. I know they are in a mess."

Calvus looked ferocious. "I told you to let me help you with that." He reached for the rolls of parchment in my hand.

I pulled them out of his reach. "Don't be so forward. Even Ethan knows better than to force me into complying."

Calvus grabbed my arm and hauled me forward until our bodies almost touched. "A Roman man would have had you properly married, with a babe in your arms, by now."

I moved back hastily. "If you say one word against Ethan, I won't ever let you back into this house."

"Just give me the book!" he screamed.

"No!" I took another step back.

He had turned a dull red. The veins in his neck stood out. For a moment I thought he might hit me. I felt as if the world had tilted on its axis. The hairs on the back of my neck stood on end.

Calvus was breathing rapidly. The muscles in his arms bulged and I saw that he was flexing his fist. With his training and brute strength, he could kill me with one blow. And who would be able to challenge him? Who would bring a charge against a Roman centurion? He could concoct any story he pleased and get away even with murder. My throat turned parchment dry.

"Calvus," I said, trying to infuse calm into my voice.

"Shut up." I could sense the struggle in him, as if he was

fighting hard to bring himself under control. Then he seemed to get ahold of whatever violent streak was driving him. His breathing quieted. To my stupefaction, he gave a short bow as if I were a great lady, then walked out.

I stood trembling, astonished by what had taken place. Calvus had a fierce temper; I had always suspected that. But he had gone too far. It made my blood turn cold when I remembered the way he had touched me and the way violent anger had twisted his lips into a chilling snarl. His passions ruled him beyond reason. Beyond self-control, even. I would have to find a way to curtail his visits to our home. Once, his presence had made me uncomfortable. Now, I felt downright fearful.

Late that night, I brought my father's books and receipts into my chamber, intending to study them further. I wanted to prove to Calvus that I had no need of his conceited help. I fell asleep before I had unrolled a single parchment.

The sound of shouting roused me from a deep slumber. Dazed with exhaustion, I grabbed a thick veil and wrapped it around me before running below stairs to discover the source of the disturbance. Joanna followed at my heels, eyes large in her white face.

"What is it, Elianna?"

"I don't know." The shouting grew louder and more distinct until I could finally work out the words.

"Fire! Fire!" someone was screaming.

SIXTEEN

We went through fire and through water;
yet you have brought us out to a place of abundance.

PSALM 66:12

AN APPALLING SIGHT awaited me close to the entrance of the house. Smoke was rising out of my father's office in wispy billows. The chamber was on fire.

Inside that fiery room sat our whole supply of new merchandise. Joanna's dowry was going up in smoke before my eyes. I froze, unable to think for a moment. Viriato, who had taken to staying at our house when he worked late, appeared next to me, his chest half bare, his hair sticking out in every direction, his scar thick and vivid on his pale face. He made a fearsome vision. I turned to him as if he were God's own angel of salvation.

"Viriato! What shall we do?"

He ignored my question and dashed inside the blazing

chamber as if he could blow the fire down with the breath of his lungs. I screamed, certain he was running to his death. Coming to myself, I organized the servants to bring buckets of water and blankets and sent Joanna to warn my mother, hoping to keep both out of harm's way.

Before we could run to Viriato's help, he stumbled out, coughing and wheezing. In his arms, he held a great pile of fabric. He had tried to save some of our stock.

I rushed into the chamber with a bucket of water, knowing that the sight of a young woman facing the inferno would encourage the servants to overcome their fear and join me. The water in my hands vanished in a moment with hardly any effect, and I stood uselessly for the space of a heartbeat and stared at the growing blaze around me. Wood furnishings and fabrics filled the chamber. The fire ate them up with voracious hunger, growing bigger the more it consumed.

I grabbed a blanket and shoved it into a servant's bucket until it grew saturated with water, then started to beat at the flames. I was fighting to save our whole house now. We had a narrow window of time to prevent the fire from spreading to the rest of the building. My family would lose everything if we failed.

"Make sure my father is safely out of the house," I yelled at Joel above the din that surrounded us. "And my mother and Joanna and any of the older servants who may still be in bed. See that no one remains in the house."

The wet blanket proved more effective than water alone, and soon other hands joined mine as we beat at the conflagration with all our strength. Several of the servants were quickly overcome by the smoke and had to leave. The fire was winning. My strength had begun to wane, but I could not give up. If I walked out of that room, the servants would soon follow me and we would lose everything. For all his valor and strength, Viriato alone could not overcome such an insatiable fire.

I couldn't see the far wall now; the smoke had grown too thick. Without warning, my foot caught against a low table and I stumbled. I threw out my hands in a precarious bid for balance, but I could not steady myself. Horror filled me as I fell forward into a wall of fire. I felt its heat touch my face, felt it lick at my hair and eyelashes. Smoke and heat smothered the rising scream in my throat.

A pair of hands snatched me with brutal force from behind and lifted me off my feet.

I flew into the air for a moment and then landed against a hard chest with a thud. My eyes were streaming with tears. I could not see whose arms held me or carried me away from the inferno.

"Elianna! God have mercy! You almost died before my eyes!"

"Ethan," I choked. "Ethan, we need to go back there."

"I am going back. You are staying here."

"No, Ethan."

Ethan shoved me against the wall, his hand hard against my chest as he held me imprisoned. "If you say *no* to me right now, I will bind you with ropes and dump you outside; do you understand me, woman? And I will lose precious time doing it."

I stared at him mutinously.

"Elianna, I have brought more servants with me. Viriato and I will handle the fire. But if you are in there, the two of us will be so distracted about your safety that we will endanger ourselves needlessly. Do you want that responsibility on your head?"

My eyes widened. I shook my head violently.

"Then stay here. And let me deal with it. Promise me."

"I promise."

It almost killed me, keeping that promise, staying outside, knowing Ethan and Viriato and the others were risking their lives to save my home while I stood in safety and did nothing to help. From where I stood, I could see into the room. I began to despair. The flames seemed unquenchable.

Those servants who could no longer tolerate the heat and smoke of the chamber scurried about the rest of the house, emptying it of valuables lest the fire spread. I joined them, dragging carpets and tapestries and furniture into the courtyard before running back inside to fetch more.

I could not understand how this calamity could have come upon us. There had been no lamps burning in that chamber when I walked out. I had checked the lampstand myself. No one should have gone into my father's office after me. No one had any business in there late at night.

To my unspeakable relief, the tide turned within the half hour. Somehow Ethan and Viriato and the fresh group of workers Ethan had brought with him from his home managed to subdue the flames before they spread into the rest of the house. My father's office lay in utter ruin, but the rest of our home was safe.

Ethan and Viriato looked exhausted. "Are you hurt?" I asked, as soon as they came out.

"Don't fret, mistress," Viriato said, rubbing his head with the fresh towel I had fetched. "I am too robust and Ethan is too stubborn to let a little thing like a fire overcome us. Hardly a scratch on either one."

Ethan drew me under the light of the lamp. "You have burned your lashes and your brows." He touched my forehead gently and I winced at the flash of pain that pierced my flesh. "You've singed the skin. Let me see your hands." He grabbed my wrists and turned my palms over; even I grimaced at the sight. They were blistered and bloody.

"Look at what you've done to yourself."

He made me sit down on the bottom stair and had a servant fetch ointment and clean cloths. With feather-soft strokes he wiped my hand and brow and applied the ointment. I tried not to flinch from the pain.

To distract myself I said, "What started the fire? Could you tell?"

"No. The whole place is annihilated beyond recognition." He took a gulping breath. The soot on his face did not hide his bone-white pallor. "You could have been killed, Elianna. You almost were. Seeing you topple into that wall of fire . . ." He shook his head and left the rest of his sentence hanging.

Before I could answer, Viriato brought the large bundle of fabrics he had managed to pull out of the chamber. Dropping them at my feet, he knelt before me. "I am sorry, mistress. None of this can be salvaged. If the fire didn't get them, the smoke did. There is no way to repair any of it."

I grabbed the corner of a fabric sitting on top of the bunch and pulled. "Not the green with the silver thread! Not the green!" The sight of that beautiful length of cloth, the best thing I had ever produced, blackened by soot and pockmarked by burning embers was my undoing. I put my head in my half-bandaged hands and started to weep.

"Joanna's dowry!" I wailed.

Ethan let me cry my fill. When I ran out of tears, he cupped my chin in his fingers and forced me to look at him. "This must stop. You can't go on like this, on your own. I don't want you to. You think you are protecting me by refusing to marry me. But it hurts me more, having to stand aside and watch you suffer. Enough, Elianna. I want you to marry me. I will help you with the care of your family. We will manage, with God's help."

I opened my mouth. Before I could say a word, he pressed two fingers against my lips to silence me. "I know your favorite word. You are about to say no. Think again, Elianna. I could hold our contract over your head. Threaten you with the courts. But I won't have to. All I have to tell you is that you are breaking my heart by refusing me."

I slumped against him.

"You want to protect me from pain? Then marry me."

I looked up to see eyes bright as gold coins daring me to refuse. I realized I did not want to. I had run out of fight, out of pride, out of arguments. More than anything, I wanted

Ethan. Nodding, I whispered, "I am bringing you a world of trouble for a dowry."

He flashed a smile that made my insides melt. "So long as you come to me, I'll take any dowry you bring."

Viriato rubbed his hands together. "Does this mean we are finally going to have some roasted lamb around here?"

I had forgotten he still sat near us and had witnessed the whole exchange. My sandals seemed to offer sudden fascination, and I bent to adjust them. "After this fire, you should thank God if I can afford to serve boiled turnips," I mumbled.

He rubbed his belly. "Then I suppose suckling pig would be out of the question?"

"Yes!" Ethan and I cried together. I grinned. For the span of a whole hour I made myself believe that my troubles were coming to an end.

⁂

"Thank the Lord you took those lengths of fabric with you, or there would be nothing left," I said to Joanna as we scrubbed the walls. Every corner of the house seemed to have become covered in oily ash. Our home stank of its pungent smell. We had been cleaning for three days straight and it still would not leave.

"I wish I had left everything in the workshop. Our whole stock would have survived if I had."

"We should praise God for sparing our lives." Joanna adjusted the knot in her scarf. "And we still have a roof over our heads."

"You are right, little sister. Things could have been much worse. Sometimes I forget that reality. And I forget to be thankful, too."

"Elianna? Did we lose the money for my dowry in the fire?"

"Don't fret about that. Ethan and I will take care of you and Chuza."

"I am sorry I am a burden to you."

I dropped my rag and wrapped my arms around her tiny waist. "How can you be a burden to me? You are God's sweet blessing."

"I want to help. Put me to work in the workshop. I am certain I can learn quickly."

I laughed. "We aren't that desperate yet. I might give you some embroidery as soon as we have more fabric."

The afternoon had turned unusually hot; you couldn't tell we stood at the threshold of winter. I felt sticky with sweat; the smell of soot clung to every part of my body. In my chamber, I washed quickly and pulled out a fresh tunic from my chest with haphazard haste. A rectangular piece of purple fabric, caught in the folds of the tunic, floated in the air before landing on the carpet. For a moment, I did not recognize it. It was a deep shade of purple, with just the right hint of scarlet. Where had I seen it before? And then I remembered.

Lydia's gift.

Months had passed since the night she gave it to me. Of course it had sat in the protection of a closed chest. Still, the color had not faded; the texture remained soft and inviting.

Its vibrant, supple folds hinted at extravagance. I rubbed it between my fingers thoughtfully.

"Joanna, put on your veil. We are going to visit Master Ezer."

❀

I stopped to talk to Ethan first, seeking his advice before plunging ahead with my plan. This new scheme offered both opportunity and danger. My father, I knew, would have avoided exposing our trade to such risk. Ethan was a different kind of man. More daring, more willing to try new things, and less fearful of failure. He never took foolish chances. But he did not allow a good opportunity to pass him by, either.

I knew that if he agreed with my scheme, we stood a chance at recouping our losses from the fire. A sliver of a chance. A tiny shadow of a chance. But a chance.

Ethan listened to me patiently, as he always did, before examining Lydia's cloth with care. The corner of his mouth tipped up. "We have everything to gain and little to lose. You should do it, Elianna."

"Are you certain? It's the last of our money. And if I am wrong . . . !" I shook my head. "I could bury my father's business for good."

"Or save it. It's a promising plan. Worthy of my clever Elianna." He touched the tips of his fingers to the back of my hand in a brief caress. "Now go and speak to my father."

I had lost all interest in speaking to his father. I wanted to linger and ask like a foolish child if he really thought I was clever. And he knew it, the wretch. I could tell from his wolfish smile that he hoped I would ask for further assurance so that he could pounce on my desire for compliments with a teasing retort.

I sniffed and walked away. It didn't help to have his laughter ringing in my ear as I turned my back.

⁂

"Yes, I did cave in and order some of that purple dye in the end, in spite of my best intentions to resist it. Ethan talked me into taking a gamble. The dye arrived last month, but as I feared, even Ethan has not been able to sell it. No one wants to take a chance on a new dye from an unknown supplier. Especially purple. Many of us have at some point tried Thyatiran purple and been disappointed. Eumenes's dye may be half the price of the royal purple derived from shells, but it is still quite an outlay of money. Our merchants prefer to spend their coin on surer prospects." Master Ezer scratched his chin. "Are you interested in trying it, Elianna?"

"Perhaps. How much do you have?"

Master Ezer's supply was thankfully small. I took a deep breath and plunged. "I will take the whole of it."

"Don't want any competition?" He gave me a toothy smile.

"Not just yet, Master Ezer."

"I will give it to you for what it cost me, including taxes and transport. I need not make any profit just yet." He held up his hand to silence me as soon as I opened my mouth. "Hear me out, child. Once the other merchants see how well your fabric sells, they will be climbing the walls of my shop to

196

get their hands on the new supply. You are doing me a favor, you see, promoting a dye I could not sell at the best of prices.

"In fact, I am so certain of your success that I will place a large order with Eumenes in time for the arrival of the spring wool. After seeing your substantial sales, others will want a taste of the new color. Then it will be my turn to make a little profit of my own."

I knew his generosity had more to do with pity than business acumen. Given our enormous loss in the fire and the fact that I would finally be his daughter-in-law in less than a month, he wanted to come to my aid while sparing my pride. In truth, for the sake of my family, I could afford no pride. I accepted his generosity without demur. In spite of his help, I was risking the last of our available cash to pay the modest sum Master Ezer had demanded.

I prayed that I would not bring ruin to my family. *Lord, for the sake of Joanna and Ethan and my mother and father, please bless this enterprise. Please don't allow me to commit an error that will bring greater hardship upon the head of my family.*

That was when the trembling started. I began to shiver even in the heat of the day, and not even the warmest clothes could stop the quaking of my limbs.

SEVENTEEN

For the enemy has pursued my soul;
he has crushed my life to the ground;
he has made me sit in darkness like those long dead.
therefore my spirit faints within me;
my heart within me is appalled.

PSALM 143:3-4

FOR THE FIRST WEEK after the fire, we dined at Master Ezer's house every day. Jerusha had pronounced our home uninhabitable for seven days and insisted that we eat there.

I found the mealtimes awkward, for I could not forget Avigail's harsh words. *Joseph died under her care,* she had accused. What had she said that was untrue? Yet I could not forgive her. Resentment and a dread of another tongue-lashing made me keep as far from her as I could.

It proved difficult. She and Daniel often joined the rest of the family, bringing with them their baby. They had named him Isaac, which fit the child to perfection, for he smiled often, showing off his toothless gums.

One evening I arrived at Master Ezer's home, wilting

and disheveled, for I had had no time to change my clothes after my long hours of labor. Mistress Jerusha had invited a large company, most of whom were Avigail's relatives, visiting from Galilee. Embarrassed by my rumpled appearance, I found a spot toward the lower end of the spread, as far away from the guests of honor as I could manage. To my surprise, Avigail joined me, Isaac at her breast.

"What do you think of my son, Elianna?" She turned the baby in her arms so that I could see his face better. Isaac flashed his wide smile, fat cheeks dimpling.

I shook my head. "He could melt a stone with that smile. You are truly blessed."

"If you had married Ethan instead of making him wait all this time, you could have had one of your own by now."

I sealed my lips, reciting David's words in my mind: *"I will guard my mouth with a muzzle, so long as the wicked are in my presence."* As far as it concerned me, Avigail was *the wicked.* Saul's medium in Endor had probably been a close relation. And yet, what would it gain me to offend her? It could only cause exasperation for Ethan and his brother, Daniel.

Close to the head of the wide spread laid out on the floor, I noticed a young woman seated with her hands folded in her lap, her feet tucked demurely beneath her. She lifted her head for a moment. Her large brown eyes fixed on Ethan before she lowered them. Her cheeks turned red. A few moments later, she sought him out with another mute glance. Ethan had moved to the far side of the chamber by then. She searched the room, her eyes wide until they found him. I recognized that look—hungry, longing. I must have looked at Ethan the same way a thousand times myself.

"Who is that young woman?" I asked Avigail. "The one with the cinnamon veil and brown tunic."

"That is my cousin Sarai. She and her parents have come from Galilee to visit Jerusalem."

"She is very pretty."

"Yes. Even Ethan says so, and he is hard to impress."

"Ethan said that?"

"This very morning." Avigail caressed Isaac's cheek. "I think if it weren't for the fact that he honors the covenant made between your father and his, he would look her way with more interest than he allows himself now. It is selfish of you, Elianna, to keep him hanging for so long. He is neither able to enjoy the joys of marriage nor free to pursue them with another."

"The wedding is to take place in a month, Avigail."

"You've said that before. I will believe it when it actually takes place. You are almost nineteen! Soon you will be past marriageable age, if you are not already. Poor Ethan. It is only his honor that binds him to you."

I sprang to my feet. "Pardon, Avigail. I forgot to give our steward some important directions."

I grabbed Joanna by the hand and dragged her with me. "We are going home."

Joanna stuffed the rest of her bread into her mouth. Her cheek puffed up to one side. "But I haven't finished eating, Elianna! They are about to serve fowl with capers. My favorite. Can't you wait a little?"

"No. You can stay if you are so hungry. I am for home."

"What are you doing?" Ethan blocked our path, his brow puckered in puzzlement. "Surely you can't be leaving yet. You barely ate anything."

"I am tired," I said.

Ethan didn't budge. His brows lowered. "Was it Avigail? I saw her sitting next to you. Did she say something to offend you again?"

"Peace, Ethan. I only wish for my bed."

Ethan hesitated for a moment, then swiveled to the side and swept an arm before him with mock formality. I noticed Sarai staring at us, her lovely face softened with sweet yearning. She seemed like an amiable young woman. I wished she would get on a cart and drive all the way to Egypt and remain there to keep the pharaohs company.

Once our orders of fresh wool and flax arrived, work on the new fabrics consumed every spare moment. The inspiration behind my plan came from the Lord's Temple. As a woman I had, of course, never set eyes on the curtain that separated the Holy of Holies from the rest of the Temple. But I had heard its description read from the Book of the Law. Thick, twined linen of blue and purple and scarlet yarn with cherubim skillfully worked into them.

Lydia's purple scarf had put me in mind of that reading, and I had determined to create wool and linen fabrics in various shades of those three colors, only. No greens, yellows, oranges, or pinks for us this season. Instead we would focus on three principal colors, presented together to potential buyers in order to enhance each one. If the Lord had chosen those three colors to hang next to each other, I felt certain the result would be something deeply appealing to the human heart.

Further enhancing my scheme was the affordable but high-quality purple. No one in Jerusalem had access to that dye but us. We would sell an absolutely unique offering, accessible to anyone with a reasonably good income, unlike the well-known purple derived from sea snails that only the wealthiest of aristocrats could afford.

As we created our first set of samples in wool and linen and artfully arranged them in swathes against a wooden background painted in gold, it became obvious that each fabric magnified the beauty of the others. Like the scales of exotic fish from faraway lands I had heard Ethan speak of, our fabrics shimmered with beauty and grace, melting from one shade into another.

Most of our customers ordered all three colors. They simply could not choose between them. We had more orders in that first week for our collection than we had received for any other offering we had produced in years past.

Some of the awful fear that I had been carrying began to melt away. I finally started to believe that I had not bankrupted my father's business and, indeed, had saved it.

I thought of the hand of God that must have carried this plan and his wisdom that had been at the very root of it. For the first time I acknowledged that God himself had saved us. Not my cleverness or Ethan's boldness, but the immeasurable kindness of God. How many times had we come to the brink of disaster and he had brought us through? How many times had this business almost sunk beyond recovery and he rescued us? I gave a prayer of thanksgiving that afternoon when Viriato brought me the full stack of orders he had been collecting for several days.

Ethan came the morning our first pieces were finished and ready for delivery. He chose a length of purple linen and another of scarlet and set them aside for his personal use. When he insisted on paying full price for each length, I lost patience.

"You shall not pay me. In a week, when we are wed, all this will belong to you. I must say I did not suspect you would fancy these shades. I have never seen you wear anything this colorful."

He smiled. "Much too feminine for me. It is a gift."

"Who is it for?" I asked suspiciously. I did not like the idea of him buying such glorious fabrics for another woman. They were not for Jerusha, who preferred plainer colors and declared herself too old for such vibrant shades. An unbidden image of Sarai's face floated before my eyes.

He laughed out loud. "Never mind that. Just sell me the cloth."

I scowled. "Fine. Give me your money, if you insist. It will return to your purse next week."

He ignored my outburst, which goaded me further. "She must be very ugly," I said, as I noted down his order in my scroll.

"Who?"

"The woman for whom you are purchasing these."

He sprawled on the couch and reached for a grape. "What makes you think that?"

"Only an ugly woman would need this much luxury to make her look acceptable," I said, forgetting that only hours before the beautiful Claudia had ordered a chestful of similar colors.

He plopped another grape into his mouth. "She is as skinny as a broom plant, and I am quite certain she has warts."

"You are lying! I can tell by the way you are trying to hold in your laughter. Who are the fabrics for? Tell me!"

"They are yours, you goose. You will look beautiful in them. Not even the queen of Sheba in all her glory could compare to you, arrayed in these colors. If your mother and mine work together, they might be able to make you a tunic in time for our wedding."

"Queen of Sheba!" I stared at my stained shoes poking out from under the folds of my long skirts. "Maybe more like her slave girl, fresh from a backwater village." In spite of my words, I flushed with pleasure, amazed that his first thought had been for me rather than business when he had seen our creations. I started to grin and then stopped. "I do not have any warts!"

"You shall have to prove that on our wedding night."

※

The next day dawned with no warning of the catastrophe it brought. The sky looked the same as it did every other morning; the birds sang the same noisy song they did with every other sunrise. How could I have known that hours thence my whole world would collapse around me? How could I have suspected that my heart was about to shatter into jagged pieces? Nor would I have believed that by my own hand and my own choice I would bring this disaster upon us.

I rose from bed earlier than I wanted, dressed quickly, and dashed to the workshop. My mother and Jerusha had agreed to take care of all the wedding details between them, leaving Ethan and me free to deal with our increasingly demanding trades. Near noon, Viriato left to meet with Ethan; I did not expect to see either of them until later that evening for supper.

I returned to the house for a quick repast and to write a letter to a trusted flax merchant, requesting another order. Because we ordered our flax already seeped and dried, we could receive shipments at any time during the year. Dried flax did not have to depend on the harvest season, but could be stored for months.

The letter took longer than I expected as I could not locate the merchant's previous accounts in my father's papers. One of the graces of God the night of the fire had been the preservation of the account books and papers. I had carried them to my room that night with the intention of working on them. But for that opportune accident, they would have burned to ashes in the fire along with everything else, throwing our affairs into frustrating confusion.

Finally I found the papers I needed and finished composing the letter. I decided to visit my father for a short while, telling him about our sales in the new colors and how our income ensured that we would have enough money to secure Joanna's wedding.

I ran my hand through his thinning hair. "Ethan and I will be married in a week, Abba." And he would not be present to see it. Would he have cared, if he had been healthy enough to attend?

I was on my way to the workshop when Calvus stopped me in the garden. He had not been to the house in several weeks. I guessed that he felt uncomfortable about his own conduct during our last interaction when he had screamed at me and stormed off. His absence had been a relief to me. I wished he had continued to stay away.

He planted himself in my path to prevent me from walking on. I attempted to dissuade him with a forceful glare. As always, however, Calvus was immune to my annoyance.

"I am told you almost perished in the fire," he said.

I crossed my arms over my chest. "Disappointed?"

"Don't be foolish. It would have been a terrible waste for something so beautiful to have been destroyed."

I rolled my eyes.

He grinned. "Always impervious to my honeyed words. Tell me, do you know how the fire started?"

"No. That remains a mystery."

"Perhaps you forgot to extinguish your lamp."

"Of course I did not. I did not start that fire."

"Well, it came from somewhere. Perhaps Jupiter sent you a thunderbolt from the sky because you are so vexing."

"If any thunderbolts were to come from your imaginary gods, they would be headed your way, Calvus. No doubt you are much more deserving of their wrath. Now, I must get to the workshop. Even if you have time to linger and do nothing, I need to keep busy if I am to pay the mountain of taxes that keeps your Caesar happy."

I don't know why I goaded him. Growing up in a nation that had tasted the sting of conquest for almost a hundred years had taught us to keep our resentment to ourselves. I had never treated a Roman with such flagrant disrespect.

Instead of stepping out of my way, he stepped closer. I could feel the calluses in his skin as he drew his finger softly down my brow, where the fire had left a red mark. "Must have hurt."

I moved back. "Calvus, you know better than to touch a Jewish woman. Please let me pass."

With a sudden move, his hands clasped about my arms and pulled me forward. I started to struggle, my heart thumping in alarm. His hold felt like steel shackles around me. "What are you doing?" I choked, kicking at his shins. My blows landed against the hard leather of his boots, hurting my feet more than his legs.

"What I should have done months ago. Teaching you a lesson."

"I don't need a lesson. Leave me be, Roman."

He laughed and pulled me against him. "You smell good. You look even better. And now I am going to find out how you taste."

I knew he was playing with me. But I did not know how

far his unpredictable nature would take this awful game. To my horror, he placed his lips against mine. His kiss was hot and indescribably invasive.

I struggled with my whole might. Bile rose up in my throat. At some point in our wild wrestling, my veil had come undone and fallen to the ground. Calvus shoved his hand into my hair and pulled with vicious strength. I squealed with pain.

"Be still and I will stop hurting you. One kiss. That is all I ask. Stop struggling and it will be over before you know it."

I pushed at him with hampered arms and tried to bite him. He laughed. "You know little about men. This struggle merely incites me to more. It is in your own interest to hold still. Who knows? You might even like it. I doubt your Ethan has ever touched you like a real man."

"Pig," I spat.

"You will regret that. When I turn my hand against your precious family, you will regret your sharp tongue and wild ways."

His words scourged me like the iron hook at the end of a Roman whip. I stopped struggling. He could do it. He had the power and authority to make life unbearable for us. I stood there, trembling with rage and impotence as he kissed me with a cruel intimacy that made me hate him more than I had ever hated another human being.

Then, with sudden force, we were ripped apart. Confused by the jolt of our separation, I blinked. What I saw made me wish for death. Before me stood Ethan and Viriato. They were both trembling with uncontrollable rage. Their faces were stamped with the violence that boiled in their blood.

I knew in that moment that nothing would ever be the same again.

EIGHTEEN

Be gracious to me, O LORD, for I am in distress;
my eye is wasted from grief;
my soul and my body also.
For my life is spent with sorrow,
and my years with sighing.

PSALM 31:9-10

BEFORE I COULD MOVE, Calvus crouched, pulling out his Spanish sword with such speed that his movements became a blur. In his other hand, he clutched a short dagger. His jaw stood out in a pugnacious square of bone and muscle, the veins purplish beneath his shadowed skin. His lips were still wet from our kisses.

"No!" I screamed and threw myself in front of Ethan like a shield. "Stop!"

I was seeing cinnabar mines. Imagining Viriato and Ethan as slaves on a galley ship. If they didn't die of a sword wound right now, they would surely perish as slaves. I thought of my Ethan languishing in the poisonous air of a sulfur mine and choked as if I were breathing that very air.

"Move, Elianna," Ethan said with deadly quiet.

211

Viriato took a step forward, his massive body tense and ready for battle. The mild-mannered Viriato I knew had vanished. This man looked like a volcano about to burst with red-hot lava.

"Keep out of this, Viriato. This is my fight," Ethan said.

Viriato clenched his fist. For a moment he hesitated irresolutely, as if unable to obey Ethan's demand. Then he gave an infinitesimal nod and stepped away. Ethan wrapped his arms about my waist and lifted me bodily to set me aside.

My mouth turned to ashes. He was about to get himself killed. His life would be destroyed even if he survived physical battle with a Roman centurion. Love and terror for him rose up like a storm in my heart until I could not breathe. He stood at the edge of a precipice, about to shatter himself against the craggy rocks at the bottom.

For my sake, for the sake of revenge and masculine pride, he was about to ruin his future. I could not stand aside and do nothing. I had to stop him at any price. In the urgency of the moment, I could think of only one way. One sure defense. Even then I knew. I knew the price I would pay. I knew I was about to destroy my own world.

"Ethan, listen."

"Be quiet and get out of our way. Viriato, hold her and don't let her loose until we are finished."

"Ethan, I wanted him! I wanted him to kiss me."

He came to a stop. His eyes had turned very dark, like brown soil on a frozen winter morning. "You lie."

"Did you see me struggle? Did you see me try to fight him off?"

"He held you." His voice didn't sound sure anymore. Doubt had started to crack through his confidence. "He held you imprisoned."

"He did not. He asked to kiss me. I gave my permission freely."

Ethan's skin had turned pasty. Sweat stood out on his brow. "Why?" It came out a whimper, a soft, keening sound of pain. Sharper than a dagger, that little word sliced me to my very soul.

"Because I wanted him."

Ethan shook his head, looking confused. "It's not true."

"Why do you think I kept delaying our wedding? It was him I yearned for."

Decimus Calvus had straightened out of his battle pose, holding his weapons in a relaxed grip. Softly, he started to laugh. "I was looking forward to a good fight, woman. You are cheating me of the pleasure of breaking a few of his bones."

"Leave him be. There's been enough damage today." Enough to last my whole life. I felt as if my veins were slowly filling with ice. As long as I live, I will never forget the look in Ethan's eyes. That dazed look of betrayal and anguish, mixing with the lingering embers of rage.

Ethan took a shuddering breath. Without another word, he turned on his heel and walked away. Viriato gave me a hard stare. A wave of nausea overcame me. Swinging around, I fell to my knees and retched until my convulsing stomach emptied what little I had eaten. I laid my head against the bark of a tree, weak and shuddering. I had no strength left.

Calvus extended a piece of clean linen to me. I slapped at his hand. "Leave me be."

"Come, mistress," Viriato said, pulling me to my feet. "Come into the house."

I nodded and followed him, leaving Calvus in the garden. To my relief, the Roman let me go without objection. I moved in a fog, unaware of my surroundings, pressed forward only by Viriato's urgent manner. He saw me inside the house, told me to bar the door, and left at a run. I knew he had gone to Ethan to try to comfort him. Comfort him for the anguish I had caused him.

When the violence of my emotions subsided a little, I considered writing Ethan a letter, confessing the truth. Surely he would believe me. Now that the immediate rage of the moment had cooled, he would be more reasonable. More willing to forget Calvus's violation. I could not bear for Ethan to think so ill of me. I could not bear to leave him to suffer the anguish of betrayal.

The more I pondered the choices before me, however, the less confident I became. This was the Ethan who did not forget or let go of what mattered to him. The Ethan who had set aside every last copper coin I had paid him because of his stubborn pride. The Ethan who insisted Viriato come and work for me because *my* money had purchased his freedom. Ethan was single-minded when he wanted something.

Would such a man let go of Decimus Calvus's offense? Would he just walk away for the sake of peace and sanity?

The Ethan I knew would not forgive Calvus's invasion with impunity. The man who had approached my attacker with chilling, intractable violence would not let this go.

Nor would Calvus, with his uncertain temper and changeable moods, back down. He would not apologize. Would not try to calm the waters of the storm in Ethan's chest. He would churn them all the more. There would be a fight. The Roman would destroy Ethan. Even if Ethan won the battle, he would be arrested, put in chains, sold into slavery, and sent to a slow death in a godforsaken land too far for me to ever find.

I could not chance it. I could not trust Ethan to know the truth and walk away. Jewish men did not accept the molestation of their women by Roman soldiers. Even a hundred years of occupation had not turned them into tame dogs, accepting their master's blows with equanimity. Ethan would demand justice. And he would not receive it from Rome. They would be unlikely to punish a centurion for daring a bit of frolic with a Jewish maiden. No. Ethan would not turn to Rome for help.

To protect him, I must wound him myself. I must cheat us out of the happiness of marriage. Our future together sacrificed for the sake of a future for him. I turned cold at the thought of life without him. Never to set eyes on his beloved face again, never to kiss those lips that spoke such kindness to me, never to hold the hands that had been my strength and guide through life's hardest moments. That was my choice, and I had no other.

It occurred to me that the Lord had finally sprung his punishment upon me. With one stroke, he had ripped away my happiness. I had known Ethan deserved a better wife than me. It seemed God agreed. I thought of the sweet Sarai, waiting in the shadows, waiting for the chance to love Ethan. She would surely make a more worthy wife and mother than I ever could. There would be no trouble attached to her like iron chains, no financial worries, no smeared reputation, no shade of a dead brother always accusing. The day would come when Ethan would thank God for escaping a life shackled to me.

I rolled up the empty parchment again and put away my ink without writing a single word. Dry-eyed, I sat in the darkness far into the night and bid love good-bye.

The certificate of divorce arrived a week later. A young scribe brought it to our house and would not surrender it to any hand but mine. Ethan, it seemed, had decided to set me aside quietly, without a scandal. For all that he thought me an adulteress, he had no heart to bare my shame to the world. My life could go on, unchanged. I would never see him again, except perhaps in passing. A glimpse of him at the Temple or in the street. He was gone from me forever. And he had chosen to do it without causing me harm.

It made my love for him grow even deeper, until there was nothing left but the unfulfilled hunger of it. A hundred times a day I told myself that I would go to him and vindicate myself in his eyes. I would beg him to leave Calvus alone and forget that dreadful day. And a hundred times I quashed those longings. In truth, I had become convinced that God wanted better for Ethan, and it was by his will that we had been separated.

My mother and Joanna stared at me with incomprehension when I told them of the divorce. They had no knowledge of what Decimus Calvus had done. I did not wish to cause them more anxiety than they already had to contend with, given my father's condition.

"I do not wish to marry. Ever," I said to them. "It is unfair to keep Ethan hanging any longer. I wanted him to be free to marry another, have children, go on with his life."

"But you love him!" Joanna cried, tears running down her smooth cheeks.

"I do love him," I said. "But I still don't wish to marry him." My lies were piling up higher by the hour.

"I do not understand you, Elianna," my mother said coldly. "Marriage is not only about you. You should have thought of your family before you made such a foolish decision."

She did not speak to me for three days after that. I could not blame her. Unmarried women did not simply ignore the wishes of their parents and make or break legal marriage covenants. But what else could I have said to her? The truth? She would have run to Ethan within the hour with the story. Should I have told her Ethan's version of the events? That I had kissed Calvus by design? I shook my head. Better she think me rebellious and headstrong than a shameless adulteress. It would kill her to believe I had defiled myself with a Roman.

Life had to go on. Joanna's dowry still had to be raised, our taxes paid, our expenses met. I drowned myself in the work as much as I was able. What had once satisfied, delighted, and distracted now became a wooden, grating chore I had to accomplish for the sake of my family. I had no joy in my labors.

Without Ethan and Viriato I did not know how we would survive. I could not meet with customers. Joel helped where he could. But his skills were too limited.

One morning, two weeks after my divorce, Viriato arrived at the house.

I stopped in my tracks. "What are you doing here, Viriato?"

"I've come to lend a hand, mistress."

"Don't be foolish. Ethan will never forgive you. Leave before he finds out."

He rubbed the back of his neck with a broad palm. "He is the one who sent me. He knows you need my help."

I gulped through the lump in my throat. "That much is true. How long can you stay?"

"As long as you need."

"Then stay and welcome." I had no pride left. I had moved beyond dignity, beyond self-respect. It didn't seem to matter that before God I was innocent of the sin of adultery. Shame still covered me like a leper's wounds. I could not scrape it off.

I took a long, shuddering breath and steeled myself to look into Viriato's eyes. I expected to find accusation. Disgust. Distaste. I found none. Instead, he gave me a sad smile and extended his hand. "Come, mistress. Let's not waste more time."

TESSA AFSHAR

Without Viriato, we would no doubt have faced bank-
ruptcy. Once again, he took on the full burden of interact-
ing with the customers. Within a month, we had recouped
our losses. Within six, I had made enough money to pay for
Joanna's dowry and satisfy Caesar's tax collectors.

I had saved my family from absolute disaster. In the process, I had paid a steep price. I had grown weary to the marrow of my bones. Body and soul, weary. I was not yet twenty,
but I felt like a brittle branch about to snap.

✲

Joanna's wedding loomed ahead in two short weeks. As happy
as I was for her, the thought of losing Joanna's companionship robbed me of sleep. I had lost Ethan, and with him,
his parents. Jerusha, who had been like a second mother to
me, now fled from me like one face to face with a violent
criminal. Once, I ran into her in the mikveh. At the first
sight of me, she gathered her things and rushed out, her hair
streaming wet behind her. By piercing her son's heart, I had
pierced hers. My mere presence opened that gaping wound.
I felt like my very being had turned to poison, causing pain
and sorrow wherever I went.

There was no time for friends. I had not seen Claudia in
weeks. It seemed easier to avoid the Jewish companions of
my youth. They would bubble over with questions about my
divorce. Questions I could not face or answer.

Joanna alone remained ever my faithful supporter. If my
mother made a sharp retort, she defended me. If Ethan's parents ignored me in public, she called their actions biased and

cruel. Some nights, she would brush my hair until her arms ached and sing in my ear to soothe me. We had become more than sisters. We were companions of the heart. But she would leave me soon. Viriato came close to being my friend. Still, he was a man, and I could not speak to him of the deeper things of my soul. It would not be proper.

I once asked him why he did not revile me for what I had done. "For Ethan's sake, you should despise me."

He crossed his arms in front of his chest. "Because I saw you after Ethan left. Saw you sick and overcome with more sorrow than I have ever seen on a face so young. I do not understand why you betrayed him, but you have surely paid more than enough already. Besides, that pig of a Roman has never shown his face around here again, and that's something. It is obvious that he never made you happy. Did you send him packing?"

I sighed. "I never invited him in the first place."

Viriato straightened to his impressive height. "Did he force himself on you, after all? Were you lying? If ever I find he—"

"Peace, Viriato," I said hastily. "I did not court him. But once he came, I could not resist him."

Better to grow my pile of lies than risk the lives of those most precious to me.

NINETEEN

You who have made me see many troubles and calamities
will revive me again; from the depths of the earth
you will bring me up again. You will increase my greatness
and comfort me again.

PSALM 71:20-21

MY MOTHER, JOANNA, AND I traveled in a hired caravan
to Tiberias, Herod's brand new capital built on the shores
of the Sea of Galilee. My father had to be left home in the
care of trusted servants, his condition too precarious for such
a journey. Viriato came with us, both to chaperone and to
protect us on our long journey. Besides, the food at Joanna's
wedding promised to be a delight to his discerning appetite.

The Jews refused to call the new capital by its Roman
title, referring to it instead by its old name, Rakkath, a village
mentioned by Joshua himself in his book. Herod Antipas had
rebuilt that ruined village and transformed it into a Greek
fantasy, with spas constructed around mineral hot springs, a
stadium, and a splendid palace to suit his luxurious tastes.

It was said that no good Jew would be willing to live there, for an ancient cemetery had been discovered under its foundations, and the Pharisees declared the whole land unclean because of it.

Since Master Shual served as steward in Herod's palace, he could not be so choosy as the Pharisees would have wished. His family was from Capernaum, north of Tiberias. But the wedding was set to take place in Tiberias, where Chuza and his parents had moved. Joanna would live with them in the addition Chuza had built on his parents' home near the palace.

Chuza had arranged for us to stay in a rented house during our time there. Joanna's trunks, containing her new clothes and rich lengths of cloth I had managed to set aside for her, had been sent ahead to her new home.

On the morning of the wedding, Chuza's mother and younger sister accompanied us to the bath for the ritual washing ceremony. Joanna glowed with joy as we washed her hair and adorned her with jewels. The scent of orange blossoms clung to her smooth skin as we massaged oil into her supple limbs. Her long hair was braided, and we looped gold and silver beads into the silky tresses.

Back in our temporary lodgings, we dressed her in her wedding clothes, starting with a blue tunic heavy with gold embroidery, sewn painstakingly by Joanna's own hands. It had taken her months to complete it. Over the tunic, we placed a large purple mantle attached to her shoulders with gold rosette pins, draping it elegantly around her. We painted her eyes with kohl and added a touch of color to her lips and cheeks. She was crowned with a gold diadem as befit a queen.

Then with slow care we placed a large, opaque veil over her head and face, as tradition required.

We were ready in the early evening when Chuza showed up to collect her, his enthusiastic friends in tow. They made a great deal of noise on their way to the house, blowing trumpets and singing their jubilant songs, so we weren't exactly surprised when they reached the door.

Chuza wore a striped linen tunic cinched at the waist with a belt set with precious stones that twinkled in the lamplight. His cloak matched Joanna's mantle. I had sent him the fabric as a wedding present. On his head, he wore a golden crown, as though he were a monarch, for brides and bridegrooms were to be queens and kings on their wedding day. He took Joanna by the hand, and though he could not see her through that dark veil, his face lit up at the touch of her hand.

Chuza's friends had bedecked the road with burning lamps all the way to Master Shual's house, where the wedding ceremony would take place. Chuza led Joanna with a protective hand, mindful that she could not see well beneath her veil. The rest of us followed, cheering and laughing, teasing the couple when they moved too slowly, and when they sped up to please us, we teased them for being too eager to arrive at their nuptial chamber.

The wedding feast lasted seven days, with rich wine and meals that satisfied even Viriato's fastidious tastes. We sang love songs and listened to the music of the harp and the lute. My favorite memory from that first evening is of the moment Chuza lifted Joanna's veil. His eyes turned round, filling up with moisture when he first saw her sweet face.

One of Chuza's friends sang David's psalm of love, with comical motions that had us doubled over with laughter. He walked over to Chuza, looking soulfully into his eyes, and sang, "You are the most handsome of the sons of men," and then fell at his feet and bowed as though to the potentate of the world, pretending to kiss Chuza's leather sandals.

For the next stanza he turned to Joanna and sang, "The king will desire your beauty. Since he is your lord, bow to him." Then he stopped the song and said, "Go on, little bride. Bow."

When Joanna complied with a dainty bow of her head, he cried, "That won't do! Try going lower. Chuza will need a lot of bowing if he is to be happy."

After the singing concluded, the noisy crowd hushed for the long-awaited moment when the groom declared his intention to claim the bride. Chuza took off his cloak and spread it over my sister to symbolize his lifelong commitment to her. Then, quoting the prophet Ezekiel, he pledged his covenant to Joanna:

"'When I passed by you and saw you, behold, you were at the age for love, and I spread the corner of my garment over you and covered your nakedness; I made my vow to you and entered into a covenant with you . . . and you became mine.'"

Joanna could not look away from Chuza. Their love seemed a tangible thing, holy, sure, loyal. Happiness for my sister welled up within me. At the same time, one corner of my soul shriveled with agony for my own barren life. Once I had dreamt of Ethan speaking those words over me. I would never have that joy now. Bitterness rose to choke me. Bitterness against Decimus Calvus, whose selfish games had destroyed my life. If I could have cursed him to death, I would.

⁂

We saw Joanna happily settled in her new home before returning to Jerusalem. I missed her already. Who would hold me in the night to assuage my loneliness and comfort my fears now? Who would make me special meals and remind me of the good things of life? God had blessed her with the desire of her heart. But her absence left another void in my inmost being.

So many losses. So many absences. And I had nothing with which I could fill the emptiness they left behind.

The day after we returned, my father's friend Gamaliel came to visit him. His popularity as a religious teacher and leader had continued to grow in the past years, keeping him too busy for casual calls. He had not seen my father since the accident. I showed him to my father's chamber.

"I'm afraid he is not well today, Master Gamaliel. He will probably sleep through your visit," I said. I would drop a kidney if he did wake up. Even Gamaliel, for all his holiness, did not carry such a bag of tricks as that. Miracles were the dominion of the old prophets. Israel had not seen a real marvel from God in hundreds of years.

Gamaliel knelt by my father's bed. His brow puckered. "I had not realized he was as bad as this. They say he continues to work."

"The workshop has been busy," I said.

He gave me a sharp glance from under bushy eyebrows.

"I see. I will pray for him. And for you, Mistress Elianna. It seems you have your hands full."

"Thank you, master."

I left him to his prayers. A shiver of discomfort ran down my spine when I remembered the shrewd look he had given me. Not much escaped those eyes, I was sure. He must have noticed that the man lying on that mattress had slipped far beyond the waking world. One word from him, and our business would collapse. He possessed that much influence.

At least Joanna was safe and settled. I still needed to take care of my parents, however. If we lost the trade, we would also lose the house. Without income, Roman taxes could not be paid. I shook my head. Would our financial pressures never cease? Would money always have a stranglehold on me?

Gamaliel found me in my father's old office. I sprang to my feet when he entered. "Master Gamaliel," I stammered. "I . . . was just looking for some papers for my father to look over later." The lie came out of my mouth in stilted syllables.

"No doubt. No doubt. Be at your ease, child. Your father is blessed to have a daughter he can rely on in his hour of trouble."

My clenched muscles relaxed infinitesimally at that pronouncement. I continued to stand like a tree trunk, not knowing how to comport myself. Women did not often receive the honor of a visitation from a member of the Sanhedrin.

"Your betrothal to Ethan Ben Ezer was annulled, I am told."

I felt the color leave my cheeks. "Yes, my lord."

"He never said why."

"I am sure he had good reason." I would have drunk a chalice full of ink if it meant I could avoid this conversation.

With no small apprehension I saw him settle into a chair. Crossing his legs, he looked at me expectantly. "Why do you not explain it to me?"

"Perhaps it would be best if you asked him."

He shrugged. "I choose to ask you."

"He deserved a better wife." I stared at the fringe of the carpet.

"In what way?"

"Master Gamaliel?"

"Yes, child?"

"I cannot speak of this."

"What if I were to tell you that I would not reveal your secret, no matter what it may be? There would be no punishment, no stoning, no condemnation. Merely a confession between you and me."

"I don't understand. Aren't teachers of the Law supposed to uphold the righteousness of Israel? Aren't they responsible for the moral well-being of its people?"

He smiled. Under the thickness of his mustache and beard, that tiny contraction of the lips was almost lost. "Why don't you let me worry about my responsibilities? I have given you my word. What do you have to lose?"

My knees began to shake. The thought of sharing my secret just once with a living soul, sharing it with impunity, without fear of endangering Ethan's life, proved too great a temptation. My words tumbling out in an awkward jumble, I told Gamaliel the truth about what had taken place on that dreadful afternoon and the tragic decision I had been forced to make.

Gamaliel covered his face with the palm of his hand. "If you had told me earlier, I would have tried to intercede on your behalf. I would have reasoned with Ethan and made sure that he would not retaliate against the Roman. In the place of your father, I would have done my best to help you." He shook his head. "It is too late. I can do nothing now."

I frowned. "What do you mean?"

"Ethan was betrothed last week while you were in Galilee for your sister's wedding. The wedding is set for a month hence. They don't wish to wait. I cannot meddle in their affairs now. He would be caught in an impossible position. The new contract is legal and binding and cannot be broken even by your tragic tale."

My knees gave out and I sank onto the stool opposite my guest. I had known this day would come. I thought I had prepared my heart for it. But nothing can prepare you for a stab from a dull knife.

"Is it Sarai?" I asked.

"Yes. You know her?"

"She is lovely."

"She seems very smitten with him. I pray she will make him a good wife."

"I pray he will be happy. More than any man I know, he deserves that." My throat ached. My head ached. My soul ached.

"I brought something for your father. But perhaps you can use it more." He gave me a thick sheaf of rolled-up vellum. "Various readings from the Law and the Prophets. I had thought it might cheer and guide him in his sickness. But I suspect he is well past that. I pray the words in these pages shall bring you comfort."

"You are giving the Scriptures to a woman?"

He slapped his thick fingers against his knees and rose. "I think in this case, God would not disapprove."

After he left, I thought of Master Gamaliel's words to me: *"In the place of your father, I would have done my best to help you."* I had no father to help me. To protect me. To provide for me. To give me guidance. I had no father because he lay unconscious and sick. But in truth, long before his accident, I had lost my father. I had lost him one sunny day on a hilltop, when I had failed to care for my brother. At the core of my life's troubles lay this wound. I was fatherless.

Master Gamaliel's scroll was written in Koine Greek, not Hebrew. After having been enslaved in Babylon for more than a generation, many of our people had forgotten their native tongue. We spoke Aramaic and understood Greek. But Hebrew had been lost to the average Judean. I could not read it and only had a cursory understanding.

The Greek tongue came easy to me, however, and I began to read Gamaliel's scroll with a passion I had never known for God's Word. For the first time, the Scriptures began to resonate in my soul not merely as a set of rules I had to obey, but also as an impartation of comfort.

You who have made me see many troubles and
    calamities
  will revive me again;
  from the depths of the earth
  you will bring me up again.
You will increase my greatness
  and comfort me again.

Would the God who had allowed so much calamity and trouble to be heaped upon me truly comfort and revive me? A tiny ember of hope kindled within me.

Until then, I had a form of religiosity based entirely on performance and lacking any heart. I was fully aware of the deficiencies in my life. I had sinned in countless ways. My own father never forgave me. What was the point of trying to draw near to God? Who wants to approach a God who will only remind you of what a failure you are? Who wants to draw near to the voice of disapproval and condemnation? I had run as far from him as I could since Joseph's death.

Now, as I read the Scriptures that Gamaliel had brought me, I began to realize that there was more to God than an angry judge. I could not fully accept that his love extended to me, but I began to hunger for more of him. Aspire that he might one day forgive me and restore me. Caring for my family wasn't enough to satisfy me. The work to which I had once devoted myself had disappointed me in the end. I came to realize that the God I found in the Scriptures might be my only source of comfort. I read his Word voraciously and clung to that spark of promise.

TWENTY

O God, save me by your name,
and vindicate me by your might.
O God, hear my prayer;
give ear to the words of my mouth.

PSALM 54:1-2

DROUGHT CRIPPLED JERUSALEM that summer. The winter rains had proven stingy, and the waters of the Gihon, the spring east of Jerusalem that bestowed its bounty upon us, banked low. All the pools in Jerusalem, including the upper pool, the lower pool, the old pool, and the King's Pool, which had been channeled into the spring of Gihon, were at a low ebb. Lack of water was always a real threat in Palestine. It made our people restless. We were too aware that our lives hung in the balance when our springs and rivers began to dry up.

Roman oppression, despite its severity and injustice, did bring us a few advantages. Besides better trade and improved roads, they offered us their aqueducts and built us larger, more efficient pools. Godless and cruel they might be, but no one could deny they were exceptional engineers. We were grateful that the rectangular pool of Siloam, with its dazzling architecture and elegant columns, was large enough to supply many of Jerusalem's residents with water, even during a season of drought.

Our workshop depended upon generous supplies of water in order to function. Dyeing fabrics often required several thorough washings. I had to pay a bribe more than once in order to provide for our needs. I was beginning to understand that running a business came with a constant stream of problems. Trouble was not an oddity or exception. The life of a merchant was pervaded with unforeseen challenges as a matter of routine. Only those who could meet the demands of new problems on a daily basis could survive in trade. Good planning helped. But life came with too many surprises for even the best of plans to foresee. I was kept busy from morning to night, trying to keep our business afloat.

One afternoon Viriato arrived with Claudia and Titus in tow. "I have not seen you in over two months, you truant friend," Claudia said. "What have you been doing with yourself?"

"Forgive me, Claudia." I rolled back the vellum I was studying. "I have been sorely remiss. And Titus! How wonderful of you to visit as well."

"Visit, nothing. I need a new wardrobe. I have been summoned to Rome."

"No! Are you finally to be given a position worthy of your talents?"

"Or have my head chopped off. Who can tell with Sejanus at the helm? Either way, I aim to go looking my best. They shall not accuse me of having turned into a country bumpkin during my absence from Rome."

I surveyed his elegantly clad figure. "That would be an impossibility. Is Claudia coming with you?"

Claudia cried, "Yes," while Titus very emphatically declared, "No" at the same time. I looked from one to the other and swallowed a smile. "I see the matter is still being negotiated. Viriato, shall we start a wager? What odds do you give Claudia?"

Titus groaned. "Please, Elianna. Do not encourage the woman. It is simply too dangerous for her in Rome. If good news greets me, I will send for her. If an ill reception awaits me, I want her out of the way of danger."

"If there is any danger to you, my love, I would all the more be at your side." Claudia removed a stack of papyri from the desk and daintily sat against the edge. She tried to look at ease and lighthearted, but I noticed the tracks of dried tears against the pallor of her face. Titus, too, when I observed him more carefully, seemed tense and apprehensive beneath his normal smile. The trip to Rome alarmed them both more than they wished to reveal. I frowned, worried for their safety.

"Tell me, Viriato, shall you lay odds on my husband or on me?" Claudia said.

Viriato shook his head. "Neither, mistress. I am not a

betting man. I work too hard for my money. Besides, no matter which one of you I choose, one of you will be offended by me. Those are not good odds."

Titus and Claudia laughed. Claudia picked up Gamaliel's gift, which I had just set aside. "Are you still working on those troublesome accounts, Elianna?"

"The only accounting recorded in that book concerns the one we will one day have to give to God. Those are some of our Scriptures."

She placed the roll back next to me with haste. "I beg your pardon. I meant no disrespect."

"Would you like to hear some of the words I have been studying lately?"

"Is there anything in there about disobedient wives?" Titus asked. "If so, I should like to hear what punishment your God accords to them."

Claudia sniffed. "I am more interested in what it says about disobliging husbands."

"Perhaps we can leave husbands and wives to a later date. I had just finished reading this psalm when you arrived. It was written by our greatest king, David. He wrote it when he was still a young man, before he became a powerful monarch. As a warrior, he had saved Israel from great danger and had grown popular with the people because of it. He was talented and handsome, champion and poet and musician rolled in one. God had blessed David.

"At that time, the king over Israel was a man named Saul. Saul grew jealous of David until he could no longer bear the anguish of his envy and set out to destroy the young man who had become his rival. This psalm is not merely a poem. It is a prayer. A prayer that has lasted over a thousand years. As long as men like you, Titus, are being pursued unjustly by powerful, despotic rulers, the prayers of David breathe life and power into our hearts. Listen. Here is what he said to the Lord:

"O God, save me by your name,
    and vindicate me by your might.
O God, hear my prayer;
    give ear to the words of my mouth.
For strangers have risen against me;
    ruthless men seek my life;
    They do not set God before themselves.
Behold, God is my helper;
    the Lord is the upholder of my life . . .
I will give thanks to your name, O Lord, for it is good.
    For he has delivered me from every trouble."

"Did your God save David from his enemies?" Titus asked.

"That he did. Once, David had the opportunity to kill Saul stealthily. But he refused to raise his hand against the Lord's anointed. He would not become wicked in order to destroy wickedness. He trusted God to protect him. To vindicate his reputation and his life. And God did so. Saul died in a terrible battle. He paid for his sins in the end, as we all shall, no doubt. As Sejanus will one day. David, now—he ascended the throne of Israel and lived to be an old man and became a father to many sons."

"I like this God of yours. He seems less mercurial than the ones we have in our pantheon. Too bad he will have no interest in helping a Roman."

I shrugged. "Who knows the mind of God? You remember the great Persian king, Cyrus?"

"Of course. We had to study many of his battle strategies when I was a boy at school. Was he a follower of the Lord?"

I grinned. "No more than you, I should imagine. Just before Cyrus rose to power and eminence, one of our prophets by the name of Isaiah spoke a prophecy about him, promising him God's help.

"I am the Lord, and there is no other,
     besides me there is no God;
I equip you, though you do not know me.

"God vowed to give him victory, you see, Titus. Although Cyrus did not know the Lord, God pledged to go before him and level the ground that he might be triumphant, for he would one day help our people. Perhaps the Lord will do the same for you."

I could not understand my own actions. Why speak of the Lord to Romans when I barely spoke to him myself? I realized that I had come to believe in the mercy of God, believe it for Romans even, though I still could not grasp it for myself. I loved Claudia and Titus in spite of their dreadful heritage. I cared not that they were Roman. I wished them to have the salvation of our God and the help of his hand. I wanted them safe from the murderous ploys of their enemy, Sejanus. Who was greater than the greatest man in Rome? Only the Lord.

"Why does your God insist that there is no other god? Even Jupiter for all his power acknowledges the existence of other gods." Claudia played with the stem of a fig. "He sounds very limiting. It has to be him alone, to the exclusion of all others. Why should I give up Juno and Apollo and Venus if I want to pray to your God? Why can't I have them all?"

"Why have you forsaken all other men in order to be with Titus? Because he is your husband, and your heart and your body belong to him. You need no other man. He loves you, and he alone fulfills your needs. It is the same with the Lord, only more so, for he is a thousand times more loving, more protective, more glorious, more powerful than your wonderful husband. He would not put up with you chasing after other gods any more than Titus would accept you taking lovers."

Titus threw his head back and laughed. "Well, that puts you in your place, my love. I begin to understand this God a little better, I think." He played with the leather strap of his belt. "Would he receive an offering from me, do you think, Elianna? A libation in his honor? Perhaps it would soften his heart toward my cause."

I scratched my forehead. "I am no teacher of the Law. But as I recall, one of our greatest prophets, Samuel, once said that to obey is better than sacrifice. Why do you not pray and ask him for his help? Instead of an offering, you can promise him your heart. Your obedience."

Viriato, who had been silent until then, chortled. "She is as bad as Ethan. He is forever trying to convert me into a Jew. Even Sarai says he is turning into a priest."

I stiffened at the mention of Sarai. By tacit agreement no one in the house ever spoke the name of Ethan, never mind Sarai, who was utterly taboo. Viriato turned red. "I beg your pardon, mistress. I did not mean—"

"Peace, Viriato. It's of no matter. I shall have to grow used to hearing her name."

Claudia wrapped her long arms around my waist. She did not know why I had broken my betrothal. I suppose she could see for herself that I was haunted by misery over it, whatever the cause.

I tapped her arm in a gesture of affection and walked out of her embrace. "Shall we look at some fabrics for you, Lord Titus? I have several lengths that will make Sejanus green with envy."

🌺

The day of Ethan's wedding dawned thick with clouds, though it never rained. The sky remained gray and unyielding.

I could not work. I could not eat. I could not focus. For the first time since Joseph's death, I walked to the hilltop where the bee had stung him. I sat on the dry grass, remembering the horror of that day. At least Ethan lived. He had been spared the suffering of slavery and death. I had done that much for him. He had the chance for a new life. For hope and joy and a future.

But what of me? What would become of me? I could

see no future for me. I would never be married. Never have children. Never really belong to anyone. All the success in the world could not alter that fact. I could create the most elegant fabrics the world had ever seen, save my father's business from ruin again and again, gain a reputation for excellence unequaled in all of Jerusalem. It still would make no difference to the lonely ache in my heart. I felt rejected and abandoned, marooned in a world that barely saw me. A great wave of self-pity washed over me.

An urgent cry roused me out of my melancholy musings. "Mistress Elianna! Come! You are needed at home. Come right away!"

Alarmed, I sprang to my feet. "What has happened, Joel?"

"Your father, mistress." He shook his head.

Once again, I ran down that hill, shoeless and panicked, burdened by approaching death.

*

I knelt by my father's side, listening to his slow, tortured breathing, while my mother wept and beat at her breast. I prayed with all my strength that he would open his eyes, look upon me, and call me daughter again. I felt that if he acknowledged me just once as his, his own daughter, his own child, then I could bear anything. I could bear the emptiness of my life, knowing he had forgiven me in the end. Knowing he had claimed me and I belonged to him again.

He died without saying a word.

He slipped out of our lives with one final shallow breath. Gamaliel had arrived by then and prayed for him as he lay dying. He would be unclean for seven days now, having touched the dead, and would have to go through the painstaking process of purification with the ashes of a red heifer before he could return to his duties. Not many members of the Sanhedrin would be willing to bear so much inconvenience for the sake of a boyhood friend.

We laid my father to rest next to Joseph's bones. They would be together now, I hoped. My father's grief had finally ended. Mine was just about to be multiplied.

TWENTY-ONE

A man's spirit will endure sickness,
but a crushed spirit who can bear?
PROVERBS 18:14

WITH MY FATHER GONE, I could no longer pretend to work under his direction. There may be places in the Roman Empire where an unmarried woman could be the acceptable head of a business. Jerusalem was not amongst them. The workshop would have to be sold. For four generations, my father's family had maintained this trade and made a success of it. I was the one who lost it. In the end, I failed the unspoken expectation of those generations. Without my father, I could not save their hard-won achievements.

My father's health had been fragile. He had held on to life by a thread as thin as spider silk. But the shadow of his presence had been enough to allow me to continue in trade. Now that he was gone, I could devise no way of managing our workshop without the illusion of his authority behind me.

As long as I had had Ethan behind me, I knew that even if we lost my father, I could continue with Ethan's help. As his wife, I would have had even more freedom than I had had as an unmarried daughter. The day I broke off my betrothal to Ethan, I knew that I would lose the family business as well as my dream of marriage to the man I loved.

A part of me had already prepared to let go of the workshop. For many weeks, my heart had grown disengaged from the work that had once been my hiding place. But losing it was still a blow.

I felt responsible for the men and women who had labored in our workshop over the years. I wanted to ensure that our workers would continue to be cared for, to have employment if possible. I could not sell the business to just anyone. I had to be sure the new owner would care for our people.

I asked Viriato to speak to Master Ezer. I knew Ethan's father might refuse me; he had every reason to hold me in contempt. But I had no other recourse. He knew everyone connected to our trade. He would be able to find us the right buyer. "For the sake of his friendship with my father," I told Viriato, "tell him to help us."

Of course the house had to be sold with the business. It sat on the same parcel of land. Such a purchase required a large outlay of cash. I worried that we would not be able to find a buyer, for as I had come to learn from personal experience, merchants rarely had this much coin to spare. I knew I would have to accept any offer, even if it proved unreasonably low. Without the income from the workshop, I could

TESSA AFSHAR

maintain neither the cost of the taxes nor the upkeep of our many servants.

Master Ezer sent his response a mere three days after receiving my plea for help. "He says he has found a buyer for you," Viriato said.

"Who is it?"

"That, he will not say. Apparently the buyer wishes to remain anonymous."

"Why? For what purpose?"

Viriato shrugged. "Master Ezer said to tell you that he can be trusted."

It went against the grain, giving up our inheritance into unknown hands. In the end, what choice had we? I signed the contracts and received an unexpectedly large sum of money for my pains. More than fair. Astonished, I wrote Master Ezer a letter of thanks.

My mother grieved more over the loss of her home than the death of her husband. She had said her good-bye to him bit by bit, at his sickbed. She had grown accustomed to his loss over the long months. But she was not prepared for the loss of her house.

We planned to move to Tiberias so that we could be near Joanna. It was the one bright spot of my life, the knowledge that I would be able to see my sister again so soon.

I found my mother packing a trunk the next morning, filled with papers. "What are these?"

"Your father's accounts and receipts and who knows what. He never threw anything away. You might need them one day, Elianna. You never know."

"Perhaps we should give them to the new owner. If they are related to the business of the workshop, he should have them."

"I haven't gone through them. They are above my head. I do know that there are private papers mixed in here. Perhaps you can sift through them and leave behind what you wish."

The thought of dealing with accounts turned my stomach. "Let's bring them with us to Tiberias. I will deal with them later. If I find anything of worth for the new owner, I will return it to him then."

My mother rubbed her left arm and shoulder. There were dark circles under her eyes, and her once-pretty face looked ravaged with early lines. I felt a stab of pity for her. She had lost more than I had in the past few years. I thought of enfolding her in a comforting embrace, but she had never been a tactile woman. I could not remember the last time she had hugged me, and I knew that if I tried to hold her in my arms now, she would turn into a block of wood.

"You are tired, Mother," I said gently. "Why don't you lie down for a few hours? Keziah can bring supper to your chamber."

The next morning, Mother rose out of her bed later than usual. Her skin looked gray and ill. "Go back to bed at once," I said, alarmed, and sent for the physician.

"It is her heart, I believe," the physician said after completing his examination. "She needs more rest."

I snorted. A whole house to pack. Servants to dismiss. A journey in a caravan all the way to Galilee. How was I supposed to provide more rest for my mother? I insisted she stay in bed the whole day and tried my best to assure her that we could take care of every detail without her.

That evening, I began to menstruate. It was not my time of the month. I could not have been more vexed at the inconvenience my body had wrought. Menstruating women were considered unclean. My mother remained constrained by her heart and I by my untimely bleeding. I crossed my arms and barked orders, frustrated that I could not help. The bleeding stopped after three days. It seemed a simple enough aberration in the function of my body. And yet something nagged at me. A faint buzz of worry I could not shake followed in my wake.

A week later, even though the bleeding had stopped and I could now be considered clean, I decided to make a hasty journey to the pool of Bethesda in the north of the city, near the Sheep Gate. This pool was famed amongst our people for its curative properties.

A great number of invalids had gathered around the pool, seeking healing for their various ailments. Some sat; others lay on mats, waiting, hoping. According to legend, an angel of the Lord went into the waters and stirred the pool at certain seasons. The one who went in first after the stirring of the water would be healed of her ailment. I sat and waited, looking about me with widened eyes. The lame, the blind, the infirm, the paralyzed lined up in the five porticoes, filling every space, faces drawn with anxiety and pain, desperate for healing.

I never attempted to enter into that pool, even when the waters did stir with a delicate agitation that seemed to come from nowhere. How could I take away the chance of another who was truly sick by making my way into those waters first?

It occurred to me that my own life, blighted as it seemed to me, had yet many blessings to offer. I retained my health, my sight, my strength. I had a mother and a sister who loved me. I had life. I left the pool of Bethesda more thankful than I had been in many days.

What shall I say of our departure from the only home I had ever known, except that it was tearful and wrenching? We took our leave of each household and workshop servant; I was astonished by the show of their deep sorrow when they bid me farewell. These people loved me, I realized with a jolt. I was not merely their mistress. I had grown precious to them.

I had set aside a bit of coin for everyone as an expression of appreciation for their faithful service to our family. In addition, I had managed to find a small length of inexpensive fabric as a personal gift for each one. To my amazement, their eyes filled when I handed them the fabric; men and women clutched at the simple gift and reminisced about the time we had woven each piece. I wished I could have taken all of them with me to Tiberias. How I would long for their company.

Just before leaving, I received a letter from Claudia. She had managed to wrangle Titus's permission to accompany him to Rome. I had hoped to hear from her soon, worried about the outcome of their precarious position.

*Perhaps your God has chosen to work a miracle, for I
have no other way of explaining our good fortune. Titus
has been forgiven. We are to remain in Rome for the
present. Future travel back to Palestine is not out of the
question, however, though it will be under very different
circumstances, I hope.*

*I miss you already, my dearest Elianna. Write to me
and tell me your news whenever you can. Have you and
Ethan worked things out, after all? I cannot believe that
you truly wished to divorce him! It is plain enough that
you love him as deeply as I've known any woman to love
a man. Forgive me for meddling. I wish only for your
happiness.*

*Your friend,
Claudia*

She knew nothing about Decimus Calvus. I had given her
the excuse I had given everyone—that I simply did not wish
to be married since the circumstances of my life prevented
me from entering a happy and equal union. I had not wished
to burden her with my troubles, knowing how her own dif-
ficulties weighed on her.

I wrote her back, expressing my delight at her news.

*My separation from Ethan is indeed permanent. You may
be surprised to know that he is already married to another.
It is for the best, Claudia. He deserves a good wife who will
bring him joy. I think Sarai is the right woman for him.*

It made me cringe to see those words before my eyes in plain black and white. Somehow, they made my loss seem irrevocably real. I let her know of our imminent move and included the directions to our new house so that she could maintain a regular correspondence if she chose. I sealed the letter and placed a kiss for my friend over the wax. Who knew if I would ever see her again in this lifetime?

Once again, Viriato accompanied us to Galilee. He came only to see us safely through the journey, refusing to allow us to go alone, even though we had hired a large and well-defended caravan. Afterward, he intended to return to Jerusalem and Ethan, where he belonged.

Chuza had rented a modest house on a dead-end street for my mother and me, close enough to his own home that we could walk to visit Joanna whenever we wished. With its two chambers, walls of undressed stone, cobbled floors, and a garden the size of an old carpet we used to keep in our formal hall, the house was a far cry from our comfortable circumstances back in Jerusalem. Still, there was a flat roof that made a lovely bed on a warm, starry night. It sufficed for our needs. Having no income, I wanted to ensure that our funds would last throughout the years, so that we would never become a burden to Joanna and her husband. Better to live modestly now than risk poverty and debt in the coming years.

Of the servants, only Keziah came with us. She was an orphan, raised in our home since childhood. It would have broken her heart if we had left her behind. I felt grateful for her quiet, uncomplaining presence. She was a piece of home I could keep. For years, I had only seen her as a useful worker, faithful, sweet-natured, and obedient. After Joanna married, Keziah had seemed to take note of my despondence. Without a word, she started to take on Joanna's small ministrations to me. She cooked me special meals, brought flowers into my room, combed my hair gently until the tangles came loose. I took Keziah with us because I grew to see her as more than a mere servant. It was one of the best decisions I ever made.

The day after we arrived at our new house, we had to bid another good-bye, this time to Viriato. "So, you are leaving us. Who will replace my giant?" I said on the frosty morning of his departure.

He grinned, making the scar pucker under his eye. "I will come back and make sure you aren't in too much trouble."

My eyes brimmed. "Take care of him, Viriato. Make sure he is happy and well."

He rubbed his face with a broad palm. "I will do my best, mistress."

I nodded. "Try not to land yourself in any more mines. Avoid Roman soldiers at all costs."

"I have found a better way to take my revenge; don't you worry. I double the price when I sell them our goods."

I laughed. "How I shall miss you. Write me when you can."

Viriato grimaced. "You complain you cannot read my writing."

"Write short letters, then. And try to make them legible."

We were laughing when he left, but my heart cracked at the pain of it. It was my twentieth birthday, I realized.

"I am concerned for Mother. She is fading," Joanna said as she helped me hang Ethan's Babylonian tapestry. "She pants when she takes three steps."

"The physician said it was her heart. She needs to rest more," I said, frowning.

"How can we force her to do nothing? That would kill her outright. You know how our mother has to keep busy."

"Perhaps we can arrange for a day at one of Tiberias's spas? The warm springs of Emmaus are famed to have curative powers."

Joanna brightened. "That is a marvelous idea. I shall ask Chuza to arrange it."

She still lit up like a lampstand at the mention of her husband's name. After five months of marriage, they appeared more in love than they had when they first became betrothed. If Joanna spent three hours with us, she began to complain that she missed Chuza. I had at least done this one thing right. I had managed to ensure that she could marry her beloved.

The spa visit did not cure Mother. Neither did all the rest we pressed upon her. Before winter ended, she was lost to us. Joanna and I, along with Chuza, traveled hastily to Jerusalem so that we could lay her remains to rest with her husband and son according to her wishes.

Master Ezer and Jerusha came to the burial. They remained woodenly polite. Their eyes never met mine. I could not blame them, of course. Even if Ethan had not shared the full story of what he had witnessed, they knew that I had trampled on my promise and hurt their son abominably. How could they soften toward me now? How could they forgive my betrayal?

I had learned from the years of living with my father that the greatest consideration I could offer them was to disappear into the background and cause as little offense by my presence as possible. They seemed to appreciate my unobtrusive silence, though they left as early as custom allowed.

I sat alone by that tomb and ached. Father, mother, brother, husband, home, work, friends . . . gone. How would I bear the burden of so much loss? I could not even weep anymore. It was as though my tears had dried up after too many calamities.

How I longed to feel that I truly belonged to someone for just one moment. I knew Joanna loved me, but she belonged to her husband and his family now. He had become the center of her world, as rightly he should. I was a mere extension. An afterthought. One day, perhaps, I would be the maiden aunt who spoilt her children. That would be the extent of my family.

⚜

We returned to Tiberias that same week. The day I arrived at my new home, now empty save for Keziah and me, I started to bleed.

My body turned traitor.

It wept blood as it mourned the destruction of every love. It hemorrhaged inconsolable sorrow.

And I became unclean.

I became like Egypt with its ten plagues. Instead of frogs and locusts, God had sent me death, betrayal, loneliness, sickness, and isolation. At every turn, a new plague visited me.

For years I had known in my heart that I was unworthy. Guilty. Sinful. Now my shame became a public thing, evident for all to perceive. My touch made others unclean. I became a burden rather than a blessing. I became an outcast—an object of disgust and pity.

TWENTY-TWO

If a woman has a discharge of blood for many days, not at the time of
her menstrual impurity, or if she has a discharge beyond the time of her
impurity, all the days of the discharge she shall continue in uncleanness. . . .
Every bed on which she lies, all the days of her discharge, shall be to her as
the bed of her impurity. And everything on which she sits shall be unclean.

LEVITICUS 15:25-26

"KEZIAH, YOU DON'T HAVE TO STAY with me. I will find you
a good home, here in Galilee or back in Jerusalem if you prefer. It cannot be pleasant serving a woman deemed unclean."

Twelve months had passed since my sickness began. Twelve
months of hopes crushed. There were days in those months
when the bleeding stopped. I would spend hours wondering, hoping I was free of this scourge. According to the Law,
seven days needed to pass from the time of menstrual impurity before a woman could be considered clean once more.
But I never had seven uninterrupted days of recovery.

Once, I had four whole days of freedom. And then it
started again, the cycle of my torment. There were days
when my symptoms were light, barely there, a faint reminder
that I could not be a full part of our society. Other days, I

hemorrhaged until I could not move. My body had turned into a prison. I could not escape it. I could not leave it behind. I remained chained, held captive by its broken bars. I could not even go to the synagogue or celebrate the Passover in the community of our people.

I felt it unfair to hold Keziah to my restricted life. I rarely left the house, lest my touch inconvenience others. My world had shrunk to the four walls of our home. I could not work. I could not offer help to anyone.

Keziah shook her head, a fat braid bouncing down her back. "No, mistress! Don't send me away. I would rather remain with you in your sickness. Where would I go that would be better than here? You never mistreat me. Who would be as kind to me as you are?"

I sighed. "For now, then, you may remain. But you might change your mind if I find no cure."

"You will find help, mistress. I am sure of it. God will heal you."

I couldn't help smiling at her vehement faith. "It has been a whole year, Keziah. And I have seen three physicians already. One eminent enough to serve Herod the tetrarch. No one seems to know what to do for me."

"You have to be patient like Abraham and Sarah."

I groaned. "They waited over twenty years! Stop trying to cheer me. You will make me cry."

Keziah laughed. "Well, I have a surprise for you. And it will cheer you, I promise."

"What surprise?"

"You will see."

I threw my hands in the air and sat down to write a letter to Viriato. He wrote at least once a month, giving me news of Jerusalem. Lydia's purple, for that is how I had come to think of it, had become the rage, fulfilling Master Ezer's best expectations. They were kept busy with the new increase in their business. I had a sense that Viriato held back more than he revealed, but then I knew that there were lines neither of us could cross. We never discussed Ethan or Sarai.

I asked him once about my father's workshop and the house. He assured me that they fared well, and the workers were content with their new situation. He never referred to the new owner. I suspected it might be Master Ezer himself. I could not think of a better arrangement, though how he had managed to accrue enough cash to pay us so generously, I could not fathom. I had given half the income to Joanna and Chuza. The other half would have to see me through the rest of my life, though if the physicians had their say, my life had better be a short one. They ate up denarii the way fish drank water. And you had to pay them whether they cured you or tortured you without results.

I was midsentence in my letter when a knock sounded at the door. I frowned. Joanna would have come in without waiting for an invitation. Keziah opened the door, and there on the threshold stood my old friend, Viriato.

I shot to my feet with a small gasp of delight. The old familiar grin slashed across his bear of a face. "The blessings of the Lord to you, mistress."

"The Lord, is it now? Why didn't you tell me you were coming?"

He walked in and tried to sit on the cushion I had just abandoned. "No!" I cried. "Don't sit there."

He gave me an inquiring look. "Are you saving it for the Roman governor?"

I flushed with embarrassment. I had not written him of my illness. I could not bear the shame of it. "It is unclean, Viriato. Sit on the couch. It's comfortable and large enough even to suit a giant like you."

His brows knit together. "I like this cushion," he said. "Your cleanliness laws bother me none, mistress." He plopped himself on my cushion.

Speech abandoned me for a moment. "Now you've done it. You won't be able to interact with other Jews until you purify yourself."

He stretched his colossal legs and made himself comfortable. "I care not. But there is something I do wish to know. Why did you not tell me you were ailing? I would have come sooner had I known."

I threw Keziah an accusing glare. Her big smile vanished and she made herself busy with the dough for our evening meal. "Will you get out of my seat, you big Lusitanian? I have nowhere else to sit," I said.

"Why don't you occupy the couch if it is so comfortable?"

I stamped my foot like a two-year-old. "Because I am unclean. Joanna can sit on the couch when she comes to visit so long as I don't touch it."

"I see." Viriato moved so I could sit on the cushion. He turned to sprawl on the couch instead.

"No!" I cried.

"What now?"

"You have become unclean by touching my seat. You cannot lie on the couch any longer. Not until you purify yourself."

He groaned. "Truly, I never thought to say this about anything. But this is worse than your food laws. What happens if someone touches you?"

"They become unclean."

"What, even a loving embrace from your own sister?"

"Unclean."

"What if they wear cloth you have woven on that loom in the corner?"

"Unclean." My jaws clenched. "I think you are beginning to comprehend. I am unclean. Impure. My presence disgusts people."

Viriato rubbed a clumsy hand against the back of his neck. "Mistress, never say that."

"It's the truth, Viriato. I have a bleeding sickness. For a whole year, it has plagued me, and I have no hope it will end."

"I am sorry to hear you have been suffering, Mistress Elianna." I saw pity well up in his big brown eyes.

"You should pity yourself. Now you will have to wash all your clothes, bathe yourself, and you will still be considered unclean until the evening. It's a real inconvenience."

"Excellent. Since we are both unclean, let us go all the way and eat whatever we wish. We can repent later."

I dissolved into laughter. I could not help myself. "You

and your stomach. You allow it to get in the way of your walk with God."

"Well, that and the fact that he wishes to cut off bits of my body I have no interest in giving up."

I bit my lip. All at once, talking about my bleeding disease did not seem so awkward. Viriato had no shame. I had Keziah fetch another cushion and Viriato sat next to me as we talked into the evening.

He stayed at an inn in Tiberias for a whole week. Every day he visited us, bringing with him cheer and the amusing stories of our trade. The poor man had to bathe and wash his clothes every day before returning to the inn after sunset. He did it without complaint, though, and when I objected, he said, "Bathing and fresh clothes merely serve to make me more handsome. You should see the fuss the women make of me when I arrive at the inn."

"I am sure they think you irresistible. Have you found yourself a wife yet?"

"Shackle myself to one woman? I have more sense than that."

He tried to laugh it off, but I knew that he longed to have a family. It would be hard, in Judea, where most of my people would rather starve than give their daughters to Gentiles.

"God has someone for you, Viriato. Someone who will not feel like a shackle, but be a great blessing to your life. Wait on the Lord and he will give you the desires of your heart."

"I could say as much to you."

Viriato's visit was like a breath of air, bringing me new strength and encouragement. After he left, I decided to try another physician. I had given up on them when the third one gave me a concoction that made me vomit for three days straight. He had the nerve to charge me the equal of a month's wages for that cure, even though it made no shadow of a difference in my condition.

I sent Keziah to purchase a fat roll of parchment; I had decided to write down an account of my life. It kept me occupied for days on end. To my surprise, describing these events brought a measure of relief. The parchment bore the weight of every sorrow with uncritical impartiality. The pen became my friend.

With some trepidation, I asked Chuza to find me another physician. Most physicians mixed the spiritual realm with their physical treatments and thought nothing of handing the patient a bowl of medicine dedicated to some foreign god or blessed by a magical incantation. They demanded libations to this idol and the worship of another.

I could have none of that. The Law forbade God's people from seeking the help of mediums or witches. Turning to any form of idolatry was also considered a grave sin. The Lord condemned the practice of magic under any circumstance; there was no such thing as good magic.

A few physicians chose to focus on herbal remedies and surgical means, however. Their curative powers relied solely on the physical realm. These I could consult. Sometimes I had to travel a long way to find one. To my relief, Chuza managed to locate a healer famed for producing good results, right in Tiberias. He had been summoned to attend Herod's wife, who suffered from a stomach disease.

Sira had been trained in Greece and had taken, according to him, an oath to ensure ethical treatment of his patients.

"What does this oath contain?" I asked.

"Amongst other things, I have promised that the sick under my care will suffer no hurt or damage, that I will comport myself and use my knowledge in a godly manner, and that my visit shall be for the convenience and advantage of the patient."

I gave a wan smile. "Then you are welcome in my home."

It turned out that Sira's ethics came at a steep price. I paid the money and prayed that healing would come my way.

"Do not fret," he said to me when I described all the previous treatments that had produced no results. "I have many remedies for your condition. If one doesn't work, we shall try another."

Impressed by the breadth of his knowledge and his obvious confidence, I put my trust in him. He made up my first remedy from a mixture of gum of Alexandria, alum, and a special crocus, famed for its healing powers. Sira bruised and pounded these together in a mortar, creating a dense paste the size of a silver coin. This concoction he then dissolved in wine and gave to me. I had tasted worse.

For one week, I drank a fresh preparation of this remedy and waited to see if it would take effect.

Joanna came to visit me one morning during this trial period. I noticed she glowed with a new happiness. "I am going to have a baby," she told me before she had time to sit down. Never had I been so frustrated with the limitations of my condition. I could not hug her or hold her as I wished.

"May the Lord be praised!" I cried. "I am so happy for you, little sister. Is Chuza beside himself?"

"His feet have not touched the ground in two days."

"And his parents? They must be well pleased."

"His mother won't stop crowing about her son's virility. I cannot fault her for that, since it is my wonderful husband she praises."

"I wish I could be of some practical help, Joanna. Do you think if I wove some linen and wool garments, and Keziah washed them with ritual care, Chuza's mother would allow you to use them for the baby?"

Joanna shrugged her shoulders. "I care not what she thinks. My baby will wear whatever his talented aunt decides to make for him. Did you bring any dyes with you from home?"

"A few samples—sufficient for the needs of a new babe. We can bleach a few pieces white and I have blue dye and a bit of Lydia's purple left."

Joanna clapped her hands. "Marvelous. I shall have the best-dressed child in all of Judea."

Sira's first remedy proved ineffective. But at least it made me no sicker than I had been before we started. The next treatment was made up of Persian onions. Sira was very precise about the amounts of each substance he used. "Nine logs. No more, no less," he said to me as he measured onions and wine with care. For several hours, he allowed the onions to boil in wine over a low flame.

When I had finished drinking a full cup, he said, "Arise from thy flux."

I arose, but the flux continued. He made me drink the onion-soaked wine three times each day for a whole week, to no avail.

For some months now, I had felt pain and discomfort in my belly. Cramps would often assail me. They were not so powerful that I was overcome by the agony. But I found that even moderate pain, when it comes against the body hour after hour, week after week, leeches the strength out of the bones. I grew weaker with each passing day.

The constant bleeding did not help. Sira prescribed more meat in my diet to give me extra nourishment. Whatever nourishment I took with my food, however, I seemed to lose immediately to the hemorrhaging of my womb.

A new worry added to my physical discomfort. Joanna had not been to see me for four days, which was unusual. I assumed that her condition had made her feel too ill to come abroad. I sent Keziah to inquire after her welfare.

"They wouldn't let me see her, mistress," she said when

she returned, huffing from her speedy walk. "They would not even let me through the doors, but kept me waiting in the courtyard like a stray dog."

TWENTY-THREE

Turn to me and be gracious to me,
for I am lonely and afflicted.
The troubles of my heart are enlarged;
bring me out of my distresses.
Consider my affliction and my trouble,
and forgive all my sins.

PSALM 25:16-18

MY HEART SANK. I suspected that they wished to guard Joanna and the babe she carried from being exposed to my ailment. I could not blame them for wanting to protect my sister from harm, nor would I interfere in that intention. How severe life was going to seem, deprived of my sister's company for all the months of her pregnancy. The thought of it made me turn cold with dread. I would find my days excruciatingly lonely without her.

I remembered a passage I had read in Gamaliel's parchments not two days before:

Bless the Lord, O my soul,
and all that is within me,
bless his holy name!

Bless the Lord, O my soul,
    and forget not all his benefits,
who forgives all your iniquity,
    who heals all your diseases,
who redeems your life from the pit,
    who crowns you with steadfast love and mercy,
who satisfies you with good so that your youth is
      renewed like the eagle's.

These were mere words to me. As yet, they held no substance. No truth. No comfort. How could God forgive *my* iniquity? He certainly had not chosen to heal my disease or redeem my life from the pit.

For a fleeting moment, I wondered if I could ever learn to bless the Lord in the way King David intended. To trust in him. Though he smite me, to cling to him and believe in his goodness. To rest in him though weariness overwhelmed me. If I could learn the secret of such a faith, then even if I lost Joanna's companionship, I could hold on to God and know his encompassing peace.

The next day, a note arrived from Chuza. I collapsed on my cushion when I read the contents.

Joanna had lost her baby.

He did not say so in the letter, of course, but I knew that his family blamed me for the loss. The curse of my illness had somehow caused Joanna to miscarry the babe.

I wept bitterly for the first time in months, knowing how keenly Joanna would feel this loss. I was impotent to bring her the smallest measure of comfort while bound by my own illness. From that time, Chuza's mother forbade my sister to set foot inside my house. Her animosity made me more determined to find a cure.

⚹

Sira's next remedy required that I walk outside the city and stand at a crossroads. He would not tell me what I was to do there. We left at noon, when the heat drove most people indoors. Sira had chosen a specific spot, though I did not know the significance of it. At the intersection of two small roads, both unfamiliar to me, he came to a halt.

"Stand here," he said, pointing at the center of the road. Thankfully, there were no animals or pedestrians in the way. I took my place where he indicated. He took out a wooden chalice from his sack and filled it with wine.

Handing me the chalice, he commanded, "Drink." I took a sip. It tasted like normal wine. "Now look at me," he demanded. So I looked up. He had an intense expression that I found perplexing.

Before I could ask what we were meant to do next, a huge man rammed into me from behind, screaming incomprehensible words. The hairs on the back of my neck rose. I had never had such a fright in my life. Shrieking, I pulled away from the man's bruising force and threw myself at Sira. I thought perhaps some monstrous demon had struck me. When I turned around, I saw that my attacker was a normal man, large and prepossessing in size, but clean and neat and apparently in his right mind.

In a nasal voice, he said, "Arise from thy flux."

"What?" I cried, before collapsing on the ground, shivering from reaction.

Sira squatted in front of me. "The fright was part of the treatment. We believe that the body releases healing humors when a great fear comes upon a patient. How do you feel?"

"How do I feel?" I stuttered, wanting to give him a fright of my own. "I feel like my legs have turned into feather pillows. You are a crazy man, you realize? I suppose you will charge me extra for this particular cure."

"As a matter of fact, that is true. I have to pay Samuel, you see."

I was frightened, all right. But I was not healed. Thankfully, Sira did not repeat that particular remedy for a whole week.

※

The following week there was another unexpected knock on our door. When Keziah, who promised she did not know who stood on the other side this time, opened it, we found Joanna. She appeared listless and wan.

"Joanna!" I leapt to my feet and ran to her, careful not to touch her with the merest whisper of my skin. "What is it? Has something happened?"

"I missed my sister. I have come to visit."

"Has your mother-in-law lifted her ban?"

Joanna shrugged. "She banned me from setting foot inside your house. I have not placed a single dainty slipper over this threshold, have I?"

I laughed. "I hope you will not get yourself into trouble with your husband's family on my account."

"I could not bear to stay away longer, Elianna. I am so sad, and you know how to cheer me."

I exhaled. "I am sorry, my love. I am sorry you lost your precious babe. I am praying that God will give you another quickly."

She nodded and gave a watery smile. "Is there no stool in your house that we can set outside the door here while we talk? I cannot stand for a whole hour."

For several days, this became our habit. Joanna would come and sit outside my door, and we would talk. Sometimes we spoke of ordinary things, and sometimes we talked about the heartaches in our lives. We held on to each other with love, with compassion, with pity. We had nothing practical to offer one another. The poultice of love proved enough. Our aches were deep, but love was deeper. In time, hope emerged victorious over our fears.

"When does Sira give you his next potion?" Joanna asked on a hot afternoon.

My shoulders slumped. "He has sent a letter to inform me that he had to leave for Ephesus on urgent family business. He won't return until next year."

"Oh no!"

"He has sent me a long dietary list. Things I am to eat and those I should avoid for the next few months. He assures me that good diet alone might provide a cure."

"And if not?"

"He says there are still a few things we can try upon his return, and I am not to give in to despair."

"I like this Sira. He sounds like a good man."

I shrugged. "For a physician."

We giggled. It was good to laugh at the absurdities of our lives.

"Is this a private feast or can anyone join in?"

"Husband!" Joanna gasped. From the spreading red stain on her cheeks, I guessed she had never told Chuza how she spent her afternoons.

"I wondered where my wife had disappeared to again. I guessed this would be a likely spot."

"I never went inside the house, as you see. I kept my promise." Joanna's voice trembled. I realized that in spite of her apparent disregard for her mother-in-law's wishes, she felt apprehensive about defying her command.

"I am sorry, Chuza," I said. "I am at fault. I should have sent her home when she first came. It was selfish of me to encourage her."

Chuza rubbed his chest with an agitated hand. "Peace. It would be cruel to come between two sisters who love one another so deeply. I do not demand such a sacrifice. My mother, now—she is another matter."

Joanna reached for Chuza's hand. "You won't tell her?"

"Of course not, Joanna. I know my mother intends the best. That does not mean she is always right. I saw how unhappy you were when you lost our babe. Then you started to smile again and be my old Joanna. That's when I began to suspect that you might be visiting Elianna. She is good medicine to your soul, whatever my mother might believe." He wrapped his arm around Joanna's shoulders. "Have you another stool for your brother, Elianna?"

He did not even ask if the stool Keziah fetched was unclean. How blessed we were the day Chuza married my sister. "Tell us news of the palace," I said, happy for new company.

"My father, you may know, is considering stepping down from his position as steward to Herod. His joints trouble him, and he is often in pain. I do what I can to help, but the steward has to perform many tasks personally. Yesterday, he petitioned the tetrarch to give me the position of steward instead."

"And what did Herod say?"

"He will think on it."

"Which means he awaits a fat gift as incentive," Joanna said.

Palace business, I realized, was just as sordid as the less-exalted kind. "Will your father provide one?"

"I believe so. My father wishes to take on a lesser position requiring fewer physical demands, without giving up the prestige of being part of the tetrarch's household."

"I wish I could help," I said wistfully. "In the old days, I would have woven you some splendid lengths of cloth, glorious enough to suit even Herod's rich tastes."

As winter drew to a close, Viriato called on me again. I had been sick for over two years now. The constant bleeding and pain had made me thinner and I often felt tired. Worse than the symptoms that dogged my every waking hour was the plague of loneliness. Sometimes I felt starved for just one touch. One tiny embrace. But being with Viriato was like taking a dose of invigorating medicine. He made me forget that I was ill.

There had been a shortage of wool that year due to a terrible plague that had struck the new lambs in Palestine, killing many. We commiserated over the loss and laughed about the many absurdities that such a shortage had created.

"We have had to import wool from Italy. The prices are so high after paying the Roman taxes that only the very rich can afford new lengths of wool this year. Men's tunics have grown shorter, and last week, I saw a Roman lady wearing a tunic that only came to the middle of her calves."

"No!" I laughed. "What a spectacle that must have made. What did her husband say?"

"He praised her for her pecuniary zeal if not her modesty. She became very popular with the men. Just before I came, I saw several ladies with shorter tunics. They had actually cut their old, long skirts."

I shook my head thinking about the cold, wet days of winter and how inconvenient a pair of bare legs would prove in such weather, as the poor had good reason to know. "Why would any man want to ogle a pair of goose-pimpled legs, white from cold?"

Viriato shrugged. "The temperature of a woman's skin has no effect on a man's ogling tendencies."

I grinned. "Men are a mystery to me. Let us speak of something I understand. How fares the workshop?"

"It does well. They don't produce the ingenious fabrics you designed while you ran it. But the quality remains good, and the workers are secure."

I nodded. I could have written Joel to ask for more information had I wished. By now, he most likely knew the identity of the new owner, even if the man himself never set foot on the property, but hired managers to do the work for him. I did not have the heart to discover that final mystery related to my past. Better leave the secret in Master Ezer's hands.

"How is Ethan?" The question leapt out of my mouth before I had time to think better of asking it. I don't know what made me violate my own unspoken ban on the subject of Ethan. I suppose my longing to hear about him finally surpassed my pain at the very mention of his name.

Viriato lowered his eyes. "They are expecting a child, mistress."

I swallowed past the ball of misery rising in my throat. This, after all, was why I had set him free. I wanted him to have a good and full life. My sickness only affirmed that decision. If he had married me, he would be chained to my side, too dutiful to divorce me. He wouldn't have a child. He wouldn't even have a wife. Not really. Decimus Calvus had done both of us a favor.

"I am happy for him. He always wanted to be a father."

"I am expecting a baby again!" Joanna bounced on the balls of her feet, too excited to sit on the chair we had set out in expectation of her visit.

I clapped my hands. "Praise the God who saves us! I knew he would bless you again." My arms felt empty for want of holding her.

"Start working on those baby clothes again, Sister. Wool and linen both, I think."

"Joanna." My voice wobbled.

She stopped midstream in her excited chatter, alerted by the grave tone of my voice.

"I have given this much thought, for I knew this moment would come." My eyes welled up and for a moment I could not speak for fear that I would lose all control and start wailing. I took a deep breath and tried to clamp down the flood of emotion that threatened to drown me.

"Joanna," I tried again. This time my voice emerged stronger. "I do not wish you to return here while you are pregnant."

She shook her head, her eyes wide. "You can't mean that."

"Listen to me. You will want to know that you did everything in your power to take care of this little one. You will want to have no shadow of guilt placed upon you while you are pregnant."

"I need you, Elianna. Do not forbid me from seeing you! Your condition has no bearing upon mine." Tears started rolling down her cheeks.

My heart was breaking. But for her sake, I could not fall apart. I could not give in to her frantic pleas. I had to be the strong one.

Why does goodness sometimes cut sharper than a sword?

"My beloved sister, we cannot be certain of that. There is a mystery to such matters. Let us take care that you and the babe will remain safe. I will pray for you every day. Write to me as often as you can, beloved."

"Elianna!" She reached a long arm toward me.

I shut the door in her face before she could touch me. Leaning against it weakly, I bit hard on my lips to keep from sobbing.

All my severe precautions were for naught. Months of separation, of isolation, and Joanna lost her baby anyway.

It was the most awful loss imaginable, for it meant I could no longer see my sister. She lost her baby and I lost her. I withdrew from her in order to give her a chance at having the desire of her heart. I kept my door closed to her visits from that moment. Perhaps if she had not come to see me at the start, at the time she had conceived, she would have been able to keep her child. Perhaps my very presence had brought a curse upon her. I did not wish to be responsible for that. I thought if I stayed away from her completely, she might have a chance at happiness. I had little to give except my absence. This, I offered her, though it was like robbing myself.

She wrote, begging me to reconsider. There were few things in life I wanted more than to surrender to her pleas. But for her sake, I refused. I would not bend. I would not soften.

Now I had only Joanna's letters and Keziah for company. I did not even have the comfort of writing Joanna anymore. I refused to allow her to touch anything I had touched.

TWENTY-FOUR

Is there no balm in Gilead?
Is there no physician there?
Why then has the health of the daughter of my people
not been restored?

JEREMIAH 8:22

IN THE THIRD YEAR of my illness, Sira returned from
Ephesus. "I have brought a new crocus from Greece. It is
famed for its healing powers."

"You know I shall try anything short of witchcraft."

He waved a hand. "We have all we need in my pouch."

My medicine included a mix of cumin and fenugreek,
plus an addition of Sira's new crocus, for which I paid an
astronomical sum. These he boiled in water and, after clarify-
ing, gave me to drink.

"Arise from thy flux," he shouted at the top of his lungs
after I swallowed the last drop. Even as I rose from the floor,
I felt blood leeching out of my body.

"Early days, yet," he said when he saw my stricken face. "We shall do this for a month."

A month's worth of his concoctions made no more difference than the first batch had. His famed crocus failed me.

"We still have another remedy to try," he said to me. He tried to sound jovial, but his tone was more subdued than I had ever heard.

※

Viriato wrote to tell me that Ethan had a daughter. Rachel. Typical of a man, he included none of the information I longed to know. Did she have Ethan's eyes? Did she smile often? Did she get along with her cousin? Did she sleep well at night?

How Ethan would treasure this little one. He was just the man to father daughters. Tender, accepting, protective, and yet willing to allow the kind of freedom that most of Jerusalem would frown upon. Though she was not my child, I felt an odd tenderness for her. I would never set eyes upon Rachel. But I loved her, because she belonged to Ethan. I added her to my prayers. Every day I blessed her as if she had come from my own womb.

※

"This remedy is more complex than the rest." Sira adjusted his spotless tunic.

I rolled my eyes. "How much shall it cost me?"

He threw up his hands. "How can you be so prosaic? What is money when your health is at stake?"

"My health would like to maintain a roof over my head and food in my belly. How much?" He named a price that made me sit down. "Sira, can you not devise a cheaper cure?"

"To tell the truth, mistress, this is my final effort. I have saved it for last because it is the hardest. It is what you need; I am convinced of it."

What could I do? If I did not comply, I would have to acknowledge defeat. Then for the rest of my life I would wonder if I had missed my one opportunity for healing.

"Lead on, physician. I pray the Lord may bless your efforts."

I had to hand it to Sira. He worked hard on that cure. He had hired a servant to dig seven trenches in a piece of land that he had hired from a farmer. Each trench was deep enough to hide a grown man from view when he stood in it. At the bottom of the pits he had carefully arranged piles of dried wood mixed with fresh branches, still bearing green leaves. "From vines not yet four years old," he said. "They have never been pruned."

I could see why this particular remedy had cost so much. He lit the vines on fire until smoke began to rise from each pile. Giving me a cup of new wine, he took me by the hand to the first pit and lowered me carefully into it. I coughed from the acrid smoke as I sipped from my cup. He pulled me out, saying, "Arise from thy flux" before leading me to the next trench and lowering me down again. Seven times he did this. My eyes burned, my skin grew hot, and my clothes stank from the smoke rising from the young vines. The wine and the fumes were making me dizzy and a little nauseous.

But I stopped bleeding.

One, two, three, four, five, six days passed. I began to dream of all the things I would do when I was declared clean. Free to walk outside without worry that those around me would look upon me with distaste. Free to visit with Joanna. To embrace her and talk to her all day if I wished. Free to start working again! Free to have a full life. Oh, how happy I was. How filled with hope.

The seventh day dawned. My final day before I could go to the priest and be declared free of my disease. One hour before sunset, one single hour before freedom could come to me, I began to bleed again. This time the bleeding was so heavy, I could not rise out of bed for a week. Feeble and unsteady, I lay on my mattress, unable to believe that I had come this far without being released from my suffering.

A dark cloud of despair descended upon me on that seventh day. It choked life and hope out of me. That night, I slipped a knife into my bed and hid it under the covers. When Keziah had fallen asleep, I took it out and stared at it for a long while, wondering if I would have the courage to cut my wrists and end the misery of my life the way Romans did. They found a strange kind of honor in suicide. We Jews believed life belonged to God and the taking of it was a grave sin.

Fear of having to face his displeasure unto eternity made me sheathe the knife that night. But for ten days, I kept it with me in bed. I took it out after the lamps banked low and Keziah's soft snores filled the chamber. Each night, I had a decision to make. Live or die. I stared at the glittering silver metal of that knife, knowing my destiny rested on its sharpened edge. Each night, death wrestled with life. In the end, life won. I could not bear the thought of Joanna's grief, or God's punishment. But that dark blanket of despair did not quite leave me, lingering through my every waking moment and sometimes even haunting my dreams.

⚘

Thank God, the heaviness of my hemorrhage subsided after several weeks, though the bleeding continued. Some days, it would come to a complete stop, only to resume after a few hours. Everyone in our neighborhood now knew that I was unclean.

Once, when Keziah had fallen sick with a fever and cough, I had to fetch water from the well myself. Though I went at the noon hour in order to avoid the crowd, I found myself waiting while a Jewish woman filled her jar. Catching sight of me, she frowned. "What are you doing here?"

"I need water."

"That's disgusting! You can't touch the well."

"I did not intend to. I brought my own—"

"I care not what you brought. Leave here, or I shall cry out and bring the whole neighborhood down on your head. A good beating will teach you to spread the pollution of your body amongst decent people."

I took a deep breath to control the anger that longed to leap off my tongue and decided to leave. I had no defense to offer that would change the woman's mind. It was useless to remain and argue.

As I turned on my heel, I saw a woman with dark hair, dressed in a simple brown tunic and mantle. "Give me that," she said, grabbing my jar from my hand. From her accent I guessed her to be of Syrophoenician origin.

Many foreigners lived in Tiberias at that time. Because of the Pharisees' declaration that the city was ritually impure due to the presence of an old graveyard beneath its foundations, most truly pious Jews refused to live here. In the absence of sufficient inhabitants, Herod had invited the Gentiles to take occupation. With such Greek attractions as a stadium and hot natural springs, foreigners were more readily drawn to this city than other parts of my country.

We Jews lived alongside them in peace, though we managed to keep to ourselves and they kept their own counsel. We had few social interactions outside the bounds of necessity.

I stood, mouth agape, not understanding the woman's intention.

She marched to the well and drew out a heavy bucket of water, filling my jar with it carefully, all the while glaring at my Jewish tormentor. Returning, she handed the filled jar to me. My Jewish neighbor spat on the ground to show her indignation and huffed off.

My words of thanks floated in the wind as I turned to express my gratitude to the Syrophoenician woman and saw that she had already moved on. She did not even linger to see how grateful I felt.

It came to me that my Jewish neighbor, by keeping the Law, had added condemnation to my already wounded heart. This woman who was a Gentile, living outside the strictures of our Law and the salvation of the Lord, had gone out of her way to help me. She had extended compassion and mercy to a complete stranger.

I thought of the goodness of the Law, for it was from the Lord and given to make us righteous. What had we done with its God-given grace to turn it instead into a weapon against the sick and the helpless? How had we twisted the glory of God's precepts to such a degree that foreigners and unbelievers had grown more compassionate than the people of God?

I had not set eyes on Joanna for over a year. Even Keziah was not allowed to visit her, lest she carry upon her some part of my sickness. Joanna wrote me every day—short notes, long letters, tearstained missives, and happy, news-filled ones.

Chuza had been given the post of Herod's steward. This was a complex and unique role, different from an ordinary household manager. It placed Chuza in charge of Herod's entire staff of servants. Even the bodyguards had to report to him in matters of expense and their daily concerns. His varied responsibilities kept him busy in the palace, but having grown up under his father's tutelage, he knew the intricacies of his work and dealt well with the acerbic tetrarch and his many demands.

Though I read each one of Joanna's letters repeatedly, I could not answer any of them lest the parchment on which I wrote make her unclean. From me, she received only silence and prayers.

I spent many of my hours spinning wool and weaving on my simple loom, which I had brought from Jerusalem. I even began to develop homemade dyes, experimenting with cheap plants available in the market. The cloths I created surprised me with their simple beauty. I was able to sell some to the Gentiles living near me. They were more impressed by the quality of my products than the uncleanness of my womb. I could not make a proper living with one loom and a weak pair of hands. But the extra income from those fabrics helped pay our daily expenses. And it kept me sane to remain busy and useful in a minor way.

In the fourth year of my sickness, Joanna wrote to say that she was with child again. Fear and rejoicing wove in equal measure through the words of that letter. She had learned too well how her hopes might be dashed and could not trust this promised happiness. This time, at least, I knew that I had done everything in my power to protect her from my disease. Keziah and I prayed every night for Chuza, for my sister, and for the babe growing in her womb.

Four months into her pregnancy, Joanna lost the baby.

She ran to my home a week later, looking terrifyingly thin and sad. It had been such a long time since I had set eyes on her. To see her so diminished and ill-looking ripped something inside me.

I shoved the door wide open and ran to her and pulled her into my arms. What was the point of turning her away now? Her babe had been lost in spite of every precaution I had taken.

After years of deprivation, I finally held her in my arms,

weeping over her agony, barely able to believe that I could touch her. I caressed her hair, wiped her tears, kissed her cheeks, held tight to her fragile hands. I don't think I let go of her for the whole span of that afternoon. I don't believe she let go of me either. We clung to each other like two little orphan children instead of grown women who had seen too much of the world.

Chuza joined us that evening. He did not come to fetch his wife back home, but to find solace. Holding Joanna in his arms, he cried too, wrenching male tears that would shatter a heart of ice. Their pain was like a tangible thing, a sharp-taloned beast that ate away at their lives. I could do nothing to assuage it.

The next day I went to a scribe and dictated a letter. This way, the missive would not be tainted by my ritual unclean-liness. Chuza and Joanna's plight gave me the boldness to attempt this insane idea when I would never have tried it on my own behalf. I wrote to Gamaliel, highly respected member of the Sanhedrin, beloved teacher of the Law, and asked for his help. A woman with an issue of blood, cursed by God, unwanted by our society, reached out to one so high and asked for pity, for hope, for intercession. I suspected he might ignore me. I could not blame him if he did.

A month later, his answer arrived. "Come," it said simply, "And bring your sister and her husband with you."

It took Chuza a few months to disengage himself from his responsibilities as steward in Herod's palace. We journeyed south in an Egyptian caravan. Foreigners paid no mind to the religious delicacies that my illness offended. I was back inside Jerusalem's walls after five years of absence. I had left in defeat. I returned crushed.

✤

"Healing is in the hands of God," Gamaliel said, when he came to visit us at the inn Chuza had secured. "He can give it through miracles if he so pleases, or he can use physicians as his instruments of grace. Either way, the power belongs to the Lord."

"What does it mean when he withholds healing, Master Gamaliel?" I asked.

"Who can understand the mind of God? I know some Pharisees act as though they do. They say sickness is an indication of God's displeasure. A sign pointing to the stricken man's sin. A portent of faithlessness and unrepentance." He shrugged. "It is not so much that these are not valid possibilities. But I think we underestimate God if we believe we can comprehend in full measure his every action. Although sometimes sin can cause sickness in the body, it is not always the case. Nor is lack of faith the only reason the sick are not healed."

"Why then, my lord? Why is my wife so stricken?" Chuza asked, his voice hoarse from holding back tears.

Gamaliel played with the tassel hanging from the corner of his garment. "I do not know, young man. Perhaps God has a reason for tarrying. There may be a lesson in this delay more important for your soul than having a child."

"Will you pray for them, master? Will you pray for Joanna and Chuza that they may have a healthy child?" I asked. "Perhaps the Lord will hear your prayers."

He turned to me. "And what of you? Do you not seek prayer?"

I lowered my head. "Perhaps I am not deserving."

"Rabbi Hillel once said, *Judge not your friend until you stand in his place.* It is not for me to judge you, Elianna. What I do know of you is good and generous. You too shall receive my prayers on this day."

I covered my mouth with a trembling hand. "You shall become unclean if you touch me."

"A good bath and a few hours apart from the noise and demands of life never hurt a man. Stop your fretting."

"May the Lord bless you, Master Gamaliel."

"Before I begin, I have a question for you. Have you passed judgment on God, any of you? Do you harbor anger and resentment against him for not healing you all these years? For taking Joanna's children before they were born? For so many losses in your lives? Do you hold him accountable?"

I opened my mouth and closed it again like a gaping fish. "Who am I to pass judgment on God?"

"I did not say it was the right thing. I asked if you had done it. The heart does not always abide by the rules of righteousness. That is precisely why we offer so many sacrifices in the Temple."

"Perhaps I have considered him cruel and uncaring at times. I think mostly for Joanna's sake."

"Then you must repent. You must learn to see him as

he is, Elianna, not as your experiences declare him. Not the indifferent thief of dreams your heart accuses him of being. You must come to know him the way the captives in Babylon came to know him. Know him deep in your soul as the One who has plans for you—plans for your welfare and not for evil, to give you a future and a hope. This is not a lesson that can truly be grasped in our seasons of happiness. You must learn these truths about God in the captivity of suffering and sickness, just as the captives in Babylon had to learn them while under the yoke of their conquerors. You must learn to trust him when there is no earthly evidence why you should.

"Even if I pray for you today, your body may not be healed. But your heart, Elianna, can start mending today. Your soul can prepare for the plans God has yet to unfold for your life."

Gamaliel prayed for us with simplicity and faith. We all repented before God for our stony hearts toward him. We promised to love him even if he withheld the desires of our hearts from us.

"The Lord spoke a precious promise through the prophet Jeremiah," Gamaliel said after concluding his prayers. "'For I will satisfy the weary soul,' he said, 'and every languishing soul I will replenish.'

"You are weary, my children. You are languishing. I want you to understand that the Lord's heart rises up to you in a special way, for his intention is to satisfy you. He may yet restore to you the years the locusts have eaten. Do not give in to despair, but trust the Lord with all your heart. Do not lean on your own understanding."

What a peace comes at the end of surrender. What a relief there is when you stop striving against God and the world and yourself. I was at the end of myself. And yet, in a strange way, I had only started the most important journey of my life. Like Job I would learn that the Lord was a restorer of fortunes.

The day Gamaliel prayed for me, my body was not healed. It continued to hold me trapped in its leaking prison, unable to escape. But the heavy blanket of desolation that had plagued me to the marrow of my bones was ripped off, leaving me free to experience peace once more. God himself had torn away the darkness, opening a way for me to start my halting journey toward him. He had seen my weariness, and he intended to satisfy me.

TWENTY-FIVE

*For I know the plans I have for you, declares the LORD, plans for welfare
and not for evil, to give you a future and a hope. Then you will call upon
me and come and pray to me, and I will hear you. You will seek me and
find me, when you seek me with all your heart. I will be found by you,
declares the LORD, and I will restore your fortunes.*

JEREMIAH 29:11-14

BEING IN JERUSALEM meant that I could see Viriato. He
came to us wearing a purple cloak and a fine linen tunic.

"Purple, Viriato?" My eyebrows shot to the middle of my
forehead. "Ethan must pay well these days."

"A good servant is hard to find." He could not hide a self-
satisfied smirk.

"You are hiding something. I can tell. Out with it. Tell
us this secret."

He shrugged, trying to seem casual. "I received some
money from home. My father passed away a few years ago.
I invested my share in business with Master Ethan. It was
a struggle at first. But we've been doing well for some time
now. That is all."

"I forget that you came from an affluent home."

"My father was a merchant, like yours. He owned sheep and sold wool. Middling rich, at best. While he lived, the cash was tied up in land and flocks. At his death, my brother wished to dissolve the business and sold everything. That is how I came to have ready money. Even so, my share of the inheritance would not have amounted to much if Ethan had not added his own money to mine. He sold a piece of land he had purchased some years ago. The property had appreciated in price and he made a hefty profit."

"I am happy that the Lord has blessed you, Viriato. Do you work in wool or in dyes?" Curiosity had got the better of me. What business had my old friend invested in?

"Some of both." He drew out a sack he had hidden under his cloak. "I have brought you a few presents."

"Presents?" Joanna cried, brightening.

"Yes, mistress. This one is for you." He pulled out a length of deep green linen, the perfect foil for Joanna's delicate coloring. "You and Master Chuza can fight over it. I only have the one length for you."

"Clearly, my devastating beauty is better suited for such a rich color," Chuza teased.

Joanna pulled the fabric out of his hold. "Clearly, you have been dreaming again, Husband."

"And these are for you, Mistress Elianna." He placed before me two lengths of wool, one a pale blue, the other a delicate pink. Both were shot through with silver thread. I gasped. They were as magnificent as anything my father's workshop had ever created.

My heart began to pound as I fingered the weave. I could have recognized that particular warp and weft anywhere; they were a signature of our own workshop. "Oh, Viriato! You and Ethan bought my father's trade?"

"We did, mistress."

"Why did you not tell me?"

"We were not sure of our success at first. Our capital was limited, and without your talent behind us . . ." He shrugged. "We thought it best not to give you too much hope before we knew that we could survive."

I gulped past my tears. "You have made a success of it, I can tell."

"It took a good deal of time and hard work. But yes, mistress. The workshop has done well for us this year."

"You better stop calling me *mistress*. Indeed, it is more fitting that I should begin calling you *master*. You have made me very happy with your news. I cannot imagine a better outcome. To have you and Ethan at the helm of my father's old workshop removes the sting of losing it."

"I am relieved you feel that way, Elianna. I had worried you might be hurt by our decision. It is another reason why I chose to keep the news from you for so long."

"Hurt? Why should I be hurt when your generosity provides for me even now?" Then a thought occurred to me that gave me pause. I swallowed hard and tried to keep my voice steady. "Do Ethan and Sarai live at the house?"

"No. He refused. They live in an addition Ethan built on his father's house. We use your old home mostly for customers. I occupy a small wing."

"Which room did you take?"

He scratched at his scar, a sure sign he felt uncomfortable. "Truth be told, it's your old chamber, mistress. Ethan said it had the best light."

Joanna and I burst into laughter as we thought of him in our old surroundings with their very feminine furnishings. "Do you sleep on the bed with the frothy white linen and gold embroidery on the cushions?" Joanna asked.

Viriato scowled. "I have not had time to attend such things and make the necessary changes."

The image of Viriato sleeping on that delicate bed with its womanly adornments proved too much. Joanna and I dissolved in merry giggles while Chuza made a noble effort to remain unaffected and Viriato frowned like a bear.

❧

Upon our return to Tiberias, Joanna and I began to study the Scriptures Gamaliel had given into my keeping five years before. Sometimes Keziah would join us, and Chuza as well, when his duties allowed. One afternoon, Joanna and I had just finished reading the story of our people's escape from Egypt, with the pharaoh and his army in hot pursuit and an impassable sea before them. One of the greatest miracles the Lord had performed for our people was the parting of that sea.

"Can you imagine passing through with a great wall of rushing water on either side of you?" Joanna asked.

"Perhaps it is a little like you and me," I said.

Joanna stretched on the couch. "What do you mean?"

"Our forefathers had many dangers to contend with at that hour. On either side of them rose a wall of water the likes of which none has ever witnessed again. The wind raged; the sea churned threateningly like a lion ready to fall on its prey. The army of the pharaoh sat on the edge of the land, intending to pursue them. How easy it would have been for our people, through every step of that perilous passage, to set their eyes on these dangers. How easy to give in to fear and discouragement. Instead of looking upon the salvation of the Lord, they could have been overcome with dread and given up.

"You and I can do the same, little sister. We can put our eyes on your barrenness or my sickness. We can focus on the dangers that pursue us. Your concern about Chuza's parents as they grow colder toward you, and your fear that one day Chuza himself may turn away. I can center my attention on my body's weakness and the cure that seems to evade me year after year. I can drown in my dread of poverty as I expend a great fortune upon remedies that fail.

"These are the rushing waters of our lives, surrounding us like a churning wall on every side. They are the army of our Pharaoh. But instead of growing distracted and fearful, we can choose to set our eyes on the path that the Lord opens for us. One step at a time, we can go forward, and learn to be faithful in suffering."

In the sixth year of my flux, Viriato came to Tiberias for business, though he stayed three extra days to spend time with

Joanna and me. One morning when we were alone together, I asked him about Rachel.

A sparkle lit up his eyes. "She is just shy of three years old, and more trouble you shall not find in such a small package if you look the whole world over."

"Does she speak?"

"Quite a lot, though only her parents and little cousin seem to understand her. She has a very sweet lisp. Next to you, she is the most determined female I have ever met."

"Has you wrapped around her little finger, does she?"

Viriato gave a sheepish shrug. "Me. Her father. Her grandparents. Just about everyone who meets her bends over backwards to do her bidding. It is a good thing she has so much charm; when she doesn't get her way, she screams the house down."

I played with the fringe of my cushion, imagining a pretty girl with a fierce temper. "Does she throw many tantrums?"

"She could be used as a secret weapon against the Roman army. Her shrieks can pierce the ceiling. Only Ethan can manage her. She minds no one else and isn't even scared of the Pharisees. Once, I pointed to a particularly fierce-looking Pharisee in his black robe and long beard and threatened to give her to him if she did not behave."

"What did she do?"

"She stuck her tongue out at the man. I dare Caesar himself to make that child do what he commands. If she were not so winsome, we would all have to run away to a different country."

I placed a hand over my mouth to cover my laughter. "She can't be that fierce."

"Well—" Viriato gave a fond smile—"I am quite her slave, I admit. She is brave and charming. But even I cannot whitewash over that temper of hers."

An image of Ethan chasing after a delightful little girl, trying to subdue her wildness, made my belly flip. Would I ever stop loving him? "Ethan must be so happy."

Viriato's face became grave. "Sarai is sick."

I leaned back with shock. "How sick?"

"They do not expect her to last through the year, Elianna."

She did not. In less than six months, she died. The young, pretty girl with hungry eyes chasing after Ethan, the mother of his beautiful daughter, was laid to sleep with her fathers. They buried her somewhere in Galilee, Viriato told me, so that she could be near her mother, who had died not long before.

For a few days, while seeing to her funeral arrangements, Ethan must have been close to me. Several hours' walk at most. I wished I could have comforted him. I wished I could have dried his tears. Instead, I settled alone on my unclean cushion and shed my unclean tears for a man I could never touch again.

When I had been sick for nine years, I went through my small house and gathered every valuable object I owned. Clothes, jewels, carpets, gold and silver plates and goblets, precious reminders of the life I had once lived. I stripped the walls of their tapestries and made a pile in the middle of our room.

"Will you help me sell them?" I asked Chuza.

"Why do you not allow me to help you? Joanna and I have not spent much of her inheritance from your father. We can spare the money. You are my sister, Elianna. It is my duty and privilege to look after you."

I smiled. "Don't think I do not appreciate your generosity. But I prefer to use my own money as long as possible. A day may yet come when I will have no option but to turn to you for help. Let us pray God will intercede before that. In the meantime, there is a small fortune in that pile. It will see to me and Keziah for several years." Of course that was only true if I did not have to pay any more exorbitant fees to physicians.

Chuza pulled a hand through his thinning hair. "These are your memories from your childhood home, Elianna. Surely it is too painful to part with them."

"I hold my memories in my heart, Brother. These things do not mean so much that I cannot let them go."

There was one piece about which I could not say the same. It happened to be the most valuable object I owned. It was also the most precious to me. I could not find the strength to let it go. I could not bear the thought of looking at a faded patch of wall, without this final reminder of the man I would always love. Ethan's rare Babylonian tapestry, I held on to and treasured.

Without warning, Joanna and Chuza's lives were disrupted by an unforeseen challenge in the palace. After years of being married to the princess Phasaelis, Herod Antipas set her aside because he had fallen in love with his brother's wife, Herodias. Herodias must have felt the same, for she in turn divorced her husband in order to marry Antipas. The scandal of it rocked our country for a good while. Kings weren't supposed to set such a bad moral example. Chasing after one's own brother's wife was frowned upon even by the most lax of Jews.

With the advent of these unpopular changes, the well-run routine of the palace household turned on its head. Phasaelis ran off to her father, King Aretas. Herodias and her alluring daughter, Salome, took up residence, bringing with them unreasonable demands and onerous requirements. Poor Chuza spent long hours in the palace, trying to smooth the ruffled feathers of the many household servants who had taken an instant dislike to Herodias. He spent even longer hours figuring out ways to appease the new lady of the house.

From one day to the next my brother-in-law did not know what new crisis he might have to face. Many nights, he could not even come home. I knew Joanna felt lonely and concerned for her husband's work. We spent many hours praying during those months. Though they were arduous times, they brought us closer to each other and to God.

Chuza escaped from the weight of his job whenever he could and joined us for prayer. He said that those prayer times saved his sanity. They did not save his hair, however. He began to lose it in handfuls until you could see his scalp clear through. Fortunately, Chuza was so attractive that even with thinning hair he did not lose his charms.

After Chuza gave me the money from the sale of my furnishings, I dragged myself to another physician, this one a Greek who had set up his business in southern Perea. He had come to gather minerals from the Salt Sea, having heard of their restorative powers, and remained long enough to build a reputation as a clever man.

Traveling never came easy for me. Constant bleeding made me weak; I needed rest more often than other women. Jews did not like to travel near me lest I touch them by accident and make them unclean.

Moreover, the expense of caravans and inns and road levies, added to that of medicines and physicians, became another concern. Once my funds from the sale of my furnishings dwindled, I would have nothing left with which to support myself.

I chose to bear the expense of this particular journey because Anaximander the physician had healed several cases that had been considered incurable. Equally important, he had little interest in evil spirits and incantations. He believed disorders had natural causes and would therefore also have a natural cure.

He took copious notes when we met for the first time, asking questions so awkward I thought of walking out a few times. The man had no sense of propriety. His long, pale forehead shone with sweat as he wrote on his rolled-out parchment. "Acute effluvium of blood. Chronic pain in the lower abdomen. Crisis lasting nine years. Repeated relapse of

patient after occasional bouts of freedom from hemorrhage."
He spoke out loud as he wrote, as if I actually could understand what confounding words such as *effluvium, chronic,* or
relapse might mean.

"Have you noticed if certain foods or activities exacerbate
your condition?"

"No."

He rolled up his sleeves. I saw him open a plain box made
of olive wood. Inside sat a menacing assortment of metal
instruments: long and short, fat and thin, oblong and spoon-
like, designed to pull and push and cut flesh. "I must examine you."

"Examine me?" I asked faintly.

"Ah. You Jews and your preoccupation with modesty.
How am I to diagnose you properly without looking for the
cause of your illness? Your servant girl may stay if you wish."

"If you think it indispensable."

I lay back on a couch, stiff with embarrassment. Examine
me, he did. He poked and prodded and sniffed and stared
and stopped in the middle of his torment to take more notes.
Tears dribbled down my cheeks. I would as soon slap him as
pay the man.

"There is an imbalance in your humors. If we bleed you,
we will restore balance to your body."

"Pardon, Anaximander, but you did hear the part about
my being here because I am bleeding? For nine years?" I threw
my hands up in the air. "How will more bleeding help that?"

"You know nothing about it, woman. Do you wish to be
cured or not?"

I shrugged. What harm would losing a little more blood do me? "Proceed, physician."

He made me turn over on my belly. With a sharp razor, he cut five precise lines deep into the flesh of my back, where it dipped lowest. I grimaced. I could feel my blood drip down my side. With a deft movement, Anaximander caught the flow in a thin-lipped bowl. Protecting his couch from the stain, I guessed. He sat near me and watched as my life seeped out of me in slow rivulets. Keziah slumped in the chair near me, looking whiter than salt, chewing her nails.

I began to feel weak and dizzy. The physician must have finally grown convinced that I had lost enough blood to suit him. By pressing a linen towel into the cuts, he stopped the flow. I only wished it were as simple to stop the flow of my flux.

"You must rest for seven days. Drink broth made from the flesh of a young bull five times a day. At the end of that period, use the mud that I have packed in this kerchief to create a warm poultice over your belly and lower parts. This mud comes from the Salt Sea and has great restorative powers. Apply it for at least three full days, making sure to keep it warm that whole time. Finally, bathe in a churning river, preferably when it is cold. You shall be cured if you follow my instructions with care."

I was certainly cured of the heaviness of my purse.

Keziah helped me walk back to the quarters we occupied during our stay in Perea. If not for her strong arm around my waist, I would have collapsed in the street. The additional loss of blood had made me so dizzy that my steps wobbled as we made our way back to the inn. I collapsed in my bed and lost consciousness for twelve hours.

Keziah waited by my bed with a bowl of rich broth when I awoke. She had procured this delicacy with some difficulty and at great expense. It tasted marvelous to my parched throat. I stayed in bed for seven whole days without putting up any argument. It wasn't merely that I wished to follow the physician's instructions to the letter. I felt too weary to move. Anaximander's remedy had nearly done me in.

At the end of seven days, Keziah made the poultice of mud according to the Greek's instructions and, after warming it over the fire, handed it to me. This proved to be a wonderful treatment for one's most hated enemy. The mud stung upon contact with the sensitive skin of my lower abdomen. But for three days I gritted my teeth and applied it faithfully as he had instructed me.

We had to walk almost two hours to arrive at the Jordan River for the final stage of my treatment. We picked a spot that seemed to have the strongest current, the water churning and frothing vigorously. I could do nothing about the temperature. To me it seemed more than cold enough. Stepping ankle-deep into the water, I gasped.

"Are you certain, mistress? It looks deep in that spot."

"I will be fine," I said, not certain that my assurance would prove true. *Lord God, please preserve me,* I prayed. *Please pour your healing balm into me and restore me. Take away this plague of blood from me forever.*

I stepped deeper until the water reached my thigh. Grabbing hold of a long branch, I held on for dear life, resisting the pull of the current that tried to wash me away. Cautiously, I stepped forward; the water rose to my waist. Without warning, my foot slipped and I sank.

I did not know how to swim.

For long moments I struggled underwater, my body waving and undulating painfully, my lungs screaming for air. Somehow, I managed to find a foothold again and stood. The current had moved me deeper into the river and now I stood chest-deep. Taking long, gasping breaths, I remained still until the pounding in my chest quieted down. Then I closed my eyes and abandoned myself to the washing of the water.

Use this river to make me clean, Lord. Wash away my shame. As you rebuilt the crumbled walls of Jerusalem during the time of Nehemiah, reach down and rebuild this ruined body.

By the time I emerged from the river, I felt spent. To my delight, for a whole day and night my body did not bleed. Then the flux returned, making me a captive more than ever, for after Anaximander's treatment I grew weaker than before and could not regain even my former strength.

After paying Anaximander and covering our expenses in Perea for two weeks, my funds once again grew alarmingly low. Soon I would be unable to maintain my own house. What could I do?

Joanna and Chuza promised to help me so that I might remain in the house, but I considered this too great an expense. Joanna already had more than enough trouble. She had not become pregnant again since her last miscarriage, and her mother-in-law, Merab, wanted Chuza to set her aside in favor of a more fertile woman. Chuza had remonstrated with her, but how long could a man withstand a mother's constant nagging? If I accepted financial help from Chuza, I would only add to the condemnation Merab heaped upon my sister.

One night as I studied the Scriptures, I came upon a passage from the prophet Isaiah:

Come, everyone who thirsts,
    come to the waters;
    and he who has no money,
    come, buy and eat!
Come, buy wine and milk
    without money and without price. . . .

I wondered about those words for a long time. The Lord was promising provision to those who feared that they would go hungry and thirsty. *"If you have nothing, come to me,"* he was saying. *"I will be your provider."*

But there was more than a practical assurance in God's words. He wasn't merely saying that in our poverty, he would provide. He had more for us. After making the promise about filling our hunger, the Lord of heaven gave a strange command: *Hear, that your soul may live.*

God wanted to fill the hunger of our souls.

Come and buy that which will bring life to your soul. It costs no money to become whole. The famine of your heart can be satisfied the way an empty belly can be filled.

I hugged the roll of parchment to my chest. Heretofore, my greatest needs had seemed physical ones. My flesh needed healing. My finances needed restoring. These were necessary to my well-being, to my survival even. And yet were these truly the most important needs of my life?

I remembered with sudden clarity Joseph's death and the guilt I had never been able to overcome, though so many years had passed from that tragic day. As if it were only yesterday, I felt again my father's blame and his constant rejection. I relived the grief of his injury and death, and my mother's loss. The pain of Ethan's wrenching abandonment overwhelmed me once more.

If the soul had blood to shed for every wound, I would be a mangled carcass now. More than a roof over my head, more than a healed body, I needed to have my soul restored. The Lord promised that this was possible. It was free. It was available. But I did not know how to obtain it. How did you go about finding wholeness and holiness when you were this unworthy? My flesh might have been unclean, but my heart was even more so.

I had no spiritual currency with which to come to God. I had no righteousness, no true depth of prayer, no great understanding of his Word. My sin was ever before me. Yet here was this incomprehensible promise: *"He who has no money, come, buy."*

TWENTY-SIX

With God we shall do valiantly;
it is he who will tread down our foes.

PSALM 108:13

ONE RAY OF JOY pierced the troubled clouds of my life. I received a letter from Claudia informing me that she and Titus would be visiting Judea soon. Better still, they had been invited to remain at the palace of Herod Antipas for a full week, so she would be a Sabbath-journey's walk from my home. Of course, it took two whole months for her to actually arrive at my door. How those sixty days crawled and tarried!

I could tell Claudia was shocked by my appearance. We had not set eyes on each other for eleven years. I was thirty-one years old and a far cry from the vibrant girl she had known. I had lost weight; my skin had grown white and pasty. And nothing could hide the frailty of my body, which forced me to sit after only a little activity.

"Oh, Elianna!" she cried and burst into tears before taking me into her arms. It had been so long since someone who loved me had touched me with tenderness. I still refused to allow Joanna any contact with my skin lest her womb be contaminated by my malady. Even Keziah was not allowed to come near me; it was the only thing I could do to protect her from being polluted by my illness. Heaven knew she already had to bear with our neighbors' scorn for the mere indiscretion of living with me.

After a moment of consternation, I leaned into Claudia's embrace and started to weep. I loved the Roman arms that did not reject me, but held me tighter and grew damp with our tears.

Finally, we drew apart and dried our eyes. "Tell me about Titus. How is he?"

"He fares well. Elianna, I cannot explain what turned the tides of our fortunes or why our former enemy, Sejanus, decided to forgive Titus and think of him in a favorable way.

"The years have not been kind to the emperor. Tiberius has all but retired from public life. This keeps Sejanus very busy; he practically runs the empire. Who knows how many seditious plots he has had to undo? Perhaps he grew to appreciate my husband's honesty. At least he knew that Titus would not stab him in the back while speaking a vacuous compliment."

"What does Titus do now?"

"He has been appointed a praetor, as we hoped."

"Isn't that an army commander?" I asked, settling myself on my cushion and leaning against the wall.

"It can be. In this case, Titus is a magistrate who works

through the tribunal. We have been stationed in Sicilia for some years. I think Sejanus is thinking of sending us back to Palestine soon."

"Oh no! I am sorry, Claudia. I know how you hated it here."

The generous mouth flashed its charming smile. "I hated seeing my husband sink under the weight of an inferior position. As praetor, he shall enjoy the rank and influence due his abilities. We shall be very happy here.

"Do you know, I believe that your prayers may have opened the door to good fortune for us. Remember how you told us about your God and the way he helped Cyrus the Persian? Titus still talks of it."

I shook my head. "I am glad that story made an impression."

"Indeed. Titus has a very positive view of your God, unlike most Roman officials who are stationed here. They only perceive him as a source of trouble—an agitator of revolutionaries."

Claudia adjusted her skirt as she stretched her feet. "My husband seems strangely drawn to your God. He even visited the outer courts of your Temple in Jerusalem once. It made him very popular with certain Jewish officials, though he had not gone to gain favor. He went to satisfy his own curiosity."

"Titus could get along with anybody. Even your cruel Sejanus could not resist him for long."

Claudia slapped her thigh and sat up straight. "I almost forgot. Guess who we ran into while at Herod's palace here in Tiberias?"

"Chuza?"

"Well, yes. But I did not mean your sister's husband. I was referring to Decimus Calvus. Remember him?"

"Yes. I have a vague recollection," I said through frozen lips. I had not seen the man or heard of him in over ten years.

"He has been transferred to Galilee recently. Time has graced him with favor. He has been promoted to senior centurion and commands a cohort."

"He is here in Tiberias?" I emptied my voice from the dread that chilled me to my bones.

"Indeed. You might run into him, Elianna. This is not such a large city."

Would I never be rid of that man? "I doubt our paths shall cross. I rarely leave the house."

"Do not be shocked by what I am about to say. Once, I thought he liked you. A lot. He often stared at you with that narrow-eyed, thoughtful look men get when they want a woman."

"The Lord spare me from such liking." I could not suppress a shiver.

"You disapprove of him? Because he is a Roman?"

"Because he is untrustworthy."

"I am sorry to hear it. I confess, when I ran into him this week, I thought . . . that is, I hoped you might be open to a new relationship. Calvus is divorced, you know? And you are as pretty as ever. Prettier, even, with a kind of fragility that is sure to please a man."

My eyes snapped open. "Have you lost your mind?"

"Why not? You would make the best of wives."

I groaned. "First, he would make a terrible husband. I would rather have a bleeding disease. Oh, wait. I already do. That should count for the second."

Claudia giggled. "I have so missed you. We must find you a new physician. If you were in Rome, you would have been healed ten times over by now."

"I once had a physician trained in Rome."

"What happened?"

"I was a lot poorer when he left."

Claudia made a noise between choking and laughter. "What of this prophet everyone is buzzing about?"

"What prophet?" I couldn't help sounding bored. Apart from the topic of brilliant physicians, nothing irked me so much as talk of new prophets. Because of my sickness, folks felt it their duty to point out any self-proclaimed holy man who poked his head out of a bush in the wilderness. I was content with reading the proclamations of the Lord as spoken through the old, established prophets. I was content with his Word. New prophets had little to offer but empty promises and trouble.

"He is one of yours. Everyone is astonished by the miracles he has been performing all over the Galilean and Judean countryside. The blind see, the dumb speak. Genuine miracles, by the sound of it."

"Have you seen one?"

"Well, no."

"There you are. By next year, he will be forgotten and I will still be sick."

My two best friends happened to come to Tiberias within a few days of each other. Several weeks earlier, Viriato had written to say that he would arrive in Galilee for business and intended to stop at my home to see me. The evening we expected him, a knock sounded at the door. I had sent Keziah to pick up provisions for our meal. In order to save my dwindling funds, we normally ate very simply, and except for Chuza's generous gifts of occasional wine and pastries left over from one of Herod's feasts, our regular diet was unsuitable for someone with Viriato's healthy appetite. I planned to feed him a stew with real meat that night. None of the usual watery barley soups for our giant.

At the sound of the knock I ran to the door, already beaming with the anticipated pleasure of seeing my friend. Flinging the door open wide, I cried, "You are early and I have no food to offer you yet."

Decimus Calvus grinned at me from the other side of the threshold.

"What an enthusiastic welcome," he drawled. "A man could grow used to such a smile, even without food on the table." He was garbed in daunting military gear, his scarlet cloak flung over one shoulder, chain mail and leather belts covering his torso. His plumed helmet was tucked under one arm.

I took a hasty step back. "What are you doing here, Calvus?"

"I am stationed in Tiberias now."

"So Lady Claudia told me when she visited. What brings you to my door? Surely you know I have no wish to see you."

"But I have every wish to see you." He brushed past me as he stepped inside, closing the door behind him.

"Get out," I said through gritted teeth.

"Is that any way to speak to a man who has spent days searching for you?"

"I do not know why you would waste your time with such a task. We have nothing to say to each other."

To my vexation, Calvus threw himself on the couch and stretched his legs as if he owned every cubit of the house. "Sit down, woman. I have things to say to you."

"What things?"

"I hear you have been sick."

"Yes. Happy?"

"Don't be an imbecile if you can help it. Why would I be happy? I never wished you ill."

I sniffed. "You caused me more harm than anyone on this earth."

He shrugged. "I am in a position to undo the damage I unintentionally may have brought you. Though, in truth, I did you a favor. That Ethan you had your heart set on was—"

"If you say one false word about him, I am walking out."

He lowered his eyelids. "Let us speak of more pleasant topics. I have been promoted, you know."

"I can see." I gestured toward his impressive uniform with its gold embellishments.

"And I divorced my wife."

"I am sorry to hear it. How unpleasant for you."

"On the contrary, it was the most pleasant thing that has happened to me in years."

I bit my lip. "You are a strange man."

He sat up. The illusion of relaxation vanished in one moment. Hard muscles clenched as he leaned forward. "Not at all. I never wished to marry her in the first place. My father pressed me into the arrangement for financial considerations. We owed her family a large sum. They cancelled our debt when I married her."

I could not help feeling sorry for any woman whose hand could only be purchased through a hefty bribe. Gingerly, I sat on my cushion. "Was she fearsomely ugly?"

"Quite the reverse. She looked like Venus. She had also earned the reputation of a harlot before she had seen her sixteenth birthday."

I gasped. "I am sorry."

"Not as sorry as I to be chained to such a strumpet. I tried to make the best of it. There was no best; her wild ways continued even after we married. I would have divorced her then, except the law required that I return her dowry, which I might add was a great deal of money to sweeten this dreadful bargain made in Hades. But I had already spent every denarius and had no hope of earning such a large sum any time soon. I volunteered for service in Judea to get away from her. And to find a way to earn enough to rid myself of her permanently. I have finally managed to do so."

I drew my legs up. "I am glad you are free of your misfortune. But I cannot see what it has to do with me."

He abandoned the couch and squatted before me on the floor. "I have always wanted you, from the moment I saw you biting and scratching and fighting like a tiger against that grimy thief. You were beautiful. Courageous. Bold. And yet so pure. You were the antithesis of the wife who chained me. In spite of the years of your absence, I have never forgotten you. The fates have brought me here, where you live. I mean to take their offering this time." He grabbed my chin with a callused hand and forced me to look at him. His face—clean-shaven, lean, and well-formed—revolted me.

"Let me go, Calvus."

"I am asking you to be my woman. I want to take care of you. You don't need to live in this hovel anymore."

I slapped his hand away from my jaw. "You do not seem to understand the nature of my illness. I cannot be any man's woman, even if I wished. Which I don't."

"I know. So you bleed a little. You Jews are too delicate about matters of the flesh. I will take you as you are. It matters little to me."

I choked, coughing until moisture filled my eyes. "Have you no shame?"

"No." He leaned forward and tried to kiss me.

I slapped him as hard as I could. "You should have learned the last time you tried that—I have no interest in you."

"As I recall, you allowed me."

"I had no choice! I did what I needed to do in order to protect my family. In order to shield Ethan and Viriato from your violence. I know what you would have done to them with little provocation. This time, I have no one to shield.

315

Leave me be, Calvus. You make my stomach turn. You always did."

"Liar!" He leaned into me until I was flattened against the wall. I was too weak to put up much of a fight. His lips landed on my cheek when I turned my face, pushing against his chest with ineffectual hands.

"Kindly take your hands off her, Centurion. If you please."

Viriato! I had forgotten him completely. He stood in the threshold of my house with the door wide open behind him, framing his great body in the light of the moon. Not again! Not this scene of horrors, threatening the lives of those I loved.

Calvus released me and rose to his feet slowly. It dawned on me that Viriato wore a smile and stood as peaceful as a lamb, no weapon anywhere in sight.

"Leave us alone," Calvus spat.

"I am afraid I can't do that." Viriato crossed his arms.

"You wish to be arrested?"

"For what crime?"

"Whatever you like, former slave. Don't think I can't land you in a cinnabar mine again."

I groaned and covered my face with my hands. A sudden noise made me raise my head. To my utter shock, there stood Titus with a host of soldiers at his back.

"What goes on here?" he asked, his tone cold.

Calvus straightened and slapped his forearm against his chest in a formal salute. I remembered that my friend now occupied a position of high rank.

"Nothing worthy of note, my lord. Just visiting an old friend." Calvus's masklike face did not betray any emotion.

"Elianna, did this centurion give you offense?"

I thought hard. Titus would not always be here. It would not be wise to make an enemy of Calvus any more than I already had. "He made me an offer, which I refused. I believe he was about to leave, my lord."

"Don't let us detain you, Centurion," Titus said. He spread a hand in a courtly gesture. "The door is this way."

Calvus turned white around the lips. Before he could step outside, Titus spoke. "Decimus Calvus?"

"My lord?"

"I overheard your final comments to Viriato. Know that I have taken note of your conduct. Should anything happen to that man or to Mistress Elianna, I will not rest until I have seen you answer to Rome's justice. Do we understand each other?"

"With perfect clarity."

Titus then dismissed the soldiers who had accompanied him. "May I come in?" he asked with civility, as though it were an ordinary night and a few friends had gathered for a casual conversation.

I sagged against the wall, shaking with reaction. "Please. And may the Lord bless you for rushing to our rescue. How did you come to be here so quickly?"

"I happened to run into Viriato on the street only moments before he came to your house. He overheard enough of your conversation with Calvus to grow concerned and ran back to fetch me. I am glad I was here to help, Elianna. Has that man made a nuisance of himself before?"

"Longer than any of us realized," Viriato said, his voice faint.

TWENTY-SEVEN

It is good for me that I was afflicted,
that I might learn your statutes.

PSALM 119:71

VIRIATO HAD OVERHEARD most of my exchange with Calvus. He now grasped more fully the events that led to my divorce from Ethan. I saw no sense in hiding my secret anymore. In halting sentences, I told my friends what had taken place so many years before.

"Why did you not come to me?" Titus asked, white with anger. "It is common enough for our soldiers to make pests of themselves with local women. The gods know we discourage them. There are rules against such behavior."

I drew a calming breath. "What could you have done then, Titus? You had your own troubles to contend with. Sejanus breathed down your back, and you did not know if you would survive from one week to the next. Besides, back

319

then, you would have had no authority over a centurion in spite of your patrician origins."

"Why did you not tell *me*, then?" Viriato said. His voice was anguished. "I would have helped you and Ethan."

"How? By attacking a Roman official and landing your-self in another abominable mine in some forsaken land? I could not live with that. I could not buy Ethan's and my happiness at the cost of your destruction."

"So you sacrificed your own happiness for the sake of our freedom?" Viriato said.

"Someone had to pay that price. I could not trust you and Ethan to remain cool. Even if you managed to control yourselves this time, what of the next? I worried that Calvus would not stay away. I feared he might renew his attentions, whether because he wanted me or merely to provoke a fight with you two. He is a volatile man who flips from kindness to violence without warning. You and Ethan would remain in danger as long as Calvus stayed in Jerusalem."

"Elianna!" Viriato cried. "When I think of what you lost in order to shield us . . . it is worse than the mines, I tell you. Knowing what you suffered for my sake, without ever telling anyone."

"Rest easy, my friend. Calvus did us all a favor. Would you have wanted Ethan saddled with a wife like me? At least, free from me, he was able to have a child. A sweet girl he adores. He experienced the love of a good woman for some years. What could he have had with me? An ailing wife he could never even touch. A barren woman with nothing to offer. If you ask me, you should write a letter to Decimus Calvus and thank him from the bottom of your heart." I tried to look lighthearted as I spoke, but my eyes stung with unshed tears.

⁂

One afternoon two weeks later, Keziah told me that she had to fetch water.

"But we have plenty."

"I wish to do laundry." She scratched her arm and looked away.

I frowned. "Keziah, you finished the wash two days ago. We have nothing that needs washing."

"I forgot my old tunic. I won't be long, mistress."

She slithered out before I could ask another question. I shook my head. She must feel cramped and restrained, stuck indoors with no one but me for company most of the time, I thought, and resolved to send her abroad more often. I pulled out my roll of parchment and had started to write the account of Decimus Calvus's extraordinary reappearance in my life when a sound made me look up.

Ethan stood in the room. He must have come in silent as a cat for me not to hear the door open and close. At first, I thought he must be a figment of my mind. I blinked and stared. To my utter stupefaction, he did not disappear.

"Ethan?" I croaked, my voice barely a whisper.

He strode toward me without a word and, before I could object, grabbed hold of my hands and hauled me into his arms.

"Ethan! I am unclean!"

He cradled my head against his shoulder. "I have never known a cleaner woman."

I struggled to get free of him. I felt defiled by my sickness; it horrified me to touch him with this bewildering intimacy. He subdued my attempts to pull away. "Be still, Elianna. I have dreamt of this moment for days. Let me hold you for a few moments longer." He reached for my fingers and held the hands that had ached to be held for so long.

I had not laid eyes on him for eleven years. But everything about him felt as familiar as it did when we were young. The scent of him. The timbre of his voice. The feel of his arms around me. The hardness of his chest, the softness of his breath as it stirred against my temple. I was shivering like a leaf caught in a thunderstorm.

"Viriato spoke to you?"

"As soon as he returned." He pulled away long enough to gaze at my face. "Why did you never tell me? Why didn't you explain afterward, when the dust had settled?"

"Could the dust ever settle on such a matter? I was afraid for you: your sense of justice, Calvus's mercurial temper. No good would have come of your knowing. And later, when you were betrothed, it did not matter."

"Of course it mattered! I thought you had broken faith with me. Knowing the truth would have freed me of that pain, at least."

"Knowing the truth would have confused you. What could you have done? Break your covenant with Sarai? Remain with her and feel guilty about me? No, Ethan. I made the right choice for all of us. I have never regretted it.

When I fell ill, I knew that we were never meant to belong to each other."

Ethan stepped away and pulled an agitated hand through his hair. I noticed that there were faint threads of silver at his temples. He was thirty-seven years old, I realized with a pang. Our youth had flown so quickly, lost to us forever.

"I heard of your sickness a few years ago. How long has it been?" he asked.

"Eleven years."

"Eleven years! Have you tried many physicians?"

"Everything possible. I fear I have run out of true alternatives. The last physician insisted that I spend a week in the temple of Asclepius. Of course, I could not do that. I would rather receive the silence of the Lord than the healing of an idol."

"Oh, Elianna." Ethan cradled my cheek in his palm. "I am truly sorry for what you have suffered."

"It has not all been bad, Ethan. I have grown closer to the Lord because of it, and that is a treasure I would not lose."

He nodded. "I can understand that. I have felt the same many times." He sighed and gestured toward the couch. "May I sit?"

"I shall have to be inhospitable and refuse you." I gave a wobbly smile. "Having touched me, you'll have to go through ritual cleaning first. I keep that sofa and most of the other furnishings in the house unpolluted by my touch for the sake of Joanna and Chuza as well as Keziah." I tapped a wide cushion sitting on the floor beside mine. "You can sit here, if you wish. Since it is after sunset, I fear you will be considered unclean until tomorrow evening, even if you wash yourself and your clothes when you leave tonight. I am sorry for the inconvenience I have caused you."

"You speak of the inconvenience of ritual cleaning to *me*? When I know what you endured on my account?" He shook his head. "I abandoned you, Elianna. When you needed me most, I walked away." He fisted his hands. I saw they were shaking badly.

"We both know that is no fault of yours."

Ethan lowered himself on the cushion near me, his movements awkward, as if someone had punched him hard and his body hurt. "When Viriato told me what you had done, I was assailed by such a tumult of emotions, I hardly understood what I felt. At first, I felt guilty, and then deeply angry. Perhaps there is a shade of that anger still left in me. I know you lied in order to protect me. But, Elianna, you took our whole future into your own hands. Without consulting me, without including me, you made a decision that changed our lives irrevocably."

I felt my face redden. "Ethan, what else could I have done? You were about to attack Calvus and get yourself killed, wounded, or arrested. You weren't in any state to listen to reason. Nothing would have stopped you short of what I said."

"I grant you, in that moment there was little else you could have done. But what of later? An hour, a day, a week after that horrible afternoon? I had calmed by then."

I rubbed my forehead. "Had you? How could I have been certain?"

"You should have trusted me."

"I was tempted a hundred times to come to you and confess. Then I would think, to what purpose? I could only bring you trouble, Ethan. In the end, I felt you deserved better in a wife."

Ethan brought his fist down on the floor, making me jump with the force of its crash. "That was my choice. I loved you, Elianna! Loved you more than my own life. You ripped my heart out with your decision."

"And my own! But you are alive. You have enjoyed a good life. You married an excellent woman. You have a beautiful daughter. With me, you could have had none of those blessings."

His eyes captured mine. In the lamplight they looked very dark, glittering with emotion. "I never stopped loving you. Even when I thought I hated you, the love was there, just under the surface."

I wiped a tear. Another escaped. "You were good to me, Ethan. The quiet divorce, your decision to speak no ill of me in public. And you sent Viriato to me. I was grateful for the many considerations you showed me, given what you thought I had done at the time."

"You must have been so lonely. Did you ever tell anyone?"

"Only Gamaliel, after my father died."

"You told Gamaliel? What did he say?"

"He surprised me with his gentleness. A few years ago, I saw him again; he prayed for me. That I might be healed. For Joanna, too." I told Ethan about Joanna's longing to have a child. I knew she would not mind Ethan knowing.

"What of Calvus? Has he shown up again since the night Titus threw him out?"

"To my great relief, he has not. Ethan, you will not go anywhere near him? Please?"

"After the sacrifice you made to keep Viriato and me safe from that man, I could not bring myself to touch a hair on his head. You have cured me of all desire for revenge."

I smiled. "I knew God would use me to build your character."

The wind was strong that night. It beat against the lattice of the windows, whistling its fierce tune and blowing dust inside. "I wonder where Keziah is. She left to fetch water. That was an age ago. I pray she is not caught in this weather." I started to feel uneasy over her safety.

Ethan pulled on his ear. "I might have something to do with that."

I glared at him. "I take back what I said about your character. Clearly it needs a lot more building. You involved my maid in an intrigue behind my back?"

He shrugged his shoulder. "I wanted to see you alone. We had too many things to discuss that required privacy."

"And when is she returning?"

"Do you miss her? I thought I might be a good substitute."

My belly flipped. I took a deep breath and reminded myself that I was unclean. There could be no future for us. He wasn't *my* Ethan anymore. "Tell me about your daughter. Viriato sings her praises."

A look of tenderness transformed Ethan's rugged features. "She is eight now. She can read and write."

"You taught her?"

He shrugged. "She pestered me until I did. It was hard on her when we lost Sarai. In the absence of a mother, she has grown deeply attached to my parents. But she is closest to me. She wants to do everything I do."

I laughed. "That must be a sight."

He gave a sheepish smile. "It warms my heart, seeing her follow me around. She has been the greatest joy of my life."

"I am glad you have her. I pray for you both every day."

His eyes clouded. "Do you, Elianna?"

The air seemed to grow heavy so I could barely breathe. To break the tension, I threw my hands up in the air, pretending a lightheartedness I was far from feeling. "I have a lot of free time. Which reminds me, you sly man, how is the workshop?"

"Do you mind that it belongs to me and Viriato now?"

"It was the best news I had heard in years when Viriato told me about it. I could not imagine a better outcome. You were too generous with me. Without your lavish payment for my father's business, I would not have been able to survive."

"I paid only what was fair." He looked around him, taking in the old furniture, the bare floors, the undecorated walls. "Physicians cost a lot of money, as I recall from the days Sarai became sick."

"Yes."

"Do you need help, Elianna? You know I would—"

"Thank you, Ethan. I am well provided for."

He frowned and grew silent for a moment. I could sense he had not let go of the subject, but was merely working on broaching it in a more compelling way. I didn't want him to offer me financial help. It grated on my pride. I did not wish to become the object of his charity or pity.

"It grows late. You had better be on your way, Ethan. The neighbors disapprove of me already. What with a centurion in full uniform, as well as a Roman praetor and his pack of soldiers at my door not long ago, they won't have much patience for an unaccompanied man and no chaperone here in the dead of night."

Ethan cut through my diatribe and picked out the relevant point. "Why do your neighbors disapprove of you?"

"I am unclean." I lifted my chin as I spoke to show that their scorn did not bother me.

Ethan's cheeks turned a dull red. "Are they cruel to you?"

"They keep to themselves. It's of no account. I have little interest in them."

"Elianna, please let me help you."

"No."

He let out a deep breath. His eyes had narrowed to slits. I had seen that look before. I tried to remember when, but could not. Without further objection, he rose to his feet. "The Lord bless you."

As he left, pulling the door softly closed behind him, I had a sudden recollection of when I had seen that same odd look cross his face. It was the day his new horse had thrown him. He had gotten that narrow-eyed look before getting on the back of that wild creature and taming it into an obedient, biddable slave.

TWENTY-EIGHT

Hope deferred makes the heart sick,
but a dream fulfilled is a tree of life.

PROVERBS 13:12, NLT

DESPAIR IS AN INVITATION to prayer. You can either sink or pray when it lodges at your door. I had arrived once again at the point of despair, and this time, I sank. I had no money. What remained of my inheritance would pay for a month of food and lodgings if we were careful and augmented it with my meager income from the sale of my homespun fabrics. I had prayed for God's provision so many times, yet nothing seemed to change. I only became poorer and more desperate. One morning I stopped praying and decided I needed to take action instead.

I came to stand before Ethan's tapestry where it hung on the wall. It was the only valuable item I had not sold. I knew I would be able to keep Keziah and me for a full year if I could sell it at a decent price.

"Keziah, come and help me take this off the wall."

I heard a gasp behind me. "You cannot sell that, mistress! You love that tapestry."

I sighed. "I have no choice. We are going to run out of money. Now please bring it near the window so I can examine it in the light of the sun. I need to ensure it needs no repairs."

Keziah did not budge. She crossed her arms in front of her chest. "Have you prayed about it?"

My mouth dropped open. Keziah never challenged me. I knew her faith had grown deeper in recent years. Often, she would join my sister and me, fasting and praying and asking insightful questions about the Scriptures. Though she could not read, she had a quick mind and had memorized large portions of the Law. Yet she had never questioned *my* faith.

"The time for prayer is past," I said. I knew my tone was tart, but I could not curb my tongue.

"Mistress! The time for prayer is never past. I will not touch that tapestry until you promise to pray for two weeks. Seek God's will, and if he opens no other doors, then I will do as you say."

After twelve years of living alone together, the lines between servant and master had long grown bleary. Keziah was as much a friend as servant to me. She had earned the right to reprimand me, though she rarely exercised it.

I felt my annoyance evaporate. "I have no choice, it seems. I can't touch that tapestry as I would render it unclean. And you refuse to do it."

Keziah grinned. "That sums it up. Now let us pray and ask the Lord to give you his aid."

After we finished seeking the will of God, Keziah said, "Mistress, have you heard of the new prophet from Galilee?"

I groaned. "I care not for any new prophet unless he is interested in buying my tapestry for a good price."

"They say his touch heals."

"And I say it is time for our noonday meal."

⚜

The day Keziah had promised to help me place the tapestry on sale, Ethan came to my home. I should have expected his arrival. Keziah kept in touch with Viriato and Ethan and had made arrangements with them behind my back more than once.

I hugged my elbows and hardened my heart to the sight of Ethan's beloved face. "Whatever you have to say, the answer is no."

"Some things never change, I see. Your favorite word is still *no*."

"I am well aware you and Keziah have hatched some plot between you. I told you I did not want your help, Ethan. I will manage by myself."

"I agree. And so you should."

"You do? I should?"

"Certainly. I am here for a business transaction."

My eyes narrowed. "What kind of business transaction?"

"You want to sell my tapestry. I want to buy it back. That is an irreplaceable piece, Elianna. If you are going to get rid of it, I would rather have it in my own possession."

"Oh." In truth, I could not object to his reasoning. The

piece was rare and extremely valuable. Ethan had always admired it. I could believe his willingness to purchase it for his own pleasure rather than in order to rescue me.

What followed must have been one of the most absurd transactions in commerce ever to take place. The buyer insisting on a higher price, the seller absolutely refusing the trade unless the price were lowered. If I had not been on the edge of humiliated tears during our negotiations, I would have laughed aloud.

As he put away his coin purse, Ethan said, "There is a new prophet in Galilee who wields great power, they say. Have you heard of him? My wife's cousin, Jairus, who is the leader of the synagogue in Capernaum, has heard him teach." His voice sounded casual, but his shoulders were stiff.

"Keziah speaks of little else these days," I said with a yawn.

"I fear that is my fault. I told her about the man."

"I have no interest in new prophets and dazzling miracles." I jingled my leather pouch, heavy with gold, thanks to Ethan's generosity. "This, on the other hand, shall bring great relief into my home."

Ethan saved me from homelessness that day. What he paid me for that tapestry would see Keziah and me through two more years instead of one. How I would provide for myself after that, I could not say. But for now, at least, I was safe. God had provided, though I, in my pride, did not like the means of his provision. I gave him thanks in much the same tone I had used to thank Ethan. Ungracious and resentful. The Lord did not strike me down, nor did Ethan hold it against me.

※

"They say he is a great prophet," Joanna said, her hands flapping with excitement.

Not this holy man again! Keziah would not stop talking about him. Every day she told me a new story more unbelievable than the one before. And now my sister was joining her forces.

"Joanna, you know that amongst the people of Israel, great prophets come and go with the same predictability as the change of seasons."

"He is different, I tell you. A report of him has spread throughout this region."

"Who is this man? And where does he hail from?"

"He is Jesus of Nazareth."

I frowned, not bothering to hide my skepticism. "Nazareth, that backwater village? He is probably just an ignorant peasant with claims too big for his own good."

"They say he astonishes people with his authority and knowledge. Last week in Capernaum, he was teaching in a synagogue. A man who had an unclean spirit came to that place. Jesus cast the spirit out, Elianna."

I rolled my eyes. "I wish someone would cast out the dust around here. The weather has been so dry, it gathers as soon as we clean it."

"Listen to me, Sister. That same evening, people throughout the village who had heard about this miracle brought their sick family members to him."

"Was there a long line? He must have made good money that night."

"He charged no money. And he healed every one. No matter what diseases they suffered, the touch of his hand healed them."

I frowned. "This is a tall tale, Joanna. How can you be so gullible?"

"How can you be so cynical? You have tried every physician, suffered every indignity under the sun from supposedly learned men. Will you not give this man of God a try?"

"Thank you. No."

Joanna was now twenty-nine years old. She longed for a child so badly that I feared she would fall for any fraudulent prophet with a slick tongue. I had been sick for twelve years, myself. I could understand her vulnerability. But I was determined that I would not be won over by a dishonest man posing as a prophet.

꙳

A letter arrived from Ethan. It did not mention money or the workshop or Calvus or the past.

He wanted to bring Rachel to Tiberias so I could meet her.

I am traveling with my daughter to Capernaum in three weeks so she can tarry with her mother's relatives. We will stay at the house of Jairus, the man I mentioned earlier. He is the ruler of the synagogue and was my wife's cousin. Rachel adores his daughter, Lilit. Though

*Lilit is twelve—three years older than Rachel—the two
are fast friends. May we stop at your house on our way
back from Capernaum so that I can introduce Rachel
to you?*

This request astounded me. I could not fathom the reason
behind it. Why would Ethan drag his daughter to my house?
To her, I was nothing but a stranger, a shadow in her father's
past. With this infernal sickness leeching the life out of me,
I could be nothing to her, not even a kindly aunt offering
frequent hugs and generous presents.

For all my misgivings, I could not resist the offer. The
child for whom I had prayed over so many years, the little
girl I had grown to love without ever meeting, would soon be
at my house. I could see her, hear her, know her a little. To
behold her in the flesh surpassed all my imaginings.

I also knew that this renewal of my acquaintance with
Ethan could shred my heart to pieces. He was already awak-
ening feelings and desires I had long since put to sleep. The
very sight of Ethan made me long for things I could not
have. Marriage. Family. Love. Belonging. I needed fortitude
to resist this futile temptation. I could resist offers of financial help and Calvus's empty overtures and even the appeal
of an early grave by my own hand. But how was I supposed
to resist love?

❧

"I witnessed this with my own eyes, when I traveled to
Capernaum with Chuza last week," Joanna said, her face

radiant with a feverish light. "Jesus was speaking at a house in Capernaum. Many of us had gathered there to hear his teaching. People filled the courtyard and even sat outside, near the windows, in order to hear him.

"The air inside was stale from the proximity of too many bodies. But no one stirred. He speaks with such authority that we hung on his words with no thought for our comfort.

"There was a sudden commotion above us. You shall never guess what happened next, Elianna. A group of men had brought their friend to receive prayer from Jesus. The invalid was a young man, with a thin face and dark, suffering eyes, paralyzed from the waist down and confined to his mat. They had carried his mat over to the house where we were, hoping to see Jesus, but could not get through the great crowds. So they climbed to the roof, removed the tiles, and lowered the man down through the hole, until he landed at the master's feet."

I chuckled. "What did the owner of the house say?"

"No one noticed! We were all laughing and cheering. Then Jesus motioned for us to quiet down and everyone grew still. He looked toward the ceiling and smiled. 'I see you have faith,' he said to the man's friends. Then turning to the paralyzed man, he said, 'Young man, your sins are forgiven.'"

I gasped. "He said that?"

"He did. There were several Pharisees and teachers of the Law present in the house at that time. Apparently, they did not like Jesus's pronouncement of forgiveness, for by their reckoning, only God can forgive sins. Jesus must have sensed their displeasure, for he said to them, 'Why do you question this in your hearts? Is it easier to say "Your sins are forgiven," or "Stand up and walk?"' And then turning to the paralyzed man, he said, 'Stand up, pick up your mat, and go home!'"

"Well, he is certainly bold. What happened when the young man remained on his mat, gaping at him?"

"He did not remain on his mat, Elianna. In front of our eyes, that young man jumped up, picked up his mat, and went home, praising God so loudly we could hear him halfway down the lane. Then everyone raised such a deafening cheer you could not hear anything but shouts of joy for a long time."

I frowned. "The paralyzed man walked?"

"As well as you and me. What do you say now, Sister? Are you starting to believe that Jesus is a true prophet?"

"I see that you believe it," I said with caution.

"There is something more I must tell you. He prayed for me."

"Did he?"

Undeterred by my wooden tone, Joanna continued her story. Something in her voice, her manner of speaking, even the faraway look in her eyes made the hair on my arms stand on end. This was my beloved sister I knew so well, and yet there was some intangible difference about her. Joanna had never seemed this content to me, nor had I seen such a joy in her countenance, not even on her wedding day.

"He has the gentlest eyes I have ever seen," she said. "It was like being bathed in love, having his gaze rest on you. Chuza had taken time away from work concerns to come with me, and he asked Jesus to bless me. The teacher laid his hands on my head. At first, I felt a peace I have never known. I could feel the sorrow of every miscarriage strip from me. Before long, another strange thing happened. The fears I have carried through the years fell away. Fear of losing Chuza's love and ending up alone. Fear of his parents' increasing criticism. Fear of being a complete failure as a wife. I was being washed, layer after layer, my soul cleansed of its many burdens.

"Without warning, I felt my knees give and I collapsed, crying and trembling. At that very moment I knew I had been healed. I knew I would bear a child. A healthy child."

I froze. I could not deny the deep peace that seemed to have settled upon Joanna. But the certainty of her hope alarmed me. How disappointed she would be when her expectations came to nothing. When she continued to remain barren. I remembered those nights when I had lain in my bed with a knife clutched in my hand because hope had disappointed me.

"Hope deferred makes the heart sick," the Proverbs taught. A truer word was seldom spoken. I smiled for Joanna's sake, feeling sick inside.

Sometimes the evidence of our senses and the testimony of the world's wisdom are plain wrong. Sometimes the Lord is busy forging victory when the mind expects only defeat.

I had believed in the brutal futility of Joanna's hope in a mere man. But God, who knits miracles from the fragile threads of our faith, knitted a miracle in my sister's womb.

After so many years of barrenness she became pregnant again. Never have I been so happy to be proven wrong.

I had the effrontery to remain worried and to doubt. She had lost three babies. Though she remained unshaken in her faith that this child would be born healthy, I could not help but fear she would yet again taste the bitterness of disappointment. This time, however, I was not nearly as contemptuous of this Jesus of Nazareth.

"Come with us, Elianna," Joanna pleaded with me. "Chuza and I are going back to Capernaum to hear him speak."

"I think not, beloved."

"You still doubt him?"

I laid my head on my knees, feeling weary to the marrow of my bones. "He is either a cheat, in which case it would be a waste of my time to come and see him, or a true prophet of the Lord, in which case he shall not want me and the taint of my uncleanness to come anywhere near him."

"I think you are mistaken. He is holy; I have no doubt of that. But in his holiness, he welcomes the brokenhearted, the sinners, the weak. I heard him say, 'Come to me, all of you who are weary and carry heavy burdens, and I will give you rest.' You are weary, my beloved sister. You carry such a heavy burden. Come to him, and let him give you rest."

I went still. The Nazarene's claim captured my soul as deftly as a fisherman catches fish in his nets, for those words were a close proximity of God's own proclamation through the prophet Jeremiah, which had seized my heart so long ago.

"For I will satisfy the weary soul, and every languishing soul I will replenish."

These were the words I had clung to for years. Words I did not yet know how to fully live. And now a man spoke them as if he were himself the fulfillment of them. *"I will give you rest."* An ordinary man with the power to end weariness, to dispense God's rest to those who carried heavy burdens. What I could not do for myself, this prophet claimed to be able to do for me.

Could such a promise be fulfilled?

Could I afford to ignore the offer, no matter how hard my disappointment if he lied?

TWENTY-NINE

When they walk through the Valley of Weeping,
it will become a place of refreshing springs.

PSALM 84:6, NLT

I TRAVELED ALONE to Capernaum, where this Jesus often visited. Joanna, though healthy, had started to feel the sickness that plagued many pregnant women and could not face the journey, and Chuza found himself preoccupied with the approach of one of Herod and Herodias's many banquets. I left Keziah behind because I knew she would care for Joanna. I dared not leave my sister to the ministrations of her censorious in-laws. With Chuza engrossed in his demanding work schedule, my sister would need Keziah's attentive presence.

In a way, I preferred traveling alone. I would prove a nuisance to anyone who came with me. By myself, I wouldn't cause my traveling companions an additional inconvenience with the limitations of my condition. I carried my own pillow and bedding so that I caused as little aggravation for the innkeeper as possible. With my cautious preparations, they would not have to wash everything after my departure. Nonetheless, I had to part with a good deal of denarii, which I could not afford, in order to make myself welcome.

It was said that Jesus crossed the Sea of Galilee often and spoke in different parts of the region from day to day. No one knew for certain where he would show up next. Nonetheless, the crowds managed to somehow sniff out his location and gathered around him whenever he approached. I needed only to remain in Capernaum for some days and wait for him to show up again.

In an ironic twist of God's incomprehensible plans, Ethan also was near, staying with Jairus the synagogue leader. I did not seek him out. I planned to return home in time for his promised visit. Trying to contact him in the house of his wife's relatives would prove an awkward imposition.

The two men who most consumed my thoughts were within my reach. Jesus of Nazareth and Ethan Ben Ezer. Yet I could touch neither.

I fell asleep a bare hour after arriving at the inn, depleted by my short journey. Anxiety had dogged each step of my travels. What if Jesus proved a fake? What if I was never healed? What if Ethan gave up on me and I never saw him again?

Fear is a tenacious force. Even through the coils of sleep I felt it nip at my heels. Felt it chase me down and catch me and laugh as it won.

*※

"That fellow you came to see," the innkeeper's wife said in her rough Galilean accent. "He is on the hillside teaching."

"You mean at this moment?"

She snapped her fraying rag at a fly marching over a tray of dates. "According to my servant who just walked past there, he has already drawn heaps of people. You better go before you miss the entertainment."

"Thank you. Can you please give me directions to the place?"

"One of our boys is going that way. You can follow him."

An impressive crowd had gathered around the hillside near Capernaum to listen to Jesus. I had rarely seen so many people in one place. A sea of people, squashed together, hanging on the words of this one Galilean. Male, female, child, adult, it seemed not to matter. They were all drawn to him.

I dared not go close lest I touch someone by accident and cause a furor; instead I lingered to listen alone from afar. His features were a blur from where I sat. He seemed a surprisingly ordinary man. His clothes were not fine and he wore no jewelry that I could see. I could hear his voice, which the hillside carried with clarity—deep, strong, and certain, with a sweet warmth I had never heard in another voice.

"But to you who are willing to listen, I say, love your enemies! Do good to those who hate you. Bless those who curse you. Pray for those who hurt you."

The crowd hushed, breathless, wordless. No one stirred one hair. I understood their stunned silence. The shock of those words went through me like an earthquake that utterly capsizes everything in its path. Love my enemies? Love Decimus Calvus? Do good to him? Bless Avigail, whose sharp tongue had pierced me more than once? Pray for Calvus, not that he be punished, but that he be blessed? That he prosper and be happy? Is that what he meant, this Jesus?

Then I wondered what would have happened if my father had done this for me. When I failed to care for Joseph as I should have, when I caused his death, what if instead of rejecting me, he had loved me? Blessed me? Prayed for me? How different my life might have been if my father had been able to live by these words.

But to love Decimus Calvus? He was not even sorry for his actions. He felt no shame for anything he had done. How could I even begin to forgive the misery of losing Ethan? And with him, the workshop, our house, everything we owned. One part of me truly believed that not marrying Ethan had been the best gift I could have given him. But a deeper part of my soul mourned that loss. It still cut me when I thought of it. Every lonely night, every empty day, every silent hour slashed at me with its sharp edge. Ethan was like a perforated wound that refused to close.

I was to forgive that? Pray for the one who had caused such an incurable wound and felt not one grain of regret? How could I? The answer came simple and fast: I could not.

In the days that followed, I had the opportunity to witness Jesus minister to the pressing crowds many times. Once, a centurion sent some of our people's elders to the teacher, asking for his help. The Jewish leaders speaking on behalf of the centurion pleaded with Jesus. "He has a valued servant who is gravely ill and will soon die. Please come to his aid. If anyone is worthy of your help, it is this centurion, for he loves our people and our nation. He even built a synagogue for us with his own money." Their sincere defense of a Roman centurion astonished me. Why would respectable Jews show such devotion to one of our enemies?

Jesus did not seem to share my misgivings; he went with them, a crowd following his footsteps closely. I lagged behind everyone at a cautious distance. When we were still a short way from the house, several Jewish men approached Jesus and introduced themselves as friends of the centurion.

"Lord," one of them said to Jesus, "our Roman friend has sent us in his place. We are to tell you to trouble yourself no further. There is no need for you to come within, for as he said in his own words, 'I am unworthy to have you under my roof. Such an honor is too high for me. I did not presume to come and meet you in person for the same reason. But if you would deign to speak a word right here, where you stand, I know my servant will be healed. For I too serve under the authority of my superior officers, and have authority over the soldiers in my cohort. If I want something done, all I have to do is speak the words. I say *come* and my soldiers come; and I say *go* and they go. Lord, I know it is the same with you. You only have to speak the words, for you have the authority to heal my servant.'"

The crowd gasped when they heard this unusual

declaration. Humility like this was rare to find in any man. But in a Roman?

"I am amazed," Jesus said as he turned to the crowd. "I tell you, I have not seen faith like this Roman's in all of Israel." He sent the friends of the centurion back to the house with a word of encouragement. The crowd lingered outside the door, wondering what the outcome would be. I noticed Jesus standing with his eyes closed, smiling as if he knew something the rest of the world could not comprehend. I could not remove my gaze from him. His mere presence drew me like a fire in the middle of a frozen desert.

A few moments later, the door burst open and one of the friends of the centurion flew out. "He is healed! The centurion's servant is healed! At this moment, he is sitting up and eating a big bowl of stew. He has not been able to eat in three days. He is perfectly recovered. An hour ago, he was at death's door. But one word from the master and he has been restored to health."

A deafening cheer pierced the countryside. I thought the crowd might trample Jesus in their ecstatic fervor. Like an immovable force he stood, unimpressed by the praise. You would think the ardent approval of men meant nothing to him.

I lowered myself onto a large rock jutting from the side of the road, my movements slow. What power was this? How could a mere man speak healing to someone he had not seen or touched? And yet Jesus seemed utterly unaffected by the furor of admiration he had caused. I was witnessing something untouched by the corruption of this world and it confounded me.

A woman with a warm smile approached me. "I am Mary. I noticed you sitting here alone and thought I would come to greet you."

"I am Elianna," I said woodenly. Though she seemed friendly enough, I could not welcome her amiable conversation. I worried that if she discovered the nature of my illness, she might alert the crowd and force me to turn away. But she did not seem interested in my history.

"The master always bestows blessings wherever he goes," she said. "There are no ordinary days when you follow Jesus."

"Do you know him well?"

"I accompany him and his disciples whenever I can and contribute financially to his ministry. He healed me of the evil spirits that had tormented me for years. I owe him my life."

"He allows a woman to travel with him?"

The smile blazed. It made her plain face look radiant. "There are several of us amongst his faithful followers, and he draws more disciples with every passing day. He welcomes women as readily as he welcomes men. Never have I felt so safe as when I am in the presence of Jesus."

"You have no cause to doubt him?"

"Doubt him?" She had an open face that seemed devoid of subterfuge. Kneeling by my side, she said, "He is my teacher and my Lord. More still, he is the promised Messiah. He has come to set the captives free. Once, I was such a captive. Now, I am free."

I frowned. Noticing a stain on my skirt, I rubbed at it,

distracted. But it proved too stubborn; I could not remove it. "That is quite a claim," I said. "He is not the first man to have made it."

"But he is the only one who has given sight to the blind, made the lame walk, restored hearing to the deaf. Though he wields indescribable power, he remains humble. No one is too low for him. Several weeks ago, after a long walk, when we had stopped to partake of a simple meal, the crowds brought their children to him. Children! Dirty feet; runny noses; wailing, smelly infants. His disciples tried to send them away, crying, 'For shame! Do not bother the master with these young ones. Gather them to the arms of their wet nurses. They do not need a rabbi yet.' But Jesus said, 'Leave the little ones alone. Don't prevent them from coming to me. God's kingdom belongs to them.' Then he laid hands on each one and prayed for them.

"I have seen him forgive sins, not with mere words that land in your ear like an empty puff of air, but with the power of God. When he proclaims forgiveness, lives change. People turn inside out and become new.

"His closest friends, the twelve that travel everywhere with him, once saw him calm a storm at sea with a simple proclamation. Even death cannot withstand his power. Last week, just as we were arriving at Nain in Judea, we noticed a funeral procession by the city gates. We questioned the crowds about who the body belonged to and were told that he was the only son of his widowed mother. How bitterly she wept, that poor woman. Her sobs racked her thin flesh so that she could hardly breathe.

"The master's eyes softened as he watched her distress. I love to see that look on his face, for I know a miracle is not far. Compassion becomes a weapon of warfare in Jesus's hands. No heartache can stand against it.

"'Do not weep,' he said to the widow. The woman gaped as Jesus walked up boldly and touched her son's bier. Everyone came to a standstill—pallbearers as well as the great crowd who had gathered for the funeral. They must have thought him completely insane! They were even more stunned when he said in a loud voice, 'Young man, I say to you, arise.'"

"He said that aloud? What happened then?"

Mary started to laugh, silent wisps of air escaping her open lips. "The dead man sat up."

"No!"

She nodded. "That wasn't nearly so enjoyable as when he started to speak."

"What did he say?"

"He said, 'What is all this commotion about? Mother, have you been crying? I feel a little tired. Why am I lying in this place?'

"I cannot remember everything. But Jesus took hold of him and drew him out of the bier and handed him into the arms of his weeping mother. Perhaps you understand now why I say Jesus is the Messiah. God has visited his people just as the crowds proclaimed that day."

Mary left to join her friends shortly after sharing these astonishing revelations with me. I had witnessed the healing of the centurion's servant. But could I believe what Mary was saying? The sick healed, the dead raised, the forces of nature itself bound by the power of the words issuing out of this man's lips? If all these reports were true, then even our greatest prophet Elijah could not compare with Jesus and the magnitude of his deeds.

As I walked to the inn, my steps heavy with fatigue, one thought haunted me. *"Love your enemies."* I had yet to ask Jesus for anything. I had yet to draw near enough to look into his eyes and be acknowledged by him. But irrationally, I felt he had asked something of *me*. If he had spoken my name out loud that day on the hilltop, his command would not have felt more personal. *"Pray for those who hurt you."* An unshakable conviction filled me with irresistible force. He had asked me to do this one thing. Love, love, love Decimus Calvus; pray for him. Bless him.

Likely, I would never come near enough to Jesus to receive his prayer. He might be welcoming to little children, but I doubted he felt charitable toward a woman who would bring him the disgust and inconvenience of an unclean touch. Still, I felt a compunction to do his bidding. Forgive the man who had ruined my life.

At the inn, in the corner of my small chamber with its crumbling walls, I collapsed on my squashed pillow. *Lord God, I have been walking through the valley of weeping for so long. Please transform it into a place of refreshing springs. Please, Lord, teach me how to pray for my enemy. Change my heart so that I can bless Decimus Calvus. Bless Avigail.* Then a new revelation dawned that made me stop breathing. *Help me forgive my father for not forgiving me.*

THIRTY

My beloved speaks and says to me:
"Arise, my love, my beautiful one, and come away,
for behold, the winter is past; the rain is over and gone.
The flowers appear on the earth,
the time of singing has come."
SONG OF SOLOMON 2:10-12

GOD'S SPIRIT CAN RIDE a puny breeze as well as a hurricane. My prayer was feeble and fearful. But I offered it with an honest desire to please God. I prayed out of obedience rather than mighty faith or conviction. He seemed not to care about my insufficiency, for in spite of my weakness, he showed me great mercy that day.

My struggle with Jesus's demand rose from the feeling that forgiving Calvus meant I exonerated him of all wrong. He would never have to answer to anyone for his selfish brutality. He would get away with his sins.

Then it dawned on me that my forgiveness had no bearing on justice for Calvus. He may not have to answer to me, but he would certainly answer to God for his sins. In that moment I realized why Jesus said to pray for our enemies. Poor Calvus! I would not wish to be in his shoes when he faced the Lord's wrath. For the first time, I felt pity for the man. The change in my heart astounded me.

This time when I prayed, my words flowed without impediment. I let my enemy go, and by letting him go, I myself was set free. I never realized how much bitterness and resentment I had held against Decimus Calvus until these burdens fell from me like broken chains. For the first time in years, I felt light and clean. I even asked the Lord to bless the man who had wrecked my life and caused my family to lose their home and business.

After forgiving Calvus, Avigail came easy. I laughed through that prayer, remembering some of her absurd words. I did feel sorry for Daniel and prayed much harder for him than I did for Avigail, I confess. I could not help it. Being married to her could not be easy. God's angels would find her a trial. Then again, I myself was no watered garden. No doubt, I proved a trial to the whole host of heaven on a regular basis.

When it came time to pray for my father, I had no problem blessing him. Loving him, though he was gone so many years. But to my astonishment, I could not forgive him. I could not forgive the man who had withheld his own forgiveness and blessing from me. He had robbed me of a father. I had grown up under his roof, eaten his food, worn his clothes, run his workshop, heard his words, and I had done it all as an orphan. My father had made me fatherless while he still lived, and this I could not forgive. The orphan child still wept the bitter tears of the abandoned.

❧✳

The next time I saw Jesus, he was stepping off a boat. We were by the shore of the Sea of Galilee, a Sabbath-day's walk from Capernaum. The crowds were thick that day, for his boat had been spotted an hour before, and we had gathered expectantly for his arrival. I stood on the edges of the throng, watching as he and his disciples disembarked from the simple fishing boat. No sooner had he stepped on land than the crowds descended on him, pressing in for one touch, a small blessing, a word. The noise was deafening. I watched to see if he seemed annoyed by the demanding hordes, but he was smiling, unperturbed by the constant jostling for his attention.

In the midst of that chaos, he reached down and tousled a child's bright red hair and said a few words that made the child shriek with laughter. Jesus grinned back. Even from where I stood I could see the expression on the master's plain face; it softened with tenderness and a keen, otherworldly warmth that I had never encountered before. Within me, something hard and closed off began to melt.

Who can understand the ways of faith? For more than a week I had followed this man and seen him perform miracles, heard him teach, witnessed him show compassion to the poor. And yet it was in this incongruous moment, when he gave his attention and affection to a little boy in torn sandals and a dirty robe that I came to believe. *He is the Messiah!* I thought. *He is our promised redeemer!*

Many have asked me what gave me the courage to do what I did that day. It was not courage, I say. It was desperation.

Simply, I became more desperate than afraid. And in my desperation, I learned to hope. I never stopped being afraid. It was just that hope overshadowed my fear. Looking upon this man's ordinary visage, I caught a glimpse of extraordinary love. It was such love that made hope grow—a hope like none I had ever experienced before. I wasn't wishing or dreaming or merely longing for the impossible. I stood on a bedrock of certainty. This hope would not disappoint. And the hope became a single, encompassing thought:

If only I touch his garment, I will be well. Once it entered my head, I could not shake the thought. I could not push it away. Here was my healing; this man himself was the Balm of Gilead. He was the end of my tears, the rest from my burdens. He was Life.

If only I touch his garment. I took a step forward. *If only.* I took another step toward him. *If . . .* Another step. Now I was in the midst of the crowd, being jostled with everyone else. People touched me and I had no way of avoiding them.

Before I could reach Jesus, a man arrived. His elegant robes and gold rings shouted wealth. The crowds made room for him, obviously recognizing him and giving him a place of honor. The man walked to the master unimpeded and fell at his feet. A gasp went up from the crowd. This was not a scene we saw every day. Rich men in general tended to avoid kneeling before other men. Jesus was poor—the son of a carpenter. By the world's standards, he stood far beneath such a prosperous man. Kneeling, the rich man acknowledged that by God's standards, Jesus surpassed him. Surpassed us all.

"Teacher, I am Jairus, the leader of the synagogue in Capernaum," he said.

My eyes snapped wide. *Jairus, Ethan's relative?* Wildly, I looked about, and a few steps behind the synagogue leader, I spotted Ethan. He stood rigid, his arms crossed about his chest. His face had a grayish cast. The only other time I had ever seen Ethan look so grim was the day he had witnessed Calvus kiss me.

Jairus spoke again, and I returned my attention to him, hoping he would explain the devastation so clearly etched on Ethan's face. "Please, Teacher. Come to my house, for my only daughter is dying. She is barely twelve. Come and save her, I beg you."

This must be Rachel's friend Lilit, whom Ethan had mentioned in his letter! Dying? No wonder Ethan was desolate. What horrors pursued us in this world! Compared to hers, my troubles seemed paltry.

Jairus's face, white and grimy with sweat and the dirt of the road, was lifted toward Jesus. He had no remedy save for the master. I knew only too well how human medical knowledge often failed with egregious regularity. Wealth could not expand our limitations. We were constrained by our ignorance, bound by our incurable sorrows. Helpless and utterly broken, this aching father sought a miracle.

Lilit had lived on this earth for only twelve years. With a sharp little twist in my heart, it dawned on me that she had lived the same number of years that I had been ill. A dozen years of life. A dozen years of agony. And Jesus stood between our twelve-year histories like a divine hinge that could bear the weight of our unlikely hopes.

Another shaft of pain twisted sharply within me when it occurred to me how deep Jairus's affections ran. This father's love for his daughter screamed in silent anguish as he knelt prostrate, unashamed to implore the master. Like an indictment, his love pierced my heart, for I knew I had not been loved like that by *my* father. Not after Joseph died. Perhaps not ever. I stood here, alone, with no one to implore for me, no one to weep for me. I stood abandoned, unprotected, while this father begged.

Jesus lifted Jairus up with a hand under his arm and nodded, turning to leave with the synagogue leader. That's when I knew. I was about to lose my chance at healing. The fragile hope for a new future slipped away before my very eyes. He could not have known it, but in heeding Jairus's entreaty, Jesus was destroying mine. Moments before, I had grown convinced that if I could only touch the hem of the master's cloak, I would be healed. The possibility of a new life had taken hold of me.

And now, that possibility walked away with purposeful steps. I could not bear it! I could not lose my one chance. Of course I would not touch his skin. I would not impose on him my filthy condition. He need never know, I thought. I pushed away at the bodies that blocked my path. In my desperation to get to him, I cared little about the Law, or the opinion of others.

I crept behind him and crouched on the ground. The crowds still hemmed about him, making a good covering for my bold theft. I reached my impure fingers and grasped the fraying, dust-covered edge of his cloak. It still held a bit of damp from the sea. I gasped. The noise of the crowd covered my exclamation; their bodies shielded my crime.

I felt a strange tingling in my fingers where I touched the fabric that covered him. Feverish heat rushed through me. Even when I had been about to fall into the wall of fire that consumed my father's study, I had not felt such flames. The words of the prophet Malachi echoed vaguely in my mind: *"the sun of righteousness will rise with healing in his wings."* It was as if the sun itself had risen over my body, pervading my veins, oozing heat into my blood.

I still weep when I think of that astonishing moment. I still shiver with the impossibility of it. For in the very instant that I touched him, the blood stopped flowing from my body. It stopped completely. I knew that I would never suffer from this infernal disease again. I knew it as certainly as I knew my own name.

I got to my feet, unsteady, half dazed. I knew I had to leave his presence before I was discovered. I had stolen from him. I had taken without his permission. Intending to lose myself in the crowd, I stumbled away.

Jesus stopped dead. The whole procession to Jairus's house stopped with him. "Who touched me?" he asked.

I trembled where I stood, not daring to take another step. Joy and horror mingled through me, making me weak. I was healed. But I was also caught!

One of his close followers, a burly fisherman named Simon whom they often addressed as Peter, said, "Master, the people are crowding and pressing against you. What do you mean who touched you? Who isn't touching you?"

I took a breath. Here was relief. Here my salvation. *Listen to Peter,* I wanted to shout. *Heed your friend.*

He did not.

"Someone deliberately touched me," he insisted. "I felt healing power go out of me." He looked about, intent on discovering the thief who had stolen from him. I began to tremble so violently that I could barely stand. I could not hide from the Messiah, I realized. If I did not come forward, he would know it was me soon enough. Forcing myself to move, I fell at his feet.

"It was I, master." I could barely breathe. "Forgive me. I was too unworthy to come to you and seek your help."

He remained silent. Through the veil of my tears, I could not make out his expression. I could not see if he was furious or merciful. I wiped at my eyes and took a gasping breath. I would have to tell him the truth.

"For twelve years I have been suffering from a bleeding flux. Twelve years unclean." I pressed the flat of my hands against my face and forced myself to continue. "Shunned and alone. No physician could heal me. They took my money, but they had no cure. Then I started following you, and I knew you could help me. I thought, if I could only touch your cloak, I would be healed."

I dropped my hands to look at him. "And I was, master! The instant my hand touched the hem of your garment, the flux left my body."

Brown eyes the color of good earth gazed down on me.

There was no vestige of condemnation or disgust in those extraordinary eyes. They brimmed over with compassion. Grace flowed from him. He knelt down until our faces were level. I began to weep so hard, my whole body shook.

"Daughter," he called me. For the first time since Joseph died, someone called me *daughter*. The word left his mouth and entered my soul like a shower of indescribable love. How do you explain a miracle? Words cannot capture a move of heaven. He had already healed my body. But by that one declaration, he healed my heart. He claimed me as his own.

We must have been about the same age. It did not seem to matter. He meant that claim. By making it, the hole in my heart began to fill. It filled with love! It filled with hope, with belonging, with protection. I was no longer orphaned. Rejected. Whatever my father felt for me after Joseph's death no longer held any power over me.

I don't know if he could read my thoughts. He smiled as if he knew the full content of my heart. As if my soul were a parchment he could read, and he liked what he found written there. "Your faith has healed you. Go in peace."

At once I knew why he had stopped the urgent procession to Jairus's house. It wasn't to remonstrate with me. It wasn't to create a new spectacle for the crowds or make a point. He had delayed in order to complete my healing. I had knelt down broken, sick, shattered. I rose up healed and fully graced by peace.

The Messiah had touched me. I would never be the same again. Across the crowds I sensed someone staring at me. I had been the focus of attention the whole time Jesus had been speaking to me. But the weight of this gaze, I could not shake. It was Ethan, golden eyes wide with shock. I laughed. If anything could have improved upon this moment, it was to have him there, witnessing the miracle of my healing and sharing in the glory of God.

My attention strayed to a man with gray hair who ran amidst the crowd with a shout. His wrinkled cheeks were wet with tears. "Master Jairus, I've just come from the house. Your daughter is dead," he said. "Don't bother the teacher anymore."

Ethan covered his face with his hands. Jairus groaned and collapsed on the ground. Jesus lifted him up gently. "Don't be afraid. Have faith."

The crowd made to follow him again, but Jesus would not allow them. "This time, only Peter, James, and John." Ethan followed them to the house, looking grim. I would have reassured him if he were nearer. Jairus and Ethan had no way of knowing this. But I understood better than most: that little girl was about to receive the surprise of her life.

I returned home a free woman in every possible way. My body, my soul, my spirit had received the wholeness I had longed for these many years. I understood Joanna's certainty about the health of her baby now. I had five more days before I could be declared officially clean according to the Law. But I had no doubt that my healing was complete.

That night, another surprise awaited me. As I came to the Lord in prayer, overflowing with so much praise I must have said nothing but *hallelujah* for a whole hour, it dawned on me that I had forgiven my father. There was no more bitterness or anger left in my heart toward him. More astonishing, for the first time in sixteen years the weight of guilt and self-loathing I had felt since the death of Joseph lifted away from my heart. I had spent half my life carrying condemnation like a prisoner's iron shackles. In the span of a few moments, the Messiah had cleansed me. What I could not have earned with all my efforts and rule-keeping, he gave to me for free. He had set another captive free.

Ethan, I knew, would come to me as soon as he could. I was restless for his arrival. Restless to hear about Lilit and to tell him my own story. He came sooner even than I expected, a mere day after I arrived home. Rachel was not with him, wanting to remain with her friend Lilit for a few more days.

"I promise you two shall meet soon," Ethan said as he sat on the couch and drank from the cup Keziah had served him. "I did not stop to rest, but came straight here as soon as I could." With a deep sigh, he placed the empty cup on the table.

"Tell me about Lilit."

"Elianna, if I had not seen it with my own eyes, I should never have believed it."

I laughed. "I know exactly what you mean. What happened when the master came?"

"There was a lot of wailing and mourning at the house, as you can imagine. 'Stop wailing. She is not dead but asleep,'

Jesus said. Do you know, some people were so bold as to laugh at him?"

"Did you?" I teased.

"I did not laugh. Not after watching what happened to you. But I did not really believe he could do anything. A sick child is one thing. But a dead one?" Ethan shook his head. "Jesus ignored the laughter and with a calm command sent us all out of the house and would not allow anyone to go to the child except for his companions, Peter, John, and James, as well as Jairus and his wife.

"Later, Jairus told me what happened inside the chamber where Lilit's body lay. Jesus went to her and held her cold little hand in his. 'Little girl, rise up,' he said. Jairus and his wife were torn between hope and dread. They hardly knew whether they had welcomed a holy man into their home or a madman.

"That was until Lilit stood up. She walked around when they asked her if she was able to move. She felt no pain. No fever, no weakness in her joints. All her symptoms had vanished. That child was as rosy-cheeked and hearty as the first day I met her."

"What did you all do when she walked out?"

"Well, no one was laughing, I can assure you. We were amazed, overwhelmed by this power that surpassed anything we had ever seen. There was a time when I thought Caesar was the most powerful man the world over. I know better now. One day no one will remember the name of Tiberius. No one will give a thought to Caesar. But the name of Jesus shall have great renown as long as men live on this earth."

THIRTY-ONE

You make known to me the path of life;
in your presence there is fullness of joy;
at your right hand are pleasures forevermore.

PSALM 16:11

"I HAVE A QUESTION TO ASK. But first, I want you to forget the word *no*."

I stared at Ethan, baffled. He had remained with me only a few hours last week before returning to Rachel. Today he had shown up with Rachel in tow, as promised. At nine, she had outgrown the wildness of her childhood, but not the spirit or charm.

"You are every bit as beautiful as I imagined you would be," I had said to her when they arrived, admiring the strange golden eyes, so much like her father's.

"You too, Mistress Elianna."

"I'm an old woman, practically," I had said with a smile.

"For an old woman, though, you are still pretty."

Ethan had covered his mouth with a hand and shrugged his shoulders at me. "Well, thank you, Rachel," I said and invited her to sit next to me. I had been declared clean by the priest several days earlier. Every bit of unclean clothing, cushions, and bedding that I owned, I had burned in a bonfire in our little garden that same hour.

Wearing a robe made of the pink and silver fabric Viriato had given me as a gift, I sat on the old couch, relishing the comfort of it. Small amenities still felt like a luxury to me. For the length of two whole hours, Rachel and I chatted. I asked her about her favorite activity—purchasing dyes with her father—and her favorite color—blue like the Sea of Galilee. She asked me regarding my illness, about which Ethan had spoken to her, and was surprisingly adult in her compassionate response. She had had a glimpse of Jesus when he came to Jairus's home to attend Lilit and spoke about him in an appealing mingling of curiosity and longing.

It was Ethan who had finally stopped our conversation. "Rachel, why don't you go with Keziah and pick up some wine and meat for our supper? Help Keziah get a fair price, now." He turned to me. "Rachel is very adroit at bargaining. The shopkeepers run when they see her come."

Now that we were alone, Ethan and I sat across from one another, and after an awkward silence he began by telling me to forget the word *no*.

I suspected that he planned to speak about helping me with finances again, and I felt the old prideful rebellion rise up in my chest. "No," I said.

He started to laugh. "I am a doomed man." His long-fingered hands reached for the back of his neck, rubbing in the unconscious way he had when he felt nervous. The last traces of laughter vanished from his face. He leaned forward.

"I have waited for you longer than our forefather Jacob waited for his Rachel. Before another impediment comes between us, I want you to marry me. If you count our long betrothal the first time around, we have more than fulfilled that requirement. Say yes and come with me to Jerusalem and we shall live as husband and wife. I still love you, Elianna."

My heart stopped, I am certain, though physicians would tell you of the impossibility of such an event. I had hoped that with time, Ethan would learn to care for me again. Never had I imagined that he would ask me to wed him right away. I thought about the many times I had denied him in our youth, delaying his desire for marriage and rebuffing him altogether in the end. This time, I decided, would be different. I would make up to him for all the denials of the past. "Ethan Ben Ezer, I will marry you tomorrow if you wish."

Ethan jumped to his feet. "Are you in earnest?"

"I am an old woman, as Rachel confirmed. I can't afford to waste any time."

Ethan burst out laughing. "If you are that old, perhaps I should reconsider."

Thirty-two years I had lived on this earth and I was still a virgin, God help me. I was not about to let my bridegroom spring free. "No reconsiderations are allowed. You better ask Chuza's permission, though, for he is my closest male relative."

Ethan grasped my hand in his. His fingers were warm and

strong. And I was clean enough to enjoy the touch of them without shame. "You are so dear to me, Elianna. After these long years, to know that you will finally be mine! I must find the teacher and thank him for this gift most of all, for by healing your heart and body, he made our marriage possible."

"Ethan, I believe he is the Messiah. He restored me as no ordinary man could."

Ethan nodded gravely. "I have thought the same since the day I saw Lilit rise from the sleep of death. When I saw you so transformed . . ." He shook his head. "It isn't merely your body he healed. That dark shadow that haunted you from the time Joseph died is gone. It's as if the real Elianna was lost for years, and she has now found her way home."

"Do you know the psalm, 'If the Lord had not been my help, my soul would soon have lived in the land of silence. When I thought, "My foot slips," your steadfast love, O Lord, held me up'? I've had it memorized for some years now. It captures my life over the past sixteen years perfectly.

"If not for God's mercy, many were the times my soul would have slipped into the land of silence. Empty. Hopeless. Lifeless. His steadfast love held me up, even when I was not aware. Jesus became to me the consolation of the Lord. He restored life to me and rescued me from the land of silence."

Ethan squeezed my hand hard for a moment. His eyes shone with tears. "I hope to hear him speak. They say he plans to come to Jerusalem soon."

"I could think of nothing better than going to hear him together. Perhaps we can bring Viriato and Keziah. And Rachel. And Claudia and Titus."

Ethan laughed. "If you are not careful, you might bring Calvus along as well."

I bit my lip. "I might." I was only half jesting.

"And now to practical matters." His mouth softened with a wry smile. "I do feel a little sorry for Chuza. He may lose what is left of his hair when I tell him my news. He and Joanna are so attached to you. I think they hoped you would live near them all the days of your lives. I feel a little guilty stealing you away to Jerusalem." Before I could respond, he pulled me into his arms. "Not guilty enough to reconsider, don't worry. I am in no mood to wait another day."

Chuckling, I pressed against his chest and leaned back. "Where are we supposed to live, since you are in such a hurry to whisk me away?"

"How would you like to move back into your childhood home? Half of it belongs to me now."

"What of Viriato?"

"He is welcome to live with us if he wishes. Would you mind?"

"I can't think of a better solution. He is like a brother to me."

"Then pack your belongings, my bride. I am going to visit Chuza right away."

My brow puckered. "Shouldn't we talk to Rachel first? She might not want to have a new mother. It might be better if we gave her some time to grow used to me."

Ethan gave me a lopsided smile. "Don't start coming up with excuses now. You were doing so well. I have already talked to Rachel. She is a little anxious, as you might expect. But she is as happy as I for you to become part of our lives."

❧

I was busy packing when Calvus arrived at my door. This time, Keziah was with me, and I expected Ethan to arrive at any moment. He had deposited Rachel with Joanna for a tour of the palace grounds and taken the opportunity to visit a merchant who might be interested in purchasing cloth from the workshop.

I felt no fear at the sight of the Roman. Not even the smallest shiver of alarm or shudder of dislike went through me. Since having prayed for him, I could not help but pity him every time he came to mind, which was rare. Not bothering to straighten from my packing, I said, "What brings you to my door, Decimus Calvus?"

"So it is true. You are leaving."

"I am. Ethan and I are to be married in Jerusalem as soon as we arrive."

"Did he set his mousy wife aside for you?"

I straightened with a sigh and rubbed my back. "Sarai died years ago. And she was lovely."

Calvus shrugged. "She was nothing to you." He had a whip in his hand, which he flicked against his boot. "They say you are cured."

"Do you believe in miracles, Calvus?"

"No."

"You are looking at one. A Jewish prophet healed me."

"You Jews and your prophets. There is one hiding under every bush."

I laughed. "Not like this one. He even helps Roman centurions."

"I don't need the help of some zealot from the backwaters of Galilee."

"You might change your mind if you met him," I said, and turned to the next box that Keziah had hauled out of our curtained nook. Not recognizing it, I flipped open the lid and peered inside. "Look at this! I had forgotten about this box. Twelve years ago when we left Jerusalem, my mother insisted on dragging it along with us. It's full of the workshop's old papers and account books. I bet Ethan will want to go through every scrap."

Calvus walked over and peered inside. "Make a bonfire of it. It's old rubbish. Hardly worth dragging back to Jerusalem after so long." His mouth had become a straight line, rigid with tension.

I sighed. "I fear Ethan will not agree." I closed the lid and pushed the box aside and pulled over a pile of pots to sort through. "Keziah," I called out. "Let us give the kitchen furnishings to the poor. The house in Jerusalem will already be stocked with what we need."

Keziah, who was working in the next room, said, "I have a pile here as well. I will take care of them later."

"When do you leave?" Calvus asked.

"The day after tomorrow. Early in the morning."

Calvus drew close. "You were ever a thorn in my side, Elianna."

369

I laughed. I could not help myself. "I might say the same of you, Centurion."

"Good day, Calvus," Ethan said from the door. I tensed, wondering how he would react to the Roman's visit. To my relief, Ethan sprawled on the couch, his movements relaxed and measured. I sensed the tension in his bunched muscles and watchful eyes, but that was only because I knew him so well.

"Did you have success with your merchant?" I said.

"A small one. It's not a large order, but a good start."

"So you are marrying Elianna after all these years," Calvus interjected. "You must allow me to celebrate your good fortune. There is a tavern in Tiberias that serves the best wine outside of Herod's palace, and their food tastes palatable, though it is Jewish. They have a private room. Very respectable, and visited by many of your own people. I wish to treat you both to a night out. To show there are no hard feelings. After all, we were friends, once."

Ethan sat up stiffly. "That is generous, Calvus. Unfortunately, we have too much to do before we depart."

"What? Pack this hovel? It won't take but an hour. Come now. If you wish, I will not accompany you. Just pay for your bill. You can take Elianna's sister and that maid of hers along, if you wish. The innkeeper knows me. I will leave him word to expect you."

"We will be happy to accept," I said before Ethan could refuse again. I saw no sense in provoking Calvus. He never liked being thwarted, even in such a small matter.

370

Calvus relaxed at my answer. Giving us directions to the tavern, he took his leave with abrupt haste.

"That is a strange man," I said with a sigh.

Ethan let out a slow breath. "I don't trust him, Elianna."

"Neither do I. But I see no reason to give him offense over such a trifling matter. We can go for a short time. What could be the harm?"

In the end, we went to the tavern as a family, with Rachel, Chuza, and Joanna as well as Keziah in tow. We found that Calvus had not lied when he described the private dining room as respectable, the wine excellent, and the food tolerable.

I had just tasted my first spoonful of the delicious stew when I remembered that I had intended to give Chuza Gamaliel's Scriptures as a parting gift. I would not see my brother-in-law again before our departure, since Herodias was sending him on some frivolous assignment for the whole week.

Of course, he and Joanna would travel to Jerusalem as soon as they could, but I wanted to give him the parchment as a remembrance of the years we had studied and prayed together. Those hard years when our dreams had seemed so impossible. I knew how he would cherish that roll of parchment. Foolishly, I had left it behind at home.

"I must go home," I whispered to Ethan. "I forgot Chuza's gift."

"I will come with you."

We made our excuses and raced back to the house, intending to return before the meal grew cold. A strange sight met us at the door. A bright light, like that of a torch, shone through the window. It should have been dark inside.

"Remain here," Ethan ordered before dragging the door open. I could see into the front room with perfect clarity. Decimus Calvus stood before the old box of papers I had discovered that afternoon, a blazing torch in hand, clearly intent on setting everything inside it on fire.

I walked in behind Ethan. "What are you doing, Calvus?"

"You bothersome woman!" Calvus shouted. "Why can't you just once do what you are supposed to do?"

Before Ethan could prevent me, I drew closer. "Why do you care about those old papers?" With sudden clarity, understanding dawned. "It's the account books. You want to destroy those old account books."

Calvus remained silent. Sweat glistened on his forehead. The torch dipped toward the wooden box. A handsbreadth away, it stopped.

I frowned. "You want to burn those old accounts? Go ahead. Do you think I care after all these years? What did you do? Neglect to pay my father for your purchases? Once, that would have mattered. But it is of little importance to me now."

Calvus glared. "You can't mean it," he said, as if the words were ripped out of him.

"Calvus, I forgive your debt. It's of no account."

"What if I said it was a great deal of money?"

I shrugged. "It matters not how much. I forgive your debt. Take the account books if it makes your heart easy."

Ethan pressed me behind him. "Wait a moment. This liking for fire is not a new hobby, is it, Decimus Calvus?"

"What do you mean?" I said.

"The night your father's chamber burned. We never found the source of the fire, remember? Didn't you tell me that you had a quarrel with Calvus over the accounts that day? Even then he was desperate to destroy them. It was you, wasn't it, Roman? You set fire to that chamber."

The centurion shrugged. "Was it you?" I said, shaken, thinking of the devastating loss of that night. "You ruined all our stock. I almost died!"

"I never meant harm to you," he said gruffly.

"And the horse," Ethan said as if Calvus had not spoken. "You pressed it on Elianna's father the night of Avram's feast. I always assumed that someone had tried to kill *you* by injuring the horse. But it was you the whole time. You tampered with the saddle yourself because you wanted Benjamin out of the way. You had no way of paying your debts. So you decided to kill him in order to save your skin."

"Is it true?" Even as I asked the question, I knew Ethan had arrived at the right conclusion. My voice had become a croaking whisper. "You harmed my father for the sake of money?" I thought of my father's suffering, of those months when he lay caught between life and death, shattered. For a moment, a spark of hatred for this man threatened to consume me.

"Love your enemies."

I heard the words as clearly as if Jesus himself had spoken them again. The hate dissolved, leaving only sadness in its wake.

"These crazed accusations are nothing but the workings of your wild imaginings," Calvus said through frozen lips. "Can you prove a single word before a legal tribunal? If not, you had better shut your mouth, Jew, or you will grow intimately familiar with the inside of a Roman jail."

Ethan took a step forward. "I can show those accounts. I may not be able to prove the fire or your murderous plot. But I can demand my money. The workshop belongs to me now. What you owed Benjamin, you now owe me."

Calvus lifted the torch like a weapon. Ethan bent at the knee, ready to rush him, intending to take the torch away from him. With a calm I did not know I possessed, I grabbed a burning lamp from the table near me.

"Stop this at once," I said. My voice sounded cool in my own ears. They turned toward me, both of them frozen midstep. Ethan's mouth clenched and turned white. I gave him a small smile and looked deep into his eyes. Without hesitation, I put the flame of my lamp against the papers in the wooden box and watched them catch fire. The flames licked up the dry contents with ferocious speed.

The two men grew paralyzed in the center of the room. Calvus lowered the arm that held the torch, staring at me with stupefaction.

"What are you doing?" Ethan cried. "Have you lost your mind?"

"I said I forgave him for his debts, and I meant it, Ethan."

I turned to Calvus. "Remember the prophet I told you about? The one who healed me? He said that we were to love our enemies. To do good to those who hate us. That's what I am doing, Calvus. For his sake. For mine. For Ethan's. I choose to forgive you."

"I don't understand. How can you?"

"I have made many poor choices in my life. I have hurt the people most precious to me. My father could not offer me his forgiveness. Nor could I overcome my own burden of guilt. Then this prophet—they call him Jesus—healed me. His touch made me whole again. Body and soul. Do you understand, Decimus? My guilt is gone, replaced by grace.

"I think that if I have received such an undeniable mercy, who am I to withhold it from you? Take the gift. It is from our Lord more than from me. Do not squander it, Decimus."

Calvus swallowed convulsively. I could not tell if it was the acrid smoke rising out of the wooden box or my words that caused his eyes to fill with tears. He opened his mouth to speak. No words came out. He ran past me, past Ethan, outside the door and into the night.

"You better put out those flames," I said to Ethan.

He gaped at me for a moment before rushing to the box. Everything inside was a ruinous mess by the time he quenched the fire.

It occurred to me that I had burned *his* documents, *his* account books. As he had said, Calvus's debt belonged to him now. Cringing, I said, "Are you angry?"

"Why would I be angry?"

"I ruined your chances of revenging yourself on Calvus and getting your money back."

He walked to me and drew me into his arms, cradling me against him with such careful tenderness you would have thought I was made of Persian glass.

"You are beautiful, my love. You are beautiful. Never again will I care about Decimus Calvus and the harm he has done to us. You have set me free of him."

EPILOGUE

He who finds a wife finds a good thing
and obtains favor from the LORD.

PROVERBS 18:22

AFTER YEARS OF DISAPPOINTMENT, loss, and suffering, the Lord gathered his many blessings and poured them upon me in such a deluge that I sometimes caught myself wondering if I was dreaming. Ethan and I were married in peace. Jerusha and Ezer shed tears of joy, knowing now the full extent of what had taken place over a decade ago. They welcomed me as if I were their long-lost daughter. I suppose I was. Joanna and Chuza were present at my wedding, as were Claudia and Titus. Viriato actually cried, which set me to weeping. In the end, I do not believe there was a dry eye in the whole feast.

Every bride should go through a trial of fire before her wedding. Though I would not wish my own misfortunes upon another, many good fruits came from them, and these I cannot regret. One result of my years of loneliness was how I cherished Ethan. He could say little to disappoint or rile me. I was so happy to share my life with him that nothing he did caused me to love him less. I never took a moment of our time for granted. Being with Ethan always seemed to carry with it a touch of the miraculous. My marriage overflowed with happiness not because Ethan and I never had problems, but because we never allowed them to come between us.

He did complain that my favorite word was still *no*. This charge was entirely unjustified. I did not once say no when he tried to kiss me or hold me in his arms.

Although Jesus had healed me of my disease, I did not know whether having suffered so many years of sickness would affect my womb's ability to bear children. But the Lord made my cup overflow with joy when after only four months of marriage to Ethan, I could tell Rachel that she was about to have a little sister or brother.

"Sarah was also ancient when she had Isaac, and that turned out well," Rachel said.

To my relief, we got along beautifully. I suppose she could sense that I loved her dearly, and that was enough for her, even though I was very old! Her mother had died when Rachel was so young that she had little memory of her. Though she still thought of Sarai with loyal fondness, she had no problem turning some of her affections toward me. Of course, Ethan was the star of her sky. Feeling the same, I could not fault her.

A few months later, Jesus arrived in Jerusalem. Viriato came with us to hear him, once. He had been impressed by our tales of him and wanted to see the man with his own eyes. When he found out that Jesus broke many religious rules, including healing on the Sabbath, Viriato declared that if following the Lord meant becoming like Jesus, then he would follow the Lord. To my knowledge, he never did give up pork.

Joanna had her baby a few months before me, a beautiful boy with thick dark hair and plump fingers. She named him Joseph. To my delight, she took to traveling with Jesus whenever she could, especially when Chuza was busy at work, clasping Joseph to her chest and taking him along. She said the presence of Jesus was the safest place for a child and never worried for Joseph's well-being on those journeys. I cherished her letters as she described her adventures and told me of the many lives touched by the love of our Messiah.

My daughter, Atarah, arrived two weeks later than expected. I could not begrudge the delay; I had waited so long for this impossible dream, two extra weeks hardly seemed worth quibbling over. She stole our hearts from the moment she opened her eyes and surveyed us with her sleepy gaze. Rachel admitted that even a much younger woman could not have produced a more perfect babe.

I daresay that my own story was amongst those spread throughout Judea and beyond. Perhaps one day people I have never met will hear of me and know that Jesus of Nazareth ended the endless misery of a hopeless woman with one stolen touch and a few life-transforming words.

A NOTE FROM THE AUTHOR

THE ONLY TIME Jesus addresses a woman as *daughter* is in the story of the woman with the issue of blood (Matthew 9:20-22; Mark 5:25-34; Luke 8:43-48). There are no throwaway words in Jesus's vocabulary. He selects each term with profound intention. We can therefore assume that he has a significant purpose in addressing this nameless woman in such a tender and intimate fashion.

Three out of the four Gospels tell this story, and it is a breathtaking as well as a strange one. Why would Jesus delay an urgent procession to save the life of a little girl in order to find out who had touched him? Why would he take time they did not have to call a destitute woman *daughter*? The story line of *Land of Silence* revolves around these questions. We know this for certain: Jesus healed her body. I believe, with his words, he also healed her soul.

There is very little we actually know about our main

character. Her personal story outside the sickness she suffered is a blank canvas, one which I filled with a fictional account. No one knows with certainty what caused this woman's condition in modern medical terms. There are several possibilities. I described her illness assuming she had a severe case of uterine fibroids, complicated by a few other problems such as endometrial polyps. Most of the medical treatments mentioned in this novel are based on extant historical documents.

Although Philo and several other rabbinic texts suggest that the life of women in first-century Palestine was very limited, archaeologists have discovered some evidence to the contrary. For example, we have recovered inscriptions from that time period that refer to women as synagogue leaders. Clearly, there was some complexity to the role of women at this time. I have tried to capture that reality in Elianna's life.

We don't know how the Jewish purity laws were enforced on a daily basis in Jesus's day. Although we have the biblical directives regarding the uncleanness of a menstruating woman, we don't fully understand how these laws were lived out practically. So some of the conclusions in this novel are educated guesses.

As I often enjoy doing, I have quoted another writer in this book. Merab's assertion that "it is a woman's business to get married as soon as possible, and a man's to keep unmarried as long as he can" is a quote from George Bernard Shaw.

Jesus's words welcoming little children were actually spoken after the section that tells the story of the woman with the issue of blood and, one assumes, at a later date. I have taken the liberty to include it out of order.

The character Gamaliel is based on a historical figure who plays a role in the book of Acts (5:34-39). According to church tradition, he and his son became secret followers of Jesus. Chuza and Joanna are also based on biblical characters (Luke 8:1-3). Joanna was one of the women who followed Jesus and supported his ministry. There is no evidence that she was related to the woman with the issue of blood. That was my own invention.

While the Bible provides profound inspiration for novels like this, the best way to study it is not through a work of fiction, but simply to read the original, the way Jesus himself would have done. This story can in no way replace the transformative power that the reader will encounter in the Scriptures.

ACKNOWLEDGMENTS

EVERY YEAR I GROW MORE THANKFUL for my agent, Wendy Lawton, who has made the journey of writing more thrilling than I could have imagined. What a joy to work with Stephanie Broene and Kathy Olson from Tyndale House Publishers. Thank you, ladies, for your detailed letters, your gracious wisdom, and your constant support. I am indebted to Mark Norton from Tyndale's Bible team for taking the time to answer my many historical and biblical questions.

I am grateful for dear friends Lauren Yarger and Cindy McDowell, who remain my writing partners—and partners in all manner of impossible-seeming things—and never grow tired of helping me with my first drafts. I deeply appreciate your wisdom and encouragement. Molly Chase, thank you for your capable editing, which made *Land of Silence* a better book. To Deryk Richenburg I owe the connection between Jeremiah's verse on the weary (31:25) and Jesus's own invitation (Matthew 11:28).

Warm thanks to my church in New England that is beautiful on the outside while radiating the glory of Jesus within.

For my boss and coworkers, without whose support I could not even start one book, let alone finish five, I am more appreciative than I can express.

Beth and Rob Bull, you deserve special thanks for giving up the dedication I promised you, and for the love and grace you have shown us. Kathi and Taylor Smith (who were the inspiration behind Claudia and Titus), I so appreciate the unforgettable writing space.

Last but not least, heartfelt thanks to John, whose quiet strength brought me peace and helped me finish when the race seemed impossible. What a blessing to receive from God so late in life.

I am indebted to every single one of my readers who keep buying these books. Thank you for being patient when I take too long!

ABOUT THE AUTHOR

TESSA AFSHAR was voted "New Author of the Year" by the FamilyFiction-sponsored Readers Choice Awards in 2011 for her novel *Pearl in the Sand*. Her second book, *Harvest of Rubies*, was nominated for the 2013 ECPA Christian Book Award in the fiction category and chosen by *World* magazine as one of four notable books of the year. Her novel *Harvest of Gold* won the 2014 Christy Award for historical fiction. *In the Field of Grace*, based on the biblical story of Ruth, was nominated for the Grace Award.

Tessa was born in Iran to a nominally Muslim family and lived there for the first fourteen years of her life. She moved to England, where she survived boarding school for girls and fell in love with Jane Austen and Charlotte Bronte, before moving to the United States permanently. Her conversion to Christianity in her twenties changed the course of her life forever. Tessa holds an MDiv from Yale University, where she served as cochair of the Evangelical Fellowship at the Divinity School. Tessa has spent the last seventeen years in full-time Christian work in New England and the last fourteen years on the staff of one of the oldest churches in America. Visit her online at www.tessaafshar.com.

DISCUSSION QUESTIONS

1. What is the meaning of Elianna's name? Do you know what your name means? If God were to pick a new name for you, what do you think it would be? Why?

2. How does Elianna cope with her grief and guilt? How do you cope with difficult situations in life?

3. Name four painful circumstances in Elianna's life. Have you had experiences that paralleled these issues? (For example, physical illness, feeling guilty for not helping someone close to you, the painful end of a relationship, the rejection of a loved one, etc.)

4. At the beginning, Elianna's faith is very legalistic (she tries to win God over by her effort). How does this affect her relationship with God? Have you ever struggled with legalism? How do you think you can overcome it?

5. Have you ever felt rejected by your father or someone else you looked up to? If so, how has that rejection affected your life? If you had a wonderful relationship with your father, how do you think that experience affects your relationship with God?

6. Name some of the "medical" treatments Elianna has to endure. Have you ever had or witnessed medical treatment that was difficult to go through? How did you respond (emotionally and physically)? How did you overcome or endure during that season?

7. In spite of having suffered a great deal, Viriato is not a bitter man. What do you think helps him remain positive in his outlook?

8. What drives Elianna to lie to Ethan about Calvus? Think of a situation when you felt your best option was to lie. Looking back, do you still feel that way? What, if anything, would you do differently if you could?

9. Elianna goes through a season of utter despair until life itself becomes unbearable. Have you ever had a similar experience? How do you overcome in times like that?

10. Why does Elianna choose to ignore all rules and conventions and touch Jesus? What gives her that boldness? Have you ever been bold in the midst of fear or shame?

11. Do you think Jesus still heals today? How did you arrive at that conclusion?

12. Share a few of your favorite scenes (or specific quotes) from the book and explain why these portions are meaningful to you.